I0632779

ATLANTEAN BRINY DEEP

High Table Hijinks Book Five

CHRISTOPHER JOHNS

MOUNTAINDALE
PRESS

Copyright © 2024 by Christopher Johns

All rights reserved.

No part of this book may be reproduced in any form or by any electronic or mechanical means, including information storage and retrieval systems, without written permission from the publisher, except for the use of brief quotations in a book review.

This is a work of fiction. Names, characters, places, and incidents either are the products of the author's imagination or are used fictitiously. Any resemblance to actual persons, living or dead, businesses, companies, events, or locales is entirely coincidental.

Dedicated to those who have been dedicated to me. To my success. To my friendship. To my very being. Thank you for choosing to walk this Way with me, and for allowing me to know I'm never alone even when it feels that way. Also, to my uncle, lost this last year to a freak accident. You told me I couldn't do it—out of love—and when I did, you were proud I'd made something of myself.

It was an honor to have been guided by you, Uncle Gary. I miss you all the time.

ACKNOWLEDGMENTS

I would like to thank those who have seen this series to where it is now. My editors, my betas and alphas—my friends. All of you have a part in this, whether that part may feel lesser now, or not.

THE STORY SO FAR...

Let's pretend for a second that you have no clue what the hell is going on, and that you need the refresher, that's okay. I like to know what I'm getting into as well, so we won't hold it against you.

Let's assume you remember the attack at the temple that prompted Galaxy and Marcus' initial meeting, him being medically discharged from the Marines to go home and lay low as his sergeant major investigated what he could on his own. Also, that Marcus chose to apply to work at the High Table, a bar he thought his Uncle Yen owned. There were Seelie involved, Marcus' son was kidnapped, and there was a whole shit-show of a showdown that we just won't get into other than to say that Arden, a new friend and a flame jinn, and Cassia, an oni with a penchant for fighting, also took up arms to help save the boy and the day. Merlin was there too. You know, the boy mage who would be a Warden?

They then moved on to going to the magical land of monsters, Grestal, for the High Table Council (it's an organization! Weird, right? I know.) so that they could try to find the long-lost relic of the past, the Huntsman's Mantle, said to belong to the leader of the Wild Hunt. Long story short, Marcus, Galaxy, Cassia, Arden, and Merlin had to fight through more Wardens that usually do their damned jobs in order to get anywhere close to their goals. Though with their new friend Amabala's help, they finally managed to find the damn thing and succeeded where so many others failed in reviving the Wild Hunt. After killing the embodiment of the Mantle, and claiming it through Galaxy, everyone thought they were good.

Hell, by that point, Marcus, Galaxy, and Cassia had even become a nice little thruple. Granted, it'd only been a couple weeks but hey, relationships are weird, man. They came back, dealt with no end of politicking, and then almost immediately had to go off to the land of sand and sphinxes—no, there were no sphinxes, I know. Let's call it what it is: bullshit.

While they were in Cairo, getting sandy and sunny in the dunes, word reached them that the god Janus had been murdered and all hell was breaking loose back home. If it hadn't been for their business over east, they'd have been helping protect the Table, but the others had that shit on lockdown—at least from their perspective. Thanks to some fine deductive work and more than a little help from the murderous creature itself, the group was able to find the monster that was killing supernatural creatures and leaving them out in the open for Normies to find. Spoiler alert: it was Council member Serpath's other half! Wild, right? I know.

While working on all that, they had to contend with one of Galaxy's former prison guards, a creature from Null called a Vorna who had stolen a fraction of her divinity: her Dominion. The group fought the nasty creature and one of its friends as they tried to kill a god but a strange being came through a portal, made by something so powerful it put the keeper Amabala into a near-catatonic state due to the fear she felt, and stole the beaten god from the Vorna as it tried to escape. It savaged the Vorna, then left with it laying beaten on the ground.

Marcus and Galaxy killed it and the other, regaining some of the goddess' lost Dominion and thus her memories. She was the first and most powerful before she was locked away.

With so much having happened, and a lockdown called due to the death of yet another god, three months passed with Marcus and the Wild Hunt working at the bar-turned-hostel and going to Grestal to hunt and grow stronger. Finally, the lockdown lifted and Marcus, Cassia, Galaxy, and Arden went to Japan to play.

While there to cosplay, shop, and play video games, Marcus and Arden dropped a nice gift on Cassia in the form of a reunion with a very old friend, Tsuki. Unbeknownst to them, this was the final thing she wanted before she would ascend to her place as the new Luck Dragon, the being who kept the Night Parade in check and from leaving the shadows of Japan.

Marcus met Cassia's family, her sister Kimiko and her mother Chiasa, and also the enforcer for the mysterious new leader of the Night Parade. There was fighting, bonding, and more than a little booze had before the battle with the big bad, but that wasn't all that happened. Someone was releasing videos of supernatural beings doing their spooky dookie and it was all over the internet. While Merlin, Amabala, and an ornery pair of Phone Gnomes assisted in trying to get it all taken down, Marcus and the gang found out who was masterminding it all —Zeke.

The Druid from another world had come home and had become a fixture in their lives, somewhat, as a friendly sort of threat. So long as they stayed out of his way, he would stay out of theirs and be cordial. Hell, he'd even offered to teach Marcus a thing or two about magic since he could. Well, Marcus called that favor in and Zeke asked him to join him and two more of his friends from this place called Brindolla, but the Wild Hunt was weary of the welcoming wish, and wondered if this one offer was just a way to pull them into chains and bind them. With that, they wilted at the wondrous wile and continued with their own duties with his blessing to interfere as they could, stating that what he was doing was dickish, but not without reason and he wasn't dick enough to keep them from trying to keep others alive how they could try to.

A weird sentiment, we know.

Marcus found out that once he accumulated so many points in a stat, he had Vorna blood in him all along and, with it, was able to awaken more powers that helped make him stronger. One of those powers being able to take the powers of other Huntsmen—beings created by Galaxy while she still ruled the cosmos to assist in protecting various civilizations. In finding and killing the Brindollan Huntsman, Galaxy found out that the gods of Brindolla were her children, prompting revelations that they may be able to go to other worlds to take the powers of the other Hunts for their own. Or gain help from the Brindollan gods.

After training with Zeke and receiving the blessing of the Frost Primordial Elemental, Marcus and Galaxy returned to the others to find that Kimiko was gone and the Night Parade was closing in on the temple that hid Tsuki.

The Parade, led by Cassia's estranged father Felix, who was newly powerful enough to lead, clashed with the now-bolstered ranks of the Wild Hunt and friends of the Luck Dragon. The fight was nothing short of epic with losses on both sides, one of those losses being Kimiko, her body having been taken over by Felix, who almost succeeded in killing Tsuki during her ascension prayer, but failed thanks to her planning.

Cassia summoned the lightning god Raijin and swore an oath to him in return for the power to smite her father for his role in Kimiko's death. His price being to empower the baby growing inside her for what was to come. She agreed, and killed Felix on the battlefield.

In the wake of Cassia's loss and the news of their expecting, Galaxy disappeared for a time and found out where the next Vorna on Earth might be hiding—Atlantis.

That, coupled with the outing of the supernatural world

thanks to Zeke and Theodorous, a Warden of the Heart and Ventricle of Ohio, is where the story ended with Marcus near a psychotic break.

CHAPTER ONE

I had no idea how long I had been asleep, but I could feel the movement and concern around me as if it were a palpable miasma.

It had been days since I'd been able to speak to anyone, having all but boarded myself into the basement of the Luck Dragon's temple. The only constant had been a sparse flow of warrior monks who served Tsuki coming in to check on me now and then or bringing food that I could barely touch.

Cassia was pregnant, Galaxy wanted to go to Atlantis, I still had to worry about finding Arden's family, and Merlin now had to wonder if the Wardens could be swayed so easily to the side of someone who might mean more harm than good.

All of it weighed on my mind to a point where even my training and previous experience with high-stress situations weren't enough to keep me from freaking out. But that was the problem, wasn't it?

Marcus... I could feel Galaxy trying to enter the realm of my mind like she had so many times before, but I stopped her. *Let me help you, please?*

"Help?" I laughed and stared at the same portion of the ceiling that I had been for the last three hours, then blinked as I let my gaze fall to my hands. "You mean like you've been *helping* us this whole time?"

She was quiet, letting me go ahead and speak, so I did. "You tinkered with all of our heads, didn't you?" I wasn't angry, just concerned. At least, I thought I was. "You, what? Made us more mentally malleable so we wouldn't break under the pressure you had us under to try to level up? The situations we were in wouldn't mentally scar us to the point of uselessness if you just jiggled this or that, right?"

She appeared before me from the shadows and wore her human form, a beautiful dark-skinned woman with a full figure, beautiful eyes and—

"Stop it."

She flinched and pouted. "That's you, Marcus. You're the one who finds me attractive."

"How can I rely on that?" I didn't wait to see her reaction, staring at the ground to be safe and said, "I was near a breaking point a few days ago when you first told me about Atlantis and then I wasn't. It was like, all that stress just up and vanished and I was ready to go again, but this time was different—what changed? Why am I able to clearly sense that I've been messed with mentally this time?"

I let my gaze lift at last and could tell that the question hurt her as she cast her blank stare drift downward to the dirty, grit-covered stones at her feet. "I don't know, but it's only been because I've had to expand your capability of just *handling* things." She sighed and sat on the ground, sullying her clothes in a way that should have been beneath a goddess, but she didn't seem to mind that nearly as much as she cared for my current disdain. "I've had to do it for all of you, and I've only done it in order to maintain readiness. If you and the others had been nearly this bothered in Cairo, that Vorna would have torn through all of you like paper."

"And you would have been put back into your cell," I added for her but the look she gave me as her eyes met mine was enraged. "What?"

"You put words into my mouth again, Marcus Bola." Her voice was deeper, angry and bitter as she leaned forward. "I told you that I did this out of caring, trying to help you keep your composure with all of the things outside our control. No one knew that you, someone previously considered human, could impregnate an oni. Even if Aeslyn was a fluke, no one had reason to believe you could do it, that was why there was never any protection used."

"Let's not just pretend it's just about that." It was hard to keep the exhaustion from my voice. "We've been going nearly non-stop since you were awakened. That weighs on people, Galaxy—we need rest to recover, so we don't get sloppy."

"My 'tinkering' kept you in top form, and active rests are a thing for a lot of bodybuilders, Marcus. If you truly needed a break, I would have given it to you, but unfortunately, we don't have the time for it." She sighed and closed her eyes. "Our hands have been forced and the next logical step for us is to regain some more of my lost power and work on getting Zeke and his friends home."

I blinked at her. "Wait, what?"

"I spoke with the others and they agree too." I stood and she mirrored me. "They think that the sooner we get them off Earth, the sooner things can go back to normal. There's nothing that they can do to brainwash humanity back into ignorance that they're aware of, but at least without Zeke and his friends here to interfere, the supernatural world has a chance at some sort of coexistence with the Normies."

"Do the others know what you've been doing?" She frowned at me and I pressed her from where I stood, staring into her as if I expected some sort of tell that she might be lying. "Do they know about your tinkering?"

"I've suspected it for a while now." Merlin's voice echoed in the darkness around us and his footsteps joined us. The battle with the Night Parade had been supremely beneficial and with his part in all of it, he was looking a lot more buff with his stat distribution. He carried himself better now and there was pride in his bearing.

I was proud too. He'd grown into himself and deserved his name.

"How much do you know?"

Galaxy's question had the sound of baiting to it and he smiled. "All of it. I know you messed with my mind to make me more subservient to you, and I know that you've also been messing with all of our minds to make us accept certain situations more readily."

I frowned at that, since it was everything that we'd worked to keep from him to make sure he was okay. He'd lost his life fighting by our side and was just a kid then—still. "So why does it sound like you're coming to her defense?"

"Because I can't say that her 'tinkering' wasn't warranted." His tone was matter-of-fact, almost like one would say that the sky was blue, or that Barney was purple like my favorite flavor of crayon. "A mental break, or one of us getting hung up over the littlest thing could have been deadly for all of us, and even if it could result in Galaxy being captured again, her main concern has always been us being stronger and as safe as can be. Besides, you can't say that you didn't have some modicum of an idea she was doing it—you've helped her to before. Justified as it was, it's like the pot calling the kettle black."

I was about to protest when he put a hand on her shoulder and nodded. "She could have let me die and eaten me so that I could have fueled her own growth and strength, but she saw my potential and gave up a lot for me. I'll never forget that, even if it's colored rosy by the fact that she played with my brain. I'm strong enough now that I can mainly just ignore that and be myself, but that doesn't mean I don't understand the necessity."

"So you think I should just man up and move on?" I almost laughed at that, because as many times as I had said the same damn thing to others, it was the last thing I wanted to hear right now.

"I think some therapy is definitely in order, but I will agree we're in a major time crunch at the moment." He scratched his head and shrugged. "Every moment we waste fighting with each other and bickering is a moment that the Wild Hunt is useless and that the Vorna in Atlantean proximity could catch wind of us coming for it. The more time we spend here wondering if what we're doing is the right thing, or was handled the way we would want in a perfect world, is more time for Normies to get their hands on information that could get all of our friends killed."

"We don't know what the Wardens are doing, if they were willing participants in what happened or not, but that doesn't matter with Zeke's promise to end the gods' influence." Galaxy took a single step forward and stared at me, pleading in her eyes. "We need to go and get this done right away. The stronger I am, the stronger all of you are, the more likely we are to survive this."

A scoffing snort came from my right and I found Arden standing there with her arms crossed, "Surviving is all we've *been* doing, and the mental shit she's been doing is a lot easier to understand than the mental gymnastics you're trying to win gold for jumping to the conclusions you are." She jutted her chin at me in greeting, muttering, "Still sulking, crybaby?"

That made me laugh, which got a smirk to cross her face in return as she huffed and pointed above her head. "Look, my best friend is up there trying to choose some baby names and her mother seems content as hell with Chiasa the Third. If you don't get your boy-band-wannabe-looking ass up there ten minutes ago, I'm going to have to beat the whiny bitch out of you myself."

"Is it seriously so bad that I feel so rotten about someone making me into basically a machine?"

The others watched as Arden contemplated and then huffed. "Take it from someone who was forced to do things she didn't want to while stuck in a bottle—what she was doing isn't nearly as rough as it can get."

I shook my head and grimaced at the thought of having to grant wishes that consumed my life force. "I knew there was some tinkering, some, but not to the extent that it was, but that's different. And you didn't answer my original question; do I not have the right to feel like I was misled a bit?"

"No!" Galaxy and Merlin barked simultaneously, but Merlin spoke on, "We will unpack all of this later, all we ask is that we move on to address what we can now."

"I know a good therapist if you need one." Amabala's soft-spoken voice almost made me jump. "She's helped me through some of my own issues, and I know that she would be more than happy to help you too."

I laughed at that. "There's a wizard for people like us?"

Amabala blinked and said, "Many. Merlin is a mage."

Merlin smiled at her and went to her side, patting her hand affectionately as he explained, "Wizard is what Marines call those who deal with the mind, psychologists and therapists. They're seen as magic workers. Either they fix you, or make you go poof and no one sees you again."

"Oh, so it's a bad thing?"

She was just too damn sweet to be overly sarcastic to, so I said simply, "Yes."

"Cut the bullshit, Devil," Arden growled at me and stomped closer. "You're better than all that jarhead juju you think reigns supreme."

"All I have to fall back on is what I know and my training," I answered and she shook her head. "What else is there?"

"Us." She rolled her eyes as the others closed in.

"Fine." I sighed and glared at all of them, hard. "We do this, but I need to talk to someone."

I turned and fixed Galaxy with probably the most serious knife hand I had given since I still wore my chevrons. "Stay out of my head—you can talk to me in there, and visit me, but no messing without asking first." She frowned and I added mentally with great care and tension in my tone, *I love you, Galaxy. I do. I want this to work. But messing with my ability to cope with shit and then expecting me to just be okay with it isn't okay. I would like for you to learn from this as well.*

I have. It was all she would say as she turned and walked away from me, leaving me to walk up the stairs to the main hall with the others.

I thought I had been growing stronger on my own, being a bit more badass, but how much of that was her tweaking my head? How many times had I condoned it toward the others and it could've been that she just made it seem the most practical? *Stow it for now, Marcus.*

Upon reaching the top, I was met by Chiasa, Cassia's mom. She wore her oni form, looking like a larger version of Cassia, if that was possible, and even more intimidating. She lifted her chin and stared down her nose at me, her gaze critical, "Human."

"Chiasa." I returned as I made to walk past her.

Our relationship hadn't been as cool as I thought it might have been, but then again, I had needed to retreat almost as soon as she had arrived and it had likely not boded well in her opinion. Much as I gave a shit. She would have killed her own kids if Felix the nogitsune and leader of the Night Parade had demanded it, I was sure.

As I came abreast with her, she put a hand on my shoulder. It wasn't a gentle stop, but one that rooted me to the spot as she spoke down to me, "Your plan to stop the Night Parade." She paused as if searching for words and finally she decided on, "Was good. It was a good plan."

I frowned as she nodded more to herself and left me with my bruised shoulder to watch her walk away without another exchange of words.

Without a clear way forward, I would need to find a way for us to get to Atlantis at the very least, but there was the problem of finding where the hell it was. No one knew, or at least no one I knew did. But that was likely nothing to really care about, seeing as though I had been human the majority of my life.

But I wasn't now. I had found out that I was a Vorna, one of the very creatures capable of stealing the Dominion from a god and the very beings that had managed to capture Galaxy and imprison her in that temple that had taken my unit.

Had my being okay with that been a necessity? Had it been her messing with my mind, or was that the Vorna in me coming to the fore? They had all seemed so ready for a fight, almost like it was what they were made for. To kill and destroy as much as Galaxy was able to create and make. Were they her opposites in everything?

Someone took my hand and I flinched, my right hand freezing with dark ice as Void Frost activated without a thought.

The hand was warm and I noticed that it was one of the quieter monks who bowed his head respectfully and motioned for me to come with him. He led me outside to one of the cherry blossom trees where Cassia stood and watched the city around us quietly.

Once we were within about a dozen yards or so, the monk bowed again and left me with her.

"Hey," I said lamely as I approached. She turned and smiled, in her human form, unlike her mother, but this one was the same Japanese one she'd been wearing for our stay here. Her sunglasses were the only thing that stood out about her other than that she was holding her stomach. She wasn't showing at all, but she just held it.

She came over to me and pulled me into her arms in a tight hug that I returned immediately. I went to apologize for leaving her the way I had, opening my mouth to do just that, but she just shook her head and muttered, "I know."

She held me a moment or two longer and then let me go. "I know that you had a lot on your mind. Finding out how we did would stun anyone, and then with what Galaxy's been having to do for us, that kind of thing doesn't always build well."

"Speaking of the mental shit... Are you okay with what was

done?" I watched her carefully as I spoke, gauging her reaction as best I could.

There was a brief pause as she considered the question. "Do you suppose the people down there—outside the few who are Touched or saw what happened in the U.S.—have any clue what happens in the background every day?" I ground the question through my mind and she added, "You know, like how many gods or supernatural creatures they meet who interfere, better, or batter their lives? How many gods intervene when they're making poor decisions? Who actually listens to their prayers?"

Frowning deeply, I had to admit, "Probably not?"

Cassia smiled as she touched her stomach, her hand resting over mine before I could pull it back. "Probably not, but we're lucky to know the goddess doing such for us in an almost-daily manner. She cares about us, genuinely, and wants our success. Those people down there, hell, most people in this world and Grestal, probably can't say that with any degree of certainty. Galaxy did what she thought was best and even if you're a little on edge because of that, I think she did what I would have probably suggested she do anyway." She turned her distant gaze to me, focusing on my face behind her sunglasses. "If she hadn't messed with our heads, I may have lost the man I love, and her as well."

I didn't say anything as I mulled that over, and in that silence, Cassia admitted, "But I'm glad you're here now."

"So am I." I frowned and fought the urge to touch her stomach, remembering all my friends who had hated that.

She caught me staring and took my hand to make me do it. "You're the father, Marcus Bola. Provided I'm not angry with you, or in the middle of a fight, you can touch my stomach whenever you damn well please."

That made me grin. I'd never really been able to do this with Aeslyn, and now doing it made me feel both elated and horrible. I missed Connell.

"I'll be there for everything," I blurted, as overcome with emotion at that second as I was.

She grinned. "You'd better be." She pulled me close and looked out into the skyline again. "When do we go to Atlantis?"

"As soon as possible, but you can't possibly mean to—" I stopped myself from finishing that sentence and she chuckled, "I 'bout fucked up, didn't I?"

"Almost. You're learning." She looked up at me. "Oni who carry a child fight as much as they can in order to ensure the child will be strong when they come out of the womb. Our child will be the strongest there is."

I thought about that, the little role I had in Connell's life as a child, and how I wanted to be there for this one. "What can I do?"

"Everything and nothing." She smiled wistfully. "We start by going home, and then from there, gaining enough power to say 'fuck you' to anyone we want. That means we need all of the Wild Hunt working the way it was meant to."

I nodded and she added, "That means forgiving Galaxy and moving on, Marcus." I frowned at that and she put a hand on my arm. "I know. I needed little prodding to keep going. Oni are built differently than all of you, and going from one battle to the next is almost a high to us. But in her glee at finding the next portion of her power close enough to claim, I could feel her getting sloppy and noticed she was mucking about in my mind. I was upset too, for a time, but after losing Kimiko to the Night Parade, I understand that, sometimes, feelings walk and power talks."

She looked up at me and said, "We need her to be at full power if we are to protect our child, Marcus. You too. All of us. I will protect them and make them strong. I need all of you to help me in this."

"And this is you talking and not her?"

She nodded, smiling. "She promised all of us no more messing with our heads before you ever said anything to her about it. She's set in her ways, but she's learning, just like you."

"Okay," I replied simply. "I'll call Uncle Yen and see what can happen. God knows how the High Table Council is reacting to the news about us being outed."

I pulled out my phone and it rang once before Uncle Yen picked up and with relief in his tone said, "Thank God you're okay." He shouted something that was muffled and came back, "How fast can you get back here?"

CHAPTER TWO

"Doesn't he know that we were kind of banned for thirty years?" Amabala asked curiously as we all gathered around her to portal back to Arden's place.

"He said that the ban's been lifted thanks to a certain goddess backing out of it in an attempt to regain composure with her staff." It was a small comfort to know that with Hanazuki, others had quit upon hearing what we had done when the Night Parade had come in after us and Tsuki.

"And not one fucking worker returned," Cassia stated triumphantly, her teeth flashing in the light. She smiled all the wider. "Pretty sure Hana bought a Switch too."

"Good, maybe she can help out with all these hunts." Arden sighed as she walked over to us, then pointed to Chiasa who waited nearby. "What's up with momma oni?"

Cassia opened her mouth, then clacked her mouth shut. She looked askance at me before she bowed her head slightly. "I didn't get the chance to say, but I wanted to bring her with us. At least to Columbus."

I blinked at her, my shock no surprise, but it was Merlin who said, "She tried to kill us all, Cass."

"*She* was only fulfilling her duty." Chiasa spoke loudly enough to be heard, stepping close enough to show herself but not enough to look. "I fought to protect my children, even from themselves. After that, I fought with the most powerful being who had claim to me. I have lost my daughter, and will not lose another."

She glared at all of us as if daring us to say or do more than bat an eye at her as she snarled, "I make *no* apologies."

"No one expects one," I growled back at her and she glared as I trod toward her in return. "You are welcome to come, but there will be rules."

"Marcus..." Cassia began but her mother shut her down with a lifted hand. Gentle a gesture as it was, she was quiet.

"Speak your rules, Huntsman."

I blinked, it was the first time she had used my title and with it, there was no malice in it. Only acceptance.

"You are to be no threat to anyone who is not a threat to your daughter, our child, or yourself. And that threat is to be clearly evident—not perceived on a whim, down the line, or by proxy to anything or anyone else." She nodded along with that, so I continued, "The High Table staff and the Wild Hunt are to be treated as family, if not to you, then my own, as they are important to me, your daughter, and our child. They are protectors and are to be treated as such."

Cassia groaned and muttered, "They'll all regret that."

I raised an eye at her but she just shook her head, motioning I carry on.

"Finally..." I sighed as I realized what I needed to say at that moment. "Finally, don't let yourself forget your youngest daughter."

Chiasa blinked at me quizzically, so I explained, "Kimiko was a bit hard to work with at times, but otherwise she was strong and noble. She cared about her people. I don't want to see her dedication to them cast aside or tread upon. I hope the oni here are stronger for what she tried to accomplish."

"The oni here have all resolved to give themselves to the

Mother of the Storm." Chiasa lifted her chin. "Where she goes, we all will follow."

"Mother of the what now?" Arden raised an eyebrow at all that. "You mean Cassia?"

Chiasa affirmed it. "I do." She stared first at her daughter, then at me. "All of the oni in Japan excepting maybe four, are willing to fight under her banner. And, by extension, yours."

"And how many is that?" Cassia wondered aloud.

"The dead number more than a dozen, so that leaves approximately thirty-four." She counted on her fingers for just a second, then amended it, "Thirty-three. I forgot I killed one too."

"What the *fuck*, Chiasa?" Arden cried, almost dropping her precious handheld game in the process of throwing her hands in the air.

All she had to say to that was, "They fought well, but I prevailed."

"Enough." The others looked at me as I sighed and redirected our conversation to where it was needed. "I will have similar promises from them if I can, but can you agree to this?"

She went to answer but I stopped her, making her eyes narrow at me darkly. "I want you to know this—we could be going up against a nearly god-level threat if Zeke decides that we're not worth fucking with. If he decides we're a problem, we're fucked with a capital alphabet soup and there's not much we can do about it yet. He *will* kill you if you get in his way."

She frowned at me and I added, "I know that means little to you, but Cassia wants you there for her and she just lost her sister. I would like her to have the support she needs and what she wants. Please, don't make us regret this, okay?"

She nodded once and said, "Fine." She grabbed my arm, the others stilling close to us to see what she wanted but I shooed them all away. Cassia hung back, but I couldn't make her leave like the others. Chiasa spoke softly, but clearly, "She saved you from me, your plan was sound and if I had gotten to you, I would have killed you. For her, and your child, I would kill you. But she loves you, and that is not an oni sentiment, so I allow this. Do not take my willingness to be there for my daughter to mean that I approve of you, Huntsman."

I smiled at her, and it was the most genuine smile I'd been able to muster in days. "Chiasa, I couldn't care less if you approve of me or not. If I have to kill you to keep my people and your daughter out of trouble, I'll happily take the beatings from the others and her. No one, and nothing, is more important to me than the family I have."

I waved my hand to all of them. "*They* are family." I motioned to her. "You're an acquaintance with an expiration date of your own choosing as far as I'm concerned. Take that how you will."

I extricated myself from her limp grip and walked away to join Cassia who turned to walk with me and muttered, "Why was my mother smiling so much?"

———

Arden's house acted as our lair for the interim as we continued to save and work on the blueprints for our own place, hopefully on a ley line so we could use the power from it to charge a portal to the High Table and some defenses.

It was just taking quite some time to get it all together as Arden was away from Billy and, by extension, the architects responsible for what we wanted to build. The place would theoretically look like a normal building or house on the outside, but the interior would be all us.

I had to admit, with things being how they had been lately and the last three months before that, I was looking forward to all of us having a place to call our own. Especially if the High Table could just up and ban us for any amount of time at the drop of a hat. Or try to make us turn ourselves in.

We piled into Cassia's SUV, Chiasa opting to stay behind so Kenshi could grow accustomed to the idea that she was here now as her excuse for not joining us.

When we arrived at the lot to the High Table in Columbus, the block had several men and women on it that looked almost like guards but they weren't ours.

"Wardens," Merlin grumbled immediately. "They're probably keeping an eye out for any kind of trouble, or for us. Either way, we should probably avoid them if we can."

"Back door it is." Cassia pulled into the lot and then toward the back of it so we could pile out and follow her into a secret passage that led into the bar.

It was an annoying passage that we had to file through one by one, but at least we could get in and that was the best part.

The worst part was the absolute zoo we walked in on in the bar. Televisions that were hardly ever on played the president's speech and the subsequent outing of magical kind on a loop and all of the creatures in the room in various states of inebriation watched in either shock, confusion, or horror. Some of them even in a mixed bag of all three.

"Yen!" Arden roared and the man came hauling ass out from behind the bar as the patrons turned on us and began to call out questions.

Some even hurled accusations at us.

"Enough, *enough!*" Yen snarled at them, finally barking, "High Table Order: Silence!"

The bar went perfectly quiet, the patrons shut their mouths, the televisions stopped where they were and even the jukebox cut off.

"Thank the gods all of you are okay." He pulled each of us into a hug and sighed in relief. "The council is doing what they can to try to spin this right, but it's not going well. The Wardens have had the place almost on lockdown again with their constant presence and people are freaking out."

He looked around and finally whispered, "There have even been a few not-so-veiled threats at Zeke and Theo for this."

"They earned it," Arden grumbled quietly. "I can't believe they just went and did that."

"It's a lot to take in." Uncle Yen may have looked physically younger, but he looked whipped. "The Council has asked if they can see you when you arrive, but from what you said on the phone, I know you won't be staying long."

I nodded. "Long enough to restock on weapons and things, then we go and find what information we can about, well, you know. Besides, that guy terrifies me, so I know if the council were to act on those threats, there would be no council."

He nodded and muttered, "You have guests in your room who would like to see you, and I'll text you in a minute. I think I might be able to get you some help."

"Thanks, Uncle Yen."

I walked up the stairs as the others did what they were wont to do, and walked into my room, the door unlocked already.

On a couple of chairs sat Aeslyn and Luca, while Connell played a game on the TV.

"Hey!" I said with surprise. I'd been expecting an irate brownie, but not them. Though I reached into my inventory and dumped out about ten pounds of all the chocolate candy I could find in Japan and slid it under the bed, "Eat up, Seamus. Appreciate you."

There was a loud harrumph and then a growling laugh at my expense, I was sure of it. Then I saw a fuzzy hand with long thin fingers push out three boxes of pocky, tap them, then point to Connell who looked at it with curiosity.

"That is very kind of you, Seamus, thank you." Luca bowed his head and the grunting laugh returned before I was sure the brownie had taken off. The former Unseelie prince looked up at me and I could see the question written on his face before he said the words.

I shook my head; his mother and the king had been murdered. Not without reason or cause, but they'd forced their hands. Zeke's hand.

Aeslyn reached out her hand and placed it on his, the gesture small enough that I would have missed it if it weren't for him jerking away from her.

"Swear to me you could say nothing."

"I swear it on all my power as the Huntsman." The oath was easy. I added, "So long as I played ball and kept his secret, all of you were guaranteed to be safe and that he would watch over you. I didn't know he would... do that. I will admit I hadn't considered it, but who could have?"

"The tie to the Unseelie is still there, but it is weaker and stronger than it has ever been. Like my family is gone and that blood bond has lessened, but the power of the court is the highest it has ever been." Luca seemed confused. "I don't know what to do. Without the throne, the people are in disarray."

"He took one for himself." I sighed and sat on the bed. "Made it himself. And all he wants is to punish the gods, and find a way to return where he came from."

"Doesn't he know that secrecy is better when dealing with humans?"

"Not with the gods," I stated just as reasonably. "Without faith, their power will wane and he can take it for himself."

"And what will you do?" Aeslyn asked. It was a simple enough question, but the way she asked left a sour taste in my mouth. As if she was putting this on me, somehow. "What will the Hunt do?"

I shook my head. "None of your concern."

"It's *all* of our concern, Marcus," she nearly shouted. "Your son lives in this world too. What is he supposed to do?"

"Mom," Connell called, shifting her focus to him. "He's got it. He's already not feeling great about all of this either. He had to worry about all of us while those guys had us, and he would have fought to save us. Let him do what he's going to do and have some faith in him."

I had to admit I was shocked at that.

Aeslyn rebuffed him with both a glare and a shift to a more disapproving tone. "Connell, adults are speaking."

He put the controller down and said, "Yeah, and using me as a means to manipulate my father into some kind of action that *you* approve of." Both of Luca's eyebrows shot up and Connell added, "Grandma taught me that. She taught me all of this in her classes. You weren't brave enough to go find the mantle yourself, and now you want to try to push your fear onto him like everyone else."

She tried once more, this time angry, "Connell—"

"No!" Connell spat, pointing at her in a fury of his own. "No. You don't get to use me to try to control him anymore. Stop it."

At the risk of overstepping, I reached down and put a hand on his shoulder, "While well spoken—and appreciated more than you can ever know—please don't yell at your mother for being afraid. We all are. I'm working on something, and the less you all know, the less of a threat you can be considered."

I fixed Aeslyn with a gaze of pure calm. "I have this under control to the best of my ability. You may not like giving up that control, but I don't care. All of you are mine now, and while you and I aren't the best of friends, I would hope that you have come to the conclusion that I will always hold my son's safety paramount."

I stood up and went to leave the room, but paused and looked to speak to Connell. "Would you like to come say hi to Cassia and hear some news?"

His eyes widened and he shouted, "Yeah!"

Aeslyn lifted a hand and Luca put his hand on hers. "Go ahead, son. Your mother and I need to have a discussion."

She looked thoroughly displeased, but we left anyway before their voices raised.

"Sorry about that, buddy." The words were out of my mouth before I could think not to say them.

"It's okay, Luca told me that might happen sometime. It just stinks to see it first-hand, you know?"

I nodded. "Yeah. I can respect that."

We found Cassia and her mother sitting with Arden as Merlin stood nearby watching the Wardens with binoculars.

"Cassia!" Connell called loudly as soon as he saw her and bolted forward. I expected Chiasa to make a move against him, but she just smiled and watched as he launched himself at my girlfriend.

She caught him and yelled, "Hey! What's up, man?"

"Dad said you had some news?" He looked at her expectantly and she smiled. "What is it?"

"Well, first, I brought you these." She pulled out a book bag full of age-appropriate manga and anime, then also a model-building kit. "Those are lots of fun to read and I love them, so we can talk about them when we come back, okay?"

"Wooooow!" He wanted to look at all of them but was polite—barely—and looked back up at her. "Did you have fun?"

She nodded. "Sure did. Ate lots of sushi too."

The boy's face scrunched up. "Ewww."

Comparing this kid to the one who had just read his mom the riot act on my behalf was something else.

"Yeah." I grinned at him and sat in the booth with them. "I'm not good at this kind of thing, but how would you feel about a sibling?"

"Mom and Luca?" He was confused, then when Cassia shook her head and pointed to her stomach, it clicked and he hollered, "Oh shit!"

That made all of us double take and he just laughed loudly as he put his hand on her stomach.

Chiasa found this all highly amusing as she watched the interaction before commenting, "He is a good brother already. Strong boy."

She was clearly trying to get his attention by calling him that, so he turned to her and said, "I'm Connell. Who are you?"

"That's my mom, Chiasa," Cassia explained.

The older woman nodded at her name and he bowed back. "Nice to meet you."

"Do you like to fight, Connell?" I stiffened at the elder oni's question.

"I've been in a couple fights, but Mom says I'm not allowed to go all out because I'm stronger than Normies. She only lets me play sports because Luca said it would be good to learn control in a more aggressive way."

That made the older oni cackle in delight, and I wondered what she would try to do with my son. Maybe I should warn Luca about her.

CHAPTER THREE

I blinked down at my phone, confusion apparent enough for Cassia to tap my arm. "What's wrong?"

"Uncle Yen texted me, wants to talk in his room." I stood up and looked to Connell. "You gonna be okay?"

"Yeah, Cassia's here." He smiled at her and her mother. It surprised me that Chiasa smiled back and that sent a chill down my spine.

Cassia caught my nervous glance at the older oni and shook her head. "I got him, Marcus. Go ahead."

Wary, I nodded and went upstairs to my uncle's room, the one catty corner to mine in the hall before his office and knocked on the door.

Uncle Yen's voice came through the door, slightly muffled, "Come on in, my boy!"

The door opened with ease and admitted me to the room. It was much larger inside than mine, or even what the building should have been able to contain. I just shook my head. "Magic."

"Indeed it is." Uncle Yen smiled at me from where he sat at a small desk with a pen and some paper in front of him.

"You're just in time. I was finishing this letter of introduction for you."

"Introduction? To whom?"

Anubis appeared from the shadows by the bookshelf across the room. "My brother, Thoth."

Anubis joined his lover, my uncle, at his desk and put a hand on his shoulder. "Are you certain you wish to call in this favor?"

Uncle Yen nodded. "They need knowledge I don't have, and the only hope they have is his advice." He ran his hand through his hair and sighed tiredly. "Frankly, we could all use his advice right now."

"So, what? He's just going to come to the Table and we can ask him some questions?"

Anubis shook his head. "No."

Yen agreed, "No. Knowledge gods aren't welcome here because they generally have a way of..."

Anubis actually spat on the floor, my uncle grimacing at it before waving it away with a spell and flick of his wrist, then said, "Say it as it is meant to be said, Yenasi. They poison those around them and become a..."

He looked like he was searching for the word before my uncle added in exasperation, "Downers. They become downers. Their minds don't shut off when drunk, they just talk louder and Thoth loves to hear himself talk."

So we would have to go to him. I blinked, wondering if that would be so easy and asked, "Where would we meet him?"

"Could be anywhere. A coffee shop down the street." Anubis shrugged and tilted his head back and forth before adding, "The great labyrinth of Alexander. Anywhere."

"I'm sorry, where?"

"The labyrinth of Alexander is actually where the Alexandrian library was kept," Uncle Yen explained with a smile. "Quite a few Touched of a certain level go there to research new magic and I was one. It was where I found that tome of spells I gave you."

He blinked at me as if suddenly seeing me for the first time.

"Radical change to the hair, by the way, my boy. Very…nega-N'Sync vibes from it. The girls like it?"

I snorted. "I hope so. I was more Backstreet myself, but Justin is a good singer, so I'll take it."

"Focus!" Anubis grumbled, crossing his arms over his chest. He stared at us for a moment and then muttered, "BTS is the best, stop this nonsense."

Galaxy surged from my shadow and snarled, "Can we not?" She glared at the three of us and sighed heavily, "I've been trying to give you space to sort through things, but bickering over boy bands is hardly what is needed right now."

I was almost angry with that, even if she was right, but she added, "Spice Girls changed the world."

I shouldn't have, but I laughed. She smiled softly at me, but Anubis stilled and stared at her as if she were a cobra about to spit in his direction. "Thank you, Arden and Cassia, for teaching me the new music." She considered the glaring god and then sighed. "I'm not a threat to you, Anubis. Especially not with you introducing us to Thoth."

He didn't look fazed by her speaking to him and just continued to stare until Uncle Yen smacked the other man on the leg and he flinched. "What?"

"Go see your brother, and please have him pick somewhere decently safe to meet them?" Uncle Yen shook his head and lifted a hand to stop Anubis from leaving, "Safe for *them*."

He nodded and left with a mild look of concern for Uncle Yen as we waited. "He still doesn't like me?"

"You're a deity he doesn't know, and the world has gone to shit since you woke up a little more than three months ago, so his feelings are valid." Uncle Yen crossed his arms and at us. "What's with the tension?"

I blinked at him and shared a brief look with Galaxy before looking back at him only to find him hitting me with the, *Boy, I know so much more than you know, so just tell me* look.

I was about to speak when Galaxy fessed up, "I've been forcibly resetting their fatigue and tolerance for life-altering situations since the beginning to keep them mentally healthy and cooperating in order to regain my former strength." Uncle Yen blinked at that, his eyes wide for a moment but she continued. "I knew that they wouldn't like it, but in order to keep everyone safer, I did what I thought was best."

She looked at the ground before looking back up at me. "Before, with you, it was natural and you were just driven. There wasn't as much of a need to make you want to go and do things, you just did. Almost predatory. But after the lockdown, there was a lag and I had to start actively pushing, bending, and molding your mind a bit to drive you on and make you ignore aspects of it all."

She took a deep breath and finally added, "I was wrong. I let my fear of disjunction and dysfunction among the group of you where your minds were concerned guide me instead of letting you rest and come to terms and deal with things in a natural, healthy way." She looked at me and in the smallest voice she had ever managed, said, "I'm sorry."

Uncle Yen looked at me and raised a brow. "Marcus?"

I just shook my head. "The sad thing is—I believe that." She frowned and looked at me with her big eyes and I just threw up my hands. "I believe every fucking word. But I don't know how much of that is forced because of previous tinkering, and how much of it is our bond. Do I even really love you, or was that you bored?"

As soon as the words left my mouth, I knew that had been a low blow. I wished for everything I was worth that I could take them back, but I couldn't and the hurt in her eyes as she flinched as if struck broke my heart. "Galaxy..."

She held up a hand and said, "Everything you felt for each other, all of you, was genuine. I just removed the trauma to allow you to coexist in a manner that kept you all sane."

"Enough." Uncle Yen spoke softly, but beneath that velvet tone was iron stiff resolve and will. "Sit down, both of you."

He waved and two comfortable chairs appeared behind us, both of them sliding forward to force us to sit down.

He started on me. "First of all, that was fucked." He narrowed his eyes at me as I chastely nodded agreement. "Kicking a lady when she's apologizing ain't right, especially the way I've seen all of you together. Even if it was a legitimate question to ask."

He pointed to Galaxy. "I understand the need to meddle when you're scared, but you need to trust the people you love, and who love you, to be sturdy enough to stand in the storm of the trials you face together." He grimaced. "Messing with minds is a serious crime, Galaxy. If the Wardens knew, they would try to get you locked up. The gods, as a goddess? Worse. But I'm not saying anything, because to me, I know you're genuinely contrite."

I frowned at him and he cleared his throat. "This room has a truth spell on it, it's woven into the very fabric of reality here. If I wanted to lie right now, I couldn't. Neither can you."

"Don't overthink it. It's a residual from the Tree that calls this place home." He held both of our gazes in turn and reasoned, "So you both meant what you said."

"I'm sorry I said it," I began. It was just a lot to take in. "It just sucks to know that we weren't good enough as we were to carry on the way we had. I thought I was doing great."

Galaxy tried to cut in, "You were…"

I shook my head. "We were not. We would have gone through so much more if it weren't for you." I scratched my head, an ache beginning to form at the base of my skull. "I almost just want to say fuck it and have you erase my memory of it so that we can all just carry on as we had been."

"I can't do that," she muttered just loud enough to be heard.

"Galaxy, what is it you want moving forward?" Uncle Yen asked softly. "If things were to get better, what would you want?"

She looked at me and it was almost as if he knew what was about to happen, because Uncle Yen cleared his throat and said, "Out loud, please."

"I want you to love me the way I love you." Her statement threw me through a loop. "I love you enough to risk that all for you. I love you enough to be with you and Cassia and to try to keep your family safe. I love you enough to stop pushing you toward my goals so that I can just be with you."

I frowned. "Even if it means you would remain weak?"

"Every second we waste not finding the slivers of my Dominion, we are in jeopardy from any number of beings." She had tears in her eyes now, but she shook her head and wiped them away. "Being with you and Cassia has opened my eyes to other things I want. That's why I was so driven to wipe you in a way that could be felt."

I frowned further, almost worried about what she would say but I had to know. "What is it you want?"

"I want to be in a family again." She put her face in her hands and took a deep breath. "I want to figure out what happened to my children and how I got here, but I dearly want to protect you and Cassia—our child."

"So wait, you tried to wipe me so that you could protect our child?" She nodded. "How would that help?"

"We could have gone to Atlantis and then gotten my sliver, and I would have been strong enough to help protect all of you. We could be done for a while until we find the next Vorna."

"What else was it you wanted, Galaxy?" Uncle Yen interrupted.

"I want to be with my family." She pointed to me and I could see the others in my mind. "Being with all of you has formed bonds in me that are just as strong as they are for you. I want to be with all of you."

Uncle Yen nodded, then looked at me. "And you, Marcus?"

Thinking about it, I sighed. "I want to be with all of you too. I want to get all of your Dominion so this wild chase will be over. I want to be strong enough that no one can threaten my children."

It felt wild to say that. If Galaxy and I had children, would they be gods?

Yes. They would likely be gods, my love.

I blinked at her, then blushed slightly. "I want to be strong enough to be equal to all of you for once."

"Equal for once?" Uncle Yen laughed. "The Huntsman says that?"

I grimaced and nodded.

"You need to work on that confidence, my boy." Uncle Yen continued to chuckle to himself before sighing and saying, "See, you both want to move on. Holding on to this resentment is comfortable for you, Marcus, because it's what you did with Aeslyn. Learning to forgive is hard sometimes, son, but it shows the depth of your love."

He stood up and came over to stand beside me, putting a hand on my shoulder before lowering his voice to say, "If not for others, then for ourselves. Carrying bitter hatred for too long hardens the heart and does irreparable damage. Let it go."

He patted me twice, whistling a tune I recognized from a show I'd liked while overseas, a whole lesson imparted just like that.

"I am sorry, Marcus." Galaxy faced me now. "I won't ask you to forgive me yet if you need to work through it. But if I have to give Chris or Zeke my word in order for you to trust me again and bind myself to him like that, I will."

"No." I shook my head. "He was one of the ones I want to stand equal to."

I ran my hand through my hair and grunted. "Just promise me you won't do it again unless we explicitly ask for it. And I mean *truly* ask for it." She nodded. "If this room hadn't been spelled to force the truth, would you have said any of that?"

"In front of him?" She snorted. "No. But I've been practicing this conversation the entire time I was inside you."

She leaned forward and touched my hand lightly. "I love you, Marcus. I mean that. I love Cassia too. I want this more than anything. If we can't find all of my Dominion, I will find a way to make myself and all of you strong enough that we can protect our child."

I took a deep breath and settled myself. "Fine. I love you too. Let's try to get over this, okay?"

She nodded and before I could leave the room, she pulled me back in and said, "If you ever try to hurt me like that again, I will kick you in the balls, Marcus Bola. Don't you *ever* doubt how much I love you or Cassia again. Am I clear?"

She didn't give me the chance to respond, instead kissing me until my stomach flip-flopped and my head spun. Once she came up for air, I murmured, "Yes, ma'am."

CHAPTER FOUR

When we left the room and went back downstairs, Cassia pulled us both into a hug and smiled knowingly before muttering, "Mother wishes to see Bubba Kenshi and I don't know how to tell him that she's here."

I grunted and looked over to where Chiasa sat with Connell still, the boy showing her something with his phone as she watched it with amused interest.

"Looks like we might have a moment to go and warn him if we need to?" Cassia turned to watch her mother for a moment and nodded. "I'll go and talk to him with you. Galaxy, stay here and make sure Connell is okay. She moves, let us know."

She nodded once before heading over to join the two of them as Cassia and I walked over to the bar area, then back further into the stairs that led to the basement and the hall to the other building and gym area. The barracks over there was where Kenshi was most likely holed up, and we needed to find him faster than Chiasa would allow us to if she wasn't distracted.

In the gym, we found a lot of the guards, but the were-wolves were missing. "What happened?"

Doc came out of his office and cleared his throat. "All of them are vying for control of the pack." He must not have liked the look on our faces because he sighed and said, "Jolly is stepping down as Alpha and he's taking challenges. The rest of the pack is trying to take him one on one but I don't see the old boy giving up the ghost very easily. Were you looking for them?"

I shook my head and said, "Kenshi, but thanks for the heads up."

Doc raised his eyebrows and pointed down the hall. "He's locked in his smithy."

We frowned and looked at each other. Cassia grunted, "Come."

I called back behind us as we walked off, "Thanks, Doc!"

At the very end of the hall before the stairs that led up to the mess hall, we found the locked door that Cassia motioned to and I took as the entrance to the smithy that Kenshi should be in. "Bubba Kenshi!"

Cassia knocked as she called his name again and he didn't answer, so I grimaced and touched the lock, willing Void Frost to freeze the mechanism inside before I kneed the door and pushed into the room.

We found Kenshi with his back to the door and in a meditative position on a soft mat on the floor. He sighed, "Sissy, not wanting disturbed."

"Too bad, Bubba Kenshi." Cassia sounded apprehensive to say the least, but she pressed on. "Mother is here."

Kenshi flinched and slowly turned his head so that he could cast a glance over his shoulder. "She is… here?" Cassia nodded and he growled low. "Why?"

"Kimiko…" She sniffed, lip quivering before her eyes hardened and shook her head. "Kimiko is gone. When we faced the Night Parade, I was tricked into killing her."

Kenshi was on his feet so fast that I subconsciously stepped between him and Cassia, Void Frost hardening in my fist to the point that I just *knew* I held an icy blade in my hand.

Cassia gripped my shoulder and sniffed. "It's okay, Marcus."

Kenshi stepped toward Cassia and when he reached her, he put a hand on her shoulder, pain in his quavering voice, "Sissy Kimiko fight well?"

Cassia frowned and shook her head. "She was under a spell. Her body was basically just a puppet."

Kenshi's lip quivered and his jaw clenched, as he turned back to his mat. He took a deep breath and there was a hitch to it. I could tell he was trying to get it out and he just *couldn't*. The grief was stopping it in his chest and he just couldn't let go.

After what could have been a lifetime, he screamed. The hair on my arms and neck rose as his anguished cry brought him to his knees, his caught breath continued to leak from his throat with the gut-wrenching sorrow roiling within. His voice was barely a whispered whine as he fell to his knees and wept openly.

The sound of footsteps springing down the hall toward us brought me from his pain. I tapped Cassia on the wrist and nodded to her brother. "I'll take care of them, take care of Kenshi."

"Kenshi needs no care!" The oni snarled and climbed to his feet, he turned and his humanity melted away from him, his massive bulk replacing it. "Kenshi needs revenge!"

"He's dead, Kenshi," Cassia explained. "I killed him and he cannot return to life that way."

Kenshi snarled and pushed her aside as he stepped out into the hallway toward the others. I thought he was going to lash out but all I saw was his mother standing imperiously in front of them all.

He didn't even stop, his hand forming a knife hand as he swung at her. She lifted her own and I could have *sworn* it sounded like metal clashing and clanging as he continued his assault.

What I wasn't ready for was that his other hand swept under his latest strike and gripped her shoulder, his foot sweeping her legs as he turned his whole body. He pressed his hip into her and threw her into the room he'd been in, her body colliding with the forge that he had set up.

That only served to feed his fury as she stood up and brushed herself off. She spoke to him in Japanese and I frowned as Cassia related it to me. "She's telling him that she didn't know either, but that she was also not at the battle when it happened. He doesn't believe her."

I shook my head as the two of them continued to duke it out, my mind wandering at the fight a bit as I realized that if Kenshi could handle his momma, it was no wonder I couldn't handle him.

Finally, both of them were bloodied and Cassia had had enough. She walked into the fray despite me trying to do it first and getting knocked aside, then bellowed a short phrase and kicked Kenshi in the hip hard enough that it knocked him onto his side onto the ground.

Chiasa took that opportunity and I used Embodiment of Lightning to step in front of her with Void Frost on full blast at her to freeze her where she was in midair.

She glared at me hatefully, but she couldn't free her arms at first and that just made her eyes glow molten.

"That is enough!" Cassia insisted as Kenshi climbed to his feet. "Kimiko is gone—because of me. I need what remains of my family, and I will not stand by as the two of you fight for no reason."

I almost said that was kind of the oni way of things, but figured I was better than that and stayed silent.

Cassia looked to Kenshi and put a hand on his shoulder. "You're going to be an uncle, Kenshi."

Kenshi blinked and flicked his gaze from Chiasa, to his sister, then to me. "This true?"

I looked at him and pointed to Cass. "She's the one who got knocked up, not me."

He grimaced and growled at me, then looked to his sister. "You happy?"

"Not without my family supporting me." She put it bluntly

and stared back at him hopefully. "I know you and mom don't get along the best, but if I have to do this, I want to do this with my family supporting my new one."

She turned to look at her mother whose composure had returned and said, "I will not abide being told what to do, nor how to grow my family. I will not be doing this in the traditional way." She turned to Kenshi and said, "I want you with me, but if you can't handle me like this, that's fine. If you don't want to be near Mom, that's fine too. I won't force you. But I love Marcus and Galaxy, and I love my child. I want this life with them."

He looked to the ground briefly before putting his massive hand on her shoulder and mumbled, "Congratulations, Sissy Cass. Kenshi proud."

He reached over to pull me into a hug. "Good job, Bubba Marcus."

Chiasa cleared her throat and when Kenshi looked at her, she addressed him, "I'm sorry I pushed you so hard, and that I killed your master for not training you well enough."

I blinked and realized why her son hated her so much. "Woah." I'd kept my voice low and she still narrowed her gaze at me.

"It not okay." Kenshi stood once more to his full height and glared hatefully down at her. "You took much."

He took a deep, calming breath. "Too much. Kenshi..." He paused and frowned. "Kenshi cares not for you."

He glanced at Cassia. "Kenshi be here for Sissy Cass. Need to be alone."

He turned back and clomped further back into his room without another look back in our direction.

Cassia looked like she wanted to go in after him, but I put a hand out and shook my head. "He told us what he needed, we need to respect that."

She glowered before nodding and walking off with her mother staring dejectedly after her son. I could feel a cool glare coming from the older oni as she watched me for a short time, but I just walked away as well. There was no time to deal with her shit and shortcomings. We had a lot to prepare for.

————

"Are you entirely sure you want to be here right now?"

Merlin sat with me in Arden's car; she had already gone inside to prepare things for us.

"There's no word yet as to whether Thoth will see us, and this is something…" I stopped. Stalling like this had never really been a thing for me.

Merlin put a hand on my upper arm. "Important to you?"

I nodded once and he grinned. "Marcus, it's a ring."

I shook my head and swatted at him, connecting with his shoulder but not nearly as hard as I could hit. "It's a *commitment.*"

I took a deep breath and really thought about this again. I had only ever thought about buying one other ring and it had been for the misguided notion that Aeslyn had actually loved me. I'd have bought it on a lance corporal's pay, so it wouldn't have been much, but I'd been especially careful in choosing it. But before I could even purchase it, she had disappeared.

We walked inside and went through the process of riding the elevator to where we needed to be and almost as if in a blur, we stood in front of a counter, waiting.

"And you're sure that she wants this?" Merlin was cautious as the dwarven crafter tending to us brought out another velvet-lined, pine box. Each one held an assortment of rings within that I just shook my head at. None of them stuck out to me.

I frowned and sighed. "I don't know."

Truthfully, I thought she would tell me no. But if I didn't ask, I would always wonder if that had been okay.

Galaxy supported it; she was with Cassia right now, distracting her from me being gone.

You just need to know that our bond is something that not even the bonds of mortal marriage can touch. Her touch on my mind was soothing and I just smiled at her.

"Declan, is there anything else? I don't know how well she would like something flashy like these."

The dwarven jeweler just mopped his forehead as his assistant brought yet another box for us to peruse. Even by dwarven standards, he was ancient. More wrinkle than man, and his eyebrow-ladened brow drooped far enough that he looked almost cartoonishly old.

He puckered his lips a few times thoughtfully before his wizened, higher-pitched voice crept out of his mouth, "Unless you wish to use a simple metal band, or some kind of necklace, I don't see how." He tapped his ancient fingers on the table methodically. "We have bands made of pure precious gyms, carved directly out of the stones themselves. But those are prohibitively expensive."

I nodded. I didn't have a budget but I *did* have one too. We were still trying to come up with the funds for a lair. Even with Arden's resources, it was still a shit-ton of money to come up with. Though Arden and Bill the gold dragon said they were close to lining something up.

We still needed to figure out what the hell was wrong with her sister as well, but she was petrified by Cassia's basilisk eyes.

Merlin glared at the necklaces that the dwarven crafter had offered and huffed, "We would need to have anything you get her enchanted to withstand combat as well." He caught my eye and smiled mischievously. "You know how she likes to punch things."

That made me and Declan both laugh, the old dwarf stroking his mostly-gray beard thoughtfully. "There are monsters in Grestal that could be harvested for better and stronger materials than what we have available to us here in the human world."

I blinked at him and he smiled. "The dwarves control a mountain range in Grestal and we get some materials from there." He took out a pipe and packed it full of tobacco that smelled different from what I was used to and lit it, puffing with a softening look of euphoria on his face until he coughed and added, "We can only go so deep before certain stony monsters higher than our tier begin to harass and kill our miners. I can arrange for a miner to guide you if you wanted to collect better materials that might be more suitable for your Cassia."

I grimaced and thought about it, but Merlin just snickered. "It would be pretty poetic to go and kill a bunch of monsters to make her a wedding ring."

I smirked at the thought, joking, "Here my love, a murder ring just for you." Then sighed, "Yeah, that does sound pretty appropriate, and an actual blood diamond could be cool too."

I looked to Declan who just nodded. "I'll let Magdalena know you wanna use the portal and get my boy to take you to the drop point."

He pulled out a rather new-looking cell phone and pressed a button. He grunted twice and said, "Portal use." He waited and then growled, "Don't fuckin' care, lass. It's Marcus and the boy mage. You want them lower levels cleared out or not?"

He smirked and I could see his eyes sparkling under the bushes of gray in his face as he said, "Love you too; see you for lunch in an hour."

He hung up and jerked his head to the assistant who plopped a glob of golden bands on a ring onto the table and motioned for us to follow along.

Once again, we were on our way down in the elevator that felt like it went in several directions in close proximity to each shift.

After a moment of topsy turvy tilting and tumbling, the elevator came to a halt and we walked out into a rock-filled loading and unloading bay with mining carts full of stones, ore, and ingots of varieties that I wanted to consume for myself.

"Suppose you've already told them we're going?" I raised a brow at the scene in front of me while the glow of Merlin's cell faded beside me.

"Just Amabala. She hates enclosed spaces so she won't be coming, but she said she'll let Galaxy know."

Devour anything you can, Marcus. I am hungry.

I nodded and mentally responded, *Yes, dear.*

We walked through the bay to a corridor made of entirely metal, with riveted support beams along the wall and then a door that looked to be more than a foot thick.

"This is the door to the catacombs." The assistant's nasally voice startled me as he touched the door to make it open with a hiss and a scrape that shook the floor as it slowly allowed us entrance.

The other side of the door gave way to six dwarves in full plate mail armor with halberds that leveled our way. One of them snarled, "The Stone's Kiss is softest in the mud!"

The assistant bowed his head and returned, "But to kiss the Stone in the mud is to drown before glory."

The weapon wielding warriors whipped their halberds back into a carry position and turned away to march back into a different position.

Merlin muttered, "What was that all about?"

"It was a pass phrase to let them know that we were cool." I glanced at the assistant who carefully stared ahead as I spoke. "If we had forced our way down here and his response had been different, they would have known to kill us to protect what they're hiding down here. Could have even gotten him killed. And now they're going to have to change it to keep us from using it if we somehow manage to come back from where we're going without our guide."

Merlin looked even more confused, then muttered, "Military thing?"

I nodded with a soft smile and he just sighed. "I should read more on that subject."

"You should," I returned and clapped him on the shoulder. "You're a part of a unit now, and that means we may need to begin implementing these things too."

"As long as it's not something really intensive and long as

that one." Merlin walked the hall with me and then we entered into another room that held the familiar sensation of a portal to Grestal.

The assistant went to hand us lanterns but Merlin just held his hand up. "Even without a flame to keep us seeing, it would be a beacon to anything watching."

I raised an eyebrow at him and he tapped his head. "Got a spell for that."

"Your guide will have received word of your impending arrival and should be at hand to meet you on the other side." He motioned to the portal. "Once you're there, you're a representative of the Forge, and as such will be given a contract to sign should it be good enough for you, and then a marker to locate you should something... happen."

I raised a brow at that and heaved a sigh. *This will be worth it.*

Grimacing, I stepped through the portal with Merlin at my side.

CHAPTER FIVE

The other side of the area was brightly lit for how the entrance had been on the other side of the planes.

The walls here were metal and fortified just like the Forge's had been, but there was a bottleneck to this room. The walls closest to the portal itself were lined with runes and sigils glimmering and shining at us, the back of the wall behind the tear in reality was about six feet to the portal, then another twelve to the room beyond.

After that there were ballistae, mounted crossbows as wide as an oni was tall and almost as thick. Four crossed arms were banded with metal to keep them bent and strung with steel cording.

"Those are meant to fire *once*," I muttered more to myself, unable to see the payload that they held ready to launch from where we stood getting the glaring once over from the host of guards in the room. All of the contraptions in here would be hellacious to try to get around for people on either side of the portal. I almost wanted to start something to see what they had to throw at us.

One of the guards at the far wall wearing plate mail with

metal braided into his beard waddled toward me with his great sword on his shoulder. "Hello."

He grunted and pointed to a table at the back of the room closest to our right that looked like a command center.

As we walked over there, it was hard to keep my gaze from taking it all in. There were positions above where dwarves with handheld crossbows, javelins, and spears could rain down hell on anything that came through the doors that they didn't like. Didn't mean it would matter much to people like us, but still, if it was someone else, or a monster? Good night!

There were also murder holes in the sides of the walls that would have been easy to miss if it hadn't been for the light reflecting off the metal bolt head behind one of them as I walked by. This place made Fort Knox look like a children's playground.

The dwarf tapped the papers held down by stone and Merlin poured over them for a moment before saying, "No."

He took the quill and began to scribble on the sheets. "We will not be liable for any cave-ins in the event of a fight. We will not be liable for anything lost from the miners or anyone else while we're here, and anything we find, we will keep with a ten percent tax given to the Forge as a favor because we're here to do you a service." He pointed to the dwarf and spoke quietly. "I don't know what kind of bull you're trying to pull with this, but if it was to piss us off before a fight, I dare say you've reached that end."

The man grunted and took the contracts to the room hidden behind the vault door that he failed to notice and Merlin cleared his throat. "Spelled to be harder to notice until used and then you forget about it if you don't focus on it for more than a few seconds."

"Focus on what?" I blinked at him and he just snorted. "Where'd he go? What was wrong with the contracts?"

"Fifty percent of the things we found and killed would belong to the Forge, and a whole bunch of liability crap that they wanted to try to stick us with." I frowned at him and he blinked at me. "What?"

"Contract work is hardly a law enforcement thing, isn't it?"

He shrugged. "I was always interested in it, but there were times that Wardens would get caught hunting or with weapons because of a lapse in judgment. Our lawyers are Wardens so we would learn the law as well." He smiled. "I wasn't the best at it since it wasn't history lessons or spell craft, but I did okay."

I just laughed and shook my head. "You really never cease to amaze me, Merlin."

He laughed and rubbed his head. "Thanks. Have you finished leveling up, by the way?"

I swore and shook my head. We'd killed enough members of the Night Parade and consumed enough corpses to net us a couple more levels so I grinned and pulled up my stats.

I thought about the last fight we'd been in and decided a rework was called for.

Two Brawn, two Dexterity, one Physique, two Mana and finally three for Charisma.

Level 18
Stats
Brawn: 22
Dexterity: 18
Physique: 20
Mana: 37
Charisma: 33
Points to spend: 0
Spell Points to spend: 6

I smiled at the growth and how it surged through my body, then turned my attention to my spells.

Spells Known
Physical Buff 1/6
Bolt Havoc 1/8
Mana Blade*
Embodiment*
Void Frost*

Arcane Infusion
Golem Summoning (Ice)*
Passive Abilities
Improved Golem Summoning 1/6

That was a good number of spells, I was just still sort of miffed that the ice working had made me lose some of my previous spells and points altogether. Not to mention that it ate a spell like Icy Forge.

Granted, it was easier to create whatever I wanted to with Void Frost and how intuitive it was to use. It felt like every time I used it, it was so much easier to control and make it do what I wanted instinctively.

I put five of the points into the passive for golem summoning, filling it all the way.

Congratulations!

You've improved the skill Improved Golem Summoning to the point that it has evolved into Advanced Golem Summoning!

All golems created by you will be twenty percent stronger and heartier.

I grinned at that and looked at the spell, my grin turning into a grimace. "Jesus Christ."

Merlin looked at me and asked, "What?"

"Advanced Golem Summoning is at one of twenty points!" I sucked on my teeth as Merlin's eyes widened and I growled, "More than six levels worth of spell points that have to all go to that or I'll be waiting for a while to get it."

"Well, can't you just pour into it in the background?" I frowned at him and he explained, "Constant use allows us to come to understand the spell more, right?"

I nodded, there had been times where use allowed me to gain a point. He continued to explain, "Well, points allow us to artificially learn those finer aspects to a spell and gain more faster. Personally, I have spell points to spare because I practice my spells as often as I'm able to."

I blinked. "So I should be constantly using my spells to gain things from them?"

He shrugged. "Certain spells you sort of don't have the luxury of casting and keeping active, like a massive fireball that scorches the area." He stared at me knowingly. "However, controlling an ice golem in a freezer to do menial tasks? Allowing Hollow to come into our plane and explore as she can? Constantly buffing yourself?"

I sighed. "How much of this knowledge comes from gaming and from your previous life?"

"About forty-sixty?" He grinned. "I've had new spells gain levels really fast because I experimented with the casting. But you also have to recognize that just casting a spell and experimentation with one are vastly different. The net gains from experimentation versus gaining knowledge through constant use are far superior in my opinion."

I thought about it for a short time, then agreed. Creative use of spells would be an excellent way to gain a bit more knowledge about them.

I raised my hand to summon a golem, but Merlin smacked my wrist and hissed, "You use any sort of magic in here and this place lights up like the Fourth of July. Those runes on the walls are meant to target magic users and keep them lit up to be pincushioned with whatever these dwarves decide is reasonable."

There was a heavy metal-on-stone grind and the dwarf that had left us returned with a rather young-looking one in tow who carried documents. He had a rather clean-cut look about him that I liked. The sides of his head were clean shaven and his long hair was braided from the front of his head to the back of it where a braided ponytail fell to his shoulders. His beard was clean and streaked with silver even though he couldn't have been more than thirty by his eyes.

Where had they come from?

The younger dwarf glared at Merlin and quipped, "Gen'rous deal ain't good enough fer ya?"

Merlin crossed his arms. "Nope." He smiled softly and

motioned to the papers the dwarf smacked onto the table. "We may be here for materials as well, but we aren't going to be taken to the cleaners for anything you can pull out of that beard of yours."

"I ken negate the liability, but will nae budge on finance!" He crossed his own arms and glared back. "This be *our mountain*"—he tapped the table with a thick finger as he said those two words—"Ain't nae one thing leavin' here we need an' have nae 'counted fer."

"Fellas." I put a hand on Merlin's shoulder and one on the table in front of the dwarf. "My girlfriends are sure to realize I'm not on Earth sometimes soon and I *need* the materials to make good rings. So here's what we will do."

I pointed to the contracts and said, "You free us from liability, and charge us twenty-five percent tax for everything we bring back, and we won't charge you per monster."

The dwarf looked ready to balk, so I pulled my sunglasses away and let him see the eyes of the Huntsman. "The Wild Hunt will swarm through these caverns and kill the creatures threatening your people for you. If we find anything to bring back that could belong to one of yours, we will. Take it as a show of good faith, eh?"

The dwarf quirked his head slightly and cleared his throat. "Ahem, eh, uh, aye. That'd be…" He grabbed his beard and tugged at it for a moment before finishing his thought. "Aye. I ken do tha', but ya give them beasties a real whompin', aye? Me sister were taken by one a year back. Get 'em good, Huntsman."

I blinked. *That… That was easy? And why the fuck have these things gone unchecked for a year?*

The two of them bantered back and forth as they constructed the contract. The dwarf was fairly quick, his quill enchanted to write as swiftly as he thought and within about twenty minutes, the new contract was drafted and in front of us. Though there was only one sheet, we could both sign it.

Merlin read it carefully and smiled. "Merit-based bonuses that can stack and eat into the tax? How would that work?"

The dwarf smiled grimly and cleared his throat. "Bring back a trinket ya find from any lost warrior or miner, and get some brownie points with me. Bring back the heads o' any monsters ya come across, and get brownie points with the leaders of the Forge."

He looked around for a moment before saying, "Ya find and bring back me sister's pick, and the beast what killed her's head? Taxes be damned—you'll keep the lot."

The warrior who accompanied him gasped and the younger one just fixed him with a glare. "Rigid, ya swampy bastard, ya say a fuckin' thin' to any souls anywhere, an' I swear by me beard, I'll brain ya in front o' yer mother afore I leave this stone. Aye? Ya lost kin down there too, donae act like yer all tha' much better than me."

The warrior grunted and grumbled, "I'll take up a collection. You'll get a bonus for all the armor and weapons you can bring back from our friends. I swear it."

I clapped my hands and signed the sheet of paper. "Sounds fucking great, guys. All we need now is our miner guide."

"Allow me to take you to him then." The neat dwarf took the contract that Merlin signed and tucked it into a parcel that he pulled *from his beard* and then tucked it back in.

He went to a panel on the wall farthest from the table and knocked on it six times in a rhythmic fashion before it slid backward then to the left, opening a small room where a man sat with a mug of something brown that smelled like whisky.

"Halgrin?" The man muttered, "What'd ya want, boyo? I have ore to mine, and I donae wish to be late on me quota."

"Yer quota is forgiven fer the day, Slater." Halgrin held up a hand with a smile. "Yer record intact, I assure ya. We need ya to guide these two gentleman to…"

He paused, flicking his gaze to us and Slater just grunted, "The killing floors?"

I raised a brow at that and Halgrin just sighed, grunting,

"Aye." He smoothed his hand slowly over his braided hair and added, "While yer escortin' 'em, look fer veins of ore we have nae seen before and harvest what ya ken safely fer testing. The usual."

Slater glanced at us and sniffed once, taking a swig of his whisky. "They gonna need bringin' back for liability reasons? I donae feel like havin' ta bring back more corpses."

He looked askance at me and Merlin. "Child mage looks like he takes steroids an' then there's mister sunglasses over here. I donae think a mutant has much chance down there with them monsters, boyo, sorry."

I grinned. "Sure a drunkard can handle guiding someone to more than a shitter?"

He guffawed and pointed to his cup. "Take more'n a Toddy ta do more'n steel me nerves, boyo." He tapped his chest with his thumb. "Only one brave enough ta go down there, an' it ain't without…"

I nodded, not needing to hear the rest. It left marks of its own, being in a place like that.

"We'll handle the monsters, Slater," Merlin affirmed. "You just get us there and we will take care of the rest."

He picked up his mug, tossed it back and gulped the contents down before letting out a contented sigh and then a belch. "C'mon, then. Let's go get ya kilt."

He grabbed a thermos from one of the counters, shoved it into a pack beside the door, and then shoved his way through to the outside.

Merlin and I glanced to Halgrin, who just shrugged and motioned after the miner. "He's the best and bravest we have. He'll keep up with ya, but ye'll have to do the same with him. Good luck."

I grunted and chuckled to myself before following the dwarven man who was busy hollering, "Dead men walkin'! Get the fuck outta me way, boyos."

CHAPTER SIX

The elevator we rode took us into the depths of Grestal. The stone shifted around us occasionally, like Grestal couldn't decide what it was made of in that moment.

We rode in the elevator for ten minutes, something that I had never experienced before. We could see all of our surroundings through the mesh. The majority of the diggers and miners were in the upper floors, where security seemed present but lax and more talkative from where we could see as we moved lower in the stone shaft.

The middle floors were a lot less packed, but the security there was a lot more intense and vigilant.

"Shafts leadin' up ain't all that uncommon," Slater explained unbidden. "Monsters dig up for a snack now an' again."

That made Merlin frown, and ask, "They don't just look for all of you and hunt you down?"

Slater shook his head. "Only the weaker ones dig upward." He shakily uncapped his thermos and took a sip, grunting, and added, "The stronger ones go *down* ta hunt other monsters an' materials. Reckon' ya'll see soon, we be 'bout there."

He heaved a sigh as the brakes engaged and his whole demeanor changed instantly. His shake was gone and his eyes were the clearest I had seen them, harder too. There was some stone to him now. Steeled nerves in the weirdest and most visible way I'd ever witnessed, and he'd not made a single sound outwardly like I might have.

His voice was deeper but he spoke softly, "Let's go."

He slipped his thermos back in his pack, strapped it on, and stepped through the opening doors to the floor below. Several of the lighting fixtures looked to have been attacked and broken.

Some of them even looked to have been bitten out of the very walls themselves, the stone around where they should have been looking like it was carved out by teeth.

I whispered to myself, "What the fuck could do that?"

I blinked and thought about the spell I wanted to cast, then cast Golem Summoning while I whispered, "Hollow."

My mana dipped rapidly, a third of it gone instantly and frozen over.

The golem formed in front of me close to the image that I had in mind. It looked more humanoid than it had before, and the ice was darker too. It was still shorter than me, but it didn't look like someone would be able to kick it and knock it to pieces as easily as they could have before.

The eyes shimmered for a second before I could tell that Hollow had taken over control of it.

Before she could speak, I said, "Be quiet. We're hunting monsters far below Grestal and looking for materials."

She frowned and suddenly her cool attention flooded my mind. *I can speak to you this way, as well. As long as we don't run into any fire or water jinn here, we will be fine.*

She regarded her body and I could tell she was pleased with it, *Better.*

I nodded at her and turned my gaze to Slater who watched our surroundings carefully before motioning for us to follow behind him.

"Merlin, if you have a way to keep yourself from taking serious cold damage, I'd use it." He stared at me curiously as I used Void Frost to create a scythe for myself. "I don't plan to play nice down here."

He grinned and pulled his staff out, muttering a quick string of words I didn't understand to himself before he tapped his chest then Slater's back.

The dwarf whipped around and his fist rocketed toward the staff. Merlin jerked it back and frowned, whispering, "Sorry."

"Don't do that," he ordered and turned his sights back to what was ahead.

Merlin looked at me and flared his mouth out like a child that made me snort quietly. He tapped me on the side of the head with his staff and I could see more clearly, so I took my sunglasses off and placed them into my inventory.

The tunnel we were in was large as far as tunnels I had seen, at least as wide as a pickup truck was long from bumper to bumper and just as tall. The support beams were surprisingly intact as well. There were offshoots that were marked in dwarven and with symbols that I didn't quite understand.

Nothing here came to me as suspicious or dangerous, but I knew from past experience that didn't mean shit.

We rounded a curve ahead to the left and walked for another ten minutes before Slater turned back and stared at us. He blinked, then whispered, "Ahead be where the killing floors begin. There's a monster what nested there, but dunno if it be there now. If it is, ye'll die."

I took a breath to respond then thought better of it and just asked, "What makes these things so dangerous that seasoned dwarven fighters can't even hack it against them? You have some of the finest crafters in the realms, and you're letting these monsters keep you from your mines?"

"They eat the ore down here an' their bodies take it an' purify it to make scales." He shivered and sighed. "The scales be *dense* an' *pure*. Purer than some of our best smiths can manage. The better the metal ate, the stronger they be."

He rubbed his face with both hands before retorting, "I be a miner, not a craftsman, aye? They tinker and toil up there, and they tried, I think. Materials to make the things they need are blocked by the scaled bastards."

"Did this one eat something different than the others, then?" He shook his head and I frowned. "Then why is it so dangerous?"

"It be *fast.*"

He wouldn't say anything else as he just turned and walked around the corner and into a larger chamber of ramps that slowly swirled downward toward a singular floor. In the middle of the floor, three flights down, was a graveyard of metal and bone. Armor from dwarven fighters littered the ground, some of it clean, other bits dusty and some even crusted over with blood and other matter.

It was a nest, alright. It swirled around a huge mound of ore that surrounded something sleeping in the center. Its scales looked rusted-over almost, a reddish hue that were flecked with black scales around it.

I looked at Merlin. "What the hell is that?"

"Looks like it could be a subspecies of drake, but I've never known one to eat metal. It's unprecedented."

From where we were, there was plenty of room for a fight, but this was the time to prove to Slater that his being with us wasn't a death sentence.

That and we don't have much time before Cassia starts to grow suspicious.

I sighed at the thought and noted that my mana bar had begun to thaw out. That was good, as it would mean I could gather it all back again once it was done.

Merlin grabbed my arm as I was about to walk forward and hissed, "We should study it. If this thing is just fast, we can put it into your ice and keep it, right?"

I frowned. "We might be able to keep it cool enough to take it back to Earth with us to see what makes it tick, especially since cold makes reptiles tired. But my ice will most likely kill it. Besides, if we take anything back to Earth with us, we take it somewhere it will be safe and where it won't be a threat."

He nodded and frowned. "So we kill this one and see if we can find something else?"

I nodded and he smiled. "Awesome."

I laughed at that and Slater just stared at us in disbelief. "Ya…"

His mouth moved like he had more to say but I just hushed him with a soft smile and a hand on his shoulder. "Gimme a sec."

I stepped over to the edge and allowed the shadows that nagged at me to come closer, washing over my body like a flood.

My strength grew with me reclaiming my Mantle and I looked down at the sleeping beast with a sense of almost pity before I hopped off the ledge of the walkway.

I fell quickly and, as soon as I was in range, swung my scythe with all I had, allowing it to flip me in midair to add some power to the stroke.

The icy blade sliced into its shoulder and gut before it realized what was happening and I froze it to the ground with its own blood and Void Frost. It tried to bite at me, but I caught its jaws in my hands and yanked, flexing my back and hips to twist and pull the bottom jaw out of the socket.

I gripped too hard though, the head jerking to the side with a sickening crack.

I let the head drop and looked around to ensure there was nothing else that wanted to tussle before I looked back up to Slater and Merlin.

Hollow grew out of the ice next to me and her voice held a soft tone of pride as she said, "That will do nicely."

"You like that?" She nodded oddly for a creature made wholly of ice. "Weird, but okay."

Slater and Merlin joined me where I stood a few moments later as I checked over my kill. True to what Slater had said, the scales were metal but these ones were burnished, almost like copper. Though the dwarf was a little more cautious and wary around me now.

I tapped a scale that I freed from the creature's body and handed to Slater. "Know what kind of metal that is?"

"Copper, but it ain't right." He frowned and shook his head. "It's too pure. Much more than be normal for these beasts and what's in this place."

He frowned and tapped his finger on his chin. "Thinkin' on it—ain't no copper here in these mines."

I frowned at that and examined it a bit more before putting my hand out and yanking several of the scales away and put them into my inventory.

"Are there any particularly good veins of ore around here for you to dig for, Slater?"

He blinked and thought about it as he scoured the area once more. "Nothin' new here, Huntsman. Just the usual Mithril and precious stones."

He stared at me for a moment and I saw it. "There's aura around your eyes, Slater. Can you see the ore?"

His jaw slackened and dropped, "Ya… Ya can see tha'?" I dipped my head and he blinked at me in disbelief. "Aye. I can."

"When do we start getting to the good shit then?"

He frowned and thought about it. "There be three more levels down where we started to break into platinum, an' other precious metals like gold, an' then the unknown stuff beyond, but tha' ain't been dug out yet. Those ones be a bit more rare on this side of Grestal."

"Merlin, you think you can handle the next one on your own?" He nodded and then raised his hand. "What, dude?"

"Slater, if you know of any metals that are valuable to humans like platinum, please let us have them. We need to have a bit of coin." The dwarf nodded and he raised a brow as Merlin continued, "Also, if you know of any ores that can hold, transfer, and amplify magic, we need that."

Slater scratched his beard and frowned. "May know a few. The gold an' platinum will be valuable, so ya can get into that so long as ya protect me and seein' what I just did? I think that'll be the easier part."

I nodded and motioned for him to lead the way down into the depth of the mountain, my eyes peeled for the items, gear, and remains of the dwarves who fell down here.

CHAPTER SEVEN

This time, two of the creatures hissed and spat at one another in one of the tunnels in front of us, their scales clattering against each other as they circled a man-sized hunk of stone with something colored shooting through it.

I looked down at Rocky, the fox golem that held part of Merlin's soul as a half-jinn and smiled. He could kill one of them. He'd proven it a floor up when Merlin had sicced him on one of the lead-scaled ones that had been gorging itself on a thick vein of the stuff.

That just proved that Grestal was a magic place, because lead had to be found *much* lower in large quantities on Earth. Like, the crust level shit.

The stone fox had passed into the stone and used the metal inside the vein that the metal drake had been eating to spear it through the brain. It dropped right where it was and we collected the scales for sampling.

Slater had said the lead scales were useless to the dwarves. Merlin had shrugged and collected a small bag full before I put my hand on the beast and a message spoke through my mind.

Consumable materials identified. Would you like to consume them? Yes / No?

I accepted and the scales flickered before fleeing into my outstretched hand.

I went to pull my hand away when the drake's corpse began to flicker as well.

The same message populated and I pulled it into me.

Draconic material consumed.

Staring after the two aggressive drakes getting ready to fight in front of me, I wanted to kill them all the sooner.

I glanced over at Hollow. *You want to stretch your muscles out, or are you just going to observe?*

Her head whipped my way and I could imagine her eyes narrowing at me dangerously. *I might reside in the golem you summoned, but no matter how nice it is, I will not just do your bidding, mortal.*

I rolled my eyes as she walked out into the tunnel from where she had been watching, the ice of her feet making a *tink, tink, chink*-ing noise as she moved. The farthest drake saw her coming first and hissed dangerously, making the drake closest to us attack.

The aggressor hit the one that had seen Hollow like a freight train and Hollow capitalized on it. The golem surged forward and the energy around her began to build instantly, her aura bottoming out around her feet and swirling like a storm before she stomped a foot and ice erupted from the aura around her.

Spears of cool blue ripped through the two beasts and blood froze in rivulets as it flecked the sides of the still spinning and growing spears.

She looked back at me and whispered, *Consider my 'muscles' stretched.*

I snorted. "Fine." Out of the corner of my eye, I watched Slater stare in disbelief at the display before him and then shake his head as he watched her leave my side.

A surge of warmth flooded over me and I could tell without

looking that my mana had completely thawed out. My stomach grumbled angrily and I sighed, *Gotta love a shifter's metabolism.*

I pulled out four meal supplement bars and stuffed one in my mouth before offering one to both Merlin and Slater. The dwarf took one gingerly but Merlin shook his head so I just ate that one too.

"You have yet to use your ice powers in a manner like that, why?" Hollow's questing tone grated on me, but I only had selfish answers.

"Mana consumption, really."

She frowned. "Your mana usage for ice should be almost nonexistent, mortal, especially with my blessing."

It was. "That doesn't mean I want to go around spending it like I can get it all back quickly." I jutted a finger at Merlin. "His mana reserves replenish like it's no big deal to blow your load in one go. Arden too. I need food and rest to recover mine with any sort of dependability. Otherwise it's just trickling energy back into the bucket that is me."

"You should be recovering mana faster, Marcus." Merlin frowned and looked over at me. "I mean, I can see it swirling around you as we speak. You're eating it up like crazy but it's not filling your mana bar back up?"

I shook my head and he frowned. "We need to look into that."

I nodded and grumbled that we did. "What's on the drakes?"

Merlin looked over it and grinned. "Gold." The boy mage looked at the dwarf who just raised a hand in a go-for-it manner.

Slater focused on the stone and then nodded his head off to the side of the wall. "There be a vein here, nice one. Wanna get into it an' see what it be."

"Be my guest; we've got your back." The dwarf nodded at that and pulled his pick once more from behind him but below his pack and got to work. The interesting thing about it though, was that there was only a soft noise of rocks hitting the ground and the scattering of rubble as he chipped into the wall.

"Enchanted to not make any sound. Allows him to listen to his surroundings." Merlin joined me and gave me a bag of golden scales. I looked over to the ore that had been there and it was gone as well. "We can sell the majority of this through a fence. This is going to be what we can use to pay the taxes you probably could have smooth-talked him out of making us pay."

My mouth quirked up almost like I was embarrassed. "It was pretty noticeable, wasn't it?"

"You may as well have been the bard in a table top game with advantage." I blinked at that and he stared at me. "What, you don't do the dungeons and—"

"Dragons?" I raised an eyebrow and he nodded. "Did the wolves let you into their game?" He didn't say anything and I cursed under my breath. "I keep hearing Kelty is a great DM, and I wanna play too!"

"He is, but they only invited me because I've played before." He shrugged, letting the conversation die as far as that was concerned. "Seriously though, it may pay to let you do any negotiating for anything that we need from here on out, with that Charisma of yours."

I smiled and watched as Slater made quick work of exposing a vein of what looked like crystals to me. Slater grunted and picked some for himself, tossing it into his pack before pulling out a hammer, chisel, and some wood. "Rutile. This is what ya break down to make titanium. Make an alloy of it, an' ye'll have a fine weapon, or somethin' worth sellin'."

"Could it withstand fighting against supernatural beings?" I asked and he frowned, then shook his head. "Probably not the best thing to use then, but could we take some anyway?"

He pulled his pickaxe back out after he finished marking the vein for others and dug into the vein a bit further for us.

He was about a foot into it when Merlin stilled and looked to Rocky, who was pacing farther into the tunnel. "Rocky says something is coming."

Slater grunted and said, "It be tha' one." He put his pick away and looked to us. "Titanium bastard. Scales hard as shite an' just as brutal. Wondered where it'd been."

I stared hard in the direction the fox golem watched but saw nothing until the creature screeched in a metallic, ear-splitting way that made my bones feel like they ached.

The fox fell into the stone at his feet and the drake went after him, clawing at the ground like a dog looking to get at a favorite toy. Merlin rushed forward with his sword at the ready and the staff in his left hand waving menacingly. The drake's metal-covered tail arched over its shoulder and would have crushed the boy mage if it weren't for the bluish barrier he erected in front of himself, his staff acting as a shield while his sword swept in.

The drake lowered its head and allowed the blade to ring off its scales and bounce to the side before twisting and putting all its weight into a clawed paw to shove Merlin away. The mage skittered a dozen feet back and suddenly stone spears rocketed from the ground where the drake stood. The stone cracked and sheared away where it hit, the density of the scales on its under-belly too much for the stone to take let alone pierce.

That attack only served to further piss it off. I closed my eyes and focused, and then rushed forward two steps before casting Bolt Havoc. The spell didn't take the shape of a ball of electricity this time but a small, slim javelin as it streaked toward the enraged drake. The javelin hit it and the electricity skittered over the scales along it and it just looked at me and snarled before launching itself at me.

"Titanium doesn't conduct electricity well!" Merlin spat as he crashed into the creature from the side with his shield spell active again. "Heat either, don't you know that?"

I pulled the Silvaero and loaded it with normal bullets, then remembered that guns didn't work in Grestal before responding, "I fucking eat crayons, God damnit!"

I had no other weapon for this other than Void Frost and I was glad to have it as the distraction from the mage just further pissed it off as I called to it. "Come get me, you scaly prick with legs!"

It roared again and I surged forward with ice encasing my hands in boxer-like gloves with spikes on the knuckles.

I hit the thing on the right side of the head and a blur of metal swung to my left that made me step back as Slater continued his assault on the beast.

That gave me the idea to make a club out of ice. I lifted my hand and grinned at the mimicry of a wooden club in my left hand and a pick in my right.

"Merlin, lock it down!" I could see him fling his sword into his inventory so that he could hold his staff with both hands, then yelled, "Slater!"

I swung my pick and hit the shoulder on his side as soon as Merlin had the drake held down and hit it with my ice club. The scales held on the first strike, the point slipping in the connections between scales, but then Slater smacked it. The frozen point rammed into the flesh and made the creature fight all the more furiously.

We took turns hitting the ice weapon until it was into the body and blood trickled out of it. From there, I took it in both hands and focused on pouring Void Frost through it like it was a funnel.

Feel the blood inside it turning to ice. Hollow spoke to me through our bond and her Blessing. *To have any liquid inside this creature is an invitation to the cold to make it solid—perfect.*

The blood flow within the creature grew sluggish; so did its fighting. Slater's hammer crashed into the spine of the pick again and the flesh beneath the scales cracked audibly and groaned as it fell away. Merlin stuck his sword into the drake's mouth and shoved the weapon up into its lizard brain with enough force to ensure that it would be dead right there.

"Marcus, that should be good." I blinked and glanced over at him as a cloud of his breath exited his mouth as he shivered.

"Thought you used a spell to keep yourself warm?"

He nodded. "I didn't think it would get this cold." He

looked around and, sure enough, there was a layer of frost all around us in the tunnel.

Slater frowned at me and asked, a shake in his voice, "What kinda monster be ya, boyo?"

I couldn't help laughing as I said, "The worst kind."

We plucked the salvageable scales we could off the drake's corpse before I devoured it for the Mantle as materials.

I did the same for the previously golden ones and grimaced as the sounds of another drake built from the same end of the tunnel where this one had come from.

I sighed and grumbled, "This is about to get pretty fucking annoying, guys."

———

We fought for almost twenty minutes straight as wave after wave of drakes of varying degrees of difficulty came at us. The easiest way to kill them was to freeze them in place and beat them senseless, but we varied on that as my mana needed to recharge more than Merlin's.

That was where Hollow came in. The golem elemental would freeze the drakes in place and then Merlin, I, or Slater would move in to finish the job by going for the vulnerable parts like the mouth, eyes, or nostrils.

It was brutal, hard work and it wore on all of us, but we made it to the last cleared mining floor. This one was open, more so than the others, and looked to have been dug out by the drakes themselves. They refused to come into this area, and it was because of this fact that we were able to have the reprieve we enjoyed.

"What do you think could be driving them away from this place?" Merlin muttered as he continued to write in the open journal on his lap.

I couldn't see anything in the area that stood out to me as a threat to something as powerful as the drakes. We stayed there long enough to fully recoup and then longer and had Slater take a look around.

He stopped in front of the wall at the rear of the room and blinked at it. "Stone ain't right here."

Merlin and Rocky trudged forward and sure enough, the fox golem touched the wall with his snout and the rock melted aside, showing a scene that none of us had seen coming.

There was a copper-scaled dragon laying in a crater filled with blood, caged into the ground and congealing blood by veins of ore that pierced its skin, scales and wings.

"What the fuck?" Machines and test tubes filled the surrounding area around it, computers and the like with tables covered in runes with tubes floating over top of them. There was fluid on the ground that had dried but when I looked at it long enough, it had a magical residue that reminded me of an aura.

The dragon looked weak and, as we came into the room, one eyelid opened at us, its slit eye focused weakly. "You aren't him."

The androgynous voice came from the air, but not really any sound from the mouth.

"I don't know who 'him' is, but if he comes back while we're here, I'm going to kick his ass." The dragon wheezed and shivered against its bonds, so I came forward to try to make it still. "It's okay, let us get these out of you, and we can try to heal you to get you out of here."

I looked over at Merlin and muttered, "Can Rocky move these things?"

He frowned and looked to be conversing with the golem. "He could, but he needs to get closer."

"I'll go in first then and help them remain calm." I turned back to the dragon and spoke directly to them. "I'm going to come over and help you remain still so that my friend here can get your bindings out. Just stay as still as you can and we'll get you out of here, okay?"

"It's too much," the dragon whispered tiredly. "He's taken

my blood, scales, and magic to make those… *things.*" That last bit came stronger and made the hairs on the back of my neck stand on end. "Every one they made drained me more and more…"

My feet moved slowly, barely lifting from the ground as I steadily worked my way closer as Rocky did the same from out of the dragon's range of vision.

I held out my hand, low enough not to be considered a threat and the dragon's eyes opened wider. "Huntsman?"

Teeth bared and I let the shadowed armor fall away from me. "My name is Marcus and my Wild Hunt has nothing against the dragons. I want to help you, I swear it."

The dragon was quieter for a short time, eyes closing slowly.

As soon as I was close enough to touch the nearest vein of ore, I could almost *feel* a sigh of relief from the dragon, one eye cracking open to look at me square in mine. It whispered, "Thank you."

I nodded and muttered, "Let's get you out of here, okay?"

The veins were a little further from the crater and dragon, so I had to cross a little further to get to it. As soon as my foot crossed the ledge of the crater the injured copper lay in, the blood swirled and spears of metal and stone lanced through the creature hard enough that it lifted its bulky body off the ground and into the air, the blood dribbling down it like rain.

Merlin, Slater, and I all shouted, "No!"

The eye that had met mine glossed over as the drakes that had previously been too scared to enter the room before this began to roar and hiss in delight from where they hid and watched.

I turned around in time to watch one of the largest of them sprinting straight at us with jaws wide open.

CHAPTER EIGHT

Rage—roiling, visceral, and cold—streaked through me. They stayed away out of fear for the dragon but they didn't care about the cold?

I spoke aloud, "Whoever did this will pay." Muttering to myself, I whispered, "Mako, go and keep them from leaving this area."

The shadowed form of the massive black drake skirted the other metal-scaled drakes unseen and took physical form behind them. The drakes hissed and roared in surprise as I closed my eyes and summoned the Mantle. As I did so, I used Frozen Form for the first time.

My body went numb and then I felt a chill before I was warm once more. Looking down at my body, I noted that my limbs were covered by the armor of the Huntsman, but even that was covered in thick frost.

I could hear Hollow's tinkling laughter as she bellowed, "Finally!"

Ignoring her, my muscles flexed along my arms and forearms as I let the ice cover my fists. The air in the room in front of me cooled faster and faster, the drakes crowding in and bickering in hisses and growling barks over who would attack first driving me over the edge all the more swiftly.

I gathered my strength and sprang forward, my right fist cocked back like the hammer of a revolver.

Move, I ordered my body and the ice growing at my feet pealed with sound as it shattered and the room resumed its normal speed.

The ice on my left fist shot into the closest drake and pierced the scales on its neck, then my right fist crashed forward and I sent the collected ice forth to slice into the flesh beneath the frozen scales.

Cold air swirled savagely as I leapt over the falling creature and in a fit of inspiration, I grasped it all and pulled it toward me, then stomped when I landed. Shards of ice as dense as diamonds formed and flung outward around me.

Some of the drakes screamed in anger more than pain, but I'd managed to blind a few of them as they'd stalked closer. One of the blind ones lashed out with his tail and slapped another drake into me, making me stumble slightly.

I turned and grasped the creature's head as it opened its mouth and used Void Frost to freeze it. The frozen head stilled and I ripped it from the long neck of the drake and flung it at the blind thing.

The attack hit it and startled it more than anything, its claws skirting the head and cutting into the ice as I attacked it outright. My foot kicked into the side of its head with Void Frost spiking through it as yet more drakes crowded into the room.

My mana dwindled faster as I fought on before I threw open the aperture of my bond with Merlin, the boy mage allowing me his mana to use as if it was my own, but also his control.

Spells the user is familiar with or has seen before will cost 25% less to cast.

My mana regenerated as I used Void Frost with the verve of

a madman. Cold fury reigned through me as I attacked with abandon and savaged my opponents. Any time anyone got close to me, they would be attacked by Hollow, or Rocky would be underground sending spikes of stone and metal through the ice coating the floor.

My mana refilled and Merlin called, "Close the bond so I can recover!"

I slammed the aperture of it shut and roared in defiance to the last three drakes that crawled into the room. Frost and rime greeted them and they tried to flee, but there was no running from my rage.

These things were made from that copper dragon—they would die.

I used Embodiment of Lightning to charge in front of the leader and a random casting of Bolt hit it, the spell surging through this one and frying it.

The Vornal voices returned, **Massacre!**

The bloodbath that was this carving beneath a mountain would affect the metal that formed here. This place would be an altar to my awakening. The beginning of the massacre.

My ire was pain. My rage a death sentence. My will that of destruction.

Foreign power began to well within me as my Mantle shifted almost uncomfortably. The cape I wore split and became wings. The gloves covering my hands grew claws.

The drakes screeched, their metallic vocal cords sending a cacophonous crashing colliding with my eardrums and my equilibrium suffered for a moment. The one on the right, the gold, tried to slip through the gap it had created as I fell, but I grabbed it.

My claws sank into the scales easily as I struck out at it, blood splattering the silver as it tried to bite me over its comrade's arched neck. It found my forearm as my left hand found its throat from the inside.

Cold burst from both my hands and their lives dwindled and blew out before the winds of my icy spell.

I tossed their corpses off me, the frozen bits shattering on impact with the ice on the ground before I stood.

Covered in frozen blood, bits of muscle, and even some shards of shattered scales that glittered against what little light flickered in the area thanks to Merlin and the spells still empowered in the other room.

I strode through the carnage along the ground, simply walking over rapidly cooling bodies of the fallen drakes as Merlin and Slater stared at me.

The dwarf pulled the knot cap on his head off and clutched it over his heart, "Meant no disrespect afore." I blinked at him and he cleared his throat. "Uh. Sayin' ya would die an' all that. It were tripe."

I shook my head and just walked past him to the copper dragon laying there where it had died. I put my head on its shoulder. "Sorry I couldn't save you. The drakes are all dead. At least all that came here."

I turned to Slater and said, "I'm used to people underestimating me and mine—their mistake." I took a deep breath and let my heartbeat calm. I was still enraged at the fact that someone could just come into this place and do whatever the fuck they wanted like this. But I couldn't do anything about it for now and while he'd been a bit of a dick before, Slater seemed like a decent dude. "Tell your people their problem should be taken care of and to keep an eye out for more strange creatures like the drakes."

I stared at the ground and sighed. "Is there anything here that meets the criteria we had?"

He frowned and scanned the walls before coming to one of the spikes that had speared the dragon from below. "This looks like it's good at absorbing magic." He frowned and then smiled. "Yes."

He touched the dragon. "Dragon bone is a good conductor of magic, but it can be a bit heavy. It would make a good wand, or staff. The horns too, but this one didn't have any. It was pretty young, if the lore about dragons is right."

"The young ones don't have horns until they're older than a century or so," Merlin confirmed and put a hand to his head. "This one was still young. A child."

Fuck. I mentally roared at that. So not only did someone trap this creature here to experiment on while it was wholly aware, they'd done it to a child.

"Merlin, collect the scales we need—the ones you can—and leave one of the bodies for the dwarves to study." I turned to Slater and glared into his eyes. "Bravest miner has to have a way of getting quick word to his people, right?"

He blanched and muttered something about emergencies only. I stalked closer to him and bent to look into his eyes without letting my voice waiver. "This is one of those. If they don't have someone here to look into this before we're done, I bury this whole place in the Hunt so often that *no one* will meet their quotas."

His face paled at that and he pulled a rod from his pack, tapping it into the wall closest to us both before he began to speak frantically into one end of it.

"Stone speaker?" Merlin frowned next to me. "I didn't know the dwarves still used those, but I guess under all this stone, it's the most reliable form of communication."

I nodded and closed my eyes trying to decide what to do with the dragon.

"The dragon's young enough that the magic in its bones isn't the best," Merlin muttered at me and I frowned in his direction. "If we leave it here, the dwarves will carve it up to experiment with as well. But if you want to consume it and carry it with you…"

He must have seen some kind of worry flicker over my face. "I've watched you do a lot, Marcus. I know that this hurt you since you wanted to help it. I have to admit, I'm pissed off too. If you want to carry this creature's vengeance inside your Mantle, I'm fine with that."

I nodded and walked back over to the copper dragon,

lowering my voice to attempt reverence over the outrage still coursing through me. "Your body, soul, and magic will be mine now, and I promise to find whoever did this to you and make them pay."

A weight of my own donning settled on my chest as I allowed my Mantle to consume the draconic materials that came from the copper dragon. Mako made his way back onto my body and settled quickly, thankfully, while my thoughts were on the dragon.

I didn't even know its name, but I would be sure to speak *kindly* to whoever had killed it like this.

———

It took two hours for Merlin and I to finish harvesting the scales from the drakes that I had felled and it took the dwarves all of ten minutes to dismiss us from their grounds.

"Should've let us keep the copper dragon!" the lead investigator snarled for the fourth time, grating on my nerves as we walked into the room with the drake corpses, scaleless and beginning to stink a bit as the ice melted slowly. "Fuckin' disgustin'."

I turned my gaze back at the furry little man and touched the drake closest to me, my Mantle consuming it. His eyes widened as I stepped to the next one. "No!"

"Maybe I'll just take all the spoils and clean this place up, huh?" I let the sarcasm seep into my voice as I touched a third. "Just to keep this place a little more pristine for you. Isn't that nice?"

"That's alright!" he bellowed as my fingers tapped a fourth drake. If I was being truthful with myself, I had already let my Mantle eat more than half the ones that we'd killed and run from. There were only three that we had left behind on our mad dash to find a better place to get away from the ones that had chased us to this very room.

I allowed my Mantle to eat this one too as I moseyed over to another. "Feel like being less of a dick?"

The dwarf turned crimson and stomped forward. "Do it again and I'll have you banned from here so fast—"

I raised an eyebrow at that and laughed. "Oh!" The barking laughter looked to confuse him a bit as I slapped another corpse. "Not what I wanted to hear."

The sound of metal-clad armor clanking down the tunnel toward us only emboldened the dwarf, "I'll fix you!"

I snarled and was across the room and touching the corpse nearest to him. "Think so?"

I consumed it and there was a break before the notification from the Mantle came but when it did, I grinned.

"What's going on here?" shouted one of the guards as the dwarf quickly scuttled over the ten feet between us to attack me.

The guards rushed in to separate us as I let him hit me a couple times before I kicked him away. It was more of a shove than any kind of actual strike but I made sure to give as good— if not better—than I got.

Mama didn't raise no punk bitch.

"Marcus, that's not the way to honor a contract." Halgrin tutted as I set my foot back down. "I only see a few of them here and hear there's a laboratory of sorts?"

I nodded and pulled out the large clanking bag of items, gear, and effects we'd collected from the grounds, bodies of the dead drakes and piles of… bones that we'd found along the way to this place.

I tossed it onto the ground in front of him and he frowned before pulling it out, delving through it with a hand before a small piece of something caught his eyes and he snatched it up and held it in both hands. Halgrin stood up and trudged toward me before he showed me what it was.

It was a gold and silver bead that looked like it was for a bracelet of sorts.

"My sister…" he started, tears welling in his eyes. Sniffling, he added, "She used to braid these into her mutton chops."

My eyebrows raised, but I was glad I'd been right in putting that into the bag instead of pocketing it. The others had been mostly dissolved and pitted so I'd left them. I hadn't been able to find her pickaxe, but there had been a drake leg in the area next to her where she had fallen, I guessed. Her bones were strewn about, but she'd likely been able to injure one.

I wouldn't give him that false hope though. If someone didn't die a glorious death in battle, then their memories were likely best left to those who cared most for them.

I clapped him on the shoulder and said, "Sorry I couldn't find more. I'm sure she was brave about being here."

He nodded and sniffled again as Merlin came over and handed the burly guard Rigid a bag. "Taxes. That should about cover it."

Rigid took it and tossed it on the ground beside his foot as he lifted a pauldron from the pile that nearly matched his own. "This was our captain's. You lot get gone and we guards will sing our appreciation to you."

He turned to the dwarf that clambered to his feet slowly after I shoved him away and growled, "Ought to kick your hairless ass, boy."

Rigid laid into the dwarf as I walked away with Merlin and Slater. The latter handed us something in a bag. "This was from the… things what speared that dragon. Ya oughta have 'em. 'Member, though, they siphon away mana and magic, so you gotta be careful, aye?"

I nodded and ducked my head. "Thank you for guiding us. Come to the High Table some time. I'll buy you a drink. If I don't end up making it for you."

That made him grin. "Not always for Hot Toddys, aye? Sometimes a cold drink be nice."

Merlin smiled at the dwarf and nodded. "Thank you, Slater. Be safe."

"Aye, I will." He grimaced and looked at the way back and then the dwarves behind him, "Ah. S'pose I'll be taken ya back up then."

I snorted. "Always one for an awkward goodbye, us?"

Slater and Merlin laughed as we began the trek back to the portal and back to the dwarf that would make an engagement ring.

Galaxy's voice echoed through my head as she purred, *Or two?*

CHAPTER NINE

"You don't have to worry, Marcus, I will make rings that will convey what you wish them to." The crafter walked away as Merlin muttered, then we watched Slater walk away from us once we were on the human side of the portal.

The jeweler's assistant had come and collected what we wanted to use and some specifics before taking us to the elevator.

I frowned and asked, "Can you take us to Jayvali?"

The assistant raised a brow and pressed a button before nodding once. We rode up the horridly long elevator ride in silence which gave me time to look at the notification I had earned.

Draconic Hoarding – The materials your Mantle absorbed have given you the magic that dragons hold most precious, their ability to hoard things. Discovery of valuable items on foes' corpses and in random places near your den increases drastically.

Aesthetic design for the Huntsman's Mantle obtained: Dragon's Rage.

I grinned to myself, wondering what that looked like. It was also curious that it was a named aesthetic, did that mean it provided something special as well?

"What do you have planned for Jay?" Merlin asked softly.

"I'm going to ask him to make something out of that material we got from Grestal." I glared at the wall as we continued to rise. "I'm sick of people's magic being so effective around us, so I want a weapon that can stop spells or at least drain their mana away."

"That's a good idea." The voice surprised me, as it was deeper than anything I'd heard recently and I glanced over to see the assistant staring at me. "Proper tools are respectable, Huntsman."

He waved to me and I looked down to realize I was still wearing the Mantle on full blast. "That may scare a few of my people. You may want to change."

I nodded and realized two things, the Mantle didn't want to be put away this way, and Hollow was still summoned down there in the tunnels.

Hollow?

Her focus shifted to me and I could hear something in her tone as she said, *Yes?*

What're you doing?

Summon me to you.

I waited until we were well and truly off the elevator before doing so, but I summoned another golem and said, "Hollow."

My mana froze over again and she stood there in front of me. "It worked!"

"What worked?"

She allowed the joy to seep into her tone. "That golem was left with one purpose, to mine and devour ore for you." Her arms raised and she dropped about sixty pounds of ice on the ground. "This is a huge find."

Merlin frowned at her. "What are you talking about? This is just ice." He glanced at me and said, "Are all elementals this way?"

I shrugged as Hollow glared spitefully at the boy. She looked back at me and said, "This is a moss-like ore that grows beneath the surface of the coldest areas in the universe—think freezer burn made into metal. When you fought in those tunnels in Grestal, the beast that bears that name allowed this ore to be made."

"What's it called?" I reached down and touched it, the cold it exuded almost enough to make me recoil despite the fact that I didn't feel cold much anymore.

"Ever Frozen." She lifted it and looked at it almost lovingly. "It's metal, and it's called that because it won't ever be less than frozen. It was born with these properties and will make any item forged with it have the same properties it did just as easily."

"How is it smelted?" We had nearly forgotten about the assistant and he had joined us to look over the ore curiously.

"It's melted, usually, but the heat you would need has to be enough to nearly melt the polar ice caps, and even then it will not remain in that state."

I lifted my eyebrows and muttered, "Dragon fire?"

Hollow looked at me and frowned. "Perhaps?"

I grinned and put all of the ore into my inventory. "Let's go see Jay."

––––––––

The dwarf frowned as soon as we walked in. "Heard you lot were here. Where's Cassia? I got a bone to pick with her."

"Having a girls' day. I got things for you to make." He frowned at me and I added, "New metals for you to work with potentially, as well."

That made his eyes widen and a grin spread beneath his beard. "She'll keep." He shoved the items on his desk behind it, the clattering on the ground a little jarring for how he usually acted, but he just patted his counter and made a 'gimme gimme' motion.

I put the bag of mana-devouring metal on the counter and

he poured it out to find two four-foot-long spikes still drenched in dragon blood. He narrowed his eyes at me before putting a finger into the blood and lifting it to his lips. His tongue darted out and lapped the crimson up and he nearly spat, "Dragon blood?"

I nodded. "Not something I wanted to be on it." He frowned at my statement and I added, "I need this to be made into a weapon for me. A scythe."

Jay snorted. "Turning into an edge lord?"

Merlin snickered and I shook my head. "No, just something my Mantle seems to like making." He pulled out a sheet and began to go through the process of blueprinting the piece.

We decided on what I would like and he nodded. "Will be a wicked weapon. The shaft of it will need to be heavy wood in order to be able to withstand the abuse you can throw at it."

I nodded, knowing he was talking about Thumper and her mangled body. "We will enchant the wood to be stronger if we can, but I don't know if the enchantment will last in proximity to the metal."

"Done one weapon with this before, but there wasn't quite this much pressure to work with, so it was just the blade that was lined with it." He tapped it and smiled. "In raw form, it eats all the mana around it. Worked? It eats the mana it touches directly."

He tapped his pencil on the counter a few times in thought then began to write on the margins of the sheet as he spoke. "Put a sheet of dampener under the haft to serve as a protective lining, then a metal cap to serve as a buffer between the haft and the blade."

He thought about something for a moment, then at the base of the haft, he drew a spearhead. "This will be a retractable number, never hurts to have something sneaky to help out, eh?"

I nodded, smacking the table in delight. "If you have some left over, can you make some knives? Preferably to fit someone with dainty hands and a preference for speed?"

Merlin perked up and smiled at me. "She's going to love this."

I grinned back at him as the dwarf sniffed and said, "Aye." He put the sheet aside and tapped the table. "Next."

I put one of the large chunks of the Ever Frozen onto the counter and it immediately began to cover the area around it in a thin layer of frost.

Jayvali's eyes opened wider than I'd ever seen them do so as he slowly picked it up. "Like no metal I ever seen." He examined it and after a moment of odd, curious gauging and experimenting that I wished I had never witnessed, like him flicking it, licking it, and attempting to eat it, he smiled. "Gonna take damn near dragon fire to melt this."

I grinned and leaned closer to him. "Still got that bottle?"

He frowned and I raised a brow at him and he knew instantly what I meant, turning red. "It could help."

I just grinned at him as he continued to glare at me and finally just said, "If you need Arden to help you manage to melt it down, we're happy to send her this way."

He frowned and then nodded. "That would be a good idea. The heat for it needs to be higher than anything we're capable of making here and it needs to be magical heat too, I think."

He grumbled to himself for a short time and then nodded as if deciding on something. "Scythe first. I'll get that done sooner, I think, as I'll start on it right away."

He patted the ore and smiled. "I got an idea for this. And it's gonna be great. Gimme the rest, and I'll get on it as soon as I can."

I nodded and dumped more of the Ever Frozen on his counter and he screamed in delight. I had never seen the like happen before and though I was concerned, he smiled at me and said, "Forget Thumper, lad, I'll be making something *amazing* with this."

My eyebrows rose and though I wanted to talk shit to him about it, I wouldn't be looking a gift dwarf in the mouth where items were concerned.

"Thanks, Jayvali, I appreciate it." He frowned at me and I nodded to him. "Do I need to send Cassia your way?"

He frowned deeper and then shook his head no. "Better not. I'll be busy for a bit."

I nodded at that and turned with Merlin to leave.

CHAPTER TEN

When we arrived back at the house, Arden's shouting at someone for being a damn noob nearly blew us from our feet as we walked into the door. We found Cassia inside at the table waiting for us with her Switch in hand.

I smiled at her. "Hey!"

She looked up at me and said, "Hey yourself." She stood up from her game and walked around the table toward me with her nostrils flaring, "You've been fighting, I can smell the blood on you."

I blinked at that and mentally berated myself only to have Galaxy pop up behind her and mentally tell me, *She has plenty to say about it, so don't kick yourself too hard.* She arched a brow as she looked up at Cass as she crossed her arms over her chest. *She doesn't need the help.*

I opted for the truth then. "I went and cleared out a mine for the dwarves in return for some money and materials, but we need to talk about that."

She frowned at me some more but I glanced over at Galaxy. "I don't care what Arden and Amabala are up to, I want them here. I also want the rest of the Hunt if they're available."

"They're available." Cassia grunted and closed her eyes behind her glasses. I could see the outlines of them from where I stood. "They'll be here soon."

"Good." My stomach growled and I looked at Cassia, some of her irritation and anger fading as I smiled apologetically. "Care for some take out? You craving anything?"

She thought about it for a moment then grunted, "Fried pickles, a sundae, and at least four cheeseburgers with extra onion." She frowned and then smiled. "And blood."

"Raw cheeseburgers, got it." I opened my phone and began calling around to several places I knew of that could deliver on what we wanted, then had it ready so that we could go and pick it up as soon as it was all ready in fifteen to twenty minutes.

"Okay, fuck face," Arden growled at me from the hallway. "If I've been summoned from my gaming for bullshit, then I'm lighting your ass on fire."

"Far from it." I sighed and looked at Galaxy. "Can I have Galaxy show you what we found real fast?"

"Just use my memories, Galaxy," Merlin offered quickly and then said, "If it will perfectly describe what happened, then do it. You all need to see what Marcus was like as well."

I frowned until there was a round of cautious consent given as Amabala had just come down the stairs.

Images of memories played like a drive-in movie in my head, and I could see exactly what I looked like from Merlin's eyes as I fought those drakes on my own at the end. One word came to mind as the images stopped and Amabala said it for me, "Monster."

Arden nodded as she blinked at me and Cassia just held her hands in front of her at her waist as she appeared to be lost in thought.

"Who would have the power to trap a dragon like that?" Amabala asked, then let her gaze rest on me and meekly added, "Sorry, Marcus."

I offered her a kind smile. "It's okay. And I wish I knew." I scanned the others' faces and there was a constant look of confusion and reflection. "No one knows anything?"

Arden heaved a sigh, letting her cheeks balloon out as she blew and finally said, "Unless Doctor Jekyll is real, I have no clue."

Cassia nodded. "Same. I know that there are older beings that like to tinker with things, but this is… beyond that."

"Do the gods need to know?" My question startled Merlin and Arden shook her head. "Why not? This seems like something that is a little more up their alley."

"It normally would be, if they weren't dealing with a homicidal guest that had an avatar lovingly made by gods from another realm who wants the majority of them dead and outed them to their followers and other random non-believers."

Cassia blinked and looked at a flushed Arden. "Been sitting on that one long, Ardent Flame?"

Arden's complexion mottled more. "A bit." She felt her phone buzzing in her pocket and pulled it out to look at it. "Cameras are going nuts. Everyone is here. I'll let them into the basement if you'll take these guys down there, Cassia?"

Cassia nodded and motioned for us to follow her, still remaining sort of quiet after watching those memories. We walked down the hall to the door that was almost never open and walked further downstairs.

Once we were at the bottom of the stairway, Cassia flipped the switch there and illuminated a sort of studio-like room that reminded me of a ballet recital area, where kids would come to practice and play and dance. It was… odd to find that in a basement of all places, and Arden's as well? Doubly weird.

More than six or so decades ago, Arden taught ballet to keep herself out of trouble before the High Table became an acceptable place for women to work in the public eye. Galaxy's nearly indignant explanation took me by surprise. *Sometimes she finds herself missing those children and comes in here to blow off some steam. Other times she is grateful for the escape that gaming offers her.*

Noted. Thanks for the kick in the shorts, love.

I noticed her smile from across the room and she just walked away as more lights came on and the door at the end of the room closest to the mirrors opened and allowed the other members of our Wild Hunt to enter.

A lot of the faces that I had expected were there, like some of the oni, Keith, Kenshi, Sabbath, and his two buddies. Who I didn't expect to see there among them was Luca.

I frowned at him and he just smiled. "It seemed the best way to ensure a fighting chance to keep my family safe, so I took it."

"Can't argue with that logic." I scratched my head and cleared my throat before saying, "Does, uh… does Aeslyn…?"

He shook his head. "Not to my knowledge. It would probably start a fight that I do not feel prepared for, but I cannot just stand by and do nothing."

I nodded and shook his hand. "I'll try to keep your secret safe. Though I do have to admit, I wish you would stay with Connell to keep him safe."

"Aeslyn can do that," Luca returned and, when I frowned at his response, just winked. "I didn't just marry her for her looks, Marcus."

"I would really prefer not to get into her weird double standards." It was hard to keep my chipper irritation from leaking into that, so I didn't. If she was such a capable fighter, how was it that I was in the wrong and bad for Connell?

I left it at that and just sighed, "Galaxy, can you show them?"

Galaxy nodded, showing them the same versions of memories that they had seen in the tunnels as Merlin. There was a low whistle from Keith and I growled, "Not one fuckin' word, furball."

He just cackled and turned back to the others he was with and once it was over, I asked, "Anyone know of anything or anyone that might do this to something? Has a penchant for experimenting on creatures like this?"

"Knowledge gods," someone in the crowd suggested, and a wolf I didn't readily recognize strode forward; he looked strong though. "They have a thing about taking creatures apart and putting them back together, or imprisoning them to screw with."

"Says the new alpha." Keith snickered and the man just turned to glare at him.

He turned back to me and held his hand out for me to take. "Dieter, Huntsman. I'll be taking over as alpha for Jolly."

I raised an eyebrow as I took his hand. "You're the new alpha? That means you beat the old man; he was pretty strong, right?"

"He still is." Dieter snorted and shook his head. "Don't know if it was by some fluke or by good luck, but I managed to pin him and get him to give up."

I chuckled at the thought and just shook my head with him. "I bet he didn't make it easy, either. Congratulations. And you're one of mine?"

He nodded, then grimaced, but I stopped him. "Not anymore."

The other wolves all stepped forward but Dieter held his hand up and just asked, "Why?"

"I can't control the wolves too, serving the Hunt is voluntary, and if you serve me, the wolves who serve you will feel obligated." He frowned at that, but let me continue. "As much as bolstered numbers are necessary now more than ever, I can't justify that. I absolve you of your decision to serve with gratitude and honor, Dieter. Lead your pack well and know you have a friend in the Wild Hunt."

Dieter frowned some more. "Are you certain? I mean, my loyalty is to my pack, the Table, and then the Hunt." He motioned to himself. "I've been security since nearly day one of my lycanthropy."

"That's part of the problem, I think." Cassia grunted and looked at the others, before stepping beside me. "Good call, Marcus." She looked to the other security staff and explained, "Sometimes we have to operate outside the Table. As such, I don't think I have a right to remain head of the High Table Columbus Branch Security."

There was an immediate uproar and she waited until there was a lull before going to speak when Keith walked over and stood in front of her. "I don't give a rat's scaly-tailed ass what anyone says or thinks—you're the best damn head of security we've had since Jolly himself and even then, you do damn better than he did too. You walk, I walk, and I know for damn sure a few more people will too."

There was a resounding outcry of agreement and though she was concerned, I could *feel* the pride and love radiating off her. She stared at them as they continued their cries of support and finally just muttered, "I guess I'll hold off."

"So the knowledge god thing..." I called over their cheers, much to some of their annoyance, bringing attention back to the problem at hand. "Is there some kind of precedent for this? Or is it just assumed?"

"They do it all the time." Keith snorted and rolled his eyes. "They create races of people, realms for their people, and then leave them to rot and stew for faith and their own power."

"Is there an example?"

Keith, deadpan, looked at me and said, "Humanity?"

Cassia guffawed at that and I had to admit that was both enlightening and fair as much as it was offensive. "It's happened a few times, but whenever it's caught, people tend to get wiped for it, or don't talk about it for fear of being noticed by the angry gods."

I sighed, my thoughts racing until finally I had to admit, "Alright, so I guess we have to keep waiting for Anubis to get back to us on a meet and greet with his brother." I wanted to find whoever had done this and end them—painfully. But if they were a god of some sort, that would put a little bit of a damper on my plans.

For now. Galaxy patted my rump and smiled up at me. "Someday, we might be able to stand toe to toe with a god."

I snorted. "A weak one, maybe. Though with Galaxy? Probably a couple."

"Hey, Marcus." Arden held up her wrist, tapping it irritatedly. "We only got a few hours before our shift at the High Table and I've got a raid to go do, so can we get these furry bastards out of my house before my cats piss all over the place thanks to their stink?"

Cassia's eyes widened. "That's today? Shit. Lemme go get my shit and I'll help!" She looked at me and I just snorted, but she took that as permission and hollered, "Dismissed!"

The wolves and other shifters raised their fists and howled, the sound edging over my body in a wave that crashed and left me with chills before laughing and congratulating each other.

I caught Cassia's attention before she walked off and said, "I'll get the food. You gonna be here?" She nodded and I gave her a kiss before I turned to find the new alpha waiting for me. "Dieter, what's up?"

"I really wish you would allow me to continue helping the Hunt." He looked hurt, but resolute.

I nodded. "We're awesome, I know, but leadership comes with some shit decisions. If I had my way, we would continue to operate with just the core staff, but that can't happen as our enemies continue to gather power to themselves."

He considered me for a long moment and asked, "If it were Jolly, would you say the same?"

I grunted and thought about that. "Since he was his own man, he didn't join us. But as his own man, he continued to try to help me personally how he could." I thought on it another beat or two and finally said, "Jolly as a person has an open invitation to join us, but as an alpha, no."

He grimaced and looked away before I put a hand on his shoulder and said softly, "You as a person would be welcome. But as a leader responsible to your subordinates, I won't bind your hands to take your freedom to keep them safe and healthy from you."

I looked at the wolves filing out of the room and lowered my voice a bit more, "If you want to be an ally, I won't say no. We need friends, but that usefulness goes both ways, Dieter. If you need the Hunt, you call us."

He smirked and held his hand out for me to shake. "Deal." He frowned to himself and admitted, "There's a rumor going around the shifter reddits that someone's come in and killed a few alphas to take over their packs. But they've not stopped at one and stayed to keep the territory. It's like they're searching for something or someone."

"You think they could be coming here?"

He sighed and rubbed his chest. "Don't know, but I do know that if it comes to a fight, I'll have to kill them. This person doesn't just beat the loser, they kill them in the old way."

I frowned and bellowed, "Keith!" I looked at Dieter, hitting him with an apologetic smile. "Sorry about this."

Keith appeared by my shoulder. "Yo!"

"Congratulations, you're my man on the inside of the pack, you're going to shadow and keep tabs on Dieter and the other wolves for the Hunt." Dieter grimaced and I continued, "Something happens, you're to get a hold of us right away so the Hunt can be there for the pack. Am I clear?"

Keith stood straighter and growled, "Yessir."

I grabbed the wolf by the back of the neck affectionately. "Try not to make Dieter want to kill you, okay?"

Keith snorted and fluttered his lashes at me. "Who, me?"

Dieter, Keith, and I laughed together before they left with me walking outside with Galaxy to go get lunch.

CHAPTER ELEVEN

Galaxy stared out of the window while we drove to the restaurant. Suddenly, she observed, "It always strikes me as so odd that humans claim to be so fragile, yet they drive these hulking metal and plastic monstrosities like it's nothing."

"It is a bit of an enigma, I'll give you that." She was quiet for a short time after I spoke, so I had to ask, "Are you okay?"

"I'm nervous about not having heard anything from Anubis or Thoth since he left." She sighed and stared out at the world as it coasted by us. "It's so hard knowing that a part of me is stuck in this legendary place, held there by a beast, and that it's just *waiting* for us to come and get it. Like, it's taunting us. The Vorna there has to have learned that I've escaped by now and that I'm coming. How is it preparing for us to show up? Does it care? Are we ready to face it?"

"What if grasshoppers had machine guns?"

She blinked at my question and frowned. She frowned for another moment or so before saying, "What?"

"It's stupid, isn't it? To think of these tiny bugs with automatic weapons?"

She shook her head, snorting. "How is that relevant?"

I shrugged and pulled to a stop at a stop light. "Well, we don't worry about that at all, and we know it's not likely to happen. So what's the point in worrying about this Vorna being prepared if we just go into this as prepared as we can be?"

She scoffed at my reasoning before laughing and turning to offer me the most sincere, "That was the *dumbest* thing I have ever heard, but thank you."

"Of course!" I put a hand on her thigh and offered her a lopsided grin.

"I've lived a long time, Marcus, ruminate on that for a bit."

I just grinned a bit wider. "Oh, I'm aware." I continued driving for a bit as she laughed at my antics and we just enjoyed each other's company. "Galaxy?"

She raised an eyebrow at me and I asked, "Do you know how many other Huntsmen there are out there? Can I... Can I kill all of them?"

She frowned and thought on it. "I suppose?" She sighed and rubbed her cheek for a heartbeat before adding, "I mean, I made them when I was whole, so I could make them again. But there are bound to be places that don't need them anymore, or the Mantles or the Hunt itself has been corrupted to some degree."

"So I would have your permission?" She just glared at me and I grinned again. "Nice."

"What makes you ask that?"

Her curious gaze made me almost want to refrain from saying anything, but I just grunted and said, "In the tunnels, I got mad. Real mad. The Vornal blood within me fed off that and I became something I wasn't sure I would be able to come out of and, if I'm being honest with you—I didn't care if I could come out of it." I took a deep breath and let it out quickly. "I was strong. Stronger than I've been before and with that strength came a sense of surety. I could take the power from the other Huntsmen and we could use that to protect the humans here and the gods from each other."

"Put certain people in their place, maybe?" I nodded and

she sucked on her teeth. "It takes the power of a god to fight against the power of a god, Marcus. As a Vorna, you would have a leg up, but against a fully realized Dominion, you would be hard pressed to succeed. I cannot think of how Zeke and his friends were able to take and keep the ones that they stole."

"Can they feasibly survive with them?" She frowned and I asked, "I know that the avatars they have were made by your children, gods themselves, but as vessels to power that they controlled, right? So it shouldn't be possible."

She motioned with her hand and there was a pause. "Maybe it was an accident?"

"What do you mean?"

She tapped her legs with her hands and said, "An accident. They were being attacked by the Vorna called War, correct? What if they made their vessels as powerful as possible, or designed them to hold as much power as possible, so that they stood a chance of defeating the enemies that they couldn't?"

That made a lot of sense. "I mean, if nothing else, give someone working for you the opportunity to amass power and then get them pointed at the right enemy and bam." I beat my hand on the steering wheel as someone pulled out in front of me without their turn signal, asshole Columbus drivers. "Zeke said something about our gods pulling them back here when they had *just* finished their mission in Brindoga—"

Galaxy put a hand on my arm. "Brindo*lla*."

I took the correction in stride. "Right, what if that was a cover?" I blinked at the road in front of me and lowered my voice, "What if the gods there knew they fucked up and that they had given their champions too much *oomph* and forced them to leave while they had the advantage and power to?"

I pulled into the restaurant, finding parking close to the entrance where I could go in and get the food. "If they lied to them in order to keep them complacent until they were gone, the Brindollan gods are at fault here and they should be made aware."

Galaxy puffed her cheeks out in thought, something that she

had started doing lately. "Do you think they would listen? I mean, if anyone has a reason to shift the blame to gods that they can't get to, it's us."

"It would be, but at the same time, doing so would have been a last-ditch effort to keep them from fucking with the status quo on Earth." I turned the car off and stared at the sidewalk in front of the hood. "Now? The only thing they haven't done is launch a full-scale attack on the gods or on the supernatural. We kind of owe it to ourselves to try to convince them that this could be a possibility. To Earth."

She nodded in agreement then cleared her throat. "Be sure they added the extra honey mustard. It's delicious and Cassia will kill someone if she doesn't have enough."

"You got food too, right?" She shook her head. "Did you want something?"

She snorted. "I want tacos, not burgers. I'll be okay for now."

I laughed and went inside to collect our food but on the way there, I couldn't keep myself from grabbing my phone after checking in to get my order. Opening my messenger app, I just reached out to him.

You free?

I got a message a second later that made me laugh.

Boy, this is the strangest booty call… Yeah. Want me to call?

I barely sent an affirmative before my phone began to vibrate in my hand. "Marcus?"

I raised my hand and grabbed my bag of food, walking to the car as I answered, "Hey, man."

Zeke's voice came from the receiver as he muttered, "Yo, what's up?" He paused for a second before asking, "You didn't happen to make a decision, did you?"

A soft smile spread across my lips. "I can honestly say that I don't think I'd mind working with you in present circumstances." He whooped in the background until I added, "But I think I have some news and I want to share it with you. Come to the High Table tonight?"

He groaned. "All those supernatural creatures that wanna gut me are gonna get a chance?"

I laughed. "It's a safe place, and I'll be working so we can make sure that you'll be alright. Just remember the rules, yeah?"

"Fine, but if Lucifer is there, I'm cutting loose. That guy's fucking awesome."

I watched as Galaxy sifted through the bag and looked at all the food for me as I spoke. "I doubt you'll be coming alone for this?"

He snorted. "And not get to travel with my posse? Please. Yoh hasn't been there yet and though he doesn't drink, he's awesome at a party." He moved his face away from the phone by the way his voice sounded as he said, "You're on speaker, bud. The rest of the guys dropped in for a minute to hear this for all of our peace of mind. You don't plan to attack us en route, do you?"

"Couldn't win if we did anyway, and this meeting is as peaceful as I can fucking wish it to be, man." I paused and added, "I swear it on my power as Huntsman."

There was a collective sigh of relief on the other end of the line and Zeke chipperly spoke, "Okay. Then it's a date. Gonna have to find something nice to wear."

Muu called over the phone, "You gonna put out?"

I snorted. "I'll see you there."

Muu, clearly upset I didn't deign to answer, brazenly bellowed, "You fucking *tease!*"

Zeke laughed along. "See you then."

I hung up and Galaxy stared at me expectantly. "Yes, dear?"

"If she doesn't have more honey mustard than this, Cassia will slaughter these people."

I laughed and headed back in before returning to Arden's to get ready for my shift and eat.

———

"You sure you wanna do this?" I tried to keep the uncertainty from my tone as Micah nodded. I shrugged and poured four shots in front of him.

He looked nervous and I couldn't blame him; he was about to do something incredibly stupid, but brave.

"It's only vodka, buddy. So just take two and take the other two with you." He nodded, his eyes glazing over to the point that I knew he was overthinking it.

I reared back and slapped him across the face, the resounding contact pulling him from his mind. I grabbed the collar of his shirt and snarled, "What would she think if she saw you panicking like this? Toughen up, God damnit."

Someone down the bar snorted. "I'm off duty! Stop tempting me to do bad things to you."

I chuckled and said, "Whoops, sorry. Next drink is on me."

Micah shook himself and downed the first two shots. "Good man!"

The leopard shifter took a deep breath and wandered over to Isis with the two shots. She'd actually agreed to meet him here as they'd met on a dating app and hit it off, but he was the nervous type when it came to the ladies.

He made it over to her and spoke softly as he sat in the booth opposite her.

She reached up and touched his face, the red mark making him laugh nervously. She threw a glare my way and I mouthed, *Sorry!*

She rolled her eyes and patted the bench next to her, making him join her on that side so she could speak with him a bit more intimately.

"Good job." Arden snickered at me as I poured the sour god down the way a pint of the imported stuff. "You think they're going to show?"

I looked outside where the line to get in was beginning to grow. Looked like the local Wardens were still staking us out and they had no intention of chilling the fuck out. They hadn't tried to come in, and Merlin still hadn't heard from Theodorous, so there was that as well. While it could've been a shit-show if they came, I was banking on the rules being ironclad, or them being about to get the hell out before things went pear-shaped.

"It's early yet, and the staff know that he's coming with the crew, so they'll just let him in ahead of the line." Galaxy appeared at the bar. "Hey! What's up?"

"Wanted something to drink but I don't have human currency of any variety other than your stuff, so I wanted some drinks." I nodded and pulled some cash from my wallet, throwing it into the till so she could have her selection of carbonated pop. The fiend.

She snorted and mentally brushed against me, purring, *I am. And I've missed you. Maybe we can play later?*

Only if I get to be DPS. She raised an eyebrow at me and I added, *I don't like tanking. Holding the hate is hard. I'd rather smack the shit out of something.*

Her lips parted in a wide grin as she winked lasciviously in my direction before turning to walk away.

Arden just huffed and I turned to her. "So, how's Masonai taking things?"

"Well, like most humans, he was scared at first, but since he's heard of it, the supernatural is a bit more interesting thanks to some of the suggestion stuff we've been going through."

I nodded and started cleaning a dirty glass. "He know yet?"

She shook her head and I sighed softly. "Sorry, Arden."

She just shrugged. "I'm immortal, Marcus." She offered me a soft smirk. "Not like I can't tell him some day when I feel he's ready."

"Could always make him immortal yourself," someone said, startling me. I turned to see a Hispanic man, on the shorter side, around five foot five or six standing near me across the bar. "Sorry for just listening in like that, but you guys and Chris seem to run the same circles, so I figured I could offer some advice for you."

Arden narrowed her gaze at the man. "Jinn don't do

immortality, and I don't grant wishes anymore." She frowned. "I don't know you, who are you?"

"I'm Yohsuke." He held his hand out for her to shake and she took it begrudgingly. "There are more than a few ways to make someone immortal. You could make him a vampire."

"We don't know any." It wasn't a lie, I knew a dhampyr but I didn't think she could make anyone a vampire like that, could she?

He grinned. "You know me." His eyes flashed a vibrant yellow and returned to normal. "My avatar is a vampire lord. I can make more vampires if I want."

"Why would you do that for us, and where are the others?"

He shrugged. "Muu is habitually late due to liking sleep more than anything, and Zeke had to walk his dogs real fast but they'll be here soon." He put a couple bucks on the bar. "Can I get a Coke?"

I nodded and filled a glass, offering him a straw that he took. "As to why I would offer? Mainly out of curiosity, but partially to see if we can get your help. I may not want to go back, but my brothers do. If I can get you to help us get them back, I'm in."

"What of the others?" I asked, politely, "I know three of you, aren't there three more?"

He nodded carefully. "One of us is in New York, a cop there, the other two here in Ohio. All of them awake and capable of fucking shit up." He stared me in the eyes as he finished that statement.

"That was no threat on my part, merely curiosity."

He chuckled to himself. "People can say that, but they don't know what those guys are capable of. One of them has been to hell and back and the demons he slaughtered sure as fuck know it was him."

"Talking about Balmur?" Another man joined us with a woman in white walking next to him. He wore glasses and was a few inches taller than Yohsuke, but his musculature was a bit lacking, whereas the smaller man was lean but muscular. He turned to me and raised a brow. "Checking me out?"

I snorted. "Gotta be Muu." The other man nodded and winked at me as I jerked a thumb to the menu behind me. "Pick something."

The woman next to him looked familiar but not enough for me to know her name and she didn't offer anything, contenting herself with glaring around the room.

She stared at Arden for a while, long enough for the bartending jinn to grow irritated enough to smack her hand onto the bar. "Can I get you a drink or something?"

"She's just getting ready to leave. Right, Eve?" Zeke came in, in his humanoid form, wearing a simple pair of gray gym shorts and a bright green t-shirt. She nodded and turned to walk out the front door and crossed the street.

It was there that she posted up with two of the Wardens on that side of the street, eyeing her like she was going to attack them, or vice versa.

Muu shook his head and glanced at Zeke before jerking his head to the window. "I really hope she's not going to get bored and kill those two."

Zeke snickered and rolled his eyes. "She's been bad enough lately on her own. She knows if she does something to piss me off again, I'll kill her." He turned back to me and grinned. "Hey, man. Is this purely a social call or did you have news for me?"

"I had a thought that was shared with me by Galaxy that I wanted to run by you and see what you thought of it." He raised an eyebrow and motioned for me to go on. "I think you guys were tricked."

He blinked at me and sighed. "Well, this calls for a stiff drink."

I shook up a cocktail, something simple in the flavor of a martini. I added two and a quarter ounces of vodka to the shaker, followed quickly by half an ounce of vermouth and the same of pickle brine.

I went to the hot sauce and Zeke put a hand on the bar. "Woah, there Devil Dog. I said stiff, not the stuff of my asshole's nightmares."

I snorted and added a dash of the hot sauce rather than the full three and then added the iced portion of the shaker to seal it shut. I shook it as I stared at the door where several people watched and once the twelve seconds were up, I cracked the shaker like an egg over the glass to pour the contents in with no ice.

I garnished it with a dill pickle spear rather than a cornichon and motioned to the drink. "I present to you Hillary's Dirty Little Secret, though to be a bit more apt of a name, it should be the Brindollan Gods' Dirty Little Secret."

"This doesn't bode well at all." Muu rolled his eyes but other than some sighs and rolled eyes, no one commented on it.

We moved down the bar closest to the window so that Eve would be able to keep an eye on her charge and stayed there, letting them grow accustomed to the noise before I started. "Before, when you would talk about what happened, the gods there told you that our gods wanted you back and they wouldn't or couldn't fight for you, so you had to leave in order to keep the peace."

He nodded and took another sip of his drink. "Woah! That's something. Not what I would usually get, but goddamn, it's stiff as hell."

I nodded and let his remark lead me into what I wanted to say. "Stiff. Funny you say that, because here's a stiff truth; they lied to you about the gods of Earth coming." All three of them stilled and stared intently at me. "The gods here couldn't have given two shits about you unless you were a priest or something."

"The gods here are assholes, as has been proven time and time again." Zeke sighed and turned to glare at the listener at the other end of the bar. "Yeah. I know you're one. Don't try to tell me differently. Plagues. Famine. Mass murder—fucking genocide? Allowing that shit just for shits and giggles? That's a god."

Arden appeared next to me, and pointed to Zeke. "Hey, chill the fuck out. This is neutral ground, and we can't have you trying to instigate a fight."

He sighed and motioned with a flippant wave. "Sorry. Just get a bit heated about them." He looked at me. "Two on me for them."

I nodded and Arden went to fulfill the order.

It was Yoh who spoke next. "What makes you think they tricked us?"

"The fact that two of you hold power that should have melted you where you stood." They stared at me curiously and I cleared my throat. "They made it so you could hold massive amounts of power, and in doing so, inadvertently made you a threat to their existence."

Yohsuke's eyes widened and he nearly shouted, "I fuckin' *told* you that shit was the reason why!" He jabbed a finger into Zeke's chest and snarled, "Ain't no way these raggedy bitches here wanted six fuckin' souls back, man. They fuckin' played us and then they sent us home to be threats to the gods here."

"I don't know about that last part, but it doesn't look good, that's for sure." I sighed as the others began to think about it and added, "The gods here may not be the best, but they're at least innocent if that's the case. I know it's too late to put the can of worms back in the pantry and all that stupid shit, but making more trouble is just a bit unnecessary, right?"

Zeke appeared to be mulling it over when he heaved a sigh and answered, "I don't know. But you've given us things to think upon and for that, I appreciate you." He finished his drink and grunted, "Christ in a Chrysler, that was rough. You good, man? The old fashioned you gave me before was badass."

"Things on my mind too." It was difficult not to smirk, but I lowered my voice and spoke to him, "Cassia and I just found out we're expecting."

"Holy fuck!" He grabbed my shoulders and pulled me

bodily over the bar into a hug that made the security staff bustle into the room. He laughed and shook me a bit. "Marcus, that's incredible! Are you happy about it? What's on your mind?"

I waved the guards off as the smaller man put me down then snarled, "Rounds on me!"

I rolled my eyes and smacked him. "Fucker, that means more work for me!"

He grinned and shouted, "Tip your 'tender!" He patted me on the shoulder and let me go to the other side of the bar to start pouring drinks, all of them beer. "So?"

I just smirked and after trying and failing to glare at him, said, "I'm excited and nervous at the same time. I missed so much with my first and I wanna do it right this time."

He nodded sagely. "Fair. Very fair." He took a drink and frowned. "Do oni give a flying fuck about marriage? Like, when you say 'do it right,' do you mean you wanna make an honest woman of her?"

I smiled and nodded, but quickly added, "She doesn't know. It's a down low kinda thing for now. She may tell me to go fuck myself for all I know, but I'm going to at least try."

He smacked the bar. "Fucking excellent. Absolutely excellent." He fiddled with the ring on his own finger absently as he thought of something for a short time. "When you get it, get one for you. Or fuck, I'll just make one for you myself. I'm going to enchant it for you."

I shook my head and he put a hand up to stop me. "I, King Zeke, solemnly bind myself to this oath that if I break it, I bequeath my crown to you to hold for your son should I lie and the Unseelie of this world will follow without question or fail: I will enchant your rings without intent to follow, track, bind, or ensnare you or your chosen and child."

I lifted a finger. "Or spy on."

He grinned. "Whoops, or spy on." He repeated the same phrase adding the addendum to the oath, then added, "The rings will be a gift from a father and husband who wishes nothing but happiness and health to someone in the same predicament."

I watched him carefully for a short time as he somberly sipped his beer before finally coming out with it. "You know what, man? I just don't fucking get you."

He raised an eyebrow and stared at me nearly in disbelief as I set my rag on the bar and leaned closer to him, my arm resting against the bar. "You could probably murder half the people in this place and feel nothing but annoyance, and let the other half live just to spread the story. You've quite literally declared open war on the gods after snuffing out a race of Fae you don't care for. You reveal the largest secret of all to the Normies, and you can turn into a fucking massive, goddamn dragon, and yet you're pining for a family you *know* you'll get to one way or another."

He snorted. "That was an Airy on TV, but it's as close to dragon as you can get without calling them a wyvern and pissing them off." He saw my eyes widen as I was about to lay into him. "Alright, I get it."

He held up a hand to calm me down, and spoke just loudly enough for me to hear. "I don't *like* having to be the bad guy. I don't want to kill thousands of people and put millions more in jeopardy to get home to my wife, our girlfriend, and my kids who have grown up without me—but I sure as fuck will if it gets me there."

He flicked his thumb toward the sky. "They've had time to think it over and try to help us get home—they haven't. And now that I think on it, the gods back home probably aren't too clandestine either. They all play their games and we just have to play along; well, I don't fucking want to anymore. We saved a universe by killing War and it cost us dearly. Friends, family, our own mental health? And they sent us away without even so much more than just a fucking thanks."

"Yeah, but why do all this if you can just be patient and find another way?"

He snorted. "Who else will do it if not me?" Zeke took a

large gulp of his beer and set the mug closer to me. "You? You're starting a family. You won't wanna get too deep into the shit, and the gods couldn't care less. I can't wait for Maebe, because if I do, she will come here to take me from this place and it could be centuries from now."

He sighed and rubbed his bald head before looking out into the street outside. "Telling the world was a dick move more to the supes, sure." He turned back to me and threw his hands up in a *what'll you do* kinda motion then said, "I'll admit that, but humans have a right to know who else is locked on this planet with them and what could be killing them. Now, they know. And if it serves my purpose? Fucking great."

His eyes met mine and he swore softly, "Shit, Marcus, you know better than anyone that when everything turns to shit, you fall back into your training." I nodded, and he shrugged. "Brindolla trained me to kill or be killed, and to hunt down what I wanted for me and mine. I may have been a hero to a lot of people there, but I don't have that luxury here. The enemy isn't some shadowy figure with a magic stick and an army for me to beat the brakes off of. It's the situation in front of me and the circumstances arrayed against my station as a mortal. But I'm not just any mortal anymore.

"I'm a fighter. A king. A father. A husband and boyfriend. A friend." He growled low to himself. "I have the power to enact my will on my surroundings to get what I want. So I will."

"And what about the Wardens and the government?" He frowned. "Surely they aren't going to let you run rampant."

He chuckled. "No, they aren't. The Wardens are working with the government and getting them up to speed. Won't be long before they reach out to try to broker some kind of arrangement—think some Marvel-level shit—before a civil war breaks out." He glanced back out the window as he absently sipped his beer. "For now, they have places like the High Table being watched carefully and are taking note."

"And what about Theodorous?" Merlin surprised us both by appearing and asking that.

Zeke winced, glancing over at the young mage. "The council of Wardens was less than pleased with his part in all this and while I'm too strong to go against, my protection couldn't extend to him all the time. He's been thrown in Warden jail and is awaiting trial. I think, though, that the president is adamant he wants to work with him, since he built enough of a rapport to warrant his favor by telling him the truth."

Merlin scowled for a short time and then sighed tiredly. "Sounds about like them, but I can't say he didn't know the possibility wasn't there." He dipped his head and walked away from us.

"Tough kid." Zeke took a final swig of his beer before looking at me. "I may not actively be an asshole for now, Marcus, but I'm not going to just stand by and wait either. I'll defend my friends and the humans. But I won't hunt until I think on it some more."

That sounded about as good as we were going to get, so I just said, "Thank you."

He pulled out a large sack of something hard and let it hit the table. "Think I have a tab to settle?"

CHAPTER TWELVE

"It's been four weeks since the reveal of supernatural entities living and moving among the human populace, and tensions have only grown as the formerly-hidden populace begin to make themselves known." The anchor on the screen spoke exactingly as she shrank and a video played of a dead werewolf, torn apart with chunks missing from its body, as if someone'd had a fucking snack before beating feet. "This makes the fifth werewolf corpse found in Ohio alone, specifically in central Ohio. The Wardens are investigating but have no leads as of yet. Our next story at the top of the hour: how you can ward your home from burglars *and* vampires."

One of the patrons growled in disgust. "Ugh! Turn that shit back to cartoons."

Arden snickered and rolled her eyes. "Alright, T-Pain, chill."

The man just snorted at her and said, "The man has good taste. Who wants to watch sports or some other bullshit in a gentleman's club when you can see the coyote chase that stupid chicken while someone strips in front of you? That's the life."

I chuckled at that and put the next beer in front of him before looking back across the bar to find Uncle Yen coming down from his office. He looked a bit more put together than he had been, but we still hadn't heard from Anubis about Thoth at all.

He glanced my way and put up two fingers, his usual order when he was still stressed. I poured his favorite beer, a deep amber lager, and then made him a Long Island iced tea to couple with it.

I brought it over to him as he sat down and asked softly, "Still nothing?"

He shook his head and sighed. "No. I can't even find him magically. It's like wherever he is, there's a barrier in place blocking all attempts to find him and there are precious few places that could even happen in this world."

"Have you tried calling him?" He frowned and shook his head. "Why not?"

"He carries your old phone, but the reception in the under-world is shit most of the time if he's in his offices."

"Who says he's in his office?" He sighed at my question again and I punched his shoulder lightly. "Stop overcompli-cating things and try his cell."

Uncle Yen pulled his phone out and dialed his boyfriend's number before listening, excitedly he whispered, "It's ringing!"

He stilled. "Anubis?" He stood up. "Anubis, where are you?"

I couldn't hear a response on the other end as Uncle Yen moved the phone from his ear and growled, "Someone picked it up but didn't say anything I could make out."

I grunted and pulled my own phone out to try calling my main go to for almost all tech, the Sketti-Wizard herself, Kazmeer.

"Yo! Kaz, how're you doin'?"

She laughed. "I'm good, sugar. How you doin'? I was fixin' to pop over to the Table here in a bit."

"Awesome!" I turned and walked back toward the bar and spoke softly. "Hey, I got a round or three on me if you can bring some of your equipment. I need you to track a phone number for me to see where the phone is."

"Shoot, sugar, should the Huntsman be getting his shit stolen like this?" She paused. "Wait, never mind. You're calling me from your phone. I'm off today, so yeah, I got you. Get me a beer to start with, and then we can move on to cocktails, darlin'."

"You got it, Kaz, see you soon."

Two hours after that, a woman only a couple feet tall walked into the bar with blue hair that had some rather wild purple highlights that ranged from bright and loud to darker, royal purple. It was pretty damn cool.

"Kaz!" She grinned at me, her sunglasses shimmering with the glitter on them. The outfit she wore was nice, though a little eccentric with all the pockets. It was like someone took black sequined material and added more sequins in gold and silver to it. There was a cute little badger on the shirt that had to be their pet.

The bright purple vest she wore had pockets on the outside of it, her blue jeans too, and for some reason, her handbag had multiple pockets as well. "You need a lot of pockets?"

She grinned and winked. "And then some. Boy, I got pockets in places you can't even see." Her thick southern accent just made the statement that much funnier and salacious as she marched forward. "Whatcha got for me, hoss?"

Uncle Yen came over with his phone and gave her the phone number to look at so that she could plug it into the tablet she pulled from her bag. After she had it set up, she whipped out this neat little folding Bluetooth keyboard that she opened with a flourish.

I frowned at her. "You can do all this from a tablet?"

She snickered. "*I* can do a lot with this tablet. Ain't hard at all." She tickled the keys of the keyboard and a matrix of the world popped up. "Hit that call button for me, darlin'?"

Despite his anxiety, that made Uncle Yen smile. He pressed the button and the device rang for a moment after he put it on speaker. After the fourth ring, the line picked up and the gnomish woman's fingers danced along her keyboard without ceasing.

There was a muttered statement from the other end of the line, "A strange device this, what is it, god?" There was a pause and the voice raised slightly, "A what? A cell-you-lar phone? Is it magical? Fascinating."

"Anubis?" The line ran dead after Uncle Yen's question and he snarled, whipping the small electronic across the room.

A heartbeat after that dramatic outburst, Kaz belched loudly. "Got it, sugar—they're in Alexandria, Egypt." She zoomed in on the map. "I don't reckon I can get the exact location, but that oughta be more than most people would get you with that small of a window."

Uncle Yen took a deep breath and let it out slowly. "That works fine, I think I can find him if I know at least where he is to start looking, and it sounds like he went to check out a book." He put his hand over his mouth and there was a frustrated line to his body. He was furious.

He turned back to Kazmeer and knelt so that he could grasp her hand and spoke softly so that only those close would hear it. "My dear, whatever you want to drink tonight is on the house. Thank you for your assistance in this."

Kaz just rolled her eyes and patted his chest. "Darlin', Marcus is good people, you ain't gotta do that." She looked up at me and grinned. "But a girl sure as shit ain't gonna look this gift horse in the mouth, hoss. Cassia and me are gonna get *good* and drunk."

Cassia stepped up behind her and said, "Arden will be, Kaz. I'll be sipping pickle juice and wishing I could drink."

Kaz frowned and turned to look at the other woman before her eyes widened comically and she threw herself onto her chair to look Cass in the eyes hidden behind her sunglasses. "No fuckin' way!" Cassia nodded, and you would've thought that she'd found out that the Duke wasn't dead. "Yeeeeehaw! I'm gonna be an auntie!"

Cassia plucked her friend from the chair as she hopped and

down carried her to the bar as easily as she would a child with Kaz hysterically laughing, "If this was anyone else, I'd cut 'em but not you, babydoll, c'mere!"

I just snorted at their antics and collected Kaz's gear to give to her after a moment. I saw motion out of the corner of my eye and caught Uncle Yen going to pick up his phone. If he was as smart as I knew him to be, he was thinking exactly what I was.

Anubis had to have gone searching for his brother Thoth in the great library there. That meant a labyrinth to find him.

I sauntered over to him as he stared forlornly at the damaged device in his hand and sighed. I touched his shoulder softly and said, "We'll go visit the Great Library of Alexandria tomorrow morning when all of us are at our most spry and see if we can't find him."

"I can't ask that of you kids." He took a deep breath to continue speaking, but I just gripped his shoulder a little harder than I should have and he paused.

While he stared at me, I said, "We won't be going alone. You can come and search for him too. If you can be away from the Table for that long, that is."

He opened his mouth, then stopped and instead just nodded before saying, "Thank you."

I just dipped my head once before I patted his upper back and took Kazmeer her stuff. I made some drinks until the end of the night, the ladies having an absolute ball. Kaz got *wasted* and started to rub Cassia's stomach lovingly cooing, "Baby! Oh, I can't wait to start you on critters and shootin'."

I snorted at that. "Let's let them get out of there and let them get big enough to walk and run before we put a firearm in their hands, okay?"

She cackled and waved me off as I heard the sound of a hammer clashing against metal. I grunted and pulled my phone out to see a text from Jayvali.

You up?

I rolled my eyes, remembering just such a conversation and

a joke I could make about it, but I just responded affirmative and told him I was off in twenty.

He responded with a request, *Come by the Forge. I have a surprise for ya.*

I snorted and sent him a thumbs up before I put my phone away and started to break down the bar like I would every night before I got ready to leave.

CHAPTER THIRTEEN

Mako and I landed in front of the Forge, the Mantle of my station falling away back into the shadows to await my will as I patted the massive beast. He hadn't been able to get out too often, as he didn't like changing his size and shape if he didn't have to, so he was cooped up on my skin or in my shadow.

In the weeks it had been since we had been to the mines, he hadn't gotten to stretch too much, though I tried to take him for a flight every few days if I could.

I sighed, looking up at the building in front of us and said, "If I let you walk with me in there, they'll try to kick my ass and I'll have to smack the hell out of them." A rolling growl of sorts that I'd come to associate with him trying to mimic our laughter crept out of his throat. I snorted and patted his chin before pointing to my neck, "You can ride shotgun then, and we'll stop at a burger joint on the way back as a little reward. Sound good?"

He raised his head and his fading image swarmed over me to land on my left collar bone and neck. Letting him ride here was mainly just so he got to see whatever he liked and let him know that I appreciated him. Never thought I'd have a pet.

Only you would consider a drake a pet. I chuckled with Galaxy as her mind brushed up against mine. *I would recommend stopping by a place that sells smoothies on your way home, as well.*

"Cass have another craving?"

She laughed and said, *No, it would be for me. But I guess she would like one as well. I will text you here in a bit to see it happen.*

I just shook my head and started inside. By now, I had enough clout with the dwarves to be allowed to move about the building's shops without the need for a guide. It was a definite benefit, but as they knew my face, theft would be instantly blamed on me if I were to do anything like that.

If it were anything like the games I liked to play, anything not tied down would be in my inventory, but since this was real life and I needed their good will for the most part, I left it all alone.

It would have been nice to give it all to my Mantle to see what it would do to it though.

I made my way to the floor with Jayvali's shop and found him grinning like an idiot behind the counter. "Hey there."

"Don't you 'hey there' me, you dirty shit." I lifted my phone and he started to laugh as I half-heartedly berated him. It was really just us teasing each other at this point. "Cassia sees a 'you up' text from anyone and she would kill me. You? She would kick my ass, then yours."

"Or send you up here for a date, more like." He laughed at that as I pocketed my phone and he motioned to the wood box on the counter. "I finished it all."

My eyebrows shot up and he smiled at me some more. "Took me a bit to get it all how I liked it, but I do like it. If you get some more of that ore, I'd love to work with it. The cooling effect is insanely good!"

"I thought it would be." He just threw open the lid and pulled out a barrel that he showed me. It had a handle to it as well. "Is that the barrel to a squad automatic weapon?"

"Sure as shit is! I wanna take this bad boy to our range and fire a few thousand rounds through it to see if it will last longer than the normal metal barrels, but that's not why *you're* here." He paused, then a conspiratorial tone edged into his voice as he narrowed his eyes. "Unless you wanna come lay down some lead with ol' Jay?"

I laughed. "I would like to, but I owe several powerful people food and if I don't pay up promptly?" I took a deep breath and let a feigned shiver roll through my body. "Well, I'd rather not have a pissed off oni and goddess gunning for my ass, know what I mean?"

Jay snorted, "Cassia kicks like a fuckin' mule, so I do." He grinned and winked at me before pulling out a crystalline-looking club that had bits of jagged ice circling it at odd angles and intervals like spikes. "What do you think of it?"

I grabbed it and felt how light it was. "She's going to love it." I pressed my fingertip to the ice and cut myself and smiled as the blood stained the ice a bit.

He nodded to himself. "Made with dragon fire, that's why it's nearly clear. Turns out when you use non-magical fire, or something less magical like jinn flames, it keeps its icy-blue hue."

I put it back onto the counter and he cleaned it before placing it back into the case in front of him. "Now these!"

He pulled the daggers out and I had to whistle. They looked immaculate. The dark blades were of an almost diamond shape with how sharp the damned edges were and the handles thick with knuckle dusters on them to increase grip and protect the hands. "Amabala will love those."

"She better!" He grinned and pointed to the handles of them both. "She got claws, so they be a bit wider to comfortably grip for her, but they should fit her hands perfectly. The curve is slight though, so she will have to work on her stabbing."

I nodded as he placed them both back into the crate and then pulled out a long wooden pole that had the scythe at the end of it. He chuckled darkly at it as he tossed it to me.

It was beautiful. The wood was crimson-stained and smooth, with interspersed, bone-white wrappings where I would need to grip. The metal blade itself was angled only slightly, meant more for cutting than anything but it would still work to stab. The best part was that it was sharp both on the interior and the exterior of where the blade should be.

"No one ever expects to be cut on the back swing; figured it would be a good idea." He came out from behind the counter and pointed to the very end of the shaft near the metal-capped bottom. There was a small piece that could be twisted slightly and then squeezed to eject the blade that hid inside. It was a tri-angled spear of sorts, curved and meant to be hell on a wound. "That won't heal pretty, aye?"

He laughed darkly and then took the weapon from me. "And one last thing here for you. Two of them, really."

He took the scythe from me and reached into the crate only to pull out a small satchel of leather. He blinked at it and heaved a sigh before turning to me. "Jeweler came to me and gave me these to give to you when you came to collect these."

He pressed them into my hands, then grasped my hand as he did so, looking me in the eyes to say, "I wish you'd have told me." He frowned and gripped a little tighter. "Over the years, I might have tried to shoot my shot with her, but Cassia is happy with you, Marcus. It might have been a blow to my heart, but she's dearer to me than just as a potential love interest—we're friends now."

I grasped his shoulder and said softly, "She doesn't even know that I mean to ask her." He brightened up and I cleared my throat. "If you have to say your piece to her before I ask her, I'm all for it, man. Just know that I love her and Galaxy too much to let them go without a fight."

The dwarven smith snorted at me and shook his head. "I ain't got nothin' to say more to her than she doesn't already know." He pulled me into a bear hug and then shoved me back-ward. "I'll whip your ass here to Hong Kong, boy. Tempt me like that again. C'mere and share a drink with me over it."

I shook my head and laughed. "Yeah, I can do that."

He pulled that bottle out, the Dragon's Brand whisky, and

poured two small glasses before he offered me one. I took it and he lifted his in front of his face, solemnly saying, "To love, real and unrequited, and the friendship of the bastard who has both."

I fought the urge to laugh until I noticed the sparkle of mischief in his eye before he chuckled and we both started to guffaw heartily. When we could breathe again, I lifted my glass and returned, "To us. Friends."

I sipped the whisky slowly this time, remembering what happened last time. There was a message again, but as I had no fire spells for it to augment, there was nothing it could do. The burn and ache of it was delicious this time, and I savored the flavors it had coursing through it.

We drank in companionable silence for a short time until he had me leave with the crate in my inventory with a promise. "Won't tell her, lad. But you better propose some way nice to her. Be classy about it, I think she might like that."

I nodded. "I have something in mind, but I don't know if she's even going to be interested. I have to get it enchanted, but I think I want to wait for her to accept?"

He grunted. "Good man. Now go on so I can get back to work, need to pity smith for a bit."

I chuckled as I shook my head and waved to him after collecting the crate and the small satchel. I put the satchel into my pocket and walked into the elevator to leave the man to his own devices before going to collect the food for the others. I laughed and waved as the elevator carried me down to the ground floor and to the fast-food lines that would surely be waiting.

CHAPTER FOURTEEN

I woke up with Galaxy in her cat form draped across my face, Cassia having been moving a good deal more in her attempts to get comfortable last night.

The one thing about pregnant oni was that they were a lot more prone to needing to sleep than they normally would. Cassia had boasted before about being able to go without it in the past, but now? Now, not so much.

I took a deep breath and heaved for a moment before lifting her as delicately as I humanly and inhumanly could with the strength I had available to me.

Her breath caught and she grunted before she turned to look at me bleary-eyed behind the snug sun-goggles she wore.

I grinned. "Good morning, sleepy head."

She blinked and grinned back, her massive oni teeth flashing at me. "G'mornin'."

I moved her hair from in front of her eyes and pulled her into a hug. "We need to go get ready for our trip to the library."

She nodded and sat up with a yawn, "Yep. I'm about ready, lemme brush my teeth."

I stood with her and she stalked into the bathroom. Galaxy

stood and stretched out before shifting into her elven form so she could glare at me. "You drooled into my fur, Marcus."

I snorted. "You shouldn't use my face as a pillow?" She grimaced and I held up my hands. "I know, my breath is warm and it's too tempting to leave off."

She dipped her chin and then added, "And she moves a lot more than normal too, so it makes not getting slapped in my sleep a bit more of a chore."

I snickered and she smacked me lightly. "Shower?"

I shook my head. "I grabbed mine last night; I'm gonna go check on Uncle Yen while you two get ready. But I have some things for her, so don't take off just yet."

She gave me a thumbs up and padded into the bathroom to get a shower and get ready.

Rather than walking straight into the hall, I decided to delve into my inventory and sort things out there. We would be on Earth as it seemed, so I wanted to be certain I had my guns fully taken care of and my ammunition ready if needed.

The Silvaero and Fae Frame were pristine and cleaned, loaded with one chambered, and I had most of my extra magazines filled. I took the time to fully fill the last few with the few Fae rounds that I had and then took the rest as normal rounds.

I frowned and thought about that for a moment. *Could I make rounds out of the Ever Frozen?*

Thinking about the necessary heat to melt it, it would be fine to blast it with gunpowder as it was only half from Grestal, right?

I pulled my phone out and pressed dial on Jay's number. It rang through to his voicemail and I started to leave one when my phone started to vibrate in my hand. It was him.

"What, lad?" He sounded as if he had been asleep or drunk.

"How much of the Ever Frozen do you have left?"

He grunted and muttered something before finally coming back to the phone and said, "'Bout twenty pounds?"

I pumped a fist in front of me excitedly. "Can you make bullets with it?"

He snorted. "Bullets?" He guffawed wildly before coming back with an edge of near tears to his voice. "You wanna waste that precious of a metal?"

I rolled my eyes. "I can get you more. Can you do it, or do I need to line someone else's pockets, Jay?"

He swore softly. "You get me more, I'll make a batch—one! I have projects I gotta finish and then I can make you more." He sighed and then belched before speaking again. "You got a preference on the grain, caliber, or anything?"

I thought about it. "Your choice on grain, though we may need to tinker with it due to gunpowder being essentially just useless dirt in Grestal." I couldn't keep the grin off my face as I added, "Make one for my rifle and another for the Silvaero."

He whistled low. "Let's go for that then. I'll make two dozen each, with varied grains to judge the amount of power you need for it."

"Thanks Jay. Gonna be a bit on that. Not sure how long we're going to be in Egypt on a hunt."

"I'll keep 'em for you. Later." With that he hung up and left me to myself.

With the call taken care of, I walked out into the hallway to find Uncle Yen. "Oh! I was just about to come find you."

He grumbled a good morning and went downstairs. I followed after and sat with him at the table, his features pinched with worry. "We're going to be ready soon and then we can go."

He nodded and drummed his fingers on the table until he paused and looked up at me and stared me in the eyes. "You ever just have that gut feeling that you're too late?"

"Part of that is nerves." I knew what he was talking about, though. "Sometimes that anxiety can be a tool. Other times, it eats at you like there's nothing else."

He stared at the table as I spoke and whispered, "I'm so scared of what I might find. Or not find."

"And you have every right to be, but you need to understand

this: you cannot be of use to him if you don't focus on searching for him."

He looked up at me and scowled. "I'm here for it, aren't I?"

I raised my eyebrows at him and lowered my voice to a more cautious tone. "You are. But you can't be there and focused on him if you're too worried about the what ifs."

He grimaced and thumped the table. "Damn it!" He rested his elbows on the wood and put his head in his hands.

I watched him for a few minutes calmly, quietly, and without judgment. Not everyone was capable of just shutting their worries off. Hell, I hadn't been able to when the Seelie had my son. In a way, this was probably the very thing that Galaxy had been trying to help guard us against.

Cassia and Galaxy joined us in short order with Luca, Merlin, and Amabala walking in just a couple of minutes after that.

I frowned at Luca and he just offered me a soft smirk, apologetically saying, "I'm in the dog house presently and figured I would offer some assistance as I've been to the library before. I also have some tracking experience."

I ducked my head. "Thank you." I glanced over at Cass. "Your mom is willingly staying behind?"

"She doesn't know, and Arden is keeping her occupied, said something about the library being filled with crappy memories? She was trying to show Chiasa how to play Uno to bond with me a bit better." She grinned broadly at me with a wink. "So what's up?"

"We're going to the Library of Alexandria to find Anubis. I think he may have gone there to find Thoth so we could get a route to Atlantis." I pulled the crate out of my inventory and placed it on the table. "Before we go, I've got some gifts."

I opened the crate and pulled the daggers out to give them to Amabala, the sheaths included. "These are for you."

She smiled as she took them and went through a pretty damn nice form with them and stopped, "They're so nice, thank you!"

I nodded to her and pulled out Cassia's mace. "And for momma."

Cassia cackled loudly as she took the weapon before she whispered, "Oooooh. This is going to look *so* good covered in blood and brains."

I just shook my head at her and looked at Merlin and Luca. "Y'all have weapons already." They nodded. "Ours aren't enchanted yet, but they're strong naturally so they should be okay for this. I don't know if we will have to fight, but if we do, be ready."

Luca nodded and simply stated, "Ready." Merlin nodded as well, watching Amabala for a moment before turning to Uncle Yen as he stood.

Uncle Yen clenched his fists and then took a deep breath before speaking. "Come with me."

We marched up to his office and he pressed a button on his phone before closing the door with us standing in the hall. Then, opened it and closed it again. Once that was done, he opened the door one last time and the office was slightly different.

I muttered, "Egypt." The offices of the High Table branches were all connected by magic and could be used as hubs to travel between them quickly. It was a handy trick to have, certainly.

We walked out of our hall and into the office and found a man I didn't know seated in the manager's chair at the desk. Uncle Yen nodded to him. "Thanks, Wesley."

"You got it, kid. Go find your man." He stood and motioned to the door, closing it with magic. "You need a ride?"

I shook my head. "We will be carrying him."

"Very well." Wesley stood and glanced around then looked at me with a nod. "Huntsman. Go out the back, Yenasi. The Wardens have been watching us like hawks."

"We will, thank you." He bowed his head to the other man and turned to walk out of the office and then stopped once more in the hallway. He tapped on the wall twice, then a third time a second later. Then once more a second after that and the wall faded from view only to be replaced by a stairwell made of stone.

We walked down it quietly and then I stopped him. "Gimme a second."

I reached through our bonds, mine and Amabala, and acquired her portal making ability.

She smiled and watched me as I reached out and created a portal to the place I envisioned in my mind. "Go!"

The others plunged through the portal, Amabala grabbing Uncle Yen by the shoulders to yank him through with her. I surged through the portal myself, the sensation of it never getting any easier to ignore for me.

A soft breeze blew the sands around the temple where we came out, the sun beating down on us from high above.

Galaxy spoke low behind me. "You know, I really want to destroy this place."

"Do it." I turned to her, shock on her face and motioned for her to get to it. "This place is a bad memory for you, so you should."

She looked up at the stone of the temple that once held her prisoner.

"It would take too much power from me to do so right now." She looked down at the sand with a sour expression. "Let us just be gone from this place."

She faded into my shadow and her voice echoed through me, *Thank you for understanding, Marcus. As terribly as I despise this place, I did meet you here.*

I know, dear. Her purr comforted me deeply as I looked to Merlin. "Can you point us in the direction we need to go?"

Merlin pulled his phone out and I grunted. "What, no spells?"

A harsh bark of laughter escaped from the boy mage as he gestured to the device. "Saves my mana and time."

I just raised my eyebrows at him and he pointed to where we needed to head.

I stepped forward and summoned my Mantle. "Commence the Hunt."

My power surged and the world sharpened drastically around us as the Mantle snapped over me from the shadows below me. I turned to find my uncle staring openly as the Hunt surrounded him.

Cassia stepped forward and offered him her hand. "You can ride with me, Yenasi."

He nodded, unable to speak as he took her hand and her shadow expanded to summon her mount. Mako burst from my shadow as well and I hopped onto his back, bellowing, "Let's ride!"

CHAPTER FIFTEEN

The city below flooded into view and there was nothing I could see that stuck out to me as where we should even begin to look when Uncle Yen called out, "Take us down, right there!"

He motioned toward the water in the harbor and I frowned at that. How could there be a library in the water?

We landed and he pointed toward the water down by a dock that had a bunch of people milling about to go into a huge building.

"The Aquarium?" I squinted at the building and he nodded. "Why here?"

"Because like all mythological places, ties to the mundane of now must be maintained in order to remain secret." He sighed and jerked a thumb toward the building. "You want to go to the library? You go into the waters beneath this building full of Normies to get there."

I raised my eyebrows and watched as he walked toward the water, lifting his hands so that magic roared toward him and then flared into the world around us, then suddenly the water below him split and parted so that there was a slide like in a children's playground.

"The fuck is that?"

He glanced back. "Natural mana barrier here activates as soon as anyone with a supernatural aura crosses into it, so that they're invisible to the naked eye." He turned back to the slide. "This is younger wizards and warlocks making bad decisions fun."

With that, he hopped into the slide and disappeared beneath the water that began to pool back toward it.

"No time to hesitate, Marcus," Cassia chided me and hopped into the slide. Her voice floated back up. "Come on!"

I sighed and jumped into the darkness and there was a singular blip of light and color before I felt myself coming to my feet again.

I blinked and saw that I was surrounded by stone taller than a skyscraper.

"Where the fuck is this?"

"Don't panic." Merlin spoke from where he landed behind me. He walked up to stand next to me. "This is a common sorcerous protection to put on a lair of magic like this. Also, this place is a genuine labyrinth of knowledge that you can go through, so it has to be able to confound things like gods and magical creatures."

Looking around, the vertigo I got was a lot more intense than I had imagined was possible, so I closed my eyes and spoke softly. "That's fair, I guess."

"You alright?" Amabala put a hand on my shoulder and sounded concerned, but I couldn't open my eyes without feeling nauseous.

I took a steadying breath and mentally called out, *Galaxy?*

She was there. I knew she was there. Watching me curiously, but there was nothing she would do until I spoke. *Galaxy, did you help me with the vertigo?*

I have in the past, but Mantle helped a lot more. She appeared in front of me, her cool hands cupping my face so that when I opened my eyes, all I could see was her gaze. "There we go."

"Will you take it away?" Her breath caught and I spoke

quickly. "I know what I said and I remember what you promised—nothing without express permission. Please?"

She smiled at me, her teeth flashing at me before her face surged forward and her lips pressed against mine in a kiss. Her lips moved in time with mine and soon I forgot what was happening as her tongue darted into my mouth, a dizzying sensation swirling from the back of my mind forward until I had to pull away to breathe again.

I looked up and while the distance was there, I no longer felt like I was going to fall into it.

I closed my eyes and whispered a brief, "Thanks." I could feel her nodding as it displaced my breath and grimaced. This place smelled like books, not normally an issue, but for tracking purposes the must would fill any sort of scent we had to go off of.

Merlin stopped up to where Uncle Yen stood leering about cautiously and spoke softly. "You have something of his with you, right, Yen?"

Uncle Yen pulled out a bandana, green and hideous to my eyes, and held it out. Merlin took it and began to utter a spell that I thought sounded somewhat familiar and a golden bar appeared over the bandana and flickered before pointing straight up, and then to the right from where the young mage stood.

Uncle Yen held a hand up. "This kind of spell is a personal one, right?"

Merlin shook his head. "Wardens have used it for centuries to track others. It's very effective."

"I don't care so much about effectiveness as I do originality." I frowned at Uncle Yen as he took a deep breath and added, "Original spells and magic get added to the records when used in the library. So I would recommend not using any magic you don't want others to be able to research."

I blinked at that and almost shook myself out to stop from shivering at the thought. "Has the Huntsman been here before?"

Merlin shook his head. "The library is younger than when the Mantle disappeared, if memory serves correctly." There was an edge of disappointment to his voice as he said it that almost made me do a double take. He must have seen my face because he added, "It would be nice to have you look at information like that. Think of it like an instruction manual."

I made an O with my mouth and gave him a thumb up to let him know we were cool. "So how do we get up there then?"

"Flight is hardly a new spell, Marcus." This time Uncle Yen smiled and flexed his hands, muttering beneath his breath as an aura lit around all of us. "Stay close to me, alright?"

We all nodded and as I thought about rising, the others as my guide with Luca leading the charge, my body felt lighter. My feet left the ground and my weightlessness drifted upward with the rest of the group flying in front of me. I somehow got the impression from Mako that if I summoned him, he might not be well received, so he stayed where he was curled on my forearm.

We flew for a few moments as rows and rows of books, stacks of them even, drifted by lazily. They flew as we did, fluttering from shelf to shelf, as if returning to where they needed to be. I caught sight of some others in the area looking at books and sitting almost on the shelves, a few of them glancing our way. One of them however, made a beeline directly at us.

"What is the Wild Hunt doing at the Library of Alexandria?" the man asked imperiously, his hands on his hips. He was lean, impish almost in how he looked physically, but I could tell he was more than just a Touched. "You aren't here to destroy this wonderful collection of knowledge, are you?"

"Hermes," Uncle Yen huffed at the man. "We're here to find Anubis, have you seen him?"

The god Hermes shook his head. "No. Tall, dark, and gloomy makes sure I don't see him. It's like a game we play—I don't like him, he don't like me—and we stay the fuck away from each other." With that he turned his weird pink eyes toward me and grimaced. "If I find out you so much as crease a page in any one of the books I like, I'm gonna—"

Luca stepped forward and held a hand up, calling attention to himself. "Hermes, please, you know well that I would not let that happen. I like this place as well. Let us go and leave you to read."

The god snickered and said, "Whatever. Threat stands, and stay away from Greece! If anything like what happened in Cairo happens there, no one would be faster getting to you than me."

He fluttered back to where he'd been posted up and left us to move on, well away from him before I muttered, "What a dick."

We floated and flew through the aisles further unmolested for a while, still catching the odd look here and there, but no one else came at us.

"We have to come back here!" Merlin called, the elation in his voice as clear as day. "Can you imagine all that we could learn?"

"Your book boner is showing!" Cassia teased and Merlin didn't respond to her at all, which made her grin all the more wildly. Either she'd hit a nerve, or all the blood *had* gone from his head and ears.

Can we keep our thoughts off of Merlin's anatomy? It's bad enough you're thinking about it, I have to deal with Amabala as well.

I snorted so hard it led me into a coughing fit bad enough that it changed the trajectory of my flight.

I crashed lightly into one of the shelves and the books there responded to my proximity, shuffling forward to be touched like dogs eagerly awaiting a pet and a good scratching. I grabbed a book that looked the most eager to me and looked at the spine, *An Aria of Shadows and Winter* embossed in bold black letters with a shimmering white background.

"Interesting." I put the book under my arm and pushed off the shelf and up back into the air to catch up to the others.

I shot through a section of shelves that could have been a corridor and yelped as an arm reached out and grabbed me.

Luca appeared next to Cass where she held me and grinned. "You know, I might need to hear that again."

A growl escaped my throat and that just made him smile all the more until I pulled out my Silvaero and aimed it in his direction. His eyes widened until I pulled the trigger and something in the shelves behind him screeched.

"Contact!" My weapon belched flames again as I fired another round at the dark figure darting to another shelf behind the Fae prince.

"Hold your fire!" Uncle Yen bellowed, waving his arms at me to get my attention. I stopped squeezing the trigger but maintained my line of sight on the shadows the creature hid inside of. "Librarian! Those are the librarians."

My mouth quirked into a grimace as I glared into the dark, trying and failing to outline the creature. "Looked like a gorilla to me."

He took a deep breath before putting a hand onto the slide of my pistol to push it down. I made sure he didn't flag anyone when he did it, allowing the repositioning as he explained, "They're beings of magic and paper that fold themselves into shapes that can traverse the library with the ease that they want!" He motioned cautiously to the creature that stepped from the ink blot against the shelf.

The gorilla was made of paper, like origami with words that flitted from fold to front then back again. It cautiously made its way forward with eyes of swirling words that made my hair raise with how creepy they were.

"See? He just wanted to check the book you dropped." Uncle Yen grabbed the copy I had snatched and took it to the librarian. "Follow me, Marcus."

I transferred the weapon to my left hand so it was free as Uncle Yen had my right wrist in his own hand.

The gorilla reached behind itself and pulled out a stamp. Uncle Yen held the book out and the gorilla motioned for my hand. I held it out with my uncle's hand to guide me and the stamp *swooshed* over my hand to collect my aura. The magic of the item as it moved through my space bit a chunk of my aura and then the librarian stamped it onto the first page.

My name and alias as Massacre. I didn't have the time to be concerned as the book snapped shut and pressed into my hand before the creature faded into the inky darkness.

"Once you're done with it, tap your name three times and let the book go," Uncle Yen explained as he patted my shoulder and motioned toward the others. "Let's leave exploring until after we find Anubis, yes?"

I nodded. "Kinda jumped out at me."

He smiled softly while we joined the others and I placed the book into my inventory for later.

With Merlin leading the pack, we continued on and on and on. It felt like we moved around the library endlessly. The columns and shelves all blended together until there was nothing left to differentiate from the outer shelves.

I watched Uncle Yen closely as we continued to blur toward our destination. Merlin had to recast the spell three times and there was still no sign of the missing god.

The direction of the spell changed multiple times until even I could tell we were moving in a circle.

"Something is either confounding your spell, or we're so close that the position is changing," Uncle Yen reasoned as he glared at the shelves in the center of the circle. "There were always rumors of a study. Somewhere that would allow you to use what you'd learned with the books here, but the books that I've learned from were always theoretical and I always took them home."

I pulled the book from my inventory and sighed. "Looks like I need to start reading then."

My head pounded as I continued to try to piece together the language the book was written in for the dozenth time, then slammed it shut with a growl. "The title is in *English. How* can I not understand the words inside?"

Uncle Yen took the book from me and tried to open the cover but it wouldn't open for him. "Spells and the knowledge of magic are often highly personal things, but the library we're in was designed and designated as a place to share magical *and* mundane knowledge." He put it back in front of me. "I'm not sure if this requires something to really read it or not, but the title was what again?"

"An Aria of Shadows and Winter." Just saying the name made my head pound again and I groaned angrily. "Do I have to sing? I hope I don't have to sing."

Galaxy piped up in my head, *I hope you don't have to sing.*

"No one wants to hear a sociopath strangle a cat, Marcus." Cassia spoke softly as she said it and I had to admit, my pride was a tad damaged at that.

You may not be able to hear yourself sing, but we have. Cadence is not singing. And no—not even if you call it sing-song, and I swear to me, if you start saying any kind of left or right foot shit, I will crawl out of you to put a foot back in you.

My eyes widened on their own and I glanced down at the book. I wouldn't be able to summon the Mantle of the Hunt because I didn't want to offer that kind of information about myself and my abilities.

"Do you think it requires some other source of magic to use it?"

Uncle Yen shrugged at me as the others began to look around for anything they could use to assist me, or maybe take on the job themselves.

"Got it," Merlin called in a hushed tone. Why, I couldn't tell you. A figure stepped out of the corner of the shelf, a turtle this time, and stamped it much the same way. Merlin came back to us. "Alchemical Solutions to Mundanities and Maladies."

He flipped a few pages and found something inside the text before speaking loudly. "Okay, here we go. This looks like a fun experiment, library? Do you have a lab area I could borrow?"

The library was silent and all of us watched the boy mage as if he were going to start tap dancing to some Broadway musical.

There was a shifting sound, stone grating against stone as the shelves in front of where we stood began to slowly grind to the side to reveal a burst of rooms in a wall almost as vast as one of the aisles we'd been traversing. Rows of spaces opened up and as we watched, one drew our focus.

Inside were beakers, tubes, desks with notes compiled neatly onto them and two tables with experiments already on them.

One of them was Anubis, several large tubes forced into his body at odd angles and intervals with his eyes closed as if he were in pain, and the other who I could only assume to be Thoth.

The bird-like beak and his reaching for his brother were what truly gave it away, but as I continued to stare at them, the resemblance to that copper dragon hit me and I had to move fast. I didn't want a repeat of what happened before.

I snatched Uncle Yen back toward me and began to issue orders, "Amabala, I want you sniffing every inch of this room once we finish clearing it. Cassia, Luca—with me, we're going to scour the place for who did this." I pointed to Uncle Yen and then Merlin, "Overwatch. Something moves, I don't give a flying fuck what it is, I want it contained or dead. This is too close to what happened to that dragon for my comfort."

Uncle Yen, anger clear on his face and tears welling in his eyes, just nodded while trying to get himself back under control.

We did clear the rest of the room, though the anomalous stylings of the library made it a bit more concerning to try to do that. Seemed like every time we went too far from the table where the incident had occurred, there was a shift and suddenly we were back where we started.

Cabinets filled with beakers of reagents, solvents, liquids, metals, and all kinds of other things foiled anyone's attempts to hide. There was a coat rack with a set of white coats on it, and what looked like an umbrella holder that had some wild-looking umbrellas and canes within. Hell, one of them had what could have been a demonic skull with buck-like antlers attached to it with gemstone eyes that looked to be following me whenever I moved. Investigating it a little further, I went to touch it when Merlin cleared his throat.

I frowned at him and he called out, "Best not to touch things in a place like this if you don't know where they came from. Someone may be looking for it and could have cursed it to make sure the next would-be owner never has the chance to lose it, catch my drift?"

A thrill of cold came from the direction of the bone shaft of the item and my hand recoiled without another thought. Curses could be nasty and even with a goddess supporting me and the power of the Mantle, there was no guarantee I could walk away unscathed.

I didn't see any kind of aura around anything else in the room so there was nothing shapeshifted and hidden that I could tell and decided that we had to at least be good enough to move along. I pulled my pistol closer to my chest so that I was ready to rock and roll if anything showed itself then called it, "Clear!"

I glanced over at Cassia and nodded. "Go to them and see if we can't at least get them back to rights so that we can figure out who the hell we're looking for."

While they worked to ensure that the two gods would make it, there was time enough for me to glance at the notes on the tables that I could see, and they were in yet another language that I couldn't understand. "Marcus?"

I flinched and raised the muzzle of my weapon slightly as I turned to Amabala. "Yes?"

She shook her head. "No, the place is clean. I don't smell any semblance of a portal. Not even traces. And no scent of a perpetrator in this room or any of the surrounding ones. I'm sorry, everyone."

I grimaced and sucked on my teeth for a long moment before asking quietly, "Do you think you can get us out of here by portal?"

"Portals don't work in the library, son," Uncle Yen called

out. Over at the table, Cassia was doing her damnedest to stabilize the two gods, and my uncle had his boyfriend in his arms. "As much as I want to scour this place for the shit that did this, we need to go, now."

I nodded and pulled Amabala to me. "As soon as they get outside, you get them and Uncle Yen back to wherever he tells you."

Cassia was suddenly next to me. "You aren't staying here alone."

I shook my head. "You're right." I turned and whistled sharply. "Luca! You'll be with me."

The former prince of the Unseelie nodded and responded softly, "As you wish, Marcus."

I frowned in his direction but it was Cassia who pushed first. "You want him here over me?"

I shook my head and put a hand on her shoulder, lowering my voice until only we might hear it, "I want you with me, but my uncle needs you more than me right now. You know him better than anyone, love. If anyone can keep him from doing something rash, it'll be you." She growled low in her throat and her skin began to change colors rapidly. "Please? I'll do anything you want after I get back. The only reason I'm staying is because we need to find a way to Atlantis that won't have us searching the bottom of the ocean for who knows how long."

She closed her eyes, the shadow of them visible enough behind her sunglasses that I could see what she was doing, and began to take deep breaths. Her skin began to go back to its normal, pink coloration and then she nodded once. "Alright, but if you get into a fight, I want to know all of what happens."

I gave her a thumb up and she kissed me on the cheek quickly before saying, "You'll regret that offer later, Marcus Bola."

My eyes widened at that but she had walked away to join the others in getting Yen and the gods out of here.

Luca closed the distance with me and spoke calmly. "Any clue as to where we should even begin to look? Thoth had some notes on him that pointed toward some books that might have held some information, but it looked like he was content to pour through them, and this is a *lot* of books. Finding them is going to take time we don't want to spend in here with just the two of us."

I shrugged. "Wonder if maybe they have, like, a way to look things up?" My fingers scratched my head and I realized I was well overdue for a haircut. "Maybe ask a Librarian? Oh, we can maybe see if they know who was experimenting here?"

"Could work." Merlin had taken the book with him so the room felt like it was closing slowly and we were ready to go, so we walked out into the aisle of shelves and Luca called out, "Library, I wondered if you had a way to find a book for us? Or that we could do it ourselves? And can you tell us who was using this room?"

There was a huffing and puffing behind us and the sound of goat's hooves on wood that made the two of us whip around to find a large man in a perfectly fitted three-piece suit there. His head was that of a bull, scars crossing it and one of its eyes milky as it stared at us. "Gentlemen."

"Uh." My brain stopped functioning for a long, long moment. "Uhm."

A brow raised as the horns shifted and tilted curiously. "Not all Minotaurs are evil, mindless beasts, master..." The speaking creature waited for me to reply before looking to leveler heads.

"Bola; his name is Marcus Bola." Luca bowed his head at a tilt and then said, "I am Luca and I wondered if we would be able to receive some guidance on finding a way to travel to where we could possibly find the realm of Atlantis?"

"Masters Luca and Bola, follow me." He was able to take us to the end of the aisle and then looked up, motioning with his hand in the air. After a moment of waiting, a large book about ten feet by thirteen feet hefted itself from a nearby ink blot and settled against the floor. "This will take us through the aisles to where we wish to be."

As soon as both of us had our feet planted on the book, the

Minotaur joined us and the book lifted. The motion was a little concerning at first, but we settled and soon it was like being back on an Osprey in the desert again.

"As to your question about the user of the room." The bull speaking surprised the two of us and we listened intently as he spoke. "The experiment was labeled as incomplete and though we have some scribes relating it into book format, it will take a week to get access to what was done so far."

"And the user?"

"The experiment was incomplete and, as such, the name of that person has been codified as 'secret' until the work can be published as complete. This is to help protect researchers and scholars who wish to formulate new ideas and knowledge."

I crossed my arms and frowned. "Even if we want to help?" The bull's eyes landed on me and though there was no emotion to the gaze, I knew this was his way of calling bullshit.

"Sir, you never did give us your name." Luca broached the subject politely with his hands clasped in front of himself as he watched our guide carefully. It looked to me like he was just curious, but it was the kind of readiness that most military police had when they were talking to persons of interest on base. Ready to respond if someone got froggy.

"Ah, forgive me, I didn't realize." The Minotaur bowed his head and pressed an open palm to his chest, "I am Frederick, guardian and accumulating custodian of this grand library of the magic and mundane. It is my sincere pleasure to make your acquaintance, gentlemen."

I frowned. "Accumulating?"

He nodded. "I go over the newly acquired knowledge within the library and decide where it is to go so that others like your-selves might find it a bit easier." His explanation still left much to be desired, but I left it at that.

We floated on in companionable silence for a short time before Frederick spoke again. "Are you finding your way to the land of Atlantis for business or pleasure?"

I grinned. "Business is always a pleasure if what you do is

important enough." The Minotaur's horns bobbed as he nodded sagely. "How long have you been doing this?"

He grunted and his tail flicked. "A long time, Master Bola. A long time." His bull grin was bright, but I could see an edge to his gaze as he looked out into the expanse of shelves as we moved into a massive intersection. There were others here riding along on books, I could see them floating in the distance and there looked to be Minotaurs with them as well. "Clones."

His answer to my forming question surprised me enough that I didn't bother asking and he just grinned and simply said, "Spells of all sorts exist here, some of them with uses that would be surprising." He motioned to one farthest away. "Those ones are Wardens seeking insight into American policies and media and how to exploit them. The one in front of them is seeking information about the Wild Hunt." He frowned, blowing a deep sigh through his nose as he motioned to another one that said, "He looks for something called, the sauce?"

Luca and I both frowned at that odd quest but left it alone. It was pretty wild that someone was here trying to find information about me and my power though. "Anything to be learned about the Huntsman?"

"There are plenty of legends and whatnot, certainly." He scratched the patch of fur on his chin and added almost dismissively, "Historical accountings of sightings, human recollections of sightings too. There are even first-hand accountings of what happened in the war with the dragons, though they're sparse and almost indecipherable."

I fought to keep my face clear and stayed quiet. I wondered who it was that was looking and if I would be needing to defend myself and my Hunt.

We floated on for a while longer, making pointless small talk that I cared little to remember as I kept watch of our surroundings until the book stopped floating along at all and landed in a section that was filled with scrolls.

"This is one of the older sections of the library and contains the maps of all known and even some secret locations. We have a section devoted to Atlantis in the beginning and then when it was lost." He motioned to the section to the far left. "We also have some conjecture on where the island may have gone as well."

I nodded and began to gather the scrolls when I felt a large hand on my forearm and turned to see a frowning Frederick and his furrowed furry brow. "The maps may not be taken. And photos cannot be taken either. I am afraid I must ask you to study them and maybe draw your own map in reference."

I smiled as I gently set the paper prizes on the table closest to the rack. "Thank you, Frederick." Internally, I reached out to Galaxy, knowing that being squeamish about her in my head doing stuff other than conversing wasn't an option at the moment. *Can you get this into Merlin's mind so that he can cross reference this with our own maps?*

Already on it, Marcus. Study them as closely as you can.

I unfurled the first one with Luca taking the time to do the same to a few others, drawing a piece of parchment that the Minotaur provided politely for our endeavor.

I poured my all into making sure I didn't miss anything on the first map, then went to the second one as Frederick hovered. He took what we finished with and then put it back. Voices raised down the aisle from us and he huffed, "More for maps, it seems."

He turned, his gaze shifting to the newcomers as they drifted into the space nearest us.

I glanced up at them out of the corner of my eye and saw that they were unfamiliar to me, but they didn't have the looks of Wardens. Their auras were tame as well, more so than I had ever seen even among the Touched.

There was a lull as they began to sift through some of the maps along the other side of the shelves from us and as I was finishing up the third map, there was a lance of fear through my being.

A bond tugged at my attention and, with Galaxy's

assistance, I threw it open wide. Keith was struggling to reach out to me. "Keith? What's wrong?"

"Dieter!" He gasped, it sounded like he'd been running. "Dieter was at the bar and a strange guy came in with Luci for a drink, but when he smelled Dieter, he challenged him to a fight for alpha."

I frowned, who the fuck would be doing that? And why?

"Marcus, this guy's going to kill Dieter!"

I growled and snarled, "Luca, we gotta go." I turned my attention to Frederick. "Frederick, thanks for the help, man. Is there a quick way out of here?"

He frowned and clapped his hand three times. "If this is a life-or-death issue, I can have the Librarians take you to the exit through the Ink, just don't shoot any more of them?"

"Sorry, but can we please do that? If we don't hurry, an associate of mine is going to die." Frederick nodded once and closed his eyes before two paper creatures stepped out of the Ink, as he called it. "Follow my friends here and see to it that you do not let go of them inside the Ink."

Luca and I raced over to them as darkness washed over their origami forms and then us in our race to beat the clock and whoever might be beating on Dieter.

CHAPTER SIXTEEN

I used my bond with Amabala to tear open a hole in space and time to cross the distance to where the fight was taking place, using her as an anchor. The theory of it was something I'd discussed with Galaxy, but the practice was still something to be desired.

"You coming?"

Luca shook his head, determination on his face as he backed toward the bar. "No, I will stay here to ensure that this isn't a ruse to get the wolves and the Hunt away from the Table. You go."

I could feel where they were and we were about a mile out from them. Gritting my teeth, I summoned Mako and hopped onto his back with a shout to Luca, "Catch you later, man."

His call back was lost in the wind and Mako's excited growling as he stomped into the air. The massive drake ate up ground like Cassia ate cheesy fries, his long stride devouring the distance faster and faster as the sound of people shouting reached us.

The crowd was much larger than I thought it would be, but

from the myriad of scents below, there were shifters I didn't know there as well.

"Land with Keith and Luci, Mako." The drake grumbled but started toward the two I'd indicated as I gathered my strength and hopped off into the middle of the circle where Dieter and his opponent circled each other.

My weight shifted dramatically as I sailed through the air and the ground beneath my feet cracked as I landed, the jarring impact shaking me but not enough to make me stop. "Enough!"

Dieter stepped beside me and put a hand on my chest while I eyed the stranger who crossed his arms across from us casually. "Get out of the circle, Marcus."

I turned my gaze toward him while keeping the new guy in my peripheral. "I told you we were allies, Dieter. That means helping you."

"The law is absolute in this, Marcus." Dieter was calm, even with a slowly swelling left eye, but there was an edge of something beneath his demeanor that I could only guess at. Fear, maybe? "He challenged, and I accepted. One of us has to fall and there can be no outside intervention."

"Ignorant friends are alright, Dieter," the newcomer drawled as he waited patiently.

I already didn't like him with that alone. His aura was massive, about as much as one would expect from a werewolf confident enough to challenge an alpha, but there was a tint to it that I didn't recognize.

He was shorter than most, probably about five foot four, with a red buzzed cut like the Marine Corps' typical high and tight, and a lush goatee of the same burning color. He wore a light blue zip-up hoodie that complimented his blue eyes, and dark jeans.

He saw my sizing him up and grinned, unzipping the hoodie to toss it aside. He wore a dark tank under it that he also stripped off without taking his eyes off me or his opponent. "I don't usually care for being sized up like this, so if you don't mind—I have a pack to take over."

Dieter gave me a gentle shove and, begrudgingly, I left the circle of lycanthropes. Luci stood with Keith, both of the men looking upset.

Luci began to speak as soon as I was in earshot, "Everything was great. We were at the bar getting drinks and suddenly he gets a call just before Dieter walks in and suddenly he's challenging him to a fight for alpha."

"Is he a friend or something?"

"Yeah!" Luci flushed slightly, "After my douchebag ex, I wanted to take it slow and he was so nice. Marcus, when he's not beating the shit out of people I know, he's absolutely adorable. Like a bite-size, ginger Michael Phelps!"

I almost snorted at the comparison but the guy did have a build like a swimmer.

Dieter shook himself out and stalked closer to the man. "Let's keep going."

The redhead grinned. "Happy to oblige!"

The two rushed forward, Dieter feigning a roundhouse kick to get a straight in on the man when he would've blocked but the smaller man just took the kick to the abs and grabbed the leg that hit him.

With the strength of a supernatural beast at his disposal, the smaller man hefted Dieter and pulled a Bam Bam. He whipped Dieter over his head and into the ground before doing the same on his other side, then tossed him through the air.

As soon as the larger man landed painfully on the ground, the newcomer hiked his leg up into the air and then dropped it with enough might that it would have cleaved a normal man in half.

Instead, Dieter rolled to the side and let the kick destroy the earth below him before surging up into his opponent's exposed midsection.

Dieter slammed into the smaller man and carried him a few feet as the redhead drove his elbows into the alpha's exposed back and spine.

"Why haven't they shifted?" My question took Keith by surprise and he just blinked at me.

"Pride," he explained, then motioned to the two fighters. "Whoever turns first is usually the most injured, so the longer they fight in human form, the better their odds because they'll both be fully healed otherwise."

Dieter drove the smaller fighter into the ground in a dive, a small crack echoing dimly before shouting began. The alpha got a few good shots into his opponent's face, splitting his lip and an eyebrow and his punches landed with all the strength of an enraged werewolf. The man on the ground took it, his lip splitting further as he grinned savagely before he thrust his hips upward to dislodge Dieter's position.

Dieter pitched forward and his opponent caught his flailing arm in a lock I was familiar with. It was a submission hold but he had no intention of letting the alpha tap out.

A crunch made me flinch as Dieter's arm snapped near the elbow.

The pain must have been enough as Dieter stood with the other man hanging on his arm still and began to shift.

The redhead fighter let go and rolled away as the change took Dieter and the alpha healed his wounds.

The redhead stood to cheers from the pack of strangers behind his side of the circle. "Marik! Marik!"

He lifted his arms as they called his name and turned in time to see Dieter settling to pounce. "I'm gonna end this, okay?"

Dieter just snarled and a wave of distaste roiled through the air as he charged forward, blocking my view of Marik in the process.

The alpha gathered his legs beneath him in a ferocious leap that carried him across the distance to bear down on his opponent and when they collided, I shouted, "Fuck!"

Two clawed hands had speared the wolf through the rib cage and in a Herculean display of strength, tore the alpha in half.

A blood-soaked Marik stood, still in human form, exactly where he had been with a huge grin on his face. His hands looked like adult hands on a child, the size almost comically enhanced, which made me wonder just how big his shapeshifted form would be.

He turned toward us and held one of his massive hands in the air to hush his pack as their cheers and jeers shook the ground.

"His pack is mine now." His voice carried as his bones snapped and adjusted with his own, now-unnecessary, change. His werewolf form was easily larger than the former alpha's had been and his eyes glowed a reddish color that bled with something else around the whites. It looked almost like the same green tinge to his aura.

"First order of business is the new order: all of your bonds to other organizations aside from the pack are now broken." My gut fell into my ass as I could feel the bonds to the members of the pack that had remained in the Wild Hunt forcibly snapped.

The majority of the wolves around all of us, including Keith took a knee with grunts of pain.

"Fucker," Keith swore savagely and stood to his feet faster than the others recovered. "You can't do that!"

Marik opened his arms, his teeth bared in the grin that I was beginning to associate with him just being a cocky asshole. "Don't like it? Kill me."

Keith roared and launched himself at the man faster than Luci and I could grab him. The men and women behind Marik surged forward, their changes faster than some of the ones I'd seen before.

They stood in the way, barring Keith access, but the young wolf didn't give a shit.

I had to stop him from getting himself killed. "Keith!" Growling, I cast Embodiment of Lightning and zipped between him and the other werewolves.

Instead of staying on the ground and running into my open

palm, he slid beneath me and outside my grasp, shifting his form as he did so.

He came up and caught one of the newcomers with a right hook like a bullet train that sent the dickhead screeching into the air.

One of them lunged forward with their claws and he just grabbed them and yanked past them like it was nothing.

I'd never seen the security guard this pissed off before and all the shit he talked and fun he had was gone now. This was something pure and filled with malice.

Marik raised a brow and ordered, "*Stop.*"

The command rippled through the wolves in the area like someone had dropped a boulder in the pond. Not one of the furry bastards moved, not even Keith.

"Are you challenging me, Keith?" Marik's words were cautious and concise as he spoke, weaving through his protectors toward the young werewolf.

Keith growled, fighting the order so hard his muscles moved and strained like he was under the weight of the world. He opened his mouth. "Ye—"

I did the only thing I could to protect him and clobbered him hard enough to crack his neck and knock him unconscious. The magic of the alpha's order didn't stop him from collapsing onto the ground.

Marik's careful gaze fell on me. "So close. I feel like he would have been a good second round." He tilted his head as he continued forward through his people, brushing them easily aside. "You keep getting in my way, Marcus. You want a piece too?"

"I'll kill you *right now.*" I started to go to that place I went when I made the really bad decisions.

Marik sighed. "Sadly, you aren't an alpha, or even a werewolf, for that matter, so all you would do is delay the inevitable if you killed me." He shrugged dramatically and added, "There are wolves here strong enough to take the packs under their wings and I doubt they would listen to you, Huntsman."

He glanced to the right of my shoulder and said in an apologetic tone, "Sorry to have cut the drinks short, Lucifer, but business called. I hope we can sort this out?"

Lucifer stood aghast and then his face contorted in outrage. "You can fuck right off, mister."

Marik closed his eyes and swore softly, "Shit." He appeared saddened, then looked to me. "I'm not going to go on a killing spree, if you're wondering. I'm just amassing my own power, world going to shit and everything, you know?"

"Tell me why I shouldn't just kill you and all the wolves I don't know right now." The edge of my Vornal blood was beginning to bleed through and I was surprised when he just shrugged.

"I could order all of your wolves to stop breathing?" He put his hands on his hips theatrically. "Order sixty-six type shit, you know—have them just off themselves and each other. Send the entirety of my pack into the city while you attack me to raise hell and kill as many people or turn them as possible while touting the Wild Hunts' name."

He snapped his fingers. "Know what? That sounds like a great idea!" He grinned savagely again and raised his voice, "Hey guys? Why don't all of you just go and tear this bitch u—"

I grabbed him by his throat as the Mantle surged over my body and dressed me for a fight. The wolves all unfroze and turned in unison; even the ones that had been with the High Table did the same. Glancing over his right shoulder I could see his bonds to the wolves around us and to me, which was **Curious indifference**. That was a first but as I pulled the Huntsman's powers to me and attempted to sever the bonds forcibly, something I couldn't describe forced my power away. It was like trying to grab a greased-up bubble; every attempt to wrest control just slipped off and the bonds out of reach.

Marik winked at me as they started forward and then tapped my forearm once. I growled and let him down so he could clear his throat and speak again. "Stay out of my way,

Huntsman. I might consider playing nice once I get to know you and the others, but I need to take care of myself first."

He looked me over once more and glowered as his gaze went back to Lucifer. "Him too. He was so nice."

I spoke low, my voice not muffled by the mask of the Huntsman, "I killed his last boyfriend too. I'm sensing an irritating trend." Then I recalled what Luci had said. "Someone called you—who? How did they know Dieter was there? Who the fuck are you?"

He just hit me with that grin of his. "I'm not completely ignorant, Marcus, and if I told you anything more than that I would be so much blood and mess smeared on the ground. So how about this?" He raised his voice as he shoved himself from my grip. "If Marcus or anyone affiliated with him kills me, I bind my soul to the order that all of the werewolves he's known that are under my control as alpha will die. Their deaths will be miserable and pain-filled things."

I grit my teeth and he blinked up at me casually. "Consider it an insurance policy for now." He smirked dangerously at me and added, "I wouldn't ask anyone in the pack about it either, because if they give you any information I don't like, I'll kill them."

I muttered to Galaxy mentally, *Can he do that?*

She appeared on my shoulder in cat form and hissed low. *I'm not sure, but we know other shifters who could tell us. Better to retreat and consider a better way to get him out of the way later.*

It took all I had not to throttle the little shit, but she had a point. *Maybe when we're strong enough, shit like this might not happen.*

She didn't say anything for a long while as Marik turned and gathered Dieter's body and had someone pick Keith up. "Gentle with that one, Max. He could be a good lieutenant for me."

Marik's laughter faded as he moved into the distance and loped away with all of his pack, old and new.

"We should go and let Cassia and the others know what happened…" Lucifer spoke softly, his focus on his feet.

I gripped his chin, softer than I felt I could at the moment. "This isn't on you."

I closed my eyes and threw my senses through the Mantle, ordering one of the Hunt to tail Marik. That way, if I found out that his shit talking was false, I could find him and rip him and his other soldiers apart.

He sighed and raised his eyes so that they met mine and, without blinking, said, "I know. I'm far from thinking that the fate of the world or others rests on my shoulders, Marcus. I'm far too old for that. But I can be sad that an innocent person died because I brought a hot stranger to the bar."

"You had no way of knowing." I pulled him into a gruff hug and then the world faded weirdly around us.

I blinked and looked up at the area around us and found that we were closer to the High Table. He smiled at me. "Least I could do."

I gave him another pat before heading toward the Table only for Galaxy to say, *Cassia had been told already. One of the wolves called her.*

Out loud, "How's she taking it?"

Not well. But she wants you at the Table to make sure this isn't a part of some larger scheme to leave us all vulnerable.

There was a pause in her voice like she wanted to say something, but she refrained. "Yes?"

She stepped from my shoulder and retook her human form. "I can't help wondering—if I had my Dominion, could I have prevented this?"

I shook my head slowly. "Maybe, but we can't dwell on that."

The sounds of people calling to the guards at the front of the building, trying to get in to become some flavor of supernatural to escape their Normie coil, grew steadily louder as we approached the front of the building.

"Merlin is working on trying to find the answers to where we need to go, but without some sort of key or compass to go off of, he says it will be slow going."

I put the heel of my palm onto my forehead and just grunted an affirmative to her to let her know I'd heard.

"We know that Hollow's sister was the one who was eaten. Would she have a clue as to where her sister could have been?"

The ocean, the ice primordial responded simply and less than helpfully. I sighed tiredly and walked to the front of the line, giving Kenshi and his partner Sabbath a nod as I walked past.

Both men stood a lot taller and looked more intimidating than usual so I assumed they'd heard about the wolves too.

Inside, the bar was a bit more it's usual type of environment. People drank and ate, chatting with each other and having a generally good time.

I passed through the bar, Galaxy staying to order us food while I moved up to our room. I opened the door to find Connell playing a game with Aeslyn sitting on the chair at the desk behind the TV as well.

"Dad!" Connell paused his game and came over to give me a half-hug and I took it. "Why do you smell like death?"

I tried to keep my face pleasant. "That's no way to say someone needs a shower, dude." I raised my arm to smell my pit and found I smelled alright.

"He means actual death, Marcus." Aeslyn's correction was soft and drew my attention. "He's always been able to smell death, but it's gotten worse since his powers awakened. Who did you kill?"

I rolled my eyes at the accusation and said, "I witnessed a challenge for alpha earlier. Dieter lost."

She sighed and Connell frowned. "Did you know him well?"

I shook my head, answering, "Not as well as I likely should have. I'd always seen him around but I really only just made his acquaintance when he took over for Jolly."

Connell ducked his head, his face contemplative as he sat on my bed. As he sat there, I joined him. "How's your power and control coming? I know that Mom and Luca have been trying to teach you."

He grumbled softly, "It doesn't listen well. Wants me to kill and eat things." He looked up at me sideways and asked, "Does your magic feel that way?"

A smirk crossed my face. Lately, it was less about eating things and just killing. Always wanting me to destroy the threats and inconveniences. That I was letting so many of them go lately… was irksome.

I wouldn't lie to him and told him as much. "My magic wants me to kill things. People. Nuisances. Galaxy's magic tempers it, I think, and hers is even more weird."

He brightened up. "Do you think Galaxy could give me some magic to help with mine?"

I paused, considering it. If she did, he would likely be able to actually use his magic in a way that was safer and less unknown.

I was about to mention it to her mentally when Aeslyn snapped, "No." Her outburst had surprised both of us, our heads turning toward her at the same time. "I will not have some weird creature's magic taint my son. You can't tell me that her magic isn't what made your own awaken the way it has."

"No, I can't. But I can promise you her magic isn't what whispers to me to kill people." Disgust ripped into her expression and I had to fight the urge to shout at her and her negativity. "Connell has *my* power in his blood. We don't know exactly what it wants to do, but Galaxy's power keeps mine in check."

"For now," she shot back angrily. "I won't have her gaining power over my son."

"*Our* son," I corrected dangerously. "I don't know what beef you think you have against her, but she's not some evil being bent on destruction."

She glared at me, then softly said, "But you could be."

My eyes widened at the implication and I just turned to Connell. "Galaxy is downstairs waiting on food. Why don't you go grab a burger?"

Connell just sighed and took the money I held up for him before glancing back at his mom. "Please be nice."

She gasped softly and he just walked out of the room while ignoring her.

As soon as he was clear of the door and down the hall, I glared at his mother and hissed, "What the fuck is your deal, Aeslyn?"

When she didn't answer, I stood up, my anger flooding me with adrenaline. "I've done nothing but my best with you." I put my hand through my hair as I searched for possible reasons for her to act this way. "I wanted to marry you when I found out about Connell. I loved you, and you fled. You moved on."

She snickered and shot back, "So have you, apparently."

I rolled my eyes. "Jealousy isn't a good look for you, Aeslyn."

Her eyes widened and she stood up, hand blurring toward my face, but I didn't feel like taking it on the cheek for her pride anymore. With a lazy flick of my wrist, I batted her strike aside and when her right hook rocketed forward for my nose, I just dipped my head to the left of it.

She let out a strangled cry of anger and kept trying to hit me and I just kept moving and swatting her attacks away. "Your petty insecurities are unfounded, Aeslyn. You moved on. You have a husband—who I'm actually beginning to like a lot more than I thought I ever would—and the ideal family."

She snarled and her movements got even more predictable in her anger. "You punishing me, Galaxy, and Cassia because of some perceived slight is really fucking annoying and unnecessary."

I grabbed her wrist and glared down at her with the full weight of my disdain. "I don't know why you're so insistent on being such a cruel asshole to me, but I don't care for you hurting Connell to spite me."

She gave me a haughty laugh. "Spite *you*?" She rolled her eyes exaggeratedly. "Please, the typical human—always with the motives of others being called into question because you don't agree or see their reasons."

She snatched her hand from my grasp and crossed her arms. "I don't want *my* son's magic tainted by some goddess who doesn't even know what she's capable of or who she even is, Marcus."

She scoffed and collected some of the things sitting on the desk behind her before turning back to glare at me. "It has less to do with you than you could wrap your head around, but that's very human of you."

"I'm not human anymore, Aeslyn." I glared at her in return and crossed my arms over my chest. "I don't think I ever really was. The human part of me, for the longest time, mourned losing you to some esoteric reasoning that you had. Blamed myself for you running away from the love I felt for you because I thought I had done something to scare you off. But now, the man I am today—the man Cassia and Galaxy have helped me to become—realizes that you used me. And you still are."

I smiled softly as I realized what I had said was true. "No more. I like Luca. He's a great guy, and every time I'm critical of you, everyone seems drawn to tell me about some sort of sacrifice that you made to take up the position you did so that you could protect Connell." Her gaze narrowed at the mention of it, but I just kept speaking. "But I don't care. I'm finally happy, and you keep thrusting yourself between me and Connell and my trying to help him. I don't know if it's some deep-seated resentment, trauma, or just you being a bitch—I don't care. If Connell wants something, he gets it if I can give it to him. I'm done being your whipping boy, and I'm finished letting you use him against me."

She growled low in her throat and I just stared at her. "I didn't even come up here to fight with you. I didn't even think you would still be here; all I wanted to do was meditate on some things to help with what's going on, but here you are throwing a tantrum because of... Who the hell cares?" She went to speak to me, probably to say something scathing and I just held a firm hand up. "A man died in front of me tonight, Aeslyn, and someone else would have if I hadn't stopped him. The pack is gone and the High Table here in Columbus is fucked because of it. It's no longer safe for you here. Take Luca and go figure out a place to lay low. Connell can stay here where it's safe for the time being."

She stood up and walked past me, tears in her eyes as she muttered, "It won't take long. We have safe houses we can use, or we can just return to Grestal."

"Whatever you think best for you—Connell will be safe one way or another." I let her leave, the door slamming behind me as I sat on the bed with a sigh.

I stared down at my hands for a long moment, exhausted. What the hell was I going to do if she decided to take Connell and run again? I couldn't just track him, and I couldn't leave any kind of tail for him without knowing how to in the first place.

A tail… "A tail?" I said out loud. Tracking. I could track him. I knew how to, but it would be easier with something that he could keep on his person. Something like a weapon.

I pulled out my phone and delved into my contacts for the person I wanted to speak to then pressed call.

CHAPTER SEVENTEEN

Luca and I stood in the dark awaiting Zeke, the campus lights above us cutting into the fog of our surroundings a bit.

I'd told him why I was coming here and after that, we'd walked across the street and stood for about fifteen minutes in silence. He'd spoken to Aeslyn, of course, and he also knew why we were waiting here.

Galaxy had volunteered to stay and watch over the boy while we were away, that way his mom couldn't do anything rash.

Another few moments passed and finally he said, "I'm sorry about that, Marcus."

I grunted, almost unwilling to talk about it now. "Not your fault."

"True enough that may be, I still feel awful about it." He sighed and put his hands on his hips, both of them close to a weapon of his own. "I will not try to justify her actions. That she tried to strike you is reprehensible, but I appreciate your restraint in defending yourself."

I dipped my chin at that; I wouldn't have hit her. As a Marine, we were trained to kill if necessary, trained in fighting men *and* women, and I had no qualms about defending myself against a woman. Cassia and I beat the hell out of each other often. But I wouldn't hit the mother of my child.

"I just want what's best for our son."

He nodded. "The boy deserves the best."

I smiled. "He does." I blew out a breath, pent up anger welling up and releasing with it. "Thanks for always taking care of him. It takes a pretty special guy to raise someone else's kid. There are men and women out there who fuck that up all the time, and you're not."

Luca just nodded, and then cleared his throat. "The sacrifice she made was her ability to have more children, the ability to be with the person she wanted most, and her own personal freedom."

I frowned at him and he just nodded. "Before you ask—no. It was not you. There had been an elven man she had wanted to be with before meeting you, a friend of hers since childhood. When she found out that he had been out hooking up with a mortal woman and had her fling with you in revenge, he found out about it." He scratched his head and cleared his throat. "He said and did some horrible things to her when he found out that she had become pregnant, and he threatened you too, so in order to protect you and Conellar, she came to my family for aid."

"Why the hell is losing an asshole like that a sacrifice?"

He gave me a droll look. "Love makes us all do crazy things, Marcus. I mean, you are trying to find Atlantis for the Goddess you love, and I am meeting with the man who killed the enemies of my people, took over my throne, and then killed my mother, all so I can be certain that the boy—son—I've chosen to love and raise is safe."

That made me laugh, and when we both finished laughing, I reached my hand out to him and said, "You're a good man, Luca."

He grinned back and shook my hand. "It has always been

the honor of my life and will continue to be until I die to protect our son."

I raised an eyebrow and slyly asked, "Not being married to Aeslyn?"

He snorted. "I could handle a little less of her angst at times, but she is nice to me sometimes."

We laughed again and then a chill ran down my spine and the air before us shifted until I knew there was a portal open in front of us. "Come on."

We stepped through into the throne room of the Unseelie and found Zeke sitting on his throne. "Hey guys! Wasn't expecting a call or anything just yet—you pop the question? Did you get the rings yet, first?"

I shook my head and he snapped. "Damn. Gotta find the right time."

Luca looked at me and then frowned before his eyes widened and I just held a hand up and said, "Later."

Zeke blinked and swore, "Shit, man, my bad, I thought the prince would know about it since he was here with you." He scratched his head and then cleared his throat. "Uh, if that's not why you're here, why *did* you call me for a favor?"

"It's about Connell, my son."

Zeke smacked the throne and stood up. "He okay? Heads rolling, what's up?"

I snorted. "No, but I could've done with your help a few months back when he had been taken." He grinned at that and I let my grin fade as I gave him the real reason for my call. "I was wondering if you could maybe enchant something for him. I have a feeling that his mom might do something drastic, and I want something that he can wear or keep on himself that would allow me to track him or know where he is."

"Both of us, if you please, King Zeke." The man in front of the throne looked down at the man who I hadn't noticed had dropped to a knee. Luca bowed his head, "I worry that, with my budding friendship to Marcus, she may decide that she has to run from me as well. I cannot protect Connell if I cannot find him."

"Stand up, prince." Luca looked up from the floor and stood as he had been bid to. Zeke came down to stand near us and offered the elven man his hand and said, "I appreciate the deference, but that was more my wife's thing than mine. Once I get home, the Unseelie will require a firm hand here, I mean to return your throne, so don't do anything weird, okay?"

Luca looked as if he had just received the world's most dangerous gift and went to kneel again, but Zeke just caught him under his arms and made the man stand. "Seriously, dude, it's cool. Just be chill."

Luca nodded and Zeke turned his attention back to me. "I can do what you're asking for. It'll take like, ten minutes? You have a ring or something?"

Luca raised a hand slightly. "My family has one that is in the vault, if I might go and collect it?"

Zeke nodded once and Luca left us to go and collect what he said he would. Once the elven man was gone, Zeke turned to me. "How you doing?"

I shrugged. "Doin'. You?"

He snorted and rolled his eyes. "President's really annoying the shit out of me." Instead of making me ask, he waved a hand and a table and chairs woven from shadows rose from the darkness around us before saying, "He wants to speak with representatives of the various factions of the monstrous world to come to some sort of... truce."

That made my heart speed up, because that would mean we could be left alone. "How's that annoying?"

He sighed and rested his head on his hand and then put his elbow on the table. "The gods would be included with the negotiations."

"Personal vendettas don't count as a way to keep them out?" He fixed me with a side eye that let me know I was close to a line and I spoke anyway, "Seriously, man, what's up?"

"He means to make a state for them, Marcus. The

monsters, myths, and legends who comply with the government will be made full citizens. Apparently, a few governments are already working on making that a thing." He sat back and held his hands in front of him, ticking fingers off as he named them, "Korea, India, Japan—hell, Germany, Russia, and several other places already made a statement that the Baba Yaga has full reign of what the fuck she wants so long as the deaths are warranted."

"Bet the Wardens are pissed about that."

He groaned and said, "Yeah, they are. So much so that they've already killed Theo for it."

I was on my feet before I realized it, roaring, "What?"

He nodded once. "Charged, tried, and hanged for treason. They burnt his body and blew it into my face." He grunted and amended, "My representative's face, rather. But the statement was clear enough—the Wardens are pissed, and they're doing what they can to fix this in their favor."

I growled low in my throat. Theo may have inadvertently fucked up a lot of things for the supernatural world doing what he had, but death was a pretty rough thing to be given for doing what you thought was right. Then again, the Wardens *had* been willing to kill Merlin for working with us.

This would mean Merlin's amnesty for his past fuck ups in their eyes would likely be burnt with the young Ventricle.

"That means the president will likely be sending someone barking at the High Table's door too." He nodded at my statement and it was hard to imagine a representative of the nation coming to a bar for magical creatures to offer an olive branch. "It may happen while I'm gone."

He frowned at me and snorted. "You going into hiding?"

I shook my head and tapped the table. "Searching for Atlantis."

"Ha!" Zeke's barking laughter surprised me. "I can't believe you just said that."

My eyes settled on him. "You drank with Satan, work with

the Wild Hunt, slaughtered a race of Fae, and can shapeshift into a fucking dragon—Atlantis is where you draw the line?"

He opened his mouth to try to refute that, but when he couldn't, his teeth clacked back together and he made a conceding motion with his hand. "Fair."

He was quiet for a short time and said, "How long you gonna be? And why go there?"

"To find a sliver of Galaxy's power and help her regain her memories." As to the second question, it was up in the air. "I don't really know. We're still researching where in the ocean it could be."

He frowned to himself before clapping his hands. "I have an idea, Marcus."

He whistled softly and Eve appeared over his shoulder. "Yes, my King?"

"Eve, I need a globe, or a map of the Earth. Make it snappy."

She faded from view and then reappeared where she had been with a large map. "My King."

"Thanks!" Zeke unrolled it on the table and sure enough, it was what he'd wanted. "You can go."

She ducked her head, subdued, but after a brief, flickering gaze at me, she was gone.

"If you'll make a deal with me, I'll help you in your search."

I grimaced; deals had costs. "Price?"

He snorted. "Jaded much?" I nodded and he just shook his head with a resigned sigh. "I know the gods are going to call for my head, or at the very least may try to make a move on me with the mortals and folks in charge."

He sat back and shrugged theatrically. "Can't say I blame them in thinking I'm a threat—I am." He grinned wickedly and leaned forward. "I want you to help me keep the bastards in check. All you have to do is be a character witness if you're asked to be one. I doubt that they could prove to be a threat to me, but with the monsters, it's a toss-up as to whether they'll like me being around or not."

I grunted. "But the Wardens and gods, at the very least, will be certain to try to gun for you, since you've killed some of them, and outed both." His affirmative dip of his chin made me fear for the sake of the world, not just the country. "So, vouch for you if they call on me to. I can do that. But how are you going to help with this?"

He clapped his hands on the table and stared at the map. "See, cool thing about having the powers of a god, specifically Janus, is that you get more goodies with use." He waved a hand over the map and said, "Atlantis, how do I find you?"

I laughed. There was no way that shit would work, right?

"Janus is the god of not just doors, Marcus, but the god of transitions." He grinned as a light blinked onto the map; it was in Ohio. "Okay. That's a start. That's where the closest portal to Earth from me is, fair. Now, show me how to get there."

The map blinked with smaller lights as the question echoed weirdly around us. As soon as the blinking lights stopped and I was about to give him a gentle helping of shit, they popped back up.

The lights led from the larger one in Ohio to the ocean, passing past Hawaii and then stopped over an area in the South Pacific Ocean not too far from the Philippines.

He circled it with a pen he pulled from his pocket and then frowned and swore, "Damn."

"What?"

"Something's keeping me out. Feels divine, so there are gods protecting the place." He gritted his teeth and the air around us steadily grew colder. It was comfortable for me, but when the pressure built significantly, my sight wavered, flashing and filling with black spots and flashes of stars. He let his breath go and shook his head. "Can't force the transition, but if my power is to be trusted, you'll find it there."

He sat back tiredly and groaned, "The headache is pretty rough."

"Does it make you omnipotent or something?" He raised an

eyebrow at me in question, snickering to himself and I just added, "Sorry, was just curious."

He shook his head with a wry grin. "I'm just more aware of gates, portals, and people on transitional journeys of their own. Other than that, I'm still a normal dude whose fiancée gets pissy with him for forgetting to take the trash out."

"How's that coming along?"

He grunted. "Good. The dogs are a pain in the ass, but they make her happy, so I'm good with 'em." He glanced at my hand and pointed to my ring finger. "When are you going to ask?"

"Soon." I didn't know when, but I would likely try to ask before we left. Leave nothing on the table.

Luca returned with a ring in his hands, holding it reverently. "This ring was an heirloom he was meant to receive anyway, as I'd hidden it in the vault when the attacks started. It is of very high quality and should work well for any work you might do with it."

Zeke took the ring and he whistled low. "Damn, man. Look at the rock on this thing!" His gaze flicked from the emerald bar on the item to the elven man who brought it and said, his voice comically low. "You, uh… you seein' anybody there, sugar daddy?"

Luca guffawed, longer than even I thought the joke worthy of, and wiped his eyes as he tried to catch his breath, before saying, "My wife would murder you somehow. And if she finds out about this? I am a dead man already."

I hated to admit that I agreed. I didn't fear Aeslyn, not the way he might, but I did hate to think about what she might do through Connell.

Zeke just snickered and raised a hand. "Would help if I had Hubris, but I can manage to do this."

"What does exaggerated pride have to do with any of this?" Luca's nose wrinkled in disgust as he asked the question.

Zeke shook his head. "Hubris is a scepter that allowed me a lot more ease in enchanting while I was on Brindolla. Poor fucker's probably stuck in his own plane of existence without me there to act as his owner."

He took a deep breath and began his work, mana coalescing around his finger tip to form an image that he then engraved into the gem on the ring, then he did the same with another portion of the item.

Once he finished with that, he closed his eyes and began to grimace as his focus was apparently needed for this. He dipped his hand into his pocket and pulled something shiny out to drop over the item, then grunted, "Blood. I need a drop of your blood."

We looked back and forth and he barked, "Both of you, now!"

I pulled the knife on my belt and stuck the tip into my thumb, then wiped the blade and gave it to Luca. He slid the blade over the pad of his own thumb and we offered the Unseelie King the wounded digits.

He had us both stick our thumbs over his project and tapped the back of our hands. The blood dripped off and I thought it wouldn't touch the item, but as soon as it was close to it, the droplets just disappeared and he hissed something I couldn't understand before there was a dull flash.

He sniffed and grunted before pushing the ring toward us. "Fuck, dude, that thing is a mana eater." He shook his head and when I took it, he sat at the table tiredly. "Soon as he puts it on, you'll see what it can do."

He lifted his head to look at me. "You owe me one, and I intend to collect." He turned to Luca. "I don't know how you can be useful to me and my cause yet, but I need you strong to rep the Unseelie when I let you have the Court once more. Do that, and we're settled."

Luca bowed his head and said, "As you wish it, King Zeke."

I grinned and pulled a small sack out. "Wanna keep that promise?"

Zeke smirked and bellowed, "Hell yeah, I do! Gimme another few minutes!"

He took his time, well over a few minutes, and enchanted the rings as well as he had the other one for Connell. When he returned them to me, I nodded at him and he just winked at me.

"I won't forget the help, man, thanks." He nodded and made a portal for us to step through and as he did so, he perked up.

He was up and on his feet in a heartbeat, growling, "You've gotta be shitting me."

I was about to ask him what was wrong when he grabbed mine and Luca's arm and pulled us through the portal. As soon as we were on the other side, it looked like a war zone had been visited upon the area in front of us.

"Where the fuck are we?" I called my Mantle to me and the armor surged over my body.

"Columbus, looks like High Street?" Luca shoved me aside as lightning streaked through where I had just been. "Who is attacking?"

Galaxy's voice and Zeke's fought for my attention before I bellowed, "One at a time!"

He frowned at me and said, "There's a god here attacking Muu." He reached up and snapped his fingers again. This time, Yohsuke walked out of the portal that tore space and time apart beside him and Zeke explained things to the appearing fighter. "Muu might need our help, more gods are coming."

"A chance for me to be on an equal playing field as you two fuckers? I'm in." The man laughed as he turned into a bat and flapped his way toward the destruction.

Zeke turned his face toward us as his body began to shift and become more vulpine. "You two need to get out of here—now. Don't stop for anything, and remember what I said, Marcus. This is just the beginning."

As soon as we were about to begin fleeing, with me and Luca prepared to jump onto Mako's back to fly away, the space around locked down. The portal that Yohsuke had come through shuddered and then shattered, the portal and the Unseelie elf coming through it as back up just gone.

"Fucker!" Zeke snarled and then wind whipped around us once and suddenly an angelic-looking figure stood against the dark clouds arrayed in the sky. To look at it was to look at something far too light, but grim to see properly even as close as we were and as good as my senses were now.

Four sets of beautiful wings spread out behind their back, two larger white on top with feathers that looked carved from opal with the way they shimmered, and then smaller gray ones fluttered at their waist and lower back. The armor they wore was beautiful, shimmering gold and platinum and the flaming sword, easily larger than any sword I'd ever wielded or thought to, burned with a blue flame that warped reality around it.

"Your blasphemous methods and murder of beings higher than yourselves has brought judgment to you." The armored figures turned toward Zeke and pointed their sword in our direction. "Lives were lost here because you and yours cannot simply accept divine right and rule."

I saw Zeke cross his arms, his muzzle quirking to the side in a weird smirk to respond when a familiar screeching whistle rang through the air.

My body went cold immediately and I roared, "Missile, down!"

I fell on top of Luca, shielding us with as much ice as I could but it melted as soon as it formed and Zeke just laughed, "Nah—worse."

The projectile dropped from the atmosphere, shattering the sound barrier as it collided with the heavenly being and bore it to the ground with a blast that shoved the air back toward us in a tidal wave of detritus, debris, and dust.

Zeke waved his hand and a sharp wind cut through the coming pain storm and he grinned. "That was Muu, and that fuckstick just got kabobbed. Come on, let's go see."

He picked his way through the fallout as Luca and I picked

ourselves up to follow him. I called after him, "How the fuck did he do that?"

He chuckled and called back, "Ever heard of a dragoon?" When I didn't respond, he heaved a sigh. "Kids. Anyway, think of it as a type of fighter who specializes in jumping onto the backs of dragons and driving them into the ground. That's his special thing, jumping higher than an enemy to spear them and kill them."

He laughed as he heard something we couldn't yet and said, "I'll bet a damn good weapon he's got him speared to the ground like a butterfly that an entomologist caught to study." He started forward once more and then looked back. "Armor off, man. Don't want you identified if you don't need to be."

We crested the crater that the warriors fighting had made and I saw the destruction in its purest form. The crater was larger than my mind would allow it to be, stretching farther even than I could see, and in the center of it was Muu and his opponent.

Muu straddled the armored figure and swung his fists, right, left, right, left, and another right into his helmet, denting it with each strike while he snarled a stream of searing curses.

When we got a little closer, he put his hands into the air. "All I wanted was lunch! This was my favorite Panda Express, and you *fucking obliterated it!*"

He clenched his fists together and drove them down into the armored figure's chest. "If you wanted to fight, you shouldn't have waited for me to be eating! That orange chicken looked fucking immaculate."

With each infuriated strike, the armor sank further into the Earth beneath his back to the point that Muu actually had to pull them up out of the ground while clambering off to the side.

"Don't kill him yet, Muu," Zeke called as Yohsuke appeared about a hundred yards from us.

Muu looked up and noticed us for the first time and snarled, his green draconic maw open wide in a savage grin. "Oh, I'm not going to."

He clenched his fist and the sound of metal under stress reached even my ears as he called out, "I'm just gonna pull him out of this fucking tin can and then I'm gonna take my three pounds of flesh for him fucking with my chow mein."

He pressed clawed hands to his victim's breastplate and started to try to carve through it when a thunderclap shook the world around us and lightning blinded me.

When I could see, three more figures cloaked in light stood with weapons drawn on the man. The one behind him issued an order, "Drop my brother, or I take that stumpy tail of yours as a prize."

Muu didn't even look at the speaking figure as he called back, "You'll have to wait your turn, sweetheart, Daddy's about to get his and then you can get your brother's sloppy seconds."

Zeke shook his head while muttering, "Don't do that. He hates people fucking with his tail."

I watched in rapt horror as the speaker did as he'd said and grabbed Muu by the tail. Rather than staying the stumpy mound of scaled flesh it had been, it straightened and struck like a spear, shooting into the attacker's chest.

"God powers or is that a thing he could always do?"

Zeke laughed bitterly at my question. "God powers." He sighed as the fight was on below and glanced at the two of us. "I need your hands clean of this, so I'm sending you away before more than just archangels show up."

I grinned as he made a portal, since the power that had held us all in this space was gone by now. "You owe us a badass weapon."

He rolled his eyes and corrected me, "A damn good one, and fine, I earned that I guess. Get gone, guys."

He turned and made his way toward the others as his body shifted and grew larger before a gust of power shoved us through the portal behind us.

We stumbled through the tear and into the grass of the

campus, appearing in the middle of a throng of people who looked confused and scared and all of them looked in the same direction.

Luca whispered, "Marcus, look."

I turned and stared as a plume of fire seared the sky, then a massive dragon with red scales tore off after one of the light-cloaked figures through the air. Luca grabbed my arm and shouted, "I will go find Conellar and Aeslyn, be safe!"

People screamed, crying and wondering aloud if they should run when someone appeared above the crowd. It was a man with a shimmering halo above his head, "All of you are safe, children. Believe in us, and we shall save you."

"Who are you?"

The man began to speak, a soft smile on his face, when someone leaped into the air and kicked him hard enough to send the man flying through the air.

A man with a New Yorker's distinct accent answered, "An asshole who wants to prey on your fear and use it to hurt innocent people." A figure climbed a light pole easily and then flipped up onto it to stand casually. His features blurred slightly as his body shifted and became covered in scales the color of shadow, tattoos spreading over his body where normal, human-like tan skin was visible. "Name's James, don't worry, we're gonna keep you safe from assholes like that trying to get a leg up on us regular folks."

Someone else called out from up in a tree, "Dude, we aren't necessarily 'normal' ourselves, can you blame them for being scared and confused?"

"Come on, Bokaj, you know what I meant." He looked around and then swore softly, "Where'd Balmur go?"

The figure in the tree snorted loudly. "You think he's going to miss out on the fighting? Nah. He's probably over there trying to figure out how to put a dagger or an axe in one of them."

"What the hell is going on?" someone on the ground near the front bellowed. There was a dull smattering of voices until called questions that ran over each other began to build toward full-blown panic. The crowd was about to go apeshit.

Music, loud and lilting, filled the area, words I didn't recognize right away filled my ears and the low amount of anxiety I had at the beginning of the crowds' panic rising was just gone. As if by magic.

It is *magic, Marcus. These men are the other surviving members of Storm Company and though they feel like they lack a Dominion, they are still wildly powerful. We need for you to leave.*

Voices raised in the distance behind me and I found a wave of Wardens stomping up the street en masse, swords, staves and other weapons lifted.

I turned back toward the Wardens to find a single man standing between them and the crowd and the man's hair stood on end and began to *burn* purple. The man's rough voice rang out as I began toward that direction to get the hell out of Dodge. "What do you cloak-and-dagger-looking assholes want with all these people?"

One of the Wardens at the lead spoke cautiously. "We know there's fighting, so we wanted to get the civilians out of the way and help."

The burning man crossed his arms and said, "Oh really? Help who?"

Another Warden spoke up this time, barking orders, "Get him out of the way, we need to get to the civilians to get them out of here so the gods can focus on fighting."

"Called it!" James chuckled behind us, his arms still crossed. "Balmur, do us all a favor and make sure that the good people coming to help the enemy know that we aren't fuckin' around?"

Balmur pulled a book out of his jacket and his finger began to move along the page as Wardens surged forward only to be stopped by a massive ghostly shield. He grinned and held up a single finger salute to the crowd before turning his back on them and addressing the crowd. "I can get you all further from the fighting, but you'll need to go through a spell."

The crowd began to grow even more anxious and he just

looked up at the men watching him from where they were, a silent plea for assistance. Once again, the soothing melody began anew, but there was the mighty roar of a dragon and the sound of someone screaming in the air that really fucked with the soothing ambiance.

People screamed and shouted, crying for someone to save them and when Balmur began trying to speak to them rationally, I just fought my way through the crowd, "Cast the spell and hold it open for as long as you can, we will help scare them through."

He grimaced at me and asked, "Who the fuck are you then?"

I grinned and let my sunglasses fall off my face and showed him my eyes. "I'm the Huntsman, and I know your boss."

He raised an eyebrow at that, but I used Embodiment of Lightning to throw myself into the crowd, hoping that the ball of electricity that would emanate from me would pick enemies over regular people and then did it a second time to get out on the other side where James watched curiously.

"Mako, time to make a scene." The drake screeched as he fled my body and shadow to stand beneath me as I allowed my armor to wash over me and roared, "Flee this place if you wish to remain alive!"

The crowd went bananas. People turned—fighting to get away from me and the monstrous drake, flooding toward the spell-made door that opened to another place on the other side of the now-moving horde of people.

"Thanks for the help, scary dude," the figure in the tree called out before dropping to the ground. He was a frozen-looking elf with a guitar in his hands and bow slung over his shoulder. "You, uh, you wouldn't happen to know who they're up against back there, would you?"

I motioned to the Wardens. "Wardens. And the guys Zeke, Muu, and Yoh are up against, I'm not really sure, but Zeke did say something about archangels?"

He shook his head and sighed. "Alright, looks like they could use some help, since they're all fast and shit. Thanks for the help!"

He turned and the guitar disappeared in a flick of his wrist, only for the bow to take its place as he prepared for the fight.

I turned and caught Balmur stalking toward us. "Thanks, man. Be safe." I nodded at him as he passed me quietly. "Come on Mako, let's get."

With that, I clambered onto Mako's back and we took off for the High Table and a sense of normalcy.

CHAPTER EIGHTEEN

"This…" I watched as the bar was completely and utterly silent as we walked in, the entirety of the patrons, staff, and even some folks from outside watched as Zeke and his friends battled not just four archangels, but three actual deities who had joined in. "Is not normalcy."

The scary thing is… Galaxy tore herself away from the fight, and spoke out loud but in a hushed tone, "The boys from Brindolla are *winning*."

I found Connell and tilted my head toward him so that Luca would go to the boy, but Aeslyn saw us first stomped over to us. "Why the hell were you with him, Luca?"

He frowned and responded with a raised eyebrow, "Can a man not speak to the father of his child alone?"

"*My* child, and not him." She seethed and I had to admit this was the most unhinged I had seen her. "We're leaving, Connell!"

I shook my head. "Connell can stay here. I don't know if your eyes are seeing the same things mine are, but there's a fight between gods and god killers outside. I don't want any of you out there in that, let alone him."

She snorted. "I don't care what you want, Marcus, nothing has gone right ever since you found out who we were or about this world." She called for Connell again who began to trudge forward. Luca reached out to him with both hands and slid the ring onto his finger.

The boy frowned and when he was about to say something, he stopped—Luca was in the way so I couldn't tell what he had mouthed, but when he let go of Connell's hand, I couldn't see the ring. It was as if it wasn't there, but I could *feel* where the boy was. How far away he was and a general status of his health.

I glanced back up to Aeslyn who looked confused for a moment, then muttered, "Let's go, Connell, we need to get somewhere safer."

"I feel safe here, and Cassia's mom offered to teach me karate!"

Aeslyn clicked her tongue against her teeth and ignored him, but just as she was walking by, I caught a glimpse of her shoulder and with it, the bond we shared flared with my power. The gauge said **Hatred.**

So she did hate me. Good. She was well on her way onto my shit list. As Connell walked behind her, he stopped so I could give him a hug and whispered, "Thanks, and I'll keep in touch. Galaxy gave me a gift to be able to do what I want more."

I frowned at that, but stayed quiet until he was gone. Luca texted me as he was already gone, *Thank you, Marcus. I will try to calm her. Keep you updated.*

Okay, thanks for the help. I turned to Galaxy and waited until they were well out of earshot before asking, "What did you give him?"

She smiled and said, "A small pendant that he will say is a gift from a patron, that is ensorcelled to make her like it enough to let him keep it. Because that's what it is. I also may have given him a small inventory with it."

I pulled her into a kiss and she smiled at me as our lips parted. "Thank you."

She rested her head on my chest and then looked up at me. "Cassia and I were worried when you were out there on the front lines with those angels."

I nodded, steeling myself for this and said, "I was too, and with that in mind, I need to talk to both of you. Could you come upstairs? Where's Cass?"

"She's already in your room cleaning up." I frowned at her and she shook her head and motioned for me to carry on walking through the building up the stairs and then into my room only to find it trashed. "Aeslyn left you with a little parting gift."

Cassia stood with some torn clothes in her hands and growled, "If it weren't for the fact that I like Connell, I would have kicked her ass."

"I'm not happy with her either right now." Arden's voice over my shoulder surprised me enough that I flinched and she sighed. "Sorry. We've been friends for years and years, but I seriously don't know what the hell is going on with her right now."

Cass turned and held up my shredded clothes. "Property damage and being a spiteful bitch. I'm lucky that I got up here in time to stop Seamus, he was going to throttle her."

Angry growls and hisses came from the floorboards beneath my bed and I said a quick, "Thanks, buddy."

There was a grumble in return and I took a deep breath before I just motioned to the mess and said, "We can burn all this shit and get more, it's cool, but I have something I need to talk to you two about." I glanced over at Arden and muttered, "Sorry, I didn't know you'd be coming up here and I just need some privacy for this."

She shrugged and yawned. "Okay, I'll just catch you guys at my house later on?"

I nodded to her and closed the door as she left, taking a

deep breath to collect my thoughts before I turned to face the two women I'd come to love.

Cassia stood with her arms crossed, her eyebrows knit together in concern with her eyes hidden behind her sunglasses. It pained me, now of all times, that I couldn't look directly into her eyes. We would need to see about getting that Basilisk trait of hers fixed safely.

Galaxy sat closer to where I stood in the room on the bed and watched me curiously.

"The world's gone to shit." That made both women nod, though they were a bit put off by the statement. "There are gods hunting down people I don't know whether to call friend or foe. I'm not human, and I run an organization of monsters designed to put the fear of all things that go bump in the night into humanity and monsters. The supernatural world has quite literally been kicked out of the proverbial closet of existence and mystery, and I knew next to nothing about all of this less than six months ago."

That last bit made Cassia smirk. "You've taken well to it."

I nodded with her statement. "I have, surprisingly so." I took a deep breath and then let it out as I said, "With the two of you to help me."

Galaxy grinned. "We pushed you a little sometimes." She saw my raised eyebrow and cleared her throat. "Alright, a bit more than that for some of us."

I nodded at that and then winked at Cassia. "And fought you along the way as well." That made her smile brighten from the smirk like a butterfly escaping a cocoon. "But the fact of the matter is, I had both of you at my side to make me better. I am the man I am today because you were there to help me. I'm the fighter I am today because you both guided me."

I could tell they both had something to add to that statement, but I pressed on, selfishly wanting to finish before they could allow me the opportunity to chicken out. "I don't think I would have been able to accomplish half the things I have in this world after my old one was taken from me if it weren't for the two of you, and I don't want that to ever stop."

Cassia's grin was radiant as I stared at her, and Galaxy uncrossed her legs so that she could stand up next to the other part of our relationship. "Cassia, you hone me like any blade ever has another. You've fought with me, protected me, and come to love me in a way I'm sure neither of us expected, and now you're carrying our child."

She put a hand on her stomach and Galaxy's joined it there with a soft smile. I turned to Galaxy and smiled at her. "Galaxy, you've protected us all. Even with some mistakes and hiccups here and there, you've handled my mortality and ignorance with a grace that I cannot ever imagine living without."

I took a breath and got down on one knee with the rings both coming out of my inventory in their special satchel.

With one in each hand, "Cassia, oni to be feared and mother of my child, Galaxy, First Goddess and my other half, would both of you make me the happiest man in the universe and share the rest of who-knows-how-long-we-have with me?"

The air between the three of us hung silent for the longest heartbeats I'd ever experienced in my life before Cassia just nodded and then looked at Galaxy who had tears in her eyes.

I tried not to sound terribly worried as I said, "Are you okay, my love?"

She sniffed and nodded. "Yeah, that was just really sweet and stupid." She laughed and said, "Who puts a goddess after a mother?"

Cassia chuckled and said, "The man who wants to stay alive?"

"Is that a yes?"

Both of them grinned at me and said, "Yes."

An ear-shattering scream from out in the hallway made all three of us jump as Arden screeched, "They said *yes!*"

A raucous cheer shook the floor as I put their respective rings on each hand. Cassia's ring was a simple band of an alloy I couldn't recall the name of that Jayvali had assured me wouldn't break if she punched something with her ridiculous strength. The thick, silvery band had a long row of small blood diamonds inlaid into it, and had a single red ruby in the center of them with the enchantment designs that Zeke had carved into them adding to the beauty.

Galaxy's ring was more ornate, the platinum of the band polished until it glowed even in dim light. Her diamonds flanked the black opal that was the centerpiece of her ring with a circular cut that showed off some of the shimmering innards of the precious stone that looked like the stars. Her enchantment markings had been on the inside of the band, swirling patterns that crossed my eyes to look at them and she admired all of it for a long moment.

"This is really nice," Cassia observed appreciatively as she stared at her hand. "Mother is going to hate it."

Galaxy chuckled at that and then perked up. "Many people downstairs wish to make their well wishes known." She smirked and shook her head. "Arden especially as we won her a *lot* of drinks."

I raised a brow at her and Galaxy just waved and the door opened to reveal the deliriously excited jinn. She grinned wider and said, "I knew your sappy ass would propose because I helped you hide it, but I made the bet that it would take the intervention of something more powerful to get you to actually pop the question."

I shook my head and grumbled, "I guess you won that fair and square." She crossed the distance and hugged me before moving to her best friend to screech happily about the ring on her finger.

Uncle Yen appeared in the doorway, irritation plain on his face but when Galaxy and Cassia held up their hands wordlessly, the dower expression faded to be replaced by joy and pride. "Congratulations, son. I'm so happy for all of you."

I walked over to him and accepted the hug before asking, "How's Anubis? Awake yet?"

He nodded once. "Recovering. Whoever had him was

experimenting with his Dominion somehow and used up a lot of his power." He ran a hand through his hair tiredly. "I've been doing what I can to help him recover it, but there's only so much I can do now since the public knows that he exists."

I frowned at that. "How do you help?"

He shrugged. "Help them do what their Dominion gives them power over." He frowned and then sighed. "May as well say it. He's a judge, so we watch garbage TV shows and he judges the contestants and their decisions with me. It's harmless fun, but being judgmental is something that helps him recoup."

I grunted and snorted at the same time, almost choking, but he raked me with a warning glare and then both of us laughed. It was so funny to imagine the Egyptian god curled up on the couch watching shit reality TV going, "Fuck that guy."

Uncle Yen smiled and patted my shoulder. "Just wanted to see what was going on. Tell whoever's on shift this round is on me for the four of you."

"Thanks Uncle Yen, and just so you know, I know where we need to go to get to Atlantis."

Cass, Galaxy, and Arden froze before their attention turned to me and I explained, "I made a deal with Zeke—nothing life changing I don't think!" All three of their expressions soured considerably, but I continued, "I just have to be a character witness if asked to, that's all."

Arden clapped and leaned forward while tilting her head, excitedly asking, "Oh, so you get to say he's fucking psychotic?"

I ignored that, mainly because it felt almost true, but he was still a good guy, right?

"Where do you need to go?"

"Mariana Trench." Uncle Yen whistled low. "Yeah. I don't know what to do about it."

"Get with Merlin before you do this, but you might want to make contact with a water god." Uncle Yen cleared his throat and frowned further. "I don't know any who preside over the oceans and seas. They don't typically come too far inland."

"You guys forget that I'm a water jinn now too?" Arden had

her hands on her hips. "I can help us down there better than the gods could."

Galaxy raised an eyebrow at her. "I don't know about that, but your innate attachment to water *could* do a lot of the heavy lifting for us if you spec into it a bit."

I threw my hands up. "That's going to take forever if we need to go level before going!"

Arden blushed and Cassia gasped, "No."

Galaxy nodded and growled, "Yup." When I was confused, obviously so, Galaxy explained, "She's been squirreling away points since the beginning. She had plenty to spend on leveling this aspect of her growth, but she hasn't."

"Fuck!" Arden flinched at my outburst and grimaced as I unsheathed my knife hand for the first time in a while. "You mean you've been sandbagging this whole fucking time and have the *nerve* to admonish me for forgetting to spend my points?"

She glared at me and retorted, "I'm a jinn, Marcus. I am *so* much stronger than you on your best day. My fire has gotten us through just fine. Honestly, it's awesome I have the points to spend for this to be able to help us."

I turned my attention to Cassia and asked softly, "You too?"

She said, "A point here and there, but with what Galaxy just sent me, she has, like, six levels worth of points saved away."

I was about to lose my goddamn mind when Arden snarled, "Fine! I'll blow my load on it, Jesus Christ."

She grunted, "Status, Galaxy." The goddess's eyes glowed and the screen appeared in front of Arden so that she could click things. "Can you point me to the path that will allow me to make it so you can all survive down there?"

Galaxy's chin dipped and she closed her eyes. "Demeanor of the Depths, left side, follow it all the way up. I don't know what will happen if you spend in any of them fully, but it could be helpful."

Arden cursed slightly as she spent her points, her aura growing a lot brighter as she did so.

After a moment she brightened. "Hold on." She turned to Galaxy and said, "All I had to do was spend points into the water tree to unlock air?"

Galaxy raised a brow at her and said, "I couldn't be sure, but it never hurts to do so." She frowned and then her face split in a grin. "Congratulations on upgrading Demeanor of the Depths to Ocean's Bond."

Arden must have thought we were a bit lost as she explained, "It's a spell that allows me a buff when I'm surrounded by water. Pairing that with Sea Hag's Bounty will allow me to share the buff with others."

She clicked something else and grinned wider. "And with Armored Scales, we shouldn't be affected by the pressure either."

Uncle Yen snorted and crossed his arms over his chest before glaring at Galaxy. "Is there anything you can't just hand wave?"

She thought about it for a moment, then said, "A double cheeseburger with bacon, egg, fries, and a Cherry Coke?"

He snorted and rolled her eyes and she just called out, "I really want that!"

My stomach growled and I heaved a sigh. "Yeah, that does sound good." I glanced at Cassia. "Food and drinks?"

She smiled wildly and said, "I want a root beer float."

With all of us laughing, we walked down the steps to cheers filled with joyous emotion and heartfelt warmth. The fighting between Zeke and his men against the deities who threatened them was slightly forgotten.

Tomorrow, we would inform Merlin what was going on and then prepare to go get Galaxy's power. Maybe after that, we could focus more safely on figuring out who was experimenting with things they shouldn't.

CHAPTER NINETEEN

Merlin walked into the bar room with a large knapsack and made it disappear with a flourish, his hands now empty. He grinned. "Love doing that."

"You make it look like you're a magician, which is *always* adorable." Amabala smiled at him as if he were the only one in the room and the rest of us just smirked at them.

They were adorable. Both of them. They were head over heels for each other and they'd stayed that way.

"Okay, okay, let's get ready to mount up." Arden clapped her hands and turned to look at the rest of us. "Do you know how hard it is not having Masonai around in times like this?"

Galaxy nodded. "If I thought he would be able to survive my blessing, I would give it to him just for you."

Would help to have another avid gamer with military experience in the group as well. Galaxy heard my grumpy thoughts and nodded again, enforcing that she meant what she said.

The past three days had been a blur of celebration, realization, and preparation. The items we had made were enchanted, this time by a certain old goblin with a taste for pop that made Galaxy want to weep at having to share.

I hadn't asked Zeke about the enchantments on their rings, knowing that he wouldn't be able to break his oath, but the girls wouldn't divulge either.

What I hadn't expected was to hear from Jayvali so soon on the rounds. "They act up on anything less than one-thirty grain, so it means your ranges will be more limited than usual, but it works."

I pumped my fist excitedly and then lowered my voice, "Can I get three magazines of each for my trip?"

He snorted. "No?"

I heaved a sigh and said, "Look, I'm going to a place where there are creatures who are used to the pressure of the depths of the oceans. Magic bullets would help us *immensely* there."

He snorted. "Lad, them bullets won't pierce water. You'll have to wait. They'll be worth it, and I'll make some more—just be sure to bring me more ore, aye?"

I grimaced. "Yeah, thanks, man."

He grunted and then hung up, leaving me wondering what to do. I had my scythe, but would it be okay in water?

And my ice magic… We would have to see. We had plenty of food and, with our inventories, our gear would stay dry too.

"Okay, so where do we want to go from?" Merlin asked softly. "We can go from Egypt and make our way east, or just go straight to Japan and make our way from there."

I shook my head. "It'll be a bit, but we should go from here and travel through the US." The others stared at me as if I'd lost my mind. "The more places we have on the roster to appear around the world, the more places we can help—theoretically."

The others seemed to be mulling it over so I just said, "If you have an argument or better reason for some other way, I'm all ears."

Merlin spoke up. "We should focus more on getting to the portion of Galaxy's Dominion as swiftly as possible."

I nodded, glad someone spoke up. "Why?"

He thought about it for a second longer, then elaborated.

"The gods are starting to try to test those allied with Zeke. We may not be outright allied with him, but we've been seen and known to work with him. The more ground we have to cover to get there, and the longer Galaxy goes without her full power, the more vulnerable we are."

I grimaced, but had to admit that was a fair assumption. "Valid. Thank you, Merlin." I glanced at the others and found that many of them agreed with nods or pensive stairs at the air between us all. "Japan it is."

Everyone nodded and I grabbed Merlin's shoulder. "How are we on comms?"

"Uncle Yen has a way to reach out to me with a writing spell attached to my notebook; he'll keep us abreast of things here and the status of Thoth and Anubis."

"Good." I turned to Cassia and she frowned. "How's security?"

"Bubba Kenshi has it, with more bodies coming from other branches to ensure we don't just have our skeleton crew that we do right now." She allowed a small smirk for herself. "Also, my mom has volunteered to ensure that the staff is trained and has joined them in guard duties."

My eyes widened without me realizing that it was happening, but that was probably for the better. Chiasa was ridiculously strong and driven to protect her grandchild.

"We ready?" The others nodded in unison, so I reached through my bond with Amabala to open a portal to Japanese soil. "Go!"

The group filed through, me going last, and came out in the alley where I'd met Zeke to spy on the yokai group of gangsters the Night Parade. The bathhouse was defunct now.

Being here reminded me of Cassia's sister Kimiko and I had to take a deep breath to keep from falling into a morose train of thought on it. There was nothing we could have done differently.

Galaxy grabbed my hand and Cassia took a deep breath before speaking softly. "Armor up."

My armor and everyone else's in the vicinity of her order dragged onto our bodies until we stood cloaked in the shadows of the Wild Hunt.

Once I mounted up on Mako, the others' mounts appeared too, and we were on our way into the sky to fly toward the water. The breeze was lovely even as the waters began to darken slowly as we went. The air around us suddenly felt heavy and the hair on the back of my neck stood on end, but it was Cassia who called it. "Someone just ran into the Luck Dragon! We need to get the lead out, or they'll get around her!"

I nodded and pushed Mako to go faster. "Any of you know what we might be approaching down there?"

My voice caught with the wind, but I knew they could hear me.

Merlin's voice was cautious. "I don't know about anything magical, but you said you had spoken to Zeke about it. Do you think that whatever gods deigned to guard it would have made things to protect it?"

"Only that there was something divine keeping him from opening a portal there."

He shrugged. "Assume there is something big and angry in the depths keeping invaders out and we can only be disappointed if we were truly spoiling for a fight."

"I'm constantly spoiling for a fight, Merlin." Cassia grunted, then she raised her voice and added, "Especially after the week we've had and knowing someone is trying to hunt us down right now."

Arden laughed. "That's fair." She was quiet and then said, "Hey, Marcus?"

I turned my head so I could see her and she called over, "How come you didn't kill him where he was? That Marik guy?"

Galaxy passed along my memories with a nod from me and she cursed. "That's a bluff."

I almost stopped Mako. "It is?"

"I've never heard of an alpha werewolf being able to do

that kind of shit where if they die the pack goes bananas?" She threw her hands up as if something came to mind and shouted, "If they could force them to do shit after they died, any fights for ascension for alpha could destroy the pack."

Merlin piped up. "Actually, it's not a bluff." Every pair of eyes that wasn't focusing on flying turned to the boy mage and he explained, "The battle for leadership trumps the old ruler's will. As soon as they're defeated, the new alpha has total control and any former orders are completely nulled, including the final one. Also, any orders given during a fight for alpha can be willfully disobeyed so long as a leader isn't decided already."

I cleared my throat and murmured, "Books?"

He nodded and stated, "Books." Then he cursed softly and said, "And practical application. The Wardens did some experiments in the 1800s in France between a pack with two factions within it. They forced the two to fight for leadership and then usurped both with a werewolf they felt was more loyal to them. He killed the new leader before the transfer of power was complete and the other was dead."

Cassia swore, "What the fuck!" She scowled at the boy. "How long have they been experimenting with our people?"

He shook his head and said, "Since nearly the beginning."

"Congratulations, Merlin!" Cassia surprised all of us, her voice chillingly chipper. "You've signed anything that gets in our ways' death warrant since I can't hit you or any other Warden right now."

Merlin just snorted and called back, "Happy to help."

"Arden?" She turned to me as I said her name, the sensation of something charging the air around us not getting any lighter or easier to bear. "Let's cool things off. We could use the buffs to go underwater since we can't really see what we're looking for down here and I don't want to tempt whoever is trying to get to us."

Amabala whined softly and Merlin just reached for her from his own mount. "It's okay. It's just water."

"But my fur…" She took a deep breath and said, "No. I can do this."

Arden closed her eyes and there was a flair of blue-green in her aura before the buffs hit us. I couldn't open them with my attention on forcing Mako into the water—he didn't like it either, but he listened when I threatened him with no more burgers.

With that, we crashed into the water. The water filtering in colored the world beneath the waves beautifully. The fish didn't appear to be able to see us, their swimming forms coming close enough that I could have reached out to touch a larger one that could have been a tuna or something.

You have no idea what that fish is. Galaxy's teasing made me laugh until I realized that I had been holding my breath without realizing it.

It was so hard to force myself to breathe even knowing that I could with the buffs Arden shared with us all.

I mentally counted down to one from ten and then tentatively let my breath go, trying to take a deep one to replace it. There was a tinge of salty scent slipping in, but otherwise I was fine.

"Let's get after it, Mako." The massive drake growled low and surged forward, the beast using his tail as a rudder to push his body even faster.

I glanced back and saw that the others were having a harder time keeping up until I made use of this experience to try an experiment of my own.

Sharks, I ordered and steeled my will as I stared at the horses beneath the rest of my Hunt. *I order you all to become sharks.*

The shadows shifted, sampling the water around until they appeared to be little more than pools of inky darkness before they shifted again.

Now they resembled sharks from someone's nightmares. Perfect, black teeth gnashed at the water and white eyes stared forward as lifeless as a regular shark's would.

"Woah!" Cassia laughed and the group surged forward,

almost overtaking me and Mako.

"Let's go!" Merlin whooped and laughed.

We raced lower and lower, the armor of the Wild Hunt mitigating the pressure as we approached the floor of the ocean where we were.

The closer we got, the more the pressure built until Arden had to cast her spell or we would need to go back up. With every continued push lower and lower, a flickering aural version of the protective scales became more and more present to me and I hoped nothing else.

We devoured mile after mile until the sun no longer reached this part of the ocean where schools of fish swam a wider berth above the yawning depths of the trench below.

"We ready?" I called to the others as my heart raced in my chest.

The buff timer for Arden's Ocean's Bond buff almost lapsed but she cast it again and we were good.

"Give me a second?" Merlin called and began to mutter to himself with his staff in hand. His aura flared and suddenly there was another buff.

Predator's Sight – Those affected by this spell are able to see in complete darkness without fail. Be cautious of bright lights.

"Nice thinking!" I took a moment to adjust to the vision enhancing buff and then called out, "Let's get after it, we've got a Dominion sliver to collect!"

We gathered and then I led the charge into the dull water ahead, the change almost immediate as we left the waters the world knew and then entered the unknown.

This place didn't want us here. I couldn't tell if it was the protections from some god that just didn't like people visiting or if it was just the Earth's way of telling us we shouldn't fucking be here, but either way, it almost made me too afraid to go on.

But if we failed here, Galaxy wouldn't be strong enough to keep what we wanted safe. That spurred me on, and the darkness around us was no longer as oppressive as it once was.

CHAPTER TWENTY

Even with being able to see with minimal light and then with no light, the depths of the Mariana Trench ate at my reasoning in a way that made me wonder if this wasn't the reason that no one had ever been here before. Cameras or no, just being in the thick mire of this place was enough to make me want to leave and forget the mission we were on. There were creatures that just didn't make sense, the ones you heard about watching TV, and then the ones that no camera would see that made my skin crawl.

Do you need me to take the fear away?

Galaxy's inquisitive mind brushed against mine and I shook my head. *No. I think if it's taken away, it might make me dull somehow. Can you sense anything?*

I could feel her shaking her head from within me as she stared into the scene before us. Large fish swam through the mire and murk to find prey that they could. Several of the fish with lanterns on their heads lit a passage of the wall off to our far right, their heads like flares in the sky that burned to look at. Passing something massive swimming through the light they gave off and then disappearing from even my sight made my skin feel like it was festering and a cool chill began to lance through my spine.

Unnerving as it was, we pressed on at the depth we entered, slowly dropping to grow accustomed to the pressure that crushed on the magic protecting us. It wasn't something that would just stop the pressure altogether, it just enabled us to get used to it much faster.

Over the course of a few hours, we dropped to a depth that began to wear on even Cassia's normally staunch demeanor. Everything about the place began to rub all of our nerves raw. Creatures that were see-through swam weirdly around us. Bones peeked out of crevices in the trench wall that looked like they could launch themselves at us at any time and there was this distinct sensation of dread that clung to us as if something was waiting to lean forward and gobble us up.

"Could it be Grestal?" I asked in a hoarse whisper.

Arden spoke back at a normal volume and made me flinch, "Could be. I haven't known there to be any sort of will for Grestal to eat something from down here, but then again—how much do we really know about it?"

"Not a lot, and everything we don't know could lead to us being as much a meal as the next poor thing." Merlin sighed and then flinched as Amabala's hand flew to his arm. "Yes?"

"A portal." She flexed her nostrils and then looked around. "I smell one, but it's not to Grestal, the smell is different."

"Where?" She pointed over her shoulder and lower toward the depths that edged and faded outside the spectrum of what we could see. "Why can't we see down there, Merlin?"

He glared at the darkness as it built there and then grimaced. "Magical darkness."

"Galaxy, can you feel anything from here down there?" She shook her head once more and I grimaced. "Maybe it's divine protection when something divine looks for it?"

Cassia crossed her arms in thought, then grunted. "It wouldn't hurt to check it out at least. If it's a city, it could be a portal to somewhere important. If it's just a portal, we could just mark it on our map and then keep looking around."

"Don't get careless by getting closer, though," I ordered and the group fell into formation behind me. "Magical darkness seems like an invitation for something to attack us from it."

"It's a very old and tiring trope," Arden groused and Cass nodded with her. "At least do something original, like make the area well-lit and inviting."

"You play far too many horror games to be talking shit, Arden." Merlin's teasing tone was overlaid with genuine worry as we started forward.

I summoned my scythe from my inventory and let the weight of it comfort me. The water dragged against the metal, certainly, but it wasn't too notable at first—then it began to really drag on it and the metal felt like it was bending. I put it back into my inventory and cursed as I realized I would be nearly weaponless down here under all of this immense pressure.

"Merlin, you have anything that can cut through this darkness?"

The boy mage lifted his hands and began to chant a spell and as he did so, light began to build from his chest before it flowed down his arms and clenched hands like he was praying and then shot into the depths below us, a warning to shield our eyes preceding it. The spell was lost to the ebon globule that ranged before us.

And then he spread his hands and the darkness spread, chased to the sides of the trench until the beacon of light pulsed and the bottom of the trench was visible to us and lit perfectly like we were outside on a cloudy day.

Buildings covered in coral cropped up—*out*—of the trench walls. A metropolis of homes and buildings that could have been home to millions. Barren. The coral had claimed all of it, from what I could see. But it also looked well preserved. The fish that swam in the area avoided the place as if it would kill them to go in.

And then the light brought something I couldn't quite make out from below us. I thought it was going to attack us, but it swam away from the light toward the city, and as soon as it was close enough, bounced off something and swam harder the other direction below us.

"Well, chances are good that's the wall we gotta go through, right?" Amabala caught my gaze with a wave and pointed. I followed her finger down to the only structure on the actual bottom itself, which looked like a colosseum of sorts. "You sense it there?"

She nodded and said, "I don't think I could even make a portal to get us through whatever that barrier is." She closed her eyes for a long moment and then groaned. "Just trying gives me a nasty headache and vertigo."

Grunting to myself, I let myself drift in the water as I stared at the barrier. Divine intervention kept things out, and here we were knocking on the proverbial door to try to go to a place that could be anywhere in the world, Grestal, or who-the-hell knew.

Galaxy, do we have a means of getting through that?

Inside me, she shook her head. *Nope.* We *don't have a damn thing.* Her voice took on a scary growl then. *But you do.*

Vorna stuff? She nodded and then gave me a mental shove, so I called back to the others. "I'm going to try something, so you guys just hang back for this, okay? Galaxy, I want you out of me, okay? I don't know what this could do to you."

She grumbled to herself before slipping from me and I hopped off of Mako into the water on my own. The water was dense, but I could still move through it well enough. I would have preferred Mako's strength to do it, but I wanted him safe too.

It took me a minute to get to it, but once I was there, I just glared at the barrier and tried to get a feel for it. When I couldn't do it that way, I tried touching it. As soon as the Mantle made contact with it, I heard alarm bells in my head and every fiber of my being screeched *death* if I went beyond this barrier.

Once I took my hand off it though, it stopped. There was a

decidedly annoying ring in my ears, but it was bearable. I put my hand on the barrier once more and this time I brought my will to bear on it and tried to destroy it.

Consumable energy from several Dominions available, would you like to consume it?

I grinned. "Yes."

A cavernous pit within me opened up and the energy cocooning this place, the city of Atlantis, siphoned into me through my hand like a tidal wave of power. At first, it was uncomfortable. The energy burned and thrummed against my bones in a way that ached as it filled the emptiness I didn't know was in me. Though as it continued to rush into me, it became less and less a thrumming ache and a more warm, almost caramel-like feeling of being drenched and soaked with sweet yumminess.

Did you seriously just equate the power of gods to caramel yumminess?

I didn't have the frame of mind necessary to tell Galaxy off. All I knew was that this power now felt great and I could have sung a song about it if I were talented like that.

Galaxy's voice floated through the mire of water toward me as she addressed the others. "He's drunk on it, but it looks like it's failing!"

I regained enough of my faculties that I could almost begin mentally trudging from the joy and delicious power enough to see that the barrier was flickering. But just beyond it there was movement now.

Bubbles at first, here and there, and then eyes that glowed amber and green that peered from the magical darkness still clinging to the buildings and entrances to homes.

Merlin swore. "God damnit, what are those things now?"

Some of them came from the thick shadows as the barrier continued to fail, wielding weapons like tridents and spears made of stone and what looked like shark teeth that should have come from something larger than even Mako.

The more I siphoned out of the barrier, the more of them

poured from the darker reaches of the city and arrayed against us with weapons at the ready.

These were humanoids, for sure, mermaid tails and all that kickass stuff, but their whole bodies were covered in scales that shimmered in the light that they were clearly leery of and their faces reminded me of the Swamp Thing more than human or anything near that.

"I was really looking forward to a mermaid trope, Marcus!" Arden roared, then her voice raised slightly. "What the fuck is *that* thing?!"

A hand reached out from the darkness at the far side of the singular building far below and gripped the rooftop to assist in pulling itself from the depths and I swear if I hadn't been devouring the power of the gods, I might have shit myself.

"Oooooohohohhooooo *no*," I whispered and then shouted as I saw the head coming out to glare at us. "Is that fucking Cthulhu?"

Galaxy was next to me in a heartbeat, bellowing, "I'm not waiting for a fucking invitation this time, guys—I'll be protecting you all from going insane just looking at that giant fucker." She tapped my head and the fear that built within me subsided like a budding tsunami meeting a brick wall on steroids

"Galaxy? Is there a way for me to use all this power I'm taking in?" I glanced at her with my peripheral vision as I watched the eldritch horror god surmount its containment and stand before us. "Like, I feel like I'm gonna need to blow my whole load on that thing."

Arden howled behind me, but it sounded fake as she called out, "Phrasing is *everything* right now, Marcus!"

Cassia snarled, "Shut the hell up and get ready to fight, Arden."

"I can help guide you from out here, but I don't know how the Vorna's powers work, so you're more of an expert on it than I am." Galaxy put a hand on my shoulder and then pulled it away with a hiss. "I can't even touch you when you're siphoning the magic because it starts to pull at me."

"Just keep an eye on the barrier and let me know when it's about to fail completely." She nodded at me and I closed my eyes, searching inward for my connection to the Null.

I scraped around inside me, then called out to the void, *I could really use some guidance here!*

As if that statement had opened the door, the Null surged forward and suddenly I stood there in the barren landscape staring at the birth of the cosmos.

Welcome, little brother. I searched for the source of the voice, but found nothing for a moment. Then the darkness ebbed from one portion of the land about sixty feet from me and a man stepped from it. ***You called for aid, and here I am.***

"Who are you?"

He smiled, sharp teeth flashing at me that were clearly visible even from this distance. ***I have claimed many titles throughout the eons, but my truth is Guide.***

I wondered what that could mean, but I was short on time. "Then can you guide me on how to use the Dominion I'm siphoning from this barrier?"

I blinked and suddenly he was crowding me, his features more defined as he leaned forward to sniff my shoulder and head. He stood about eight feet tall, so it was easy for him to make it look both weird and intimidating at the same time.

Ah. He leaned back and his chiseled features softened as he looked down at me with a gaze that could only be described as the stars held within his eyes. There were flecks of bright light that spanned the darkness within them that could have held the cosmos itself. ***It's you, is it? I wondered when you would finally seek help.***

"What do you mean?" With him so close and of unknown strength, I wasn't entirely certain I could take him, but I would damn sure try if he got froggy.

She is with you, Massacre. He smiled his creepy smile as he said my Vornal title and then closed his eyes. ***How apt.***

The one who carries her claims such a title and has to come here for aid. Tell me, how is she?

I shoved him and for all it did, I may as well have shoved a mountain. "You'll stay away from her."

He raised an eyebrow at me and his smile became less predatory. *Oh, little brother, I have no interest in collecting the First or even her imprisonment. As soon as I was born, I fled her gaze and influence to the farthest reaches of the stars her birth created.*

He stared down at me and then put a hand on my chest. *There it is. The Dominions you chew at are ancient for the world you come from. Nutritious. If I were you, I would ensure I devour the sources if possible.*

He clenched his fist and stared at it as he did. *Vorna, God Eaters, can claim the Dominions of others for themselves with little danger other than addiction to the taste.* He smirked at that and closed his eyes. *You'll find the strength below your stomach in a place we call the Endless. It swirls there, waiting to be used, condensed, or dissipated. To use the power, focus on the Endless within you, and pull the power to your hand, and then give it shape.*

He turned his fist from him and then splayed his fingers as he spoke. *This can be done by just pushing it out in a wave, a blast, or by a spell. I cannot begin to fathom the magic she can gift you, but I cannot imagine it will be weak or counterproductive to our power. As you grow more adept with the sensation of feeding it, the Endless will alert you to how much of a Dominion you have left before it dissipates on its own if you do not allow it to recover.*

There was a brief pause in the explanation. *It seems time is up, and you are required to give your all. When you have need of me and my Truth again, simply touch the Null as you did and call for me. I look forward to seeing what else the two of you can do.*

His grinning visage accompanied me as Galaxy shoved my shoulder again to get my attention. "It's almost all gone, Marcus!"

As I fell from the Null, acute awareness dawned within me of the Endless inside me where Guide had told me it would be. There were five distinct, but ethereal energies swirling within, in a tight formation.

Gritting my teeth, my will lunged forward into them all and corralled them to bring them forth.

"Cassia, pull stone from the wall and make a barrier with it around all of you." I focused harder on pulling the energy into the Endless and then up through my other arm and into my hand. "Arden, once it's good, push all the water inside the barrier out of it."

Cassia began to speak but I just snarled and barked, "Now!"

They're doing it, Marcus.

I nodded and then responded aloud, "I may need some divine protection, Galaxy. Can you use some of your divinity to make us immune or resistant to electricity?"

"I can try." I just grunted to let her know I heard and then I felt her magic *swoosh* around the two of us. "They're ready. Barrier falling in four…"

The army in front of us began to swim forward at the behest of the eldritch nightmare pointing toward us as Galaxy's count reached two and the incomplete Dominions inside me began to finish gathering into my open palm.

"Now!" Galaxy roared and the barrier fell entirely to unleash the swarm of monstrous swimmers on the other side, me as their target for convergence.

I threw all of the Dominion energy into Bolt Havoc and willed the lightning's energy to spew out in front of me. As soon as the magic met the water, the area around us charged with it and a scream tore from my throat as the stinging energy scoured my whole body in retaliation for my scientific hubris. Sure, it didn't spread nearly as far as I wanted it to, but with the help of the Dominions, it defied logic just enough to be mostly useful.

A massive ball of lightning torpedoed from my outstretched hand as the rest of the god energy slipped from my control and surged through the army before us. I was hurt, but not dead, and I had a job to do.

With Galaxy's help, I could keep the others safe.

A hand touched my shoulder and Cassia stood next to me with her eyes glowing so brightly behind her sunglasses that I could almost see her pupils.

"You forgot that I carry your god-blessed child within me and that they have the magic of a thunder god in their blood." She darted forward with her mouth open as the lightning began to whirl inside the army of dying fish people. "This will give us power too!"

As soon as she was closer to the lightning, a spectral semblance of the Japanese thunder god, Raijin's array of drums, appeared behind her shoulders. While it shook and vibrated behind her, she brought her hands together and a shockwave of sound crashed forward, slinging the bodies of the survivors in the lightning water toward Cthulhu.

The eldritch beast roared, the tentacles on its face shivering as its muscles bunched and it launched itself toward the fray.

"Galaxy, is that thing a god?"

She appeared on my left and scowled at it. "If it is, it can hide that fact. Think you can try the Vorna thing on it?"

The massive creature slammed into the electrical energy still shocking the water and fucking *tanked* it. Barely seeming to care that it was being singed and shocked in its frenzy to get to us. It hit the spell so hard, it fizzled out and almost made me shit myself. A notification popped for me but I didn't have time to look at it. This thing was coming.

"Time to fight, y'all!" I heard the stones behind me protecting the others crackle and then shatter as they surged from their barrier against my spell and rushed out. "If it ain't one of us—kill it!"

Arden roared, "You *fucking think?*" She swam past me so fast it was hard to follow her until she twirled in the water just before slicing her hand through one of the barely living fish monsters. "Fuck, I love this spell!"

She yanked her hand out, greenish ichor-like blood seeping from the fish man as Cassia sent another shockwave through the water into the others and finished up the fish people. That left only the big guy.

Merlin muttered under his breath and then began to move past me with his hands in front of him raised at the beast. "This is gonna suck."

His aura reared and then his magic rushed through the space and attached itself to the tentacled monster and *yanked* him toward it. As he flew toward it, he pulled his sword from his inventory and slid it along his own arm, bloodying the water trailing behind him.

The sword glimmered somewhat and then looked to solidify somehow before he lashed out at the arm that swung at him. He ducked it just in time, leaving a gash that festered with *something* behind in his wake.

That's not good. I turned to Galaxy. "Hop on, let's go kill an eldritch horror."

She grinned and faded into my body before I could swim off toward the fight.

"Got you, Marcus!" Amabala swam to me and touched my shoulder, the world about us flickering as we appeared next to the elder god's hip. "Let's get him!"

A leg sliced the water and caught me in the midsection as I floated and tried to get my bearings, sending me a bit away from the beast. But as soon as it touched me, I knew—it was no god.

For some reason, that made me *very* angry. The frigid water around my arms crackled as Void Frost formed along my forearms and made two blades that began at my elbows and grew past my hands.

A small bar of ice grew over my palm and I gripped it as the rest of the blades formed over my fists. The ice here formed and built *fast* and strong as hell.

I pressed my arms over my head and swam toward the distracted monster. I reached it and as its arm dipped low, I struck, my icy blades slicing skin and water alike. Fractals of ice grew in their wake as the damage was done and more festering disgustingness was opened from it.

Something from within it reached toward me and snatched my leg into its grasp, yanking me away from the beast. If it weren't for the fact I was in water, it would have yanked the leg from its socket but instead it pulled me toward the wound.

I twisted and sliced it from my leg and the grasping nightmare limb remained clenching painfully but I was free.

Another wash of sound that sent me careening through the water crashed into the beast and me as well and cleared me from the danger zone.

The others were doing an okay to excellent job of corralling the bastard, his attention on them and their attacks, which left me room to try something.

I reached out to the cold, frothing water around me and cast Void Frost, building what I saw in my mind's eye with my will.

A massive spike with a wicked spear on the end of it began to build slowly and then fast as I called Mako to me.

"Push this down into him, and then help keep me covered, okay?" The massive black drake dipped his scaled chin and swam up to the butt of the spear, put a paw on it, and shoved with all his might.

The frosty weapon sliced through the water as I spent the mana to make another weapon, this one as large as the other but more sword-like. I built it until it resembled a buster sword I'd seen somewhere before and was as large as the monster itself.

The weight of it was ungodly, but it could at least be steered in the right direction. I gripped the hilt of it with both hands spread to get a real handle on it and tipped it forward blade first as the tentacled beast screamed.

Mako's thoughts rushed into mine, showing he'd hit him in the upper leg near the hip and was distracting him for me with his massive tail swinging.

Hollow, how do I make the most of this?

The elemental glared out from within me and whispered, *My sister is not close here, so your magic will be less effective, but if you use that weapon as ice can be when it breaks, it will create much damage.*

I mentally shrugged, wondering what she really meant with that, but if I needed to make an ice shrapnel bomb, I could do that. It would just be dangerous.

Once the blade was completely vertical again, I stood on the hilt and crouched, shoving it down with all my might.

It sliced through the water rapidly but not so much as it could have and then the water around it gave way in a bubble of air that gave the massive floating weapon more momentum.

I saw Arden launch herself back toward the massive boss creature and swoosh her hands to make the water above the weapon crash into it and drive it down harder.

Galaxy, I need Cassia to help me.

Galaxy mentally gripped me and said, *She's a little busy with the new monsters that showed up from behind us.*

I cast my gaze over my shoulder and, sure enough, she and Amabala were battling a new wave of creatures.

Shit. Okay. I turned my attention to the jarring sensation below me and found the tentacle-faced piece of shit screeching at me with its hateful red gaze as it grabbed the blade.

I grinned and pressed my hands against the blade and forced Void Frost to travel down the ice and froze its hands to the weapon.

As if he sensed what I wanted, Mako appeared next to me at the hilt of the weapon and assisted me in shoving it through the creature's chest with a savage, satisfying glee.

"Cassia!" She turned toward me from where she was as I began to flee from the sword. "Shatter it!"

She nodded, Merlin turning his attention to her portion of the monsters so she could assist me, and grimaced as her eyes flared behind her sunglasses and clapped, this wave of thunderous sound ripping toward the creature with malice as it struck both it and the weapon of ice. The ice splintered under the onslaught and then exploded in an array of light and gore that just ate into what fight Cthulhu had left.

The water clouded with ichor disgustingness that made the fish men turn tail and run for the shadows as Amabala, Merlin, and Mako gave chase.

Galaxy swam from me to go to the dead and began to collect her toll, their bodies to be used for more experience for all of us as we had fought so hard for it.

I was just eager to see what we might find down below on the other side of the portal that our Keeper had felt.

What strange waters the rip in reality might deliver us to and still no god other than the weird one trying to get to us? Things just kept getting weirder and weirder.

CHAPTER TWENTY-ONE

After Galaxy had her fill, we took an inventory of how the majority of us were doing. Luckily, injuries were scarce enough that Cassia was able to help get everyone back to tip-top shape swiftly.

"Great work with the barrier." Cass spoke to me softly as she looked me over. I felt a little wrung out after the fight, but Galaxy had assured us both it was because I wasn't used to the effects of a Dominion. My mana usage hadn't helped either, and I was frightfully low in that department too.

"How long until I don't feel like someone took a hooked mixer to my innards?"

Galaxy and Cass both hit me with a look of both sarcastic impatience and I rolled my eyes. "This shit isn't a man-cold, okay? It fucking hurts."

Cassia's hands ran over my stomach and her healing energy sizzled through me, but there was precious little for it to cling to in order to fix. "It seems mental to me."

Galaxy nodded and added, "And I'm not going to scrub it from your mind for two reasons—knowledge of how to use it and the consequences of blowing your whole wad on a single, nearly ineffective attack need to be learned."

Arden snorted, "Phrasing." She started whistling as soon as Galaxy glared her way.

The goddess turned back to me and said, "And two, I can't."

I rolled my eyes. "Could have just led with that, love."

"Yes, well, sometimes I have to get you to learn from your mistakes the hard way." Galaxy smirked and ran a knuckle over my cheek. "You did fight well after that, though. Good work."

My head lolled to the side for a long moment and I could feel a mounting sense of urgency near me through my bonds.

"If we rest, it may help, but we run the risk of someone sending more troops to come and collect our collective hides." Merlin swam closer to us and floated there for a second, staring down at the temple cautiously. "We can't leave here without giving them time to recover and set up another viable defense, and going forward is potentially risky."

I put a hand to my head and grumbled, "Forward. Let's get through there and into whatever lay beyond. We don't want to face another army."

I took a deep moment to find myself and opened my eyes to find concerned faces watching me cautiously, then turned toward the temple and called my ride. "Mako."

The drake swam past me and I grabbed ahold of him as he did, allowing him to haul me lower toward our goal.

The massive temple almost glowed with how my sight was right now thanks to Merlin's vision buff and as we neared it, I could see why. It was a metal building that looked to have been made with copper but it was perfectly preserved.

The salt hadn't done a damn thing to it, and that could have been in part to the barrier that had been erected by the gods, but there was no telling how long it had been up. This smacked of a near carbon copy of the Parthenon to me, but I was far from an expert.

Mako took me to the door and after an inspection of my

own, I called to Merlin, "Look it over for magical locks and traps. I don't want any surprises."

The boy mage took his time, reading the symbols and carvings in the doors and the frame before sighing. "It looks safe. I can't feel anything sinister, but I also don't know anything about how to feel for the power of gods."

Galaxy stepped closer to the doors and held her hands up, feeling for energy, if I'd had to guess.

Galaxy snickered and said, "I feel something waiting, but it's weak. Weak enough that it can't be sensed by normal means." She stared at the door as her mind spoke to us all, *Cassia, I want you to do a bit of a harsh knock for me, can you do it?*

I didn't have to wonder if she would be able to as Cassia swam forward and flared her arms as far back as she could and then slammed her hands together so hard that the doors bent inward from the force and then tore from their hinges to disappear inside.

Arden hollered, "Damn!" With her shout, she rushed inside to see who could have been hiding from us and called, "They're gone! Galaxy, can you sense them?"

Galaxy shook her head and called back, "No. They're gone."

"Tear the place apart." Amabala and Merlin both paused to turn my way at the order, so I clarified. "I want to know what and who we're dealing with. If we can glean anything from this place, I want to learn what we can."

Rather than going all the way into the room, I had Mako take me in a little bit and then turned around to watch outside for anyone who might come up on us while we were busy.

Galaxy, could you understand the writing on the doors? There was a mental affirmation from her as she continued to stare at the interior from outside. *Can you help them search? I know that there's something nagging at you based on how you're acting.*

It seems so familiar to me. She stepped closer to the wall on the inside of the doorway as if entranced and transfixed by what she saw. *I could have given these runes their form, Marcus. I could have passed these very thoughts from within me to the people who created this place.*

I nodded, knowing better than to sit here and doubt her. She very well could have, and I had no right to think she couldn't have known what I knew now.

"There's something about fish people," Amabala stated as she swam toward us, a small shattered vase in her grip. "Merlin and the others are checking some of the back quarters, but other than that, there's really nothing that sticks out to me as earth shattering concerning who or what may have been here."

I grimaced but accepted that there would likely not be anything that we would be able to understand anyway and just asked, "And the portal you felt?"

She tilted her head and craned it upward toward the ceiling and as she did so, Merlin appeared with his light pointing that way.

Above us in the center of a depiction of a typhoon—the very eye of the storm itself—was a portal like nothing I'd ever seen. It was a gemstone of a creation. The typhoon appeared to be tearing the world apart, massive chunks of land being pulled into the air from the middle of the ocean to be thrown into the wind.

On the other side floated spectral figures. Beings whose entirety were covered in light of colors that I just couldn't comprehend at the moment. Some were large, others even larger. But they appeared removed from the scene somehow.

Had they caused this destruction? Or were they just complacent and content to watch as it all happened?

I ignored my musings and focused on what I could actually glean from it, or rather what others could. "Is it safe for us to use?"

Amabala closed her eyes for a long moment, straining visibly as she searched the portal with her instincts and experience assisting her. "I think so. I can't really tell where it will lead though. It feels unlike anything I've ever seen before."

My knuckles cracked as I gripped the ebon reigns in my

grasp while focusing on my breathing. A lot of unknowns ahead.

We will stand with you, Marcus. Galaxy's voice assured me, soothing my struggle ever so slightly. Not so much as to be considered invasive, just her presence calming my nerves in a way that few could.

I could trust these people with my life. I could trust them with their own lives and to look after one another.

"We go." I urged Mako upward toward the portal and stopped so the others could grab ahold of my hand and form a chain so we couldn't be separated.

Galaxy faded into me and then we all rushed through the portal.

There was no sensation of being squeezed through the tear in space and time as if you were being pressed through the cosmic zit on the face of reality and expelled, only to try to find yourself and ensure you didn't hork up all you'd eaten.

No, this was something else entirely. The transition was seamless, and as we came out on the other side still in water, the pressure around us lightened significantly.

"Where the hell is this place?" There was a light quality to the water that concerned me almost as much as the depths had. This wasn't right.

There was a mirror of the temple below us, it looked almost exactly like the one at the bottom of the trench but this one was actually green and looked to be well traveled. As if people came here all the time to leave offerings and presents to the god or gods they worshiped.

Cautiously, we swam below and observed their sacrifices.

Carvings and paintings. Goods that would keep under water. Some of it looked to be fresher than others, but there wasn't any clutter as if it had been going on for a long time. Someone had clearly been in to clean things out and make sure the oxidized temple was presentable to the flock.

Why? Who knows. But all I knew was that this was not the

place to be when someone came back to deliver their adoration for an entity who probably *did not* want us here.

Hollow, can you sense your sister?

The ice primordial brushed against my mind and sighed, *No. When you are close to whomever devoured her, I will feel her. Until then —be cautious.*

I rolled my eyes at that and almost responded sourly, but we needed to get to wherever civilization was and try to blend in.

I lowered my voice and hissed to the others, "We get out, recon, and look for wherever there's civilization to blend in with and get the lay of the land. I don't know how we'll manage it with fish people, but we'll make it work."

They nodded and we went for the entrance, swimming out of it as quickly as we could, only to find that our exit strategy had a few flaws.

We knew nothing of our surroundings other than that there was water here. So when we swam out of the building into the courtyard filled with water, that was normal.

What wasn't normal was the fact that we were in a massive bubble of water in the middle of the *fucking sky!*

"What the hell is this place?" Arden whispered softly. The sky held a blue so deep and beautiful that our own mortal sky couldn't even really compare. Just above where this temple floated in a bubble of water was a section of royal purple with the glimmering of winking stars that stretched even higher up above us.

It could have been nothing more than a backdrop to a painting, for as perfect as it was and felt. Like this was someone's ideal backdrop to a world all their own.

"This isn't Earth." I stepped closer to the barrier of water, and asked, "Is it Grestal? I don't recognize it."

"This is a pocket realm, similar to a Soul Realm." The words came from nowhere and everywhere around us, our search for the source fruitless. The voice returned. "I should warn you to return to your own realm, but I would be remiss if I did not entreat you for aid. The people here are in a predicament unlike any they have ever experienced, and we could use the aid of someone who is not mind-washed with the land and culture of this place."

My eyebrows knit into a knot and Cassia asked, "And just who are you to ask for help?"

The voice was quiet until we thought that they were gone entirely when they spoke again, "The only representative of the sleeping gods here in this place. There is a man here who tampers with the powers of those he does not know, and I dare not think of the ramifications of his actions."

The voice was quiet a second and then added, "I will send my most loyal follower to you. Please, do not be found."

My eyes widened and Galaxy bristled, *Could the person who hurt Thoth and Anubis be here?*

"Who is he?"

My question fell on deaf ears as voices raised in the distance in a song of sorts that floated toward us. Merlin went over to the side of the water bubble and stared down over the side of the little island floating inside and reported what he saw, "People with wings are flying up here and as they come up, some are breaking off and going to lower islands."

He paused and then added, "They look tired, the ones that stopped flying, as if it's hard to fly up here. I think the ones that can make it will either be really strong compared to the others, or exceptional flyers." He scratched his head and thought for a moment before speaking again. "Either way, if the others are brainwashed like that sleeping god said, then there's a chance they could be taking us straight to that guy, and we're in no condition to go straight to them with an entire realm of potential supporters."

I grimaced but nodded. "That's a fair observation. I don't want anyone to see us yet." Through Galaxy I added, *I don't exactly know if we can trust a slumbering god of any variety if that person is here, since we don't know exactly what they're capable of. Or the person they send.*

The others nodded and closed ranks around us. Arden motioned to the boy mage and ordered, "Merlin, do the thing."

He glared at her dourly before making a motion with his hands, saying a few words, and then releasing magic that clouded the waters around us and made the water still for a moment before Arden raised her own hand and made the water move like it had been before.

We waited as five figures, humans with the wings of birds growing from their backs, rose just above the globe of water containing their temple and dove in. As soon as their bodies touched the water, there was a shift of the light around them, their auras darkened and their wings disappeared to be replaced by scales and fins, fine gills grew along their necks and it looked as though they were just as comfortable like this.

What the hell are they? The thought exited my mind and no one else answered for once. After they entered the temple, their song renewed and garbled words and music rose up from below.

Marcus, if we are to escape, we should leave now while they're worshiping, lest we find out if any of them can sense our magic. I didn't want to leave with them so close for that very reason, but a distraction was as good as we were going to get in this aspect so we left.

Leaving the water globe around the temple loosed a little water down below toward some of the other islands, but once we were out of the place and out of danger, the immensity of this place crashed into me as I rode on Mako's back under Merlin's spell.

There were hundreds of smaller, cul-de-sac-sized islands floating all over the sky at varying distances and heights spiraling around three to five larger ones that could only be compared to the size of large cities. One of them was absolutely massive and was above the others with a river of water that flowed over the edge and into the center of another island in a waterfall that had rainbows decorating it in an almost-permanent way, it seemed.

"So this is Atlantis?" Cassia watched in the same shocked

awe that I did. "I never would have thought it wasn't just a city under water all the time. Even the cartoons got it wrong."

Arden snorted. "The movie was great though. It was close, I think." She grinned widely. "And Milo? Wow."

Amabala laughed at that and shook her head. "Is he the one you have art of in your room? Him and the long-haired one, with the space boats?"

"That's Jim, and Treasure Planet was amazing, thank you." Arden crossed her arms and raised a brow in challenge at the other woman who I had a sneaking suspicion probably hadn't seen the movie.

"Focus on finding a place for us to hide, guys." I found myself focusing inward and following their leads as I put my mind to work. Who could we possibly be up against here and how much shit were we in if the locals found us out before we got Galaxy's power back?

And in a place like this, where could a Vorna who ate Earth's primordial water elemental be?

CHAPTER TWENTY-TWO

The way we plummeted from the entrance to the realm and the temple containing it was much more fun than I thought it would be, considering we were still invisible.

I couldn't see the others, relying on my bonds with the Hunt to be able to keep all of us moving together toward wherever looked the least likely to be gone to.

There were several places that looked inviting, with trees and hills, and there was one even that had a home on it. The island itself was smaller than some of the others but it was a lot more viable to me than the vast majority of the options.

What do you all think of that house?

Through Galaxy, there was a consensus of assent to landing there and at the very least looking it over.

The grass was overgrown. Bushes unkempt with brambles and berry bushes of sorts erupting from them. The home looked reminiscent of what you might see in an affluent area of American cities, but there was an odd, aquatic or avian flare to it somehow that I just couldn't put my finger on.

Was it the material? It looked like it was meant to withstand height, or could it have been depth, or was it the compact height of the floors? The three-story building had a squat, six- or seven-foot height to each of them, and the roofs were covered by small slopes that lowered from the roof above it.

It could have been reminiscent of Asian roofing, but less theatrical and sloping.

We landed and hid ourselves in the tree line and large bushes while Merlin scanned the bushes and the berries on them. "Poisonous?"

I reached out and grabbed a few, sniffing them. They smelled nice. I pocketed some of them, then thought better of it and put them into my inventory instead.

"Can't hear anything inside." Amabala's ear's continued to twitch as she stared at the building for another few moments, then sighed, "Nothing. Not even a heartbeat. But the voice said something about sending someone to us. Should we have stayed still?"

I shook my head. "Had we done that, they would probably have found us." I chanced a glance at Arden and she knew what I wanted, her face becoming more and more pinched. "Come on."

"I don't want to." She crossed her arms and acted childishly. "Just because I'm faster than everyone else here doesn't mean I want to go running around the house."

I rolled my eyes and sighed, defeated. "Then make the heat mirage and I'll go looking." She grinned and did just that, the entirety of the area in front of me becoming a shimmering heat wave.

It was hard to walk around in for a second and then the heat pushed outward away from the home and formed more of a barrier for me to move through.

Walking through the now-cooler air was so much nicer on my skin. The cold never really bothered me before, but the heat had been terrible. Could it have been a side effect of Hollow's bond with me?

I didn't listen to any intrusive voices and carried on with my mission and began to peer through windows on the first story.

Furniture, low backed for support with winged users to use, looked to be the popular mode of decor and the colors were varied enough to think the person either had eclectic tastes or they just grabbed what they could or wanted. Either way, the dust that settled over the vast majority of things led me to believe the place had been long empty and could be used to hide in ourselves.

I hoped.

I reached back and waved them all forward and spent a few minutes checking the doors for any sort of traps or alarms.

I couldn't find anything, but luckily the others reached me in time to catch me before going in. Merlin pointed to just above the door to carvings that edged just this side of visible to me and as he did, they shimmered ever so slightly with an aura.

He glared at it for a long moment, then sighed, "Definitely an alarm of sorts, but I don't know the language to tell if it's armed or not." He motioned for all of us to stay here and did a brief inspection of the windows near us as well. "Good news; only the door looks to be alarmed from this side. Once we get to the other side, I'm not sure with the windows—hard to tell. So either we can stay here and figure out a way in, or we can just stay in the trees over there underground with Cassia's help and wait for nightfall."

I turned to her and asked softly, "Can you move this kind of stone and stuff? The ground doesn't feel like normal earth here."

She grunted. "I can try. I need to rest soon—I'm getting tired, and that fight with tentacles took a lot out of me and the baby."

I grimaced and motioned everyone back toward our hiding spot in the small wood and Cassia tried to move the rock, doing so with difficulty. "It's a lot denser than what you would think would be able to float freely like this. Like there are different minerals in it."

Merlin nodded. "It's entirely likely that there's a scientific explanation for why these islands all float in the air like this.

Likely just as much as a magical one with the amount of mineral in the soil. It could actually be that there is a repelling effect or even a magnetic one acting on all of them."

Arden groaned and then put a hand to her head. "Like the amount of the minerals or opposing magnetism in the stone and soil means that they float higher?" Merlin grinned happily and nodded at her, but she just closed her eyes and whined, "I've been living too long with super nerd!"

"How are negotiations coming on the house?"

Amabala's question caught Arden and me by surprise and she cleared her throat. "With the world having gone to shit a bit, it's kind of hard to get things going on a loan of any sort. Why?"

Amabala motioned to Merlin. "You're corrupting Merlin with your nerdiness, and I was just wondering." She peered over at the house in the distance. "That one looks like a nice one."

I nodded. What Arden said made sense, but I couldn't say I blamed the young woman for wanting privacy, even if the question was ill-timed. "Let's all just rest as much as we can for now and we can begin to look for how to track down Galaxy's Dominion after that."

Once the hole was ready and the others piled in, I took a steadying breath and decided to go look at our surroundings a bit more. I low-crawled toward the side of the island with greater caution than I'd ever used when low-crawling, and peered down below.

The islands seemed to drift and remain still all at the same time, occasionally figures fluttered from one to another and disappeared. I would've liked to go down below to check things out a bit more, to explore and just appreciate the ethereal beauty of this place. How many people could say that they'd been here, in this spot, to see all this majesty?

No one that I had ever heard of, that was who. Weight settled on me and I found that Galaxy had joined me. *It's beautiful, isn't it?*

I nodded just a bit and thought back, *Yeah, yeah it is. I find myself wondering what the situation was that brought all this about. Was it because of the gods? Did they do it to protect this place, or to punish them? You hear so many stories and theories, but when you've got the islands of the place staring back at you, it's kinda hard to justify those.*

It would be, yes. A soft purring reverberated on my back, comfortingly shaking me. *Those creatures looked somewhat frail. I wonder if they taste like chicken, or fish?*

It took everything in me not to chortle at the thought, shaking my head ever so slightly at her curiosity and an almost joke. *If it weren't for the fact that I can't fly on my own, and there's a Vorna somewhere around here, I would love to dig deeper into this area. See how the people tick and what their culture is like.*

A mental frown from Galaxy made me raise a brow as she asked, *Why?*

Well, we learned about the cultures of the peoples' whose countries we went into while I was in the Marine Corps, places like Afghanistan, Pakistan, Iraq—hell, even Korea—and that was fascinating to me. It was fun to learn those things and to learn to respect their cultures at least a little bit. I paused, remembering all the times that it had actually helped me to interact with the locals. The times that knowing how they thought had paid off and how many lives it may have saved. *It's an invaluable skill to be able to learn about those you're in conflict with, why not enjoy it?*

But you still went and fought them. Isn't that counterproductive?

I shook my head once again. *No. We knew we had a mission, and while it made it easier for us to keep the people we dealt with in our minds, it also helped us understand our enemies too. We knew how they thought, how they controlled and governed the locals, and what to expect of them at any given moment. How their fear mongering and threats made them the monsters that we needed to rid the world of. It wasn't always easy, but to me it wasn't necessarily any harder either.*

She remained quiet at that for a long time as I continued my prone vigil in the shadows of the large trees that grew overhead. Once she had digested that, she padded off my back with nary a word and returned to the others. I stayed for another ten minutes or so to make sure that at least from what I could see, no one was coming and then crawled back.

When I returned, I happened across Arden, who pulled out a portable game console and rolled my eyes. "You checking to see if it works?"

She grinned as she turned the volume down, the small blaring noise startling me and Merlin. "It works, alright. I got first watch, you guys rest."

I thanked her with a quiet mouthing of the word and she dipped her chin before turning her gaze toward the entrance to our small cave beneath the grassy ground and between the roots of a few trees.

The others went about various tasks, Cassia taking out some food to eat for herself and as I attended her, she fell asleep against me a lot faster than I had thought she would.

Galaxy's voice echoed into my mind, *She ended up using a lot of the child's Dominion to fight that monster. As close as all of you are to leveling up again, it won't be enough to replenish that kind of energy for her. She needs to rest if she's going to be using that level of magic.*

Understood, thank you. I paused briefly as I collected my thoughts on how I wanted to proceed. *I'm going to be doing something similar to what I did to gather the Dominion earlier and going into myself for a bit. If anything happens that you need me, let me know how you can.*

Good luck.

I offered her a soft smile as she took her cat form and laid on Cassia's stomach and legs and then I closed my eyes and called out mentally into the Null, "Guide!"

I spread my consciousness forward as his deep chuckle lingered at the edges of my perception and found myself in the Null.

———

The same figure greeted me this time, though he wasn't alone.

"This is my younger brother, Oathbound." The creature next to him looked similar to Guide, only he had chains wrapped around his wrists and ankles, bulky and uncomfortable-looking to me, but nothing that he looked to care about. *"He has volunteered to assist me in your training and education."*

"And you mean no harm to my goddess?"

He considered me for a long moment, almost to the point of me wondering whether I was going to have to fight him and kill him until he said, *"I mean no harm."*

My eyes narrowed at him as I spoke softly. "Carefully avoiding saying to whom?"

Both he and Guide smiled, then Oathbound raised his hands so that he could clatter his chains' links loudly. *"I swore an oath that changed my truth. I can willingly cause no lasting harm to anyone. Vorna, god, goddess, human. Nothing."*

"Why would you go and do something like that?"

Guide raised his hand. *"Being a harbinger of doom is something most fear. The eldest born Vorna are some of the most powerful. With the exception of two of them, War and Life, there are still many others active and very much in play. But truths are not why we have come, little brother. You desire training, yes?"*

I nodded and they both grinned in unison, Guide clapping his hands. *"Then training you shall have. Oathbound? Bind the time around us so that we get the maximum amount of training possible."*

Oathbound reached out with his hands and closed his eyes, a considerable swirling of energy and aura rising from within him, just below his navel.

"Time, Null, I bind you to my will—bequeath to me your power so that I might exert my will over the power you hold."

There was a shiver and suddenly we were no longer by ourselves. A creature made of darkness given eyes as dull and shimmery as the stars in the distance stared at us and hissed

"You would bind the time flow here while we watch our beloved ones' children?"

I flinched at the fury that they exhibited. "What the fuck are you?"

The creature turned its gaze toward me and a swath of darkened motion raised toward me, but I pushed my hand forward and used the Mantle's power to press back against it.

The white of its eyes narrowed dangerously as the power that should have sent me flying across the area just washed over me like a stinging wave of oceanic water.

"The power you wield was not given by me—who gave you that?"

"He was blessed by Her," Guide answered for me. **"So far, his power is given by the object he chose as his Vornal weapon, the Mantle of the Huntsman."**

The creature growled in annoyance. *"One of those things?"* It came closer to me and sniffed, then flinched and sniffed again. *"You are blessed by a lesser primordial, ice?"*

It sniffed me again as I nodded and went to speak, but then it grabbed me and pulled me close, *"Beloved? You've been near several of our contractors!"*

I blinked at that and tried to pull away but their grip was iron. "I have no idea what you're talking ab— Wait." I did have an idea though. Hollow had said something similar to me when I was contracted to her. "Do you know Zeke and his friends?"

The shadows did something I hadn't expected—they hugged me. *"Our beloved lives!"*

The Vorna watched with curious expressions as the shadows shook me in their tenacious happiness.

The creature grasping me pushed me back slightly. *"We need you to pass a message to him from us, and from many others, we are certain, but we will begin with us."*

"He is here to train with us, Spirit of the Null," Guide inserted cautiously. **"Though guidance is what he needs, his power is a farce of what you are capable of giving. Would you form a pact with him?"**

Oathbound put a hand out and added, *"So long as it will not change his truth."*

The creature considered it for a short time. *"Allow us to ponder this. Until then, allow us to use your shadow?"*

I frowned at that, but figured it couldn't do any harm. A small globule of shadow broke off from their mass and slithered into my shadow. Nothing felt off, though this wasn't my physical form, I couldn't feel any discomfort.

With that done, the shadowed entity that they had called Spirit of the Null was gone.

"Strange company you keep for having garnered their attention, Massacre." Guide spoke softly so that his voice didn't carry far. He turned his attention to Oathbound and tilted his head questioningly. When the other Vorna nodded, he smiled and said, *"Let us carry on with your training then, little brother. You have much to learn and time is exceedingly precious to you."*

CHAPTER TWENTY-THREE

I cracked my neck and hunkered down once more as the others waited for me to do as they wanted.

To take my Vornal form.

"I still don't know why what happened to me in the tunnels doesn't count."

The shifting that had happened then, the beast-like change that the Mantle had undergone and the ensuing dismemberment of my enemies, was all just a fluctuation in my power with it.

"Though I will admit, it was likely very close. And if you take this form, you will need to be certain that your goddess is not inside you, or close by."

I frowned deeply at Guide's warning but it was Oathbound who explained, *"Young Vorna do not differentiate food from friend very well. We see power—especially Dominions—as nourishment. The stronger you become, the less likely you are to lose control, but take the time to get there first."*

Fair enough, but I'll have to have damn good control or I'm going to be a danger to the people I care about. I sulked and then sighed as nothing was coming to me for this. "Is there like, some special thing you do to take your Vornal form? Like, a ritual or a rite?"

They looked from me to each other and then back, Oathbound snickering as his brother tried to keep his composure. *"We are **born** Vorna. We can assume our shape as easily as breathing because it is natural to us. You? Were not born as we were. Your dormant blood was awakened with the touch of the goddess and the Vorna you killed.*

"Try thinking of your truth," he offered wisely, his hands sliding to his humanoid-looking face. As they did, Guide's form shifted into that of a Vorna, though his form was different.

Where others of his ilk were tall, broad, and muscularly built, he was slim and athletic-looking, his wings much larger than the others and the horns on his head massive. His skin was dappled with almost a marble-like look to it, white with splotches of gray and black along it.

"Has anyone ever told you that you resemble Gargoyles?" They both raised an eyebrow and I shrugged. "Just a thought."

Oathbound shimmered darkly, however that was possible, and his own form revealed itself. His skin was as pale as the moon with a single, spiked, golden rod *shoved* into his chest. He looked emaciated, malnourished, and from the rod the chains were completed, giving enough slack for the creature to move, but where it came out the back of his chest, platinum ones bound him from behind as well.

I couldn't speak as he leaned forward and cheekily reasoned, *"Perhaps your thoughts would be better suited to accessing your true form as opposed to whether we can help dissipate water from a roof or not?"*

I grimaced and sighed as I thought about the things that could initiate the change, that last bit slightly confusing to me, so I just glanced over it mentally. Any change. *Something* that could pull my alternate form from within me.

I shook my head and tried to think about what was going on

with me when I was in that fight. I'd been angry. Infuriated that someone had done something like that and I hadn't been able to do anything—but that didn't feel right to me.

Had it been the fighting? The act of preparing myself mentally to kill?

When I thought about it that way, I tried to settle myself into my thoughts. That cold, blank, nearly thoughtless place that I went into to do what needed doing.

Once I began to fall into that state of mind, I realized that *this* was the truth I had been trying to find. Massacre wasn't just about my proclivity to violence, but my ability to reach for and find it to bring it out to others. Knowing that the violence was almost a necessity rather than just something that happened.

My killing the enemy brought justice. Peace. Safety. The more enemies I slaughtered, the safer those I cared for would be. The safer the innocent would be.

Safe. The thought reverberated throughout my being and that made me smile, because while I would work toward that end, ***I was anything* but *safe.***

My body shifted of its own accord. My already strong muscles, lean and steely, grew denser and moved strangely to accommodate the changes my body underwent. It wasn't painful, just different. Was this how the werewolves felt with each change? The shift from prey to predator had to be heady indeed, because I felt as though I could kill the very gods.

I chuckled to myself as I glanced down at my now dark-colored hand, ***I mean, I can. That's the point of being Vorna.***

"Yes!" Guide clapped and Oathbound just stared at me with curiosity on his features. ***"Tell me, was it your truth that brought the change within you?"***

"It was thinking of my truth and how it affected those around me."

Oathbound flexed his clawed hands, his chains rattling ominously as a mirror appeared next to him for me to look into.

Standing in the mirror stood what I could only imagine as a

demon. My musculature was still much like my own, but where the other Vorna looked like monstrous creatures with cruel snouts and leathery skin, with scales and other varying features, I was human-like.

Though my skin wasn't pale, above my hands, ivory or anything like that, it was much less actual skin and almost stone-like. Like Oathbound's, it was almost marbled, but my hands were darker. Blood.

They weren't black, they were a crimson so dark and dried that it just *looked* darker. Rivulets of crimson dribbled down my cheeks from both sides of my eyes, making a patterned pathway down to my chin where small red horns like fangs hung down off my jawline.

From my forehead, horns the same shade as my hands rose and curved slightly backward before coming to a point.

I chuckled more to myself than the others and said, "I look like some edgelord's wet dream."

Oathbound looked over to his brother and spoke quietly. ***"What is that?"***

The other Vorna shrugged, then focused on me. ***"Flex your will and summon your weapon of choice, little brother. We have much to do."***

I frowned and stared at him, "I'm going to fight you?"

He chuckled and shook his head. ***"Hardly. We go hunting."*** He stopped me before I could turn my attention from him to the Null and shook his head again. ***"Not here. This is just a hub for us. All places are tied to this place, as it is the beginning of existence."***

I frowned at that, but he clearly knew more about this place than I did. "Where do we go?"

I flexed my hand and pulled the scythe from my ring only for it to be yanked from grasp by Oathbound who immediately looked pained as he held the weapon. ***"This is not your weapon. Summon the one you chose when your blood first awakened. The one you can make better through sacrifice."***

I grimaced and summoned my Mantle. It fell over my shoulders like a familiar hoodie and they grunted, nodding before Oathbound passed me my scythe back. *"This one will be useful, but the Mantle you wear is what we will be focusing on."*

"So I'm not going to hunt a god?" They shook their heads and I asked, "Then how am I supposed to be able to fight them and absorb their power?"

"That will come to you naturally. Your weapon is weaker than you right now and the other Huntsmen who serve your goddess have begun to forget her." Oathbound spoke sadly as his brother stared into the distance. *"Now, we go to one of the planets where a cruel Huntsman sits upon a throne of his own making. Once you take his Mantle as your own, your power will grow and you might become ready to hunt a god."*

"I thought that the time distortion only worked here." The statement, borne of my concern for passing time in Atlantis and on Earth, was a bit more confrontational than I meant for it to be.

"It will stack with the passing time of the veil, do not worry." Oathbound's eyes were closed as he spoke and then he pointed to me. *"While you rest your physical body, your manifestation as a Vorna and your spirit will be able to cross the veil and inhabit a physical form on another plane."*

"How the hell is that possible?"

Guide smirked and explained, *"The veils have a nasty habit of speeding up or slowing down the timelines of individual planets or even galaxies to ensure that intelligent life cannot interact well, or interfere with each other."*

"The only reason we know about that is because of the vast amounts of time we've spent spanning the cosmos." Oathbound stared at the ground of Null as he spoke. *"You pick up a trick or two about time when you*

find out the people important to you thought you were dead because you were gone for hundreds of years when you thought it was only a decade or so."

Guide rolled his eyes and sighed. *"I keep apologizing for that, but I know how you hold a grudge."*

Oathbound smiled softly and cleared his throat. *"The place we mean to go has a rather large gap in time from this realm. With time as close to a standstill as it is here, and the difference of the veil taken into account, you should have all the time you need to train."*

I frowned. "You don't mean to come with us?"

"I am needed here to maintain the oath binding time." He grinned wider and clanked his shackles. *"I know you mean the subjects there, at least one, harm. Thus, if I go with you, I would be intentionally causing someone else harm."*

"But wouldn't it be the same if you stay here and do nothing?"

His grin widened. *"I am here to assist you in your training by giving you the gift of time. I have no way of knowing whether you will live up to your truth or not. By not acting, I am at the very least only minorly responsible for some harm, but I can deal with that discomfort. You make this journey of your own free will, I did not force you, and I am not telling you that you cannot go, or that you should go. I am only doing a favor for my brother and a newborn sibling."*

I nodded and joined Guide as he stepped past his brother and began to walk toward the slightly less-dark horizon line of Null and reached his hand back toward me.

Once my palm touched his, his fingers gripped my hand and *pulled* me along, through the stars and the shadows between, flitting past the births of new lights in the night sky until we passed something concerning.

I shouted against the wind and pulled, "What's that hole

there in the darkness? The one with purple cracks on the other side with all the debris?"

Without so much as even glancing back at it, Guide answered, *"That is where my brother War fell. Mortals challenged his truth and his armies' abilities and won. They destroyed him, and the loss was so great that it scarred the planet as he tried to pull them into the Null."*

"Why would he do that?"

He thought on it for a moment as we continued beyond it, then said, *"They had the aid of the oldest ones, and their avatars were mightier than even he, in all his mastery of his truth, could have imagined. They tore him apart and ended him—the scar he left on the planet eroding it to the point where the gods had to intervene to keep the corruption at bay."*

"How do you know all this?"

He smirked. *"The oldest ones cannot keep the prying eyes of their elders off them for long. And those who knew my brother best were paying attention."*

With that, he fell quiet and I had time to think to myself. *War. That name sounds familiar to me, but for more than just that they've mentioned him a few times to me. Where have I heard the name? And why does it feel so important?*

"Can others use the Null as a hub?" Thinking of Zeke, it seemed like the perfect way for him to get home. "I have a friend who's looking to get to his kids across the veil to… somewhere. I can't remember the name right now."

He stayed quiet and contemplative and I almost asked him what he was thinking about until our speeding flight came to a crawl. *"We pass through a thicker veil now. The time here is different and might even be faster than at the Null and your home planet. I am not certain. We will need to travel to another place if it does not stabilize."*

"How bad could it be?" He glanced back at me, his glowing eyes narrowing until I grunted, "Bad, got it."

He grimaced and pushed a clawed hand forward, nails scratching at the veil until something gave way and he grinned. *"We're through, but we will not have much time."*

I nodded, worrying slightly about my family back home, but if this meant I could keep them safer, I would do it happily.

"Where are we?"

"A place whose name I have long forgotten, but the people here are human and the like." Guide paused and frowned. *"Forgive me. I thought this was a more... uncivilized planet, but it seems they have discovered a manner of controlling the mana that permeates their environment and have created machines to assist their livelihoods."*

I gasped as we crested into the atmosphere above the planet and sure enough, they must have. It looked like something out of a steampunk novel gone mana-forged or something like that.

Massive flying monstrosities with moving parts, carrying huge blue or purple crystals in their centers, moved along the air currents as if like planes.

"Ah!" Guide clicked his fingers and grinned. *"I remember them calling it something like, Odjuret Asor, or something like that."*

"What will we do?" He frowned and tilted his head to the side. "You said the Huntsman rules here. I can't just go in and fight him, can I?"

"You could, if this were the place that I thought it still was. Now?" His glowering gaze girded my giddiness at the prospect of something happening swiftly. *"Now we will likely need to hunt them down. There are creatures here who you would do well to train yourself against, though, so we will begin there before truly looking."*

I smirked. "I can kill a few monsters, Guide."

He patted me on the shoulder and it felt like the most patronizing fucking thing anyone had ever done to me. *"Certainly you can, little brother. Certainly you can. Let's go test your mettle, shall we?"*

CHAPTER TWENTY-FOUR

I gasped and fell onto the ground, winded once again as the mana beast I'd been fighting began to dispel and leave its bounty behind.

"Three weeks," I grumbled to myself, exasperated. It took me *three fucking weeks* to manage to kill one of them. Every day, I would hunt one down and attack it, only to have it slip from my grasp because all of my spells and magical strength just didn't matter to it.

Hell, some of them had even grown stronger from eating my magical attacks and came seeking *me* out for a meal.

"You improve every day, little brother." To his credit, Guide watched every time I fought and then went to find information on where my opponent could be. His smirk was more and more infuriating every time I saw it and this was hardly any different. *"Do you mean to challenge another of them, or am I able to leave to hunt again? I think I'm getting close."*

I frowned at that, as he hadn't mentioned closing in on any information last night when he returned. "How close?"

He turned his gaze southward and spoke with confidence.

"I believe I have heard a rumor that they reside on another continent hidden in an almost-constant eclipse here."

I closed my eyes, trying to imagine what living in near-constant darkness would do for the ability to manipulate shadows that came with the Mantle of the Huntsman.

I grimaced and stood, walking over to the only evidence of my fight with the massive mana snail, a crystal the size of my fist, and grabbed it. Looking it over intently, I could feel the energy within it—mana.

Something shimmered on the ground and I grinned. It was gold and a ruby. They weren't very big, but as this was the first time I'd killed something since getting that benefit of Draconic Hoarding from my Mantle, I was still pleasantly surprised.

"Go ahead, I'll be okay on my own now." I pocketed the items for later and then turned to speak to the air, knowing he was gone already. "I'll just shift my form if it gets too heavy."

His forbidding me to use the Vorna form unless I felt like I was about to die had been the furthest thing from training I had expected.

If I was to train to battle gods themselves, then wasn't the idea to perfect my control over the form I had least control of?

His placations played over in my head. *"Your control of the form is abysmal because your control over your body is terrible. You rely on magic more than you rely on yourself."*

I didn't know how that could possibly be true since I had been using my body for more than thirty years, but he was the one training me, so I had to listen.

Now that he was gone though, I was free to hunt as I wished. There was no experience here without Galaxy to dole it out, so I would just focus on collecting as many materials as I could for my Mantle to absorb and then work on my control of my magic. Ice and shadow.

Calling my Mantle to me from the shadows at my feet so that it covered my hands in the gauntlets of my station was so much easier now, and as I walked through the forested area around me, I let it eat as it would.

Trees, rocks, the ground around me—everything.

After half an hour of devouring the world around me, I let the Mantle dissipate and walked on. The trees around me were a beautiful copper color through the leaves, the veins red like fire. They were absolutely stunning and practicing my shadow magic in the shade of their elegance was a highlight to my day now.

They led to the pond of water that I used as a place to bathe myself and I'd come to like the place. As I devoured the surroundings, it was slowly becoming an oasis in the slowly dwindling foliage of the forest.

Casting my focus outward to feel the shadows around me as I meditated, I found myself relaxing slowly. When I was home with my family, I operated from a place of fear for their safety, or from a frantic need to protect them.

Or rage. I chided myself for trying to self-delude the truth.

Those emotions and places had power, but operating from that calm place within me just felt more effective.

My left hand rose slightly so that I could turn it palm up to pull the shadows into it. I opened my eyes to find a small, swirling ball of shadows lazily floating in my grasp. As the leaves overhead shook and moved, swaying with the breeze, little tendrils of energy bled away from it as the sunlight struck it. Otherwise, it maintained the shape I focused on.

With a little more will, it shifted and formed a small spear, flickering and spinning so that I could look at all of it. Last month, I couldn't have done anything this complicated.

"Do you happen to know what happened to all of the materials around here?"

The shadows in my hand splashed coldly against my palm and then slithered back to where they'd come from as I turned my attention and focus on the person who stood next to the shore of the pond, the soft sediment at their feet crunching slightly as they paced toward me.

Their figure was covered in a golden cloak that looked like it was actually *made* of the precious metal. "Ew."

I blinked at that and they closed the distance. "Why are your eyes like that? Is it a modification that you've made? I've not seen one like it before."

It took me a second to realize that he was talking about my eyes, the Huntsman's eyes that didn't fade from my own anymore. I chuckled. "Definitely wasn't born with them."

I could just make out a mouth and chin on the inside of the hood and it was a thin line turned down at the corners. "I don't recognize that language either. Who are you?"

I could feel the Dominion radiating off this person, but as to what their power could be, I had no idea.

"I'm Marcus, and it's hard to believe that everyone would just recognize a language they're not used to, don't feel bad about it." I stood up slowly and brushed myself off. "I don't know what you mean about 'materials' though, sorry."

They stared at me calmly and cleared their throat. "That would be the case for many, yes." They nodded and turned toward the water again.

Play it cool, Marcus. Don't want to get into it with a god without Guide here to well… do his thing.

"The materials that grow here are a part of a special land tract given to the people of Alartha, the city nearby, in order to make their things." The figure moved over to a tree nearby and touch the bark. "They make things as offerings to the gods for a bountiful harvest, and the wood is used to make weapons to help them fend off the horrid creatures plaguing this planet."

They chuckled to themselves and said, their tone full of levity, "How strange that a massive swath of those materials disappeared in the blink of an eye, and here is someone with unrecognized modifications in the area of the crime and speaking a language that a god of the planet does not recognize."

I smirked softly. "That would be suspicious."

They clapped their hands, then pointed toward me, delightedly, "And unlike all the other mortals on this planet, you do not fall to your knees and prostrate yourself before the gods."

That made me raise an eyebrow. "Protocol has always eluded me without a clear rank structure."

"Protocol will be the least of your concerns, mortal." They waved a hand in my direction and gold sprang from the ground and trees around me, lashing out to grab me and hold me tight. "I have already summoned my right hand to me, and she flies here as we speak to kill you and take your corpse to my cousin for study."

They came closer, their smile hidden only partially by their cloak as they gloated. "Maybe I'll bless some of my followers with your kind of modifications."

They stood close enough to touch me now and reached out to grab my face with their hand partially covering my mouth. "You know, if you tell me what they do, I can have her be a little more gentle with you. Make your end swift?"

At this point, the molten gold had begun to cool and solidify. "I'm sorry, but they're attached. What does a god of gold like you have any interest in someone new for, hm? Are your cousins as crazed as you?"

They slapped me, and it didn't have any real power behind it from what I could see, but there was a sting that made me grit my teeth. "Mere gold? I am the god of *commerce*! Wealth! I am the Lord of Fortune and Luck!"

They laughed and sneered. "And what luck I have to have found a mortal who somehow made all the materials they'd send me disappear, with decent mods and no good sense to boot. Your luck must be shit."

Okay. No more being nice, Marcus. Time to share the truth with him.

"Well, Lord of Luck." Their attention flicked back toward me, and then something in the distance loosed an earth shattering roar that shook the ground and drew his attention.

I flexed my will and froze the gold on my body so fast and cold that the metal crackled and flaked off me. My truth raged through me and my body shifted as he turned around to catch my hand with his throat. My deeper voice growled, "Looks like your luck's just run out."

I pulled against the energy that prickled against my skin, yanking it through my skin into my very veins, and then drove my right hand straight into their stomach. From within the folds of the cloak, their body appeared and with it their life force. As I dug my hand up through the stomach into the chest cavity, the god cried out and began to try to form words.

"You don't... get to do this!" They gasped as I jerked them forward so that I could reach the heart. "Mortal! Stop, and I will let you go!"

I shook my head sadly and almost felt like I was mocking him and murmured, "I don't think you would, my friend. I truly don't. And I don't think your right hand will, either."

My fingers grasped their heart as I looked them in their eyes, the platinum gray of them pained and dulling slowly as my hand gripped and I pulled. "If you ever come back into existence, always remember that you could have left well enough alone at being curious. Your greed was your end."

I pulled their heart from their chest and threw it on the ground, to the sound of an eerily slow clap coming from behind me.

My head whipped around, expecting to find another challenger, and instead only found Guide in his human form. *"Excellently done! I knew that 'warning' would make you wary enough to be cautious, but brutally efficient. Now, the Dominion is still in the body, so all you have to do is completely pull it into yourself."*

I reached down and touched the body, seeing the aura around it flickering and guttering slightly like a candle preparing to go out.

Gathering the Dominion toward myself was easier now that the god's influence and mind were gone. It took me a few moments to truly pull the dregs into myself and then down into the area below my stomach called the Endless.

"Take a seat, and press your mind inward." Guide's

words were forceful and I shook my head, forcing him to frown. *"This is not optional, little brother. You must anchor the power within your own in order to obtain control over it."*

"Something is coming to do his bidding, and I'm going to kill it." I began to scan the horizon past the trees and the other Vorna just stared at me with confusion on his features. "He said he had something on its way to kill me."

His eyebrows shot up with surprise and he shot me a sly grin. *"Oh, I took care of that. I was getting hungry while I was waiting for you to kill the god so I made a bit of a snack of the sky leviathan that was coming to his aid. Sorry."*

Sky leviathan? I tilted my head at him as he pointed to the ground. "You were saying?"

I put my ass into the grass and sat there awaiting his instructions.

"To anchor the power and make it your own, all you must do is **lock** *it within the Endless within you."* He held a hand up to stop me from interrupting what he was saying to continue his lesson. *"Imagine your will forming a cage, or a pen of some sort. Within it, you place the Dominion—mind you, make it larger than you think you might need because the small amount you will have now will grow within you."*

I layered my focus around the nimbus of radiant golden energy writhing and floating within me and then began to push my will toward the Dominion. I began to build a fence of sorts around it with my mind. Envisioning a brick wall building around the skeletons of a wooden frame as quickly as I could manage to build it while keeping the energy firmly inside, and then another will touched my own.

Cold and calculating, this thought was deeper than the one that I'd been using. Less frantic and insightful, and more about getting the job done.

Swords of ice crashed into the stone that I'd begun to build and immediately created a barrier as crackling walls of light blue began to form like walls in the shapes of shields that touched the swords and the walls were set.

This was my power too, but I didn't think to use it this way. Would it stay?

"That was rather reckless, brother, but it will do." Guide leaned over me curiously and then smiled his humorously humorless smile as his hand touched my chest. *"It feels like it will remain cold forever. Interesting. Now, we go and search for the next lead and get away from this area."*

I grunted as I stood, sore for some reason. "Can they feel their sibling's death?"

He shrugged. *"Gods somehow always seem to know."* He flapped his wings and then turned to me with his grin in place. *"Allow me to take us to a more—well less —hospitable climate so that you can train some more. I do not think it wise for you to be going up against the Huntsman of this world just yet."*

"How are we on time?" I knew they could take care of themselves, but I was really starting to miss Galaxy and Cassia. Wondering if they were okay kept me up through the exhaustion most nights.

"It's likely been several hours on Earth, or days." He grunted and reached out to take my hand, ignoring my surprise and concern to force us into the air. *"Time is relative, brother. In the vast scope of eons that I have seen, you will see many as well—we hope."*

I called over the wind and noise, "My family needs me! They're in a place that could get them hurt with an enemy who tampers with the power of the gods!"

He called back without looking, *"Then it sounds like you need all the assistance you can get!"*

We rocketed through the air as the heavens fell behind us, lightning flashing as rain pounded the earth below and massive shadows plummeted through the clouds above and circled the area we'd been just seconds before.

Guide laughed and kicked his flight up a notch or two and it felt like the rain falling behind us was chasing us and then it was just gone.

"We escaped their notice, but let's not kill another god for a little bit, yes?"

I just nodded numbly and we shot off again.

———

Fury sliced through my thoughts at the display before me. An entire village destroyed and, in the lands surrounding it, monsters roamed unchecked.

We'd been on this new continent for weeks and I'd become much more adept at using my own strength to kill them, matching my cunning. There was a massive city not two hours from here with the capability to send soldiers to kill these beasts or at least collect the civilians to take them back for safety and security to wait out the onslaught.

But they didn't. No matter how much I didn't understand about this new world, I understood one thing—protecting the weak. And with nothing else to do, and all of my cries to return to my family and friends all but soundly ignored, I had to work and train under his stipulations. Like not using any actual weapons other than what I could make with my own power.

More than a dozen mana beasts the size of dinosaurs crashed their way lazily through the area and fought over the spoils of their attack, survivors screaming in a language I wasn't familiar with, but I understood the distress. The fear.

I glanced back in the direction I felt Guide hiding in and his almost imperceptible nod of permission sent me rushing forward.

I chose the largest and most brutish-looking one to begin my rampage against.

I crossed the hundred-yard distance with ease and crashed

into the monster with the wrath of a vengeful beast. My fist crashed into its lower jaw and a distinct, meaty cracking sound made me grin. Broken. Good.

I covered my fingertips in ice so cruelly sharp that it tore into the once-too-hard-to-puncture skin and aided me in pulling the massive chunk of muscle and mana-bone away from the top of the head. Blue-green blood splattered the ground and me as I threw it away, then launched myself back at it as soon as my foot touched the ground.

My hand soared through the bottom of its now-exposed upper jaw, then into the tiny brain above, killing it.

The others didn't react like normal scared monsters, they instead turned and rushed toward me to try to kill me and attain their place at the top of this new food chain.

Savage joy overwhelmed me as I rushed to meet them, a wave of mana and ice screeching from my outstretched right palm, the blood there turning to rime immediately.

Heavy, growing shards of ice peppered their hides with a bit of unfocused Dominion added to them to give them the piercing ability I needed. The golden energy sliced through their mana-hides like money could slice through most of life's problems and put three of them down, injuring another two.

The remaining whole monsters trampled the injured to get to me, killing one of them. I grimaced and stomped on the ground next to the shadows of the beasts and tore their shadows from them, creating a lance that I imbued with Dominion to stab some of them.

I hit three of them with ease and sliced another's back leg as it dropped a horned head to gore me.

I roared wildly and grabbed the horns, using the monster's momentum to carry me onto its head and then its shoulders so I could kick it in the spine. I covered my heel in a spike of blood and ice and drove it into the monster's spine, ending it.

Two fully healthy monsters then tried to run off, but I summoned my will and cast Embodiment of Lightning and appeared in front of them with a shield of ice ready.

I clobbered one fully in the face, driving it to the ground and tripping the other. Using the sharp edge of the shield like a shovel, I drove it into the first one's neck and then once more covered my arms in ice with god power to cut into the flesh.

By the time I finished with them, I was covered in blue-green gore and walked steadily over to the heavily injured survivor of the raid. It saw me, eyes widening in fear as I stalked toward it, shadows leaping into my upturned palm.

Once I had enough, I shot the shadow energy into the eye closest to me and pierced the brain. As the monsters dissipated, I gathered the spoils of my victory.

Mounds of gold with the mana cores slightly larger than usual, likely a part of the power of the Dominion within me. Ever since I obtained it, Draconic Hoarding had become insanely profitable.

I observed the surviving civilians as they collected themselves and began to journey out of their hiding places and ruined buildings. There were only a few who weren't horrendously injured, but other than basic first aid, I had no real way to get them the help they desperately needed.

"You are not responsible for them, Massacre." The Vorna instructor floated next to me suddenly and smiled. *"What?"*

"Why are these monsters so hard to kill again? And how come I'm having such a shit time with them, but that god was a cake walk?"

Guide closed his eyes and shook his head. *"The god was taken mercilessly by surprise. The first one is usually the one who is complacent, and I made certain that they were weak before allowing them to corner you."* His feet touched the ground and he took a deep breath. *"These creatures are imbued with power that that god was not. Dominion is a lot easier to steal for us. Mana? Aether? Not so much. Besides, I think it is time for us to make another escape to our goal."*

I grimaced. "No more training—I need to return; we should go directly to our target."

He dipped his chin in thought and I was about to snarl at him that it was my choice but he consented and said, *"I agree. You have learned much and very quickly. I will fly us to our starting destination while you focus on recovering your Dominion."*

I reached my hand out and he grasped it, taking off as the rain began to build once more over our head.

The gods had been chasing us all over the continent the last week, trying to figure out what we were and to end the threats we represented. Guide had done the majority of sensing them first, only because his ability to do so had millennia of practice and outstripped mine at every turn. Though I was becoming steadily more and more aware of Dominions and the gaze of various gods on the planet and how to avoid them.

I cast my mind inward and focused on the tenets of the Dominion inside me. Wealth. Commerce. Luck. Risk and reward.

I'd never really thought about traditional commerce before. Capitalism being how I was raised, I was familiar with it, but it wasn't to the point where I had a steady grasp of the things that *made* money. Just how supply and demand worked and whatnot.

I'd thought I was rich before all this with the money I was earning from bartending at the High Table, but the gold I had now? Sheesh.

The Vornal act of recovering a Dominion was to reflect on what it meant and how it could interact with your truth. With my battle-focused truth, money didn't really have too much of an effect on what I could do, other than getting me better gear, but with Draconic Hoarding, I could earn more money killing.

The more I Massacred, the more cheddar I earned from it. And with that cheddar, I could do the things that made fighting easier.

There was the luck aspect of it too. I could get the drop on my enemies, they could lose their footing, or just have shittier luck than me.

I watched internally as the golden Dominion of the god I'd killed—my Dominion—began to refill itself, the golden pool of power, tinged slightly with the crimson of my own power, began to swirl and grow deeper and fuller.

It would take several hours to become what it was, and several days of true introspection to be able to get past what I had now. I'd been working on it to get the energy to more of what I wanted it to become.

"Hey Guide?" The Vorna twitched his head to let me know he was listening, so I said, "How many Dominions can a Vorna safely hold?"

He laughed and called back, ***"It is called the 'Endless' for a reason, Massacre. There have been Vorna who have devoured entire pantheons before and have been perfectly fine to devour more. Why do you ask?"***

I frowned and answered honestly, "There's someone in Atlantis tampering with the power of their gods and if I can take that power from them somehow, we could fight them better, right?"

He nodded, staying quiet long enough for me to add, "Do the gods' powers interfere with one another?"

That made him laugh again. ***"Oh yes."*** He flew in silence for a short time and then spoke again. ***"Some can interfere, but others can have a slight effect on the applications of others. For instance, if you were to devour a god of battle, your Dominion of luck and commerce would feed it power because that is how your Truth is making it work. Others will overlap slightly, and some will oppose the ones you have. All it takes is practice to keep them handled."***

I offered a serene nod and did my best to fall back into focusing on it, but his next words brought me out of it, ***"You could also deepen the power if you find a similar enough Dominion to merge the two together. Could be*** *fun to mix and match, though I am not as practiced in that."*

That gave me pause. *I can make all of these better somehow?* "Who would be?"

He thought about it for a while and said nothing. After traveling for more than an hour, he finally muttered, *"I do not know right now."*

I nodded and said, "Thank you for the honesty." He dipped his chin and on we flew, him transporting us over the mass of water below us and me focusing on restoring the whole of my Dominion.

CHAPTER TWENTY-FIVE

The view from above the continent we would be invading next was stunning. Darkness swept the land as a moon floated between the planet and the sun, swept through the gravity at the exact strength and speed of the rotation of the planet around its sun. It was weird for the place to be exposed to no light whatsoever and yet it was still so lush and covered with growth.

Pale plants the same ivory of bone sprouted from the ground. Trees with thick, armor-like bark grew sparsely but they were massive.

"Is this some kind of necropolis or something?"

I didn't realize I'd spoken out loud until Guide responded, ***"I do not know, but this place is filled with creatures under the influence of the Huntsman who resides here."***

Sure enough, there were beasts and people below covered in various scraps of shadow milling about beneath us, living their own lives. Collecting plants, fighting each other, farming. It was rather disconcerting how disjointedly they moved and operated whatever it was they were doing.

"Can you sense something wrong with them?" The question was out of my mouth before I even realized I was asking it.

He didn't answer and instead flew us lower and then I saw it. Where the bands of shadow were, there was a dark energy surrounding it, and it looked to be linked to each and every being the shadows touched.

"Put me down, I want to see something."

The smiling Guide turned back toward me and said, *"As you wish."*

He flew me slightly lower still and the beasts and people began to notice me and make noise. Not normal noises either, a keening sort of scream that spread faster and faster to the surrounding area for almost a mile.

Guide dropped me and I plummeted toward them all, shifting my form so that I could use my wings to glide to the ground safely and shifted back. This shift was where the first wave of denizens rushed me. The creatures, people, and monsters didn't look normal at all, or like there was anyone home behind their eyes. Just mindless drones living a false life.

"Massacre!" I turned to look at Guide and he smiled. *"All weapons not created by you are now available to you here, but try to last without them. Think of this as a minor graduation of sorts."*

I grimaced and pulled my magic into myself and then built an ice scythe in my right hand. If I had my actual weapon, this would have been *so* much easier. But alas, I had to settle with kicking ass this way and if killing these things freed them from the adversary, so be it.

A hand touched my shoulder and I moved. My whole body shifted at the hips and my scythe sliced anything and everything in its way.

The sound of coins and other things hitting the ground made me grin, as I'd been right. *All of these creatures are under their control, but aren't summoned and worthless.*

As I surveyed the carnage I'd left around me, I grinned wider. *And they aren't protected like the other creatures are.*

There were still mana cores here to collect as well!

"Oh, this is going to be *fun*."

More shadow-touched people and monsters flooded toward me, and I welcomed the tidal wave of funds that I was about to be flooded with with open arms and a gleeful swing of my weapon.

The sea of bodies parted after a few moments and then something I wasn't expecting showed up. A massive drake, almost like Mako, but this one was longer through the body and less muscular.

Instead of the fodder allowing this new monster to attack me on its own, they rushed in first as it came in behind them.

The tactic was beautiful and if it hadn't been for the fact that I was prepared for it, I'd likely have been overwhelmed. Instead, everything around me ended up with shards of ice and shadow impaling them for twenty feet in every direction.

Their blood froze in their bodies and the larger creature crept over them, noisily stomping their corpses like autumn leaves crunched on the pavement.

I dipped under its furious swipe and attacked its stomach with my scythe, the long body twisting as the front portion landed. It moved just far enough to avoid the worst of the attack but it didn't avoid the whole thing.

Blood splattered the ground and immediately a noxious fume billowed.

I grimaced and covered myself with my Mantle. The armor and helm covered me and helped keep it from being too much for me, but it immediately made me feel nauseated.

My body moved on its own and I knew it was because the Mantle was trying to keep me from being hit. The scythe in my hand sliced to my right and more poisoned blood spilled from the draconic beast.

Its fanged mouth opened wide and a pearlescent beam of light began to circle inside its jaws before it blasted toward me.

I pulled the shadows up from below me and then crafted a thick shield of ice to back it. The beam ate through the shadow and then slammed into the ice and bounced off, slicing in half some of the other creatures that flooded forward.

That shit looked like moonlight, but how?

I didn't have time to focus on it as it was charging it again.

I repaired the shield once more and added a lip to it that made it almost like a bowl and rushed forward.

The blast crashed into the shield and hit the center, then refracted up toward the lip and bounced once more toward the ground. I changed the angle of it as it clattered forward, still breathing the attack, and hit the monster with it.

It screamed, its scales shimmering as the light touched it and then glared at me hatefully.

The shadows around me grew darker as I realized what was happening. The light from the eclipse was actually making it stronger and when the attack had hit it, it was only surprised.

And I had an idea of how to counter it. The shadows around us deepened further as I prepared my trap and threw the shield in front of myself and waited.

The weird dragon-like creature glared hatefully at me and then at my shield and I shook it a bit, yelling, "Come on, I'm on a schedule!"

The creature didn't move, so I threw my arm out and used Void Frost to create a spear behind it and jammed it into its flank. The long drake screamed and whirled, slashing at the attacker and I grinned.

It turned around and I waggled my shield again. "You come to me, or I come to you. I was serious about the time crunch."

It hissed and stalked forward, keeping itself low to the ground to the point that I could hear its stomach dragging on the earth. I had to remind myself about my plan to keep from impaling it with shadows from below and instead began crafting my next weapon.

As soon as it was close enough, the shadows sprang up and cloaked us both in the darkness I thought would cut it off from its power source.

The beast panicked, the breath weapon charging as it

swiped at me. I used Bolt Havoc to cloak the shield in lightning and threw it away from myself.

The monster launched its attack, planting its feet on the ground and jutting its head toward the former protective object. The ice splintered and shattered as the light and heat stressed it too much to keep its form. Then I struck.

The ice sword I'd been making behind the shield stabbed into its underarm, driving toward the chest and the heart on the other side of it.

Instead of using the weapon the way it was meant to be, I once more cast Bolt Havoc to drive lancing lightning through it and then burst the weapon so shrapnel scattered inside it.

The monster screamed again and this time shadows poured into its throat and spread wide in the esophagus, then became a saw. The creature whined once before the head sheared off and fell to the ground where it stood.

A sigh of relief whooshed from me and then I let the shadows fall as the mass of wealth and power began to churn from the creature's dead form to create something different. A much larger crystal, egg-like in shape, formed rather than a mana core.

I picked it up and felt thrumming life within it. "You know, Guide, this is a first."

The Vorna came to me instantly and observed it. *"I can imagine it is. That could be the manifestation of your new Dominion's luck aspect."*

His gaze fell to the gold and platinum below us at my feet and he grinned. *"What do you mean to do with your vast wealth, little brother? You do know that this is not a physical form you can take things back to, correct?"*

My mouth twitched, edging toward a frown, but I had known the likelihood of being able to keep things like this was low. It would be too good for me.

"If I can't take it with me, I'll consume it." I eyed the egg-like stone and he took it from me. "Hey!"

"I will hold on to this for you, Marcus, and see that

it gets to your true body." His grin grew as he observed it. *"Another reward for your cunning."*

I nodded and let the shadows around us fall to reveal the rest of my warmup. "Lemme take care of these guys real fast."

He dipped his chin and stood back as I created another scythe of ice and launched myself forward to carve my name in this world through blood and violence.

It took half an hour more of unmitigated, unrestrained violence to cull the monsters and people attached to the Huntsman from this realm in the area. That was, however, just this area—there were still miles and miles of living beings in this portion of the world that felt like they were connected to the thing. It would take days to kill all of them, and even longer after that to scour the continent to ensure they were all gone. I didn't want to waste that time.

Once I did end them all, I piled my winnings in a single area. Coins, gold, silver, copper, platinum—bars of precious metals, woods, and small trinkets made of material I had no idea of, scattered into a large pile taller than me.

I did the same thing for the cores I'd collected, dropping them into a large pile so that the varying sizes all mingled together and clattered as they collided. It was oddly satisfying to something within me to see them all piled in such a way. Especially in an area I had just taken through force for myself.

"Time for another lesson, Massacre."

I turned my gaze from my growing hoard and found him standing between me and my gold. My gaze narrowed at him dangerously, but he continued to watch me, unfazed by my glare.

"Gods have things their Dominions like. War gods like battle and thrive off the souls of lives taken in combat." He moved his hands and motioned around us. *"No doubt this area would be a feast for those with that sort of desire if these creatures still had their souls. Crafter gods, gods of making and cleverness would be*

content and fed by smiths, jewelers, those plying a craft or trade they made with their hands."

I frowned, trying to follow his logic, but only coming back to the fact that he was between me and my spoils.

He stepped away from my gold and I relaxed a bit more, finally able to think, then he said, *"Give me the gold."*

"What?"

He held up a hand to stop me from advancing on him and explained, *"Gold sacrificed to a god of wealth holds more weight than regular gold. I mean to offer it to you so that you can gain more from it."*

I frowned and growled, "You mean it?" He nodded and I had to think about it for a long, long while. Finally, I grumbled sullenly, "Fine, take it."

He nodded, then went and touched it, pulling a single large coin from the pile and turned to me. *"God of Wealth, may this sacrifice honor you and bring you strength as you face the coming trials that lay ahead of all creation."*

He turned back to the pile and swiped a mass of coins toward me and bellowed, *"Take this offering as a sign of respect, and bestow upon me what gift you can."*

The coins that would have pelted me disappeared in a wave of precious metal dust as they swooshed toward me, a cloud of it billowing around me like a sandstorm. The pile began to lift and spin with it, the powder soon crowding closer to my skin as it did.

"Open your Dominion to it, Massacre, and take it into yourself. The rest will come naturally."

I dipped my chin and pulled a sliver of my Dominion from the Endless within me and pooled it into the palm of my right hand. As soon as it was free of my flesh, the cloud of precious metal surged into the golden energy and continued to do so for long seconds until it was all gone.

Once it was all gone, the power bucked and tried to free itself, but I clamped down on it with my will and yanked it back into myself.

Once it rejoined the rest of the Dominion, there was a creaking and crackling within me that was wholly unfamiliar. The power brushed up against the walls that confined it and they began to crack under the pressure. Rather than reinforcing the walls, I willed them to remain and then made another icy outer wall reinforced with my power and will. Thicker and stronger than ever before and designed to contain anything that touched it.

The brewing, potent power inside the first wall broke through the ice like water from a shattered dam. It rushed the new outer walls and as soon as it touched them, shrank back as if seared somehow.

From within the writhing energy there was a call—an order almost—to bless the one who gifted us this power.

Symbols and runes I didn't understand flashed before me and began to swirl and I smiled. It was like a lottery.

"Bless you, Guide."

One of the golden symbols etched in fire rushed forward and a bit of my Dominion's strength leached from me to enforce the blessing.

He smiled. *"Thank you."* He motioned to the pile that remained. *"And the same for this one?"*

I shook my head. "I mean to feed all this to my Mantle."

He appeared surprised but said nothing as I called the weapon to myself and began to wade into the pile.

Consumable materials identified. Would you like to consume them? Yes / No?

I selected yes and the first few cores disappeared into my palms.

Mana-rich substance consumed.

Three quarters of the way through the pile, the notification I had been hoping would populate came.

Mana Siphon — While wearing the Mantle, the user's mana recovers faster than normal.

I grinned, leaving the Mantle on as I stared down at the rest of the bounty before me. I hadn't done this in some time, so the likelihood that something good came of it was iffy, but it would be worth a shot.

I took one of the smallest mana stones and put it into my mouth to eat, letting Galaxy's power do with it what it would.

But nothing happened.

"That was an odd thing to do. Were you expecting something?" Guide came over to me and picked up a slightly larger core and plopped it onto his tongue, pulling into his mouth and chewing until there was a decidedly violent crunch. He grimaced and swallowed it before growling, *"It tastes like old souls smell. That was horrible, but did you gain anything from it?"*

I shook my head and sighed. "Hopeful, as always." I held a hand out and plucked another one out of the pile that was a little larger and a slightly different color. "Let's try again maybe?"

I repeated the action, the flavor much worse this time, and I actually got a bit of a scare trying to choke it down, but still nothing happened. This time I just devoured the rest of them with the Mantle and offered Guide one last one but he shook his head and waved a hand at me. *"I fear it will not agree with me."*

I shrugged and allowed the Mantle to consume it with all the others it had eaten.

I shook myself out and stretched as my mana continued to replenish faster than it ever had and then looked to Guide. "You know where we're headed?"

He dipped his head and then jutted his chin in a northward direction.

"How far?"

He smiled. *"Not too far for someone with the powers of a god, but I realize that you've said you're on a 'schedule'?"*

I nodded and he simply smiled wider and rushed forward to grab me so that I could be flown to where we were headed expeditiously. There were *thousands* of creatures and humanoids heading toward where we'd come from and they looked ready for a fight, if my eyes were to be believed.

"Glad that we skipped that mess. Though it would have given you a severe bump in power if we could have taken the time."

I frowned at that. "You know, I have to say this—the longer I'm around you, the more human you sound." I looked up at him from where I hung from his grip. "Why?"

He flew on for a long while and then finally admitted, *"I also learn from the Vorna I am around."* He flapped his wings and the glided for a short time. *"As the Guide, it is my duty to be able to learn new paths for those I may meet. Until I met you, I had thought that I had met the last of our kind. I am delighted to be able to continue learning and passing on our knowledge and power."*

I nodded at that, the sentiment rather nice, but the Vorna didn't strike me as the type to be that way and I said as much.

His smile appeared to me to be almost sad as he turned back to me. *"Someone has to care for the monsters, Massacre."*

I nodded, considering how they addressed each other as if they were all siblings—even me. It was disarming and settling at the same time.

The clouds passed so swiftly below as he flew on, leaving me with those thoughts. He was right, in a way. Someone did have to care for the monsters.

The High Table had been doing it for who knew how long, and now that the mythological world's secret was out, there was so much just *not* being done for the monsters. They were people too, in a way.

With what the U.S. and some of the other countries were trying to do, there was a chance at them getting citizenship. Was that okay?

If they became citizens, could I kill them if they stepped out of line?

Had it bothered me to do so before? I frowned at the thought of it. Murder. Killing bad people, mainly, but still it was murder.

This isn't the time to be thinking about this, Marcus. We flew over a massive swath of bone-white plants, some of which bore a small, round, dark fruit.

Attractive as the idea to drop in and consume them all was, the scenery changed drastically to an almost wetland kind of place. Skeletal remains remained in bogs and pits that had been picked clean by bone-white versions of crows with wicked-looking beaks on their faces and glimmering green eyes.

In the middle of the nightmarish bog was a fortification. It was low, as if it would sink into the ground if it were too heavy. Along the tops of the walls every twenty to thirty feet stood a guard with what very clearly resembled a rifle, long barrels with sights on them.

"Fuck, I could've been killing people with guns this whole God damn time!"

That garnered special attention from the guards and on the corners of the structure, two behemoth launchers rose out from below the lip of the wall and loudly clanked and clacked as their caretakers turned them in our direction.

My eyes widened and I bellowed, "Fuck me *sideways*!" I clawed at the Vorna holding me, my fingers gripping his grasp. "Drop me—drop me on them, God damnit!"

He chuckled darkly as the first projectile screamed from the launcher and speared through the air directly at me. I shouted a few colorful expletives and kipped myself forward to avoid the shot.

My feet grazed the first one as the second one speared toward me and I had an idea.

"Good luck storming the castle, little brother!" Guide called as he let go, the second spear closer now.

I put my foot out and used the weapon's momentum to push me upward and onto Guide's back as I grinned and growled, "Thanks."

I heard him grunt as I leapt with my full strength, launching myself at the closest guard and his weapon.

They were skilled, a small round slicing against the outside of my quadriceps on my left leg. It stung, but it wasn't enough to stop me from grasping the end of his rifle and slamming the buttstock into his head hard enough to cave his head in.

The butt of the weapon was bent and useless now, but there were others to use.

I pulled the rudimentary trigger after aiming at the guard closest to my position. I pointed the muzzle center mass and there was a click and then nothing.

Growling in frustration, I jerked the weapon back and spun, throwing it at the guard behind me as I threw a barb of ice at the one I'd wanted to shoot.

The weapon spun and clobbered him, his shot going wide as ice shattered on the other. One fell over the wall inside and the other was frozen and fell backward.

Weapons cocked and I ducked, ice forming around me as a volley of fire-belching weapons sent a wave of metal at me.

The ice chipped as it thickened, some of the projectiles pinged away, but I wasn't shot and that was the good part. I burst upward, icy shrapnel blasting away from me as I launched myself into the air.

The ones who weren't hit reloaded, and the ballistae runners turned the weapons inward to try to spike me.

Rather than wait, I covered myself in my Mantle and roared, grasping the shadows of the world around me, the guards' own, and used them to attack. Shadows sharpened where they sat and then reared up as spikes and pierced them through their chests and necks.

The ones who faded left behind tinkling coins and goodies. The ones who didn't were too injured to offer much resistance as I walked the edge of the wall, killing them all.

My mana steadily returned the more I wore the Mantle and it brought a savage smile to my lips.

As I looked into the courtyard below, I was concerned to see that there was an entire platoon of soldiers below. Two, actually, that stood in the center as they just watched me.

Their armor looked almost mechanical and as I kept looking at them, they moved aside. With accurate and drilled steps, they parted and left an opening for someone to leave the interior of the place to address me. As I watched them moving below me, the man called up, "Stranger, the Huntsman will see you if you will but cease your attack."

I recognized this one, through my own Mantle. This was Arden's equivalent rank. Someone important and likely stronger than the riff raff out here.

I nodded silently and jumped down with ease, landing in the stones of the courtyard with a crunch. The man in more ornate armor than the others bowed his head and motioned. "Please, follow me."

I dipped my chin and did as he bid, content to observe and if anything so much as had the vaguest sense of a trap, I would kill everyone.

The walls inside were the same dull gray as the outside, there being little light in here.

Through the long hallway we walked, and nothing stuck out to me as a trap, allowing me to observe my surroundings. Still gray stone and nothing.

At the end though, there was a room twice as large as my own with a slit of glass high above that enhanced the little light available outside, making this room remarkably well-lit.

Where the bar of almost solid light hit, there was a throne that appeared to be attached to a coffin made of a silvery stone that for some reason reminded me of the moon with its craters and divots. The way it sparkled and caught the light was truly beautiful to me.

Upon the throne sat a woman of gray skin with silvery hair and fine—if not pinched—features.

She leaned back against the stone of the coffin and offered a small, tame wave of her hand at the wrist. "Welcome to the Moonlit Sepulcher, stranger."

I dipped my head, my horns drifting lower from my Mantle's helm.

She observed me calmly for a moment, content to see if I would speak, and when I didn't, a soft smile spread lazily across her features. "I do not know why yet another Huntsman can exist in this same realm; I thought I was the only one. I do not know how, either, and that annoys me, but to that end, I can see that you at least are competent."

I let my head loll to the side and she smiled wider. "This continent has been my home for quite some time after the technology of the populace here made it impossible to rule through might. Now, I simply rule through the shadows, pulling the strings of the puppets I want to maneuver as a means of entertainment." She tilted her head in a mirror of my movement and raised a thin, silver eyebrow. "I've heard the gods are displeased about something. Do they seek you?"

I remained quiet. If she knew that, she might be able to call them here and screw me into fighting against all of them.

"The brooding type?" She sighed sadly and I almost snickered; that wasn't me at all. "I have a sneaking suspicion that it's you they're upset about. But if I were to take you into the fold, they wouldn't dare touch you for fear of me. For fear of *us*."

She stood, her clothes shimmering in the light as the motion caught the beam just right. It could have been a practiced effect for all I knew, but she held up her fist. "For too long I have operated in the shadows, content to bide my time and allow the gods their due—no more. With the two of us, we can rise up and keep them in check. Maybe even join them as deities to the pathetic mortals of this realm."

She smiled and closed her eyes. "All you need do is join hands with me and choose the right side."

That made me grin beneath the helm I wore and she frowned at my continued silence. She must have taken it as uncertainty. "Well? What will you choose?"

For the first time, I spoke and fully let the Huntsman's Mantle take my voice as I said, "I choose *massacre*."

CHAPTER TWENTY-SIX

The guards in the room swarmed me, the walls themselves coming alive to the point that I genuinely thought the stone had been able to move. The camouflaged armor even had the blocky build of the wall behind it and looked like bricks.

The eight of them that rushed me took spears of shadow to the chest and I flung their bodies away from me in my eagerness to get to my counterpart. As she stood bathed in the light of the moon, her Mantle worked upward over her and she grew to a horrendous size.

The armor that covered her from head to toe made mine look like it may as well have been made out of papier mâché and was just as beautiful as the light that played off it.

She reached into the light and pulled from it a great sword that would make this room a whole lot roomier as soon as she started swinging it.

The thought of her trying to do that, the bulk of her captivating and almost-pearlescent armor hindering her movement, made me grin, and the fight was on.

The sword dissolved as soon as she swung it and I moved

forward only to find myself flying back down the hallway I'd come through.

The doors broke my fall, taking my breath as she followed along behind me. Her voice was no less terrifying than my own could have been as she hissed, "I will reward my men with your Mantle and take my fight to this world and others on my own."

I grimaced at that and took my feet, standing cautiously. "That's some neat trick you got there."

There was a savage glee in her voice as she stated, "Yes, it is. It took decades to learn it and I am *good* with it."

With her last statement, she hefted her sword and swung it at me and I disappeared, using Embodiment to move instantly in front of her, then thrust my hand forward and hit her with a fist covered by dark ice and a dribble of Dominion.

The spikes over my knuckles drove through the armor and as she scuttled backward six feet, I smiled. The blood covering the ice froze swiftly and my gaze drew up to where she watched me from behind her visor. "Same."

She stomped her foot and suddenly everyone in the vicinity stilled, her words echoed throughout the air around me as she hissed, "Commence the Hunt."

My eyes widened with the words she spoke and with them the world around me got a whole hell of a lot more crowded. It was like the Wild Hunt under her control just faded into my immediate personal space.

Luckily, I'd been preparing to fight hordes of monsters and people.

A radiating cold leaked from me, then blasted outward, freezing the warriors reaching for me on the spot. The sword flashed again, disappearing slightly in the light and lack of, as if it edged between the two and sliced through the group in front of me.

This time I was ready and watched as the glimmer of the moonlight passed through the metal of the sword and jumped backward. The very tip of the blade sliced my hip and I grimaced at that but pressed some of my Dominion into it to heal it slightly. A neat trick the Vorna and the gods could do.

The blade whirled back and I followed it around and toward the one swinging it. The other Huntsman was skilled, that was for certain. As soon as she realized that I would be making another attack, she lashed out with her foot and almost caught me in my shoulder with her heel.

I dipped under it and stabbed my clawed fingers into her hamstring and immediately cast Void Frost into the wound to sever the muscles and tendons there. The magic surged from my fist and into her wound and her Mantle pressed it back until I growled and shoved harder.

It cost me more mana to do so, but it was worth it, as her leg was now immobilized.

Her master sergeant equivalent joined the fight and swung a massive hammer at me, the head of it connecting with my shoulder hard enough that the muscle displaced painfully. The blow knocked me aside and I had to watch in frustration as the knightly man reached over and healed her wound before beginning to limp himself.

He can take the injuries of others? That's cool. Wish we had someone like that on our team. Maybe it's time to do some recruiting?

Now I knew what I had to do as the Huntsman set herself back up to summon more of her Hunt to her. I created a scythe out of shadows and whirled it in front of me dramatically as the hammer-wielding knight hobbled toward me. Hefting it into the air to swing it, I brought my left foot forward and swiped at him with it, missing him by more than a dozen feet.

"Missed me, faker." He started to charge and the shadows tangled his feet together and tripped him, making him fall onto his face so that I could pounce.

Once the blade of shadow and Dominion sliced him from mid-back to his shoulder by his neck, I offered a sardonic bow and said, "Healer dies first, sorry."

Every instinct within me roared for me to move, my body twisting impossibly to the point that I actually lost my footing as the massive great sword the Huntsman wielded stabbed through where my chest had just been as she screamed.

"How dare you kill one of mine!" She went berserk. Her sword moved to a rhythm that only she knew and wove a tale of death so broad and long that I was almost cut in half twice before I used Embodiment to get myself out of her immediate reach. As soon as I disappeared, she snarled and stabbed her sword into the ground where I had attacked her before.

If I'd gone there to attack her again, I would have been split in half, but instead I was up on the wall and heard the commotion outside. Risking a glance, my blood ran cold. "Fuck."

Monsters—beasts of all shapes and sizes—played horsey with the populace of this place and they all wore shadow armor just like the rest of her horde of followers. The riders egged the monsters on as they all came to her defense here in this small fort. Hounds ran ahead of them, their snarling visages almost enough to remind me of my branch of service's namesake earned in Belleau Wood. Their red eyes and slavering jaws sending a chill down my spine.

A war of attrition was not how I would win this fight. They would whittle me down until there was nothing left of me and she would take my Mantle for her own. I couldn't allow that. This had to end now and it would take a lot out of me to do it.

"My army is impressive, is it not?" The words sent another chill down my spine as her voice sounded closer than it should have.

I whipped around and crossed my arms as the fist connected with my forearms and launched me backward into the outer wall that the guards could've hid behind when I first came to assault the place.

My head rang loudly as I tried to stand back up, her casual walk toward me concerning. "Had you but joined me, we could use this army to march on the gods themselves after taking their precious faithful as our own." The sneer in her voice made the sorrow sound mocking more than anything else. "Now, I'm going to kill you."

No time like the present to give things a shot.

I stood up and pressed forward toward her, hoping to lure her into a close-up fight. I made a thick shield of ice on my left arm and a spear in my right hand made of shadow and began to dance forward like I was going to try to take her head on. She hefted that massive sword and as she swung at me from well outside my reach, I threw the shield down at her feet and it shattered as I threw the spear straight at her, summoning my Dominion to cast Bolt Havoc. Golden energy that smelled vaguely of melting gold leapt from my outstretched hand as her sword swung.

The god-energy-enhanced spell surged into the metal and made her scream as she had to let it go, but the damage was done.

Her hands smoked as I launched myself under her loosed weapon, grabbing the handle and twisting the heavy sword in the air to shove it into her. Spears of darkness rushed from below her, and the ground at her feet and even up her legs froze solid.

Her injured, smoking hands clapped onto the sides of the sword and stopped it from spearing through her, but it was just a feint. The real threat she faced was me appearing behind her with my fist covered in both ice and shadow. My fingers glowed golden with Dominion as they shredded through her armor and Mantle like it was butter and then I reached her rib cage.

She screamed and stomped, more of her people appearing closer, but I paid them little mind as I gripped her ribs and *yanked* with all of my considerable strength.

Bones broke and snapped outward and then I dove into her elbow deep, gripping her heart in my hand in a now-practiced motion. I used the Dominion coursing through my body to cast Embodiment straight into the sky and took her with me.

The weight of her body and armor tugged at me and I just held onto her as the people below me began to try to mount a rescue somehow. Flying monsters launched into the air as her last breath rattled from her body. Her heart's last pumping beats in my palm fed the urge to just end it and collect the bounty that I had been promised.

So I did.

Her heart crushed in my hand as if I was squeezing a tomato and I received the message I wanted.

You have touched the Mantle of another Huntsman. Would you like to take it into your own?

The way the question was posed might have been different, but my answer was the same. "Yes."

The air around me whipped furiously as my Mantle edged down my arms toward the one that still covered her body and began to devour it as I slowly fell toward the ground and the enemies below.

Memories flooded through me like last time, but this instance was a lot tamer. As if I knew what I was doing and looking for.

She had taken the Mantle for herself from her master who had brought her into the Wild Hunt and who had become complacent. As a servant of the moon goddess, a priestess for her dark mother, she was able to bend the light and use it with the darkness the Mantle commanded to great effect.

Armies razed and the world was hers until the gods decided it was time to relegate her to the darkness. She was allowed to flee.

Dishonored and wounded, she spent centuries honing her Mantle's power to the point that she was able to grow her influence and power to keep a constant tether on her subjects. With her Mantle's power, she could summon them to her at will, or just make shadow creations of them that could fight and do basic things.

After that, her campaign against the continent she had been exiled to began, and when it was complete, she would march on the other lands, or go somewhere else if she could. Anything to leave this place she had come to loathe.

"You certainly played that fast and loose, little

brother." Guide laughed as he caught me and hefted me into the air once more.

I was about to respond with equal sarcasm to his teasing when the voice in my head let me know things were finished.

Assimilation complete. Additional powers of the Huntsman's Mantle have been converted and added to your own.

Masquerade spell added to the user's repertoire. Assimilating with the user's system.

"A spell?" That caused me to tilt my head. I'd been willing to sacrifice whatever proficiency I would be gifted from it to get better with my magic, but if this was the case, I would be able to potentially gain a lot more if I found other Huntsmen and their Wild Hunts to devour.

"Spell?" Guide asked curiously as he continued to heft me into the air. ***"Spell what? Did you need to stay here any longer? The gods have sensed something amiss and are coming."***

I glanced down at the amassed army and watched from this distance as the bands of shadows faded and from the confusion on their faces, it was apparent that they were free now. And with that freedom came a fight that would likely make rivers of blood.

Monsters turned on the humanoids with them and the weapon-toting people did their best to fight back with what they had, but it was just a slaughter.

"No, Guide. I think it's time I head back to mine."

With a terse nod, he smiled and off into the stars we went.

Flying back took less time this go around, the Null known to us on an almost instinctual level. Almost like how some people just always seem to know which way was north, it was just how Vorna felt. Even as we flew toward it, I could *feel* that it was closing toward us.

"Now that you have the power of a god, Massacre, you will be known to other gods." Guide's words were softly spoken, almost as if in warning. *"I assume that you will also have the ability to know where they are or, at the very least, when they are close to you. I would recommend not killing too many if you plan to stay on Earth."*

I snorted and said, "Yeah, the ones there tend to frown upon that happening."

Speaking of staying on Earth... "Hey Guide?" He lowered his head until he could see me and I posed my question. "The cosmoses are split between veils, right? There's the Null, Grestal, the realms of other planets, I'm sure. But where do the gods dwell? I know they have their pantheons and whatnot, but do they make their own planes of existence for themselves?"

He dwelled on that silently for a long moment. *"Grestal is something that the majority of the Vorna steer clear of. It enjoys toying with our abilities in ways we do not find amusing, and is largely an existence that boggles even us."* Quietly he cleared his throat and then nodded. *"Gatherings of gods in a specific locale, world, or region is a pantheon, but they can also be responsible for the creation of their own spaces of existence within that world or region. For instance, the god that many Americans and other places like so much claims he made the planet and the entirety of the stars and everything in it. That is not the case, but they do create things. Fractured realms, at times for themselves, or places for their worshipers."*

"Okay, but how did so many gods come to exist when there are fewer in other places?"

Tiredly, Guide sighed and turned. *"The concept of creating a deity is not new, Massacre. They are birthed from the consciousness of mortals and through combined societal belief. If enough people believed in a purple pasta monster of some sort—true faith, not that edgy, all-religion-is-stupid-and-I-need-you-to-feel-less-superior-than-me-for-me-to-be-okay kind of belief —it would become an existing creature."*

That scared the shit out of me. "Is that how the monsters on our planet came to be?"

He smiled softly to himself and turned a doting eye on me. *"Let there be* some *mystery to life, Massacre—there is yet plenty for you to live until someone takes it or you cease wanting to exist."*

I opened my mouth to retort something just as sullen and truthful, but he just turned his attention back to his flying and left me to my thoughts.

The mind played a huge part in all this and so did faith. True faith. Did that mean my Dominion would begin to fade here unless fed by someone else? Was it something I would have to have my friends do occasionally?

Just focus on the mission ahead of you, Marcus. I took a steadying breath and let it out slowly before closing my eyes to focus on regaining what Dominion I had. *It will be a tool you can use if it does last, and if it doesn't, you can gain more if absolutely necessary.*

CHAPTER TWENTY-SEVEN

When we arrived back at the Null, there was nothing to find, really. It was the same dreary nightmarescape. It was no wonder Galaxy had come from this place and not returned to it.

Oathbound wasn't here, and Guide assured me that he had sent him word that we were on our way when we were close enough, and that he had left shortly before our arrival.

I dipped my head, feeling oddly for a moment as if the ground was shaking. "Thanks for taking the time to train me up, Guide. I appreciate it."

He smiled and offered his hand to me, a strange offering from the strange man I'd gotten to know a bit better over the time we'd been together. *"I appreciated having a good student. And don't forget, I will be bringing you the egg that you found."*

I almost smacked myself; I had already forgotten. "Thanks for that as well." I shook his hand firmly and he let go, turning in one swift motion and was gone just as easily as having let me go.

As soon as he was gone and I was alone, I began to will myself back into my body. It wasn't as hard to return as I had expected it to be, but the wake up was something out of a fantasy novel, that was for certain.

I woke up to several faces poised over mine with worry in their eyes and with enough grogginess that I was sure I'd have been able to go back to sleep right then and there if it hadn't been for the fact that hands were on me immediately.

Over the din of what could've been running water, I heard, "He's up!" Into the air and then being placed on my feet made me feel weird, like my body was still too heavy with sleep.

Merlin and Cassia were in front of me instantly, and poured over me with hands that roved a little too far and near for my sleepy mind to handle. "Woah, now, yes is sexy."

Cassia's face thundered into view and I could have sworn I actually heard the distant boom of the natural drum beat that the clouds made during a storm as she growled, "Shut the fuck up and stand still. We're making sure you're okay."

"I'm fine!" I yawned and stretched so hard I actually got a cramp in my left calf. "Shit!"

Cass slapped my calf and healing energy ravaged the lactic acid from my muscles and the appendage returned to how it should have been.

I looked around blearily and saw that we had changed locations. "How long—"

"Eight days, twelve hours, thirty-seven minutes, and forty-five seconds," Galaxy answered with barely-contained fury. "You've been gone for over a week, Marcus."

I blinked at that and almost whistled but figured if I did, I was pretty sure someone was going to deck me so I just cleared my throat dumbly and said, "Oh."

"Oh?" Arden parroted snidely, her eyes narrowed at me. "*Oh?*"

She stalked closer to me and showed me her tattered clothes, and the fact that she was bruised despite Cassia's healing abilities. "We had to fight an army of those flying assholes to get you off that island after they came and found us."

"How did they find us?" I shook myself out and fought to focus and clear my mind.

"We had to try to figure out where we were and where the enemy was, and if there was some way to get you out of your slumber." Merlin cleared his throat after saying that. "How could you have been gone for so long? We needed you."

I frowned at him and he pointed to my left wordlessly. Shifting, my eyes cleared and I could see into the darkness a bit better from where we hid. This was an actual cave and the entrance, where a little bit of light bled through, put a focus onto Amabala. She was injured, and laying on the ground on a mound of bed rolls with her eyes screwed shut in pain.

Concerned, I made my way to her. "Why hasn't she been healed?"

"Cassia's magic won't make whatever is wrong with her stop," Merlin explained softly, but there was an edge to his tone that was thicker and harder. Blame. "She's been suffering for days because one of the priests hit her with some kind of spell that just pours pain into her mind and keeps the wound from closing."

"They also use it to track us," Galaxy added tiredly. She yawned and looked at the others tiredly. "Get what rest you can, they will be on us again shortly."

I glanced at her and asked mentally, *How shortly?*

She blinked slowly, as if trying to think. *We've been running for five days, moving and fighting every few hours. The god that said they would send someone did, and we trusted them for a moment, until he proved to be the biggest threat.*

Memories sifted into my mind and played out. A man with a staff, older and winged like the ones we'd seen. He came to them smiling at the others as I slumbered and trained. Merlin translated as he related what had happened to his people.

How when Atlantis fell, the gods pulled their doomed denizens into their own dream-like domicile and have protected them for generations upon generations. The air and water here was so pure and filled with magic that it sped along their evolution and had given them the gift of flight, strength, and magic. Their science was nearly indistinguishable from magic, and some of it genuinely was a mixture of the two. This was a utopia.

The only problem was the one who had come and entreated the gods for their aid in breaking a curse placed upon him a few years ago. In order to garner the gods' attention and benevolence, the cursed one had shown them a great deal of knowledge and how to better use magic. Some called them prideful and arrogant, atrocities—others called them miracles.

Eventually, he had won his audience with the gods and their confidence. And then the once tight-knit community and connection that the denizens of the soul space here of Atlantis had once enjoyed with their gods was just... gone. Freakish creatures began to appear as members of the community disappeared or just vanished without a trace.

Then the fanatics who liked the cursed began to act out, calling for the deaths of those who didn't believe that a new god had been made. Then all mention of the gods themselves was gone, and there was only the Cursed.

And it was then that he smiled and focused on the ones around him, and said in impeccable English, "And his flock."

The small dugout we had made was just upended and torn to shreds as they had found us and began to work their way to the others as I lay uselessly. And then I saw it. What tied it all in for me.

We were dealing with the same person who I had seen before—or at least their work in the mountain with the dwarves and the mutated drakes.

Chimeras and other mutant creatures had been mixed into the crowd of opponents and the level of intricacies of each of them was about the same as the drakes had been. There was enough difference between them all that they looked like experiments. But they were off, somehow. Like they were earlier ones —half-done and half-not. Like the mixture of parts and abilities was subpar.

The fight had been brutal. The man—the priest—attacked Amabala specifically, as if he somehow knew she would be able to keep them moving faster. It was even more brutal than the one against the fish men and Cthulhu himself.

Not to mention it took Cassia out of the fight to make sure that I was safe in my slumbering training session.

The others had been handling themselves well. Even Amabala—injured as she was—kept up with what was being thrown at her. It was when several of the bird people pulled vials of some kind of liquid from their clothing that gave me pause. As soon as they quaffed them and tossed them aside, two things happened. Some of them got much larger and their muscles grew so dense they looked like they were about to pop, and others began to sling spells as if they had no worries about mana at all.

The craters in the ground that they left behind were enough to make me cringe and from there, it just proved that this wasn't right. Those were the performance enhancers that the Seelie had been using, how had they gotten here?

Shunting the rest of the memories, I let my breath out slowly and then muttered, "I'm so sorry, everyone. I know that at least one of you thrives off battle, but that can only last so long."

I turned back to Amabala and knelt next to her to put a hand on her forehead to try to feel out what was eating away at her. I could sense it as soon as I touched her, a nefarious energy draining her mana as it regenerated and as soon as her mana bottomed out, her life force was attacked.

Then the cycle started all over again.

"Merlin, I want you to give me something of financial value to you." I couldn't see his face as I spoke, but instead of fielding questions, I just said, "Fuck it, all of you do it."

They glared at me in confusion, Arden looking like she was about to rip my head off. However, it was Merlin who saved it. He reached into his pocket and pulled out his wallet, digging into it for cash. He pulled out a few notes, then pulled a satchel out of his inventory. "If you can get rid of whatever is ailing her, do it, please."

I nodded and then the others joined us, offering things. Arden was the last, tipping the scales with her game system. I frowned at that and she sighed, "I don't have any money on me because I was worried about it getting wet or something. If this will help, take it."

My head tilted to the side and my hand moved on its own, grasping the piece of tech and suddenly all of it burst like all the coins and other sacrifices had before and siphoned into my body. My friends gasped and then I placed my hands on Amabala's stomach and focused on Merlin's request to get rid of what was ailing his beloved.

The golden energy of my Dominion flooded her body and began to eat into the insidious parasite inside her stomach. This was the payment for their sacrifices. Once I pulled it out, I would have upheld my end of the bargain.

This was the trade. This was the commerce of their offering to me.

And my Dominion strengthened with that very thought. The parasite that attacked this poor woman was *mine* now and I was collecting my due.

The inky, disgusting slickness of it compressed under the strength of my Dominion and with it crushed as it was, I pulled it from the woman under my hands and forged it into a coin. A brown coin with green, coursing flashes through it that just *radiated* disease.

I thought about it for a moment, then placed it into the inventory ring on my hand. Observing Amabala, there was a massive change in how she presented now.

The labored breathing was gone and I could feel her life force no longer being attacked, though I knew for certain she needed to rest.

A flurry of motion outside the cave caught my attention and Cassia squared up, her torn and shredded clothes helping her cut an even more intimidating figure and I smiled at that.

I stood up and stretched, my body feeling ungodly cooped up, and joined her. "Take a break and protect everyone else here, I'll take care of them."

She frowned at me and said, "I don't know what happened with you sleeping for so long, but there are dozens of them out there at least, Marcus. They're strong."

I grinned at her. "I am too, my love." I leaned over and kissed her on the cheek. "I've missed you. I'll be right back."

There was a blip next to my foot and I could feel Galaxy trying to step into me.

Marcus? I feel a strange power within you. Did you…? Did you kill a god?

I nodded, and knelt next to her. "I did. And once I finish killing everyone outside, I'll come back in and make sure that you all are aware of what happened to me while I was gone."

She nodded and sat, her cat eyes staring up at me. *I will watch over the others and we will speak on this further. And I missed you as well.*

"I missed you too, love." I scratched her head and called my scythe from my ring and grinned.

A shape loomed in the opening of the cavern, the waterfall obscuring it slightly. It was huge, almost as large as the entrance itself. It was dead, it just didn't know it yet.

Bending at the knees, I flung myself forward and swung the scythe with a massive heave.

As soon as the water parted, flesh did as well and I could see where I was.

The waterfall near the city which was terribly close to where we *should not* have been. We were entirely too close to the city and potentially the god who tried to trick us as well, if that had even been a god.

Is that so bad? The voice was me, of course, but why it sounded hungry was beyond me. The corpse I stood over was a bear with lobster arms and armored scales on its back.

There were more monstrous chimeras with them, but what

drew my attention most were the staff-wielding feathered asshats.

There was more than twenty of them sprinkled about and they all had the same dazed look. *Are they under some kind of spell or something? Influence?*

A sigh crept out of me and then I shrugged my shoulders. *Only vaguely matters.*

A sly grin crept across my face. "I'll keep one of you alive to take me to this 'Cursed' guy."

Reaching down, I grabbed one of the dead bear's arms, pulling it with all the strength available to me and it tore from the elbow, the crab claw coming away with a jerk that made me step back.

The feathered person closest to me squawked an order to me that I barely paid any mind to until he leveled his staff in my direction and repeated his demand for me to drop my weapons.

Grinning, I motioned to the scythe with the claw. "You don't want me to drop these. They're what's going to keep some of you alive."

I pointed the claw at the one issuing orders and grinned wider. "Case in point."

I cast Embodiment of Lightning and used some of my magic to widen the claw enough that I could pinch the person in it, freezing it shut. "You're supposed to keep these things frozen."

Spells fizzled into life around me and I could just *feel* them on my skin in a way that I couldn't before.

With both hands filled with my scythe, I got to work showing this soul space exactly who they had bothered.

It was a bloodbath and it only worsened when I cast Masquerade. The entire time I let my scythe fly, their screams and cries of agony made me smile in grim satisfaction as shadow copies of my friends danced among the living and fought with wild abandon. Glad to know my soul's muscle memory was just as deadly as it was there and that I had a new spell to tinker with.

I'd made it through about a third of the available targets before someone actually managed to hit me, bloodying my lower back enough to sting and I covered the wound in Dominion and turned to see who it was. The man with the staff who I'd stuck on ice had managed to wiggle his arm free and had cast a spell at me—and looked to be doing so again.

My grimace at the dulling ache in my lower back brought me to bolt toward him, his raised hand not showing any sign of stopping or even slowing down as he frantically muttered the words to his spell. I flicked my wrist and a shard of ice slipped into my grasp and I threw it at him.

The shard just missed him, but it was enough to make him stutter with his spell and the pained scream that ripped from his throat meant he wouldn't be casting a damn thing for a second and then one of the shadows was on him.

I whipped my scythe toward a group of chimeras, but one of them caught my weapon and turned it against me with a battle cry. It was a squid-like monster with spikes coming off the bulbous upper body or head and tentacles as muscular as an ape's arms. A shield of ice formed on my left arm and my right arm from my forearm down became a sword.

As soon as the sonofabitch swung at me, I blocked the scythe at the haft and slashed with the ice sword, taking the tentacle with it. The chimeras that surrounded me rushed me all at once and I twisted my body to avoid an arm and shattered the shield violently to use the ice as shrapnel. The shards pummeled and pinned some of the monsters, and the one that actually grabbed me got the sword I released from my skin in the stomach for its trouble.

I turned at the waist and gripped the scythe, swinging myself away from the crowd momentarily before I pulled a coin from my pocket, holding it between my thumb and middle finger before pulling my hand up by my ear and snapping.

The coin sharpened at my will with my Dominion and

launched into the head of a caster ten feet in front of me. The coin pierced his skull and dropped him where stood. *Oh fuck, if that wasn't the weirdest coin slot I've ever fucking seen...*

One of the chimeras stopped and began to try to feed off the corpse before I jumped toward it and lopped off its head. I closed my eyes and tempered the rage welling within me, the hunger that drove me to want to shift and show off the new powers I had.

You know that fucker is likely watching this somehow, Marcus. Can't show all the goodies before giving them the business.

I gripped my scythe a little harder and went back to work. My weapon and I cleared out the majority of the combatants before the survivors decided to flee for their lives. Or to report back to the Cursed one.

Once they were gone, I collected my new favorite chew toy, wrapped in frozen crab and shivering all alone as he was, and hauled him inside. *I know you will all have questions, but I need to focus on getting the information I want from this guy first. Please, be patient.*

Galaxy lifted her paw to lick her claws and gave me a long stare before sighing in my head. *Fine.*

"Merlin, can you translate for me?" The boy mage stayed where he was but devoted his attention to me so that I knew he would do as I focused on the enemy in front of me. "Where is your leader?"

The shivering man spat on the ground at my feet, staring defiantly into my eyes. Merlin translated for me, though I figured the guy got it with how he stared hatefully at me.

I nodded along as Merlin spoke for him. "I would rather pull each of my feathers from my wings than tell you where our glorious new king is."

I snickered and brushed my fingers along the feathers on his wing, the observable flinch in his eyes as I did so was something that excited the Vorna in me. "I'm above torture, though." I glanced at the others, their various stages of concern for me slowly disappearing as they realized what I was saying. "They may not be, but... Tell you what."

I put a hand out and stopped Cassia from getting too close and Arden was just instantly next to him, flames roiling over her knuckles. "Are we beating him for answers? Because I've not been able to button mash in days, Marcus. *Days.* I'm about to quick-time-event his ass into a seared chicken breast."

The crazed gleam in her eyes was almost enough to distract from the fact that she was slightly melting my ice. She must have been really pent up after all.

"Relax, guys. He's not gonna talk even if we want him to." I pulled a silver coin from the ether around me with my Dominion, the burn of it familiar against my naked fingertips. "I'm going to pay him to take us to this guy."

"You can't be serious," Merlin snarled, coming to his feet so fast that I almost backhanded him before I realized he was stopping himself from getting too close to me. "These guys hurt Amabala, and you want to *pay* him?"

I grinned and said, "Yeah. A paid guide will do us wonders, Merlin."

Cassia looked wary of the idea, but when I suddenly grabbed the man by the jaw and stuffed the coin into his mouth. "I remember there being myths about putting the fare for travel after *death* on the dead person's body. But I have other ideas for you, shit stain."

Using my Dominion to shove the coins down his throat and into his stomach, I grinned wider. "Galaxy, I don't think he needs to be able to remember that, do you?"

Merlin blinked and grinned along with me. "I don't think he does either, and I've got just the thing for it."

His hand raised and he began to mutter softly before all of us closed our eyes. A flash of blue light, searing and painful despite my eyes having been closed, streaked into existence and just as swiftly it was gone.

I strobed my eyelids to get my vision back somewhat and found Merlin whispering something to the man before putting him to sleep. He helped the now-sleeping bird person to the ground before turning his attention back to me. "You have about six hours before he wakes up and thinks he was knocked out by a glancing blow and then found himself in this place. From there, he's going to feel compelled to take himself to whoever he reports to, to let them know that the sleeping one is stronger than the others."

I nodded at that and motioned to the back of the cave. "Then we will go back there and Cassia can hide us behind a wall of stone."

I bent down and picked up Amabala, carrying her back to our new hiding place before placing her onto Merlin's bedroll. Once I was done with that, I could just feel everyone's eyes on me.

I chuckled once to myself and sighed. "Yes, everyone. It's me. And some of you might be wondering what the hell happened to me, and I mean to tell you. But first, the burning question."

I stood up as the stone under us rumbled and created a wall with a few small pin holes for oxygen, turning to find expectant eyes affixed to me. "Yes, I killed a god."

CHAPTER TWENTY-EIGHT

Arden was the first to stress her disbelief. "You've got to be shitting me, Marcus. You go to sleep for eight fucking days and you come back having killed a god?"

I blinked at her and nodded once before opening myself up to scrutiny as Galaxy shifted her form and sashayed over to me. Once her hand was on my chest, she closed her eyes and I could feel her power questing for my own. Her slivers of Dominion brushing up against my full and devoured one.

Her voice started as a whisper, but as she finished speaking, Galaxy's voice rose with concern. "It's true, but how?"

"Yeah, I feel like there would be something to indicate another god being killed, even here." Merlin stared at me with disbelief for a moment. "Who did you kill?"

I pulled Galaxy forward softly and gave her a gentle peck on the forehead and began my story. "I was gone for months, and I'm not sure what his name was, but the planet I visited was far from our own and on the other side of a veil, whatever that means." I scratched my head and recounted some of what I'd been through. The training I had done and how the god had attacked me with plans to kill me first. "I can see how

Zeke had to defend himself with what happened to me just being in proximity to one, though I know how I annoyed mine."

I motioned Galaxy forward and passed her permission to share my memories.

There were gasps all around as they got a front row view of everything I went through. While they watched, I reached out and summoned a golem of ice. "Hollow."

The golem slimmed down and took on a more feminine figure before beefing up. "Yes?"

"Can you feel your sister here?"

Her holed eyes stared blankly ahead for a short time until she answered softly, "I can feel her power, but it is weak."

I lowered myself until I could look her in the eyes. "Weak because it's gone, or weak as if it's possibly hidden inside something?"

She perked up and pointed at me. "That one. She's hidden by something." She looked around for a short time, then pointed up. "Above us."

I dipped my head and focused on what I could feel around me. Galaxy's Dominion, weaker than what it should fully be. And then I felt an echo of it. Not too far above us.

The waterfall? Was that how they had the waterfall here?

That didn't make sense. How could they get a Vorna to eat an elemental and then become a waterfall for them?

What if they made them promise to do something for them? Like with Oathbound?

It made no sense. *Repeating yourself won't do anything, Marcus.*

"Galaxy." The cat twitched and then shifted until she could stand on her two feet, her elven form what she wore now. "The Vorna with a tidbit of your power is here. Close by, I think. I'm going to go and collect your Dominion for you."

She smiled. "I'll come with you."

I frowned. "I don't know if that's safe. With my powers fully awakened, I don't know if you can be inside me anymore without me accidentally consuming you."

She put her hand against my chest and sighed. "I guess we'll have to see about that, won't we?"

With that statement, she entered into me and settled herself as she always did. *Nothing wrong so far.*

There was a shift within me once more and she gasped. "What?"

Don't worry, I just see something within you. It's golden and warm. Is this... is this the Dominion you stole?

I found myself standing in the same interior she stood in and sure enough, there was a massive pile of warm gold.

"Galaxy, you inhabit my Endless?" She shrugged and I snorted. "I mean, it makes sense, but you don't feel anything? Tired? Drained?"

"I don't have my full power, but I feel no different than I normally would. It's comforting inside you."

I laughed at that and shook my head. "So glad Arden isn't here to hear that."

Galaxy chuckled with me. "So am I." She stared at the pile of golden coins and fell silent for a time.

I couldn't blame her. I had killed a god and here she was, a goddess. "You know I won't hurt you."

She snorted. "I know that." She still didn't face me. "You were gone so long, and I saw that you killed another of my Huntsmen from the memories you shared."

I nodded, more for myself than for her, but I knew she could feel the movement. "I did. Only so I could face what's coming and keep you all safe, which it seems I've done a shit job of doing so far."

I scratched my head, slightly taken aback that I had to say this. "I genuinely had no plans to kill a god."

Finally, she turned around and said, "I don't doubt that you weren't planning to. I would've known if you meant to. But with this person wielding the power of the gods and another Vorna nearby, we might have to rely on you being able to kill more. Are you okay with that?"

I blinked and retorted, "Are you?" She frowned at that.

"These gods weren't made by you. The majority of them all were made by the needs and minds of humans or lesser beings. If I kill them, is that going to be okay?"

She was quiet for a time and then whispered, "I don't know. My first thought is that necessity will prevail. If we can rouse them and have them fight their oppressor, I would like that more, but if he's able to put them to sleep like this, what's to say he's not capable of turning them against us too?"

"We have no way of knowing until it happens, and if I had to choose?" I clenched my fists and nodded to myself. "I would kill them over having any of ours being put in jeopardy."

Galaxy sighed to herself and squared down on herself, hands over her head, and groaned. "Why do I feel like just *saying* this is like offering lambs to the slaughter?"

A stillness ran through me while considering that. They essentially were. There was no lateral movement from the thought in my mind. Either they could be used to get rid of the threat, or they were a part of the threat and I would kill and devour their power to negate the threat on my own.

"Is it hubris that I don't wonder if this person can use the power against me or turn me on you?" Galaxy looked up at me as I spoke and her brows furrowed, concern evident as she thought on that. "Is it cockiness or just knowing?"

"I think it's knowing. You've killed one god and another Huntsman. Your power waxes and, with it, your abilities." She stood up and patted my cheek. "I will be going out there to collect your rewards. I can give you all the experience from those, but I can only give you partial credit for killing all of those creatures there in the other place since you consumed some of them. I'm sorry."

I leaned down and kissed her and she returned the affection with a hungry kiss of her own.

"The others are beginning to come out of your memories; you'd better be there. And if these monsters cause you to level up, you will be soon. But I think you have new abilities and spells to consider, yes?"

I returned to my outer self and watched as the others stirred from the trance-like state of watching my memories. Merlin was the first to come clear of it and considered me for a long moment. "How strong is your control of ice and shadow at the moment?"

I shrugged. "Better than ever, I'd guess?"

Cassia cleared her throat and said, "I want to see what you look like as a Vorna."

I considered shifting, but shook my head. "We don't know if my changing right now will make me a target for the Vorna in this realm as well."

She crossed her arms sullenly and grumbled, "You got to fight and train for months and this is all I get?"

There was a flurry of movement and suddenly I had a hand on my shoulder that I recognized as Guide's, and then it was gone.

"What the fuck was that?" Arden hissed and fire roiled into life from her fists as she glared around the darkness.

"Guide came to give me something." I leaned down to pick up the dragon egg and Merlin swore below his breath. "What?"

"That's a dragon egg!" Arden answered and swarmed forward. "Do you know how rare these are?"

"Rare enough that he decided to come to mythic Atlantis and give it to me?"

They glared at me and Cassia sidled closer to me, whispering, "Get it away from Arden before she collects it like she collects cats."

"I heard that, asshole!"

Power flooded into me as Galaxy's consuming the dead gave me a massive rush of experience. And sure enough, it wasn't enough to make me level up. Damn.

Checking my skills, I did see that I had one point I could spend. Seeing that my newest spell was looking a little lonely as a one of six, I spent it on Masquerade.

Masquerade — Caster summons beings of shadow to do their bidding. Number, type, strength, and useful-

ness of shadows depends on the summoner's abilities and rank of skill.

This is going to be really nice when I level it up more.

"Alright, guys, here's the deal." Cassia, Merlin, and Arden raised their brows at me and looked concerned as I spoke. "Hollow told me her sister's presence is nearby. That means there's another Vorna close."

Merlin spoke up, his exhaustion showing for the first time. "I'm not ready for another fight."

I put a hand on his shoulder. "And I don't mean for any of you to join me on this one. You all need to rest." I focused on Cassia as I said that last bit. "Even you. I can sense that you've been relying on our little nugget's Dominion, and it's weak right now. You need to rest—both of you do."

She begrudgingly sat down next to where Amabala rested and growled to herself, "Yeah, I get it."

I appreciated that she wasn't going to fight me on that.

Arden glared at me. "You're going to fight on your own again?"

Smiling, I grunted. "Only if I have to. Something is wrong that they're not moving or, at the very least, this waterfall shouldn't exist without something being weird." That made her cross her arms at me and I held my hands up. "I need to at least investigate and then I can tell you through Galaxy whether I need the help or not."

"I'm only going because I need to be there to collect my Dominion if the creature falls." Her presence startled the others as she stepped from the shadows but I'd known she was there.

Cassia touched the ground and made a hole in the wall. "Just let me know when you want back in."

I dipped my head at her and said, "Thank you."

She grinned back at me and gave me a thumbs up, which she never did, and closed the hole when we walked through it.

I found the slumbering bird person. I thought about punching him in the face again just for good measure, but refrained and instead went outside the water and began to climb up the wall of the cliff.

I realized during the climb that I had been mistaken before. We *weren't* close to the city. We were in it. This cavern was behind the waterfall that plummeted from the massive isle above us. When I realized that, I knew I was going to need Mako to get up there and called him.

The drake surged from my arm and I smiled at him. "Thanks for the ride, buddy."

He surged upward, carrying me and Galaxy within me easily, and I suddenly had a whole new appreciation for him carrying me everywhere. Something about being flown by your shoulder everywhere just had that effect on you, I guess.

"Hollow, tell me when I get close."

The ice primordial spoke directly into my mind. *Keep going. It feels like she's at the origin of the fall.*

I leaned closer and urged Mako to move faster until I came to the top of the fall and a beautiful oasis-style pool of water. In the center of it was a statue that vaguely resembled a winged creature; water flowed from the creature's open hands, mouth, and even its eyes like it was crying.

She cut an almost angelic figure, but the tail and draconic-looking wings weren't so divine-looking to me.

It was close to a Vorna, but it wasn't quite what I was used to seeing. But remembering Oathbound, mine, and Guide's appearances could be different among all of us, it was close enough that I had to recognize this thing was it.

As I came closer, the eyes of the statue moved to me and though the body stayed rigid, I could almost see the pleading in the whites of them. The wild and chaotic flickering begging me to help.

The poor thing. I dismounted and Mako stayed where he was, watching for anyone coming at my back. "You look like you're stuck, sister."

The eyes latched on to me and I could just barely gather the feeling of sanity slipping. Madness gnawing at the edges of the mind and periphery of the senses as you were forced to be still for years. *Years*. Decades. Centuries. Denied access to the Null and any sense of escape by the very powers you had desired to consume.

Whoever had forced her to stay here and provide water like this had to have been powerful, because her will was slipping and it was all I could do to pull myself out of the impending madness.

"All I can give you is the mercy of a swift demise, but if you have a way to tell me who it was that did this, I will try to avenge you." Her gaze never left mine so I offered choices. "Look to your left for yes, and right for no."

She looked to her left and I growled, "Good."

"Was it the people who live here who did this to you?" Right. "Their gods?" Left.

"I don't know their titles or powers to specify who, but was it more than one?" Left again. "All of them?" Left twice.

"All of them." I sighed and took a steadying breath. "Are there more than six?"

Right. Her eyes closed and the tears no longer looked forced. The eyes opened again and this time there was a new gleam in them, one of determination.

"If I were to break this, would you attack me?" Right. "Are you lying?" Right. Left.

"Can I even free you from this without their power?" This time, there was no movement, just a bitter stare. "I see. Then I offer you peace. Will you give me your power in exchange for a merciful end?"

She stared at me again and her eyes slowly edged to the left as more tears fled the corners of her eyes. I dipped my head and mentally muttered to Galaxy, *Be ready. This may be what gives our position away.*

I am ready, but Merlin says we have a problem that we need to solve soon, so hurry.

I dipped my head and spoke to the Vorna. "Rest in peace, sister."

I launched myself toward the fountain, ice covering my fist as I pulled the Mantle from the ground and drove the ice spike through the sculpture's chest.

Blood flecked my arm as her eyes bulged. "Sorry, but you'll have to deal with it for a moment."

I closed my eyes and began to feed just like I had with the god. Pulling the power inside the other being into myself and then into the Endless within me. There was nothing other than something cool and immense that rushed against me.

Hollow, how do I release your sister?

The primordial ice elemental's presence brushed up against me, thoughtful, curious but reticent. *Can I just release it to you?*

The burbling, tentative trickle of power trying to find a way into me faded back and then crashed into my focus.

Hollow appeared next to me, the golem held her hands out and I pulled the power into the Endless and then turned and pushed it from within me to her.

The energy flooded toward her and when it was all out of me, she held it between her palms.

"I am so sorry, sister, but you do not appear to be yourself right now." Her concern and despair were evident in her tone until it turned to frosty lightness. "I guess I'll just have to oversee your duties for you from now on."

The water swirling and rushing in her grip slowly dribbled up her arms as she siphoned the power into herself, her icy body growing slowly as she did so.

Close to her name, the interior of her body began to fill with water. As she grew and the water density lessened, she laughed loudly.

"What do you gain?" I called over her laughter, her vision filled with water.

"Power, right, and possibly even more if I do well." She stared appreciatively at her hand as the icy nails lengthened and sharpened. "When a lesser, or mixed, elemental takes over for a pure elemental, there is a short amount of time where they can ascend to their level of responsibility. If I do well enough in her previous duties, I keep the power and become the new primordial elemental for water. Then, her element and mine become more, and are tied together more permanently."

Galaxy showed herself and pointed to me. "And he benefits from this?" She crossed her arms. "Seeing as you used him to further your own agenda?"

"When I'm given an opportunity, I take it." She looked at me and smiled widely, horrific in her golem form, as changed as it was. "As my power grows, his power will too."

She considered me closely for a long moment. "You're different. More in tune with your powers, and there's something strange about you."

I shrugged nonchalantly. "Yeah. So why shouldn't I just eat you?"

She reached down and touched my head, like someone touching a pet. It almost raised my ire, but it was the power that washed through me that stopped me from pushing her hand away from me.

I opened my status screen and saw that my Void Frost spell now had a tree of things behind it that were largely open and able to be spent into with points.

"A gift. Though I doubt that you will like many of them."

I allowed that, wondering what they would be, but knowing there wasn't time. "So, not food for now, got it. So do I dispel you, or are you capable of letting yourself out of this form now?"

The horrid grin was back and she said, "I can see myself out."

The ice froze and crackled and the water washed away from the being dissipating right in front of my very eyes.

The crackling of stone and the no-longer-rushing sound of water drew my attention. I turned to find Galaxy delving into the statue. She pulled out a chunk of the stone, something darker than what was visible on the outside.

She popped it into her jaws and crunched down, the shadows around her deepening to a massive eclipse of the area.

She chewed slowly and then once she swallowed, the shadows snapped back toward her and the light permeating the soul space dimmed.

Rushing to her as she began to flag from her feet, I caught her and hissed for Mako to join us. He burst from my shadow and flew us down to our cave behind the waterfall, the water doing little to wake her from her likely trauma-induced power nap.

Mako dipped his head and neck to the point that I could slide off him, his body dematerializing into my shadow where he crawled up my leg as a tattoo and then settled as I carried Galaxy past the slumbering messenger to the cursed one and called to Cassia with a knock on the wall, "It's me!"

A slat in the wall opened and Cassia glared out. "What's the password?"

I blinked at that and I had no idea. "Uh." Considering that she looked like she was about to lunge through it, I tried, "You wanna fight?"

She grinned and reached out as the slat widened to a door and yanked me through as Arden swore vehemently as she threw her hands up. "You lost me two hundred bucks!"

My gaze landed on her and I grumbled, "You really should know better than to bet against me by now."

Merlin appeared next to Cassia and snapped to get my attention. "We have a message from your uncle." He opened the book that he'd been given and read aloud, "'Hey kiddo, I see that the book hasn't been destroyed so you must still be okay. We have an issue—the U.S. has subpoenaed you for a summit to decide the fate of the monsters, and the gods are *not* taking it well.'"

Merlin cleared his throat and said, "I asked what he meant by that and he said, 'They've begun to actively withhold their bounty in some spaces and are starting to boycott the Table for not banning Zeke and the others. They say that the neutrality of the High Table only applied to those who were a threat to humanity—not those who were a threat to the people who know about the other side of the world, as well as monsters and gods.'"

I put my head in my hands and sighed. "Can't this shit wait?"

Arden was the one to speak up this time. "No, actually. If the High Table loses its neutrality, there could be an all-out war."

"But this Cursed person is capable of fucking with the gods' powers and using them for them!" They all didn't seem shocked at that, and I had to fight not to lose my shit. "This guy is an even bigger threat than Zeke and his friends are! The Seelie drugs are here, and we don't know who made them or how they got here, but they can't have been Seelie made fresh, right?"

I scratched my head and Merlin bounced his index finger like he was thinking of something while pointing at me. "You said the Seelie at the school were going to talk to someone about getting more, right? When you went with Zeke in Japan?"

I shook my head. "No, someone mentioned something about a doctor, or something when we went to rescue Connell, but for some reason I can't fully recall it."

Merlin frowned. "Same, but it is concerning that the drugs that the Seelie had somehow made their way here. Could it be another experiment?" He blinked and pulled the book back up to his face. "Shit. They want to do this soon. Like either tonight or tomorrow, Yen says there are people at the High Table asking after you and your whereabouts."

"You made that promise too," Galaxy whispered softly behind me.

Whipping around, I found her sitting up with her arm on her knee as if she was trying to recover from something. I knelt down next to her and she put a hand out to stop me from getting too close. "We made a pact with Zeke for his help. If we don't hold up our end of the bargain, he can come to collect your power, and I do not think that even the Vorna can stop that kind of action from happening, considering the weirdness of the Fae and their power over oaths."

"Okay, we can go and try to check in on where that asshole out there goes after the fact. How are you?" She seemed dazed still as she tried to get her bearings, so I lowered my voice and asked, "Are you okay? What did you see?"

She put her head in her hands and when she spoke, she wasn't quiet about it, "I want all of you to hear this, so listen closely." She waited a brief moment to take a steadying breath, all of us watching as her shoulders rose and fell before she let a deep sigh creep out from her lips. "My children are the Brindollan Gods."

"We know that." Merlin spoke carefully, Cassia elbowing him for interrupting, making him yelp, "Ouch!"

Galaxy stared at him until he shrank a bit at the shoulders and looked away. "Sorry."

"My children are the gods that I gave birth to, and they are the reason I lost my power." I frowned at that statement. Had she sacrificed parts of her Dominion to keep them safe? Had they needed her and she had given herself up to the Vorna in exchange for their safety? She looked up at me with possibly the singularly most morose expression on her face and softly whispered, "No, Marcus. They betrayed me and gave me to the Vorna so that they could take over. The largest chunks of my Dominion reside with them. The Vorna we killed so far were sent to guard my temple here so that no one could come and free me."

"What the fuck kind of Days of Our Lives bullshit drama is that?" Arden roared, startling all of us. "Fuck, I thought my sister going crazy was bad, but damn! Why would they betray you?"

Galaxy shook her head. "I don't know." Her eyes locked with mine as she growled, "But I know someone else with a vendetta and who also seeks a way to get to them."

"You can't mean..." Merlin started and then bowed his head. "Galaxy, Goddess, you can't mean to move against your own children, do you?"

She stood to her feet and brushed herself off as she

considered our surroundings for a long moment. "Yes. At least in so far as to find out what threat I posed to them so that I can finally know who I was that they had to betray me like that."

She looked at Merlin. "You will go out to that slumbering buffoon and make him sleep until we return to make certain of what he is doing." She pointed at Arden. "There are some items outside the cave and waterfall that I didn't collect—I want them collected and brought back in here."

The others didn't move so Galaxy hissed, *"Move as your goddess commands."*

They leapt to her orders, leaving me and Cassia to watch her closely as she crossed her arms and stared at the ground for a long while without moving. Cass approached her first. "I know that you're hurt, and confused, and I'm so happy you got your power back—but please don't do that."

Galaxy blinked at the ground and raised her gaze to Cassia's sunglasses-covered eyes. "Why ever shouldn't I? They should have moved the moment I stated what I wanted because time is not something we have much of. There is nothing better to do than to ensure that the spoils of Marcus's fight and the one plan we have to find who is responsible for what has been going on comes to fruition."

I nodded at that. "Yes, I agree, but we also need to make sure we remain amiable with our friends." She turned to me and there was a look on her face that I didn't quite get for a few heartbeats and then it dawned on me. "How much of your power did you get back and could that be what's responsible for you acting entitled?"

Her jaw dropped and she squealed, *"Entitled!"*

"Yeah." Cassia sighed, a smirk dawning on her face. "You're acting like a stuck-up goddess. Isis, right?"

I nodded. "Pretty sure her friends just tolerate her, or don't invite her to shit because she can be such an uber bitch."

She recoiled as if she'd been slapped, her lips beginning to form a pout. "Am I?"

Cassia went to her and held her. "We only say this away from everyone else because we love you."

I walked over to them both and pulled them into the hug that I'd wanted to give them earlier. "We know what you just learned is fucked up, and we know you need time, just try not to make us your scratching post to take it out on, okay?"

She sniffed and whined into my shoulder, "Ugh, a cat pun?"

I grinned. "That's the girl I love. Come on, we have things to do, a lot to prepare, and you should probably apologize too."

CHAPTER TWENTY-NINE

Merlin returned first and when he walked somberly into the room, Galaxy pulled him to the side and spoke with him. I couldn't tell exactly what she was saying as she was speaking to him directly through their link, but the way he was nodding and she looked crestfallen, I could see that her apology was at least received well on his part.

The other part would be wondering whether Arden would even want to talk to her at all.

A clatter of items being dropped almost peeled me from my skin as I flinched at the noise and Arden stood with her arms crossed over her chest and her chin raised defiantly. "Done."

Galaxy motioned for her to come to her and Arden stood with her body and jaw set. "No."

Galaxy huffed quietly and started, "Arden, I—"

"No, Galaxy," Arden stated again, with her hair beginning to burn at the edges. "You drew a line, and I don't like it. I don't let any of my friends treat me that way. Not my customers, not the patrons at the bar, not even people who I know in passing. If you want to draw that line, fine, draw it. I won't cross it, but there's no going back."

I sucked on my teeth, eliciting a disgusted sneer from her. "Hey, hothead." Arden's eyes widened and I motioned toward Galaxy. "If you would listen to her, she's trying to apologize."

Her hair actually burst into flame. "And she doesn't need *you* to come to her rescue, asshole!" She pointed at Galaxy and snarled, "She's the one who made the mistake. She's the one who just got raw-dogged by horrible memories and decided to take it out on us. Just like you were taking the mind-fuckery thing out on her!"

She turned her fury at the now grief-stricken goddess and spoke in a softer tone, but all the rigid lines in her stance and the way her hair burned were a dead giveaway that she was far from cooling off. "I understand that you feel like the universe hates you, that getting shit on by the beings you created is the most terrible thing you could have probably learned. I do. I have a murderous sister and a betrayer of a brother to thank for that, and I'm not over my own hang-ups—I get it. But if you want to be friends with me still and have me at your side and your back, as opposed to kneeling and subservient, you had better damn well make sure your actions and words line up on that, Galaxy. I mean that shit."

Arden put her hands down to her side, and took a deep breath before letting it out as she huffed, "So which is it? Servant and master, or friends?"

Meekly, Galaxy slunk toward the fiery jinn and when she was close, she chanced a look at Arden and said, "Friends. I'm sorry I was being such an uber bitch like Isis would be. You deserved better than that, and I am better than that."

Arden sighed, her hair lowering from where it had been, visibly cooling as her anger seeped out of her. The jinn pulled the goddess into a hug. "Good, because I would hate to have kicked your ass and lost a valuable gaming partner. People who can keep up with me are in desperately short supply."

"Sappy moments and all that notwithstanding, we're kind of on a time crunch?" Merlin tapped his wrist as he stared down at the book in his hand once more. "We should figure out a way to get back here if the gods are used to put a Dominion barrier back up."

I'd been thinking about that. Though I could drain the barrier easier now, it was still a warning to those who made it, and I didn't want that, so I had an idea. Swirling a bit of my Dominion for a moment, I pulled a quarter from my inventory and allowed my power to surge into it.

Once the little coin felt more like me, I shoved it back into the end of the cave at the far wall like it would be a carved in structure to find somehow. As I moved away from it, I became acutely aware of where it was and that it was *there*. Just short of a god draining the power from it, I had to rely on being able to feel it and get through power from others with it as an anchor of sorts.

"Okay, let's go then." I glanced at Merlin and made a motion for him to tell me, "Where to?"

"Capital hill?" I shook my head and he said, "Get us to the High Table. We have a way there since someone gave their word."

I turned around and used my bond with the still uncon-scious Amabala to create a portal to the earthly plane, difficult, but not impossible for me now. We stepped through the portal and into the street in front of the bar, all of us moving quickly and when Merlin came through carrying Amabala, he also had a staff clutched to his hip under his arm.

"Where'd that come from?"

He glanced down at it and said, "From the priest. The enchantments on it are like nothing I've seen. I wanted a chance to study them."

The staff looked plain enough to me, but he was more familiar with these kinds of things than I was, so I had to trust his judgment. "Okay. Get her somewhere she'll be safe, and then get ready to leave. How much time do we have?"

Merlin looked at the phone he pulled from his inventory and answered, "Twenty, thirty minutes tops?"

I nodded. "Shit, shower, shave, and get ready to meet a lot

of stressed-out leaders." I chuckled at his disdain and called out, "Dress nice!"

He carried Amabala to the doctor's quarters in the gymnasium portion of the High Table, and I entered the front, Kenshi himself at the doors. "Bubba, whole lot going on…"

I nodded at him, patting his shoulder. "I get it. We're going to work on it, hang in there."

He grinned at me and took the time to show me in before turning his human scowl on the people outside.

I was surprised that everyone was remaining so calm when someone just walked out of a hole in reality, but there were guards posted outside with rifles and swords. Some were ours, the ones with Kenshi's katanas in their grasp at least. The armed guard was newer to me, especially the ones in Kevlar with helmets that looked ready for a riot.

"There you are." Uncle Yen surged down the steps toward me and pulled me into a hug, "Anubis needs to see you."

"I want to see him too, but I have to prepare to go talk to a lot of angry gods and even angrier people, and if I smell like this, I'll die of embarrassment." I pulled away and hopped up the steps and entered my room, finding it empty of people. I pulled a towel off my desk and began to strip as my uncle stood in the door to my room with his back to me. "You gonna be there through my whole shower?"

"Only to give me an opportunity to come in and tell you what I know." Anubis's voice carried from the hall and grew louder as he crouched and came through the doorway in his full god form. "The being you are going to fight has access to magic unlike anything on this planet."

I took a breath, having almost expected those words, which seemed to be a *very* popular sentiment lately. I moved away from my room and into the shower before completely taking my clothes off and turned the water on as hot as I could stand.

Steps alerted me to my godly guest moving toward me, so I held a hand out, "Say it with your chest so I can hear you, Anubis."

The god actually chuckled at that and began to speak a little louder so he could be heard over the water. "We were not even aware that he had taken our power, and we did not see him when he did. The way he takes the power and puts it under his control is almost like a suggestion that is not a suggestion. A command, if you will. He cannot interact with it directly, so he forces the god to sleep and then takes control of their ability to wield their power and uses that as a conduit."

I frowned at that as I lathered myself with soap. "So he basically used you as a focus, or a battery?" There was no answer and I snorted. "I can't hear you nodding if you are."

Uncle Yen called out, "He was."

"What I mean to say is that you need to be certain you can cut him off from his supply of power before he has the time to do what he wants to do." He paused and then softer, almost to the point that I could just barely hear him, "His experiments defy nature and her natural order. They are an affront to creation, and he does these things on a whim."

My fingers combed shampoo through my hair as the water beat against my skin and washed the grime and soap away. "I've seen some." I took a breath and heaved it out. "Gotta say, I'm not a fan."

Water turned off and I grabbed the towel to begin drying myself when Galaxy entered the room. "My turn?"

I smirked. "Warmed it up for you." The towel went around my waist and I walked out to the others waiting. Anubis, still looking sickly, was by the door with Uncle Yen, and I tucked the towel into itself to keep it wrapped around me as I searched for clothes to wear.

I had slacks and a button up, but that wasn't going to necessarily cut it when I was going to be meeting with gods, supernatural creatures, Wardens, and politicians.

The last two being the most dangerous to me at present. *Maybe I can unite them all to a different cause? Finding this guy because he's the biggest threat?*

Galaxy's voice echoed mine for a moment, then she spoke

through my mind, *It will take a lot more convincing than we can do, I am afraid. And now that you also have the power of a god within you, you will become a target of their fear and ire as well.*

A hissing sigh fled my lips and I pulled my underwear drawer open to find a pair of briefs, then put them on. Respectfully, Anubis and my uncle faced away.

"Something else I can do for you gentlemen?" There was no malice in my voice, just annoyance at not being able to be alone.

"Why do I feel a Dominion within you, Marcus?" Anubis was cautious as he asked and I could feel a tensing around him and Uncle Yen as he broached the subject. As if they expected me to attack them.

"I've gotten stronger, and while I was training, I was beset upon by a fool who had one." The truth. "I claimed it, as what I am is a predator to the gods."

I pulled the shirt over my shoulders, then my slacks up my hips, fastening the buttons slowly. Cautiously, I explained, "My blood held dormant Vornal power, the keepers who took Galaxy's power. They can eat the Dominion of gods, and claim it for their own. I devoured the god who attacked me, and took his power as my own."

Anubis held a crook in his hands and lowered his stance so that he could stand between me and my uncle. "I'm not going to attack you, or any of the gods there, without serious reason and affront, Anubis. I'm not some rabid beast who will attack any god near me."

Uncle Yen stepped around Anubis and put a hand on his weapon. "Let's all calm down here."

Blinking, I smiled. "Perfectly calm, though I wish I had a bite to eat before going to this thing."

Wouldn't be the first time you went into something hangry. Galaxy's teasing made me roll my eyes.

"I can have something whipped up for you to scarf down real fast if you like?" Uncle Yen offered and before I could answer, Galaxy had shouted a yes from the shower. He snorted and shook his head. "Answers that."

Anubis glared at me, and then shifted his whole body. Gone was the sickly-looking grim reaper of a man I had seen before and in his place stood a sun-kissed god. He wore what could have been a very traditional style of garb for an Egyptian. A skirt of darkness around his waist tied with a golden sash that had a red blob at the end weighed it down. A gold and black collar that laid around his neck, partially covering his chest, and dark hair that curled tightly into his head.

His eyes were painted like the pharaohs of the past out of the museums I'd been to. His dark eyes stayed attached to mine and he walked forward. "I weigh the souls of the dead to judge their worthiness, Marcus Bola. Their paths are based on their own decisions and their own sins and choices. I do not weigh the souls of the living, so I cannot say whether all you do is right or wrong, but I am choosing to trust you."

He held his hand out to me and when I offered mine, he grasped my forearm and pulled me close to him. His words rumbled onto my shoulder as he said, "I owe you much for finding my brother and I. Do not saddle yourself with the sins of others, please. Your uncle would be lost if anything were to happen to you."

A soft smirk crossed my face as I nodded. "I'll try my best. Just take care of him, okay?"

"For the rest of my days," Anubis responded and patted my shoulder before letting me go. "Be safe. I will lay my influence where I can; I have friends in that meeting today as well."

"Thank you." I glanced around and watched as Galaxy dressed herself under her towel with magic making her clothes. "Cassia?"

She blinked and my bond with her opened wide. "She's downstairs with her mother. She needs a moment."

Grunting, I continued to prepare myself when Kenshi walked up into my room with a box. "Ammunition from Jayvali."

"Woo!" I took it from him and opened it with glee. Inside were two magazines filled with rifle ammunition and there was a full set of rounds put into Styrofoam for my pistols.

The note within said, *I don't have more mags to give you, so just take the rounds of yours out of your Fae Frame. It will work best with these as it can handle more kick than the Silvaero. I need more ore to make more rounds, but I will make more once I'm freed up a bit more.*

I grinned at that and resolved to summon a golem to pretty much live there with him to get more ore to him. I'd have to do that later though.

I pulled my pistols out and began to dump the rounds in their current magazines before refilling them with the cool-blue-tipped rounds. They were chilled to the touch and I had to admit, I wondered if they would be able to fire at all, but shit. If Jay had made them, they'd do the job.

With the rounds placed and put into the weapons, I placed them back into my inventory and gave Galaxy the look. She dipped her chin once and I went downstairs with her to check on Cassia.

We found Cassia hugging her mother before Chiasa scowled at me then walked away.

Cass didn't even need to look at me to know I was there and she proved it by speaking to me with her back to me. "You know this is likely going to be a trap, right? If not for us, exactly, it'll be for Zeke and his friends."

I nodded. "I'd figured. Which is why you and the others are going to stay here, preparing to come to the rescue should we need you." She turned then, her skepticism on her features punctuated by worry. "I have a way to get you to me from my time on tour, but we may need wheels and that's why I need you to make sure Amabala is up and ready to go. Whatever you've gotta do to get her back from her resting, we need it."

She scowled and Merlin appeared next to me, subdued, "Don't worry, I'll be with him, Galaxy too. We aren't going to let someone else get the drop on him."

I raised an eyebrow at him, but he stopped me from

commenting, waving his new staff. "You'll need someone some-what more well-versed in politics and magical lore to make sure you don't step on any toes. Plus, having someone come with you as an aide is more acceptable than being completely on your own against the forces arrayed against us and our people."

"Not to mention the fact that the Warden orders will be there as well." Cassia sighed and rubbed her forehead tiredly. "Yeah. Okay. I'll get all of the others ready, though without the wolves, it'll be rough on us."

Arden appeared and grinned. "I have an idea about that, and his godliness isn't going to tell me no either."

She'd said it as if she was challenging me to, but she was right, and I said as much. "We need the numbers, strength, and power. I've seen what numbers can mean for the Hunt now, and we're severely understaffed. Make it happen."

All three of them hit me with that surprised-Pikachu face and I just snorted. "I mean it. Make it happen, Arden. You know my criteria, apparently, and I trust you both."

Cassia grabbed me by my shoulders and yanked me into her, her lips pressing against mine before she muttered, "I love you. If they move against you, kill all of them."

I chuckled, a smirk blooming on my face as I said, "Yes, dear." I kissed her forehead and said, "I love you too."

"Food for Marcus?" The voice wasn't familiar and I turned to see Kenshi opening the door for someone to come in with a bag and I grinned wildly, "Ah, here you are."

I took the bag and handed him twenty for his trouble, his thanks enthusiastic as he left me to unwrap the burgers, fries, and other various odds and ends. I motioned to the food. "Chow?"

Arden snatched some fries and Cass followed me to the bar to help me eat. Merlin waved us away with the excuse of nervousness and I chuckled at that, letting him leave with the promise to return in time for our ride.

The other bartender on shift, Hammond, dropped over as I

pulled the rest of my food out. "Heard you went looking for Atlantis? Well, here's the drink for it—call it a Briny Deep."

I raised a brow at him, pulling out one of the little gummy sharks and he laughed. "Had to."

I shared a chuckle with him and he watched me take a sip. It was strong and there was a slight fishy tang to it that wasn't unbearable. As I took my second sip, Hammond explained the drink, "Half-full with ice, pour in Nori-infused scotch, two ounces, top it with club soda and garnish it with more nori."

I grimaced as the taste really went for the throat and he smiled. "Fishy? Got the recipe from a couple of nerds online. Seemed exciting, so I started infusing a while ago, but this is the first time I got the chance to really use it."

I grinned at him. "It's something deep, that's for sure. But after what I've seen of Atlantis? You may want something a bit more bird-like and fluffy."

He rolled his eyes at me and said, "Yeah, right, I'll believe that when I see it with my own eyes."

"I'd put money on it." Cassia grinned and the other bartender stilled. "Too chicken?"

Hammond growled and put the cup he had on the bar. "Nope! I'll take that action. How much are we talking?"

Cassia thought on it. "Ten grand and three shift switches with no complaints and no refusal."

He countered, "Fifteen grand, and four shifts, and when I come in, I drink free for the night." He thought he'd stomped her for trying to call his bluff, but Cassia just held out her hand. The man grinned and took it. "I'm gonna be so rich! When are we going?"

I chuckled and said, "I have shit to do right now, but when I get done, you can come with us and we'll happily claim that money and time."

He laughed to himself as some of the other patrons glared at us and left us be. While I ate, I texted Zeke and he responded that he would be with us a few minutes before it was time and to get ready.

We ate quickly but not so fast as to not taste the food. It was delicious, especially compared to the food I'd been forced to eat while off planet and I was truly enjoying it. "Ah, pickles. I never knew I would be enjoying you so much until now."

Cassia snorted at that and took a massive gulp of the milkshake I'd been given before belching. "Whoops!"

I laughed and shook my head. "Cute." I considered some options and then asked, "You think I should go with my armor on?"

She grunted, nodding before she cleared her throat and muttered, "Better the non-gods have to do some digging to know who you are. They'll know you have a Dominion and they're likely to either fear or hate you for it, so at least keep the Normies in the dark."

"Fair enough."

Kenshi opened the door and called. "Bubba Marcus!" Glancing back to him, I saw that he had Zeke standing next to him in a nice suit with a grimace on his face.

Merlin, time to go. Galaxy passed the word for me as she melded with my shadow and I stood to leave. Cassia touched my shoulder and I felt refreshed. "Got some levels while you were off hunting. Improved my healing as well. If you need us, get us there, okay?"

"Of course." I grinned at her, though the nerves began to weigh on me. "Make sure Amabala is okay."

She nodded and went back to her food before getting up with her burger. "Good luck."

I offered her a stiff smile and walked toward Zeke and his friends. "Hey guys."

Zeke grinned at me. "Hey buddy." He blinked at me and his amicable demeanor stiffened and fell away as he leaned forward, his nose crinkling as he sniffed at me. "You've been... busy."

I nodded, pulling him out the door so that we had time alone, or as alone as we could be with his friends eyeing me like

I might fuck around on them. "So I got some news, Galaxy and me."

He frowned and crossed his arms. "Yeah?"

I nodded quickly and muttered, "The gods here *actually* aren't at fault for you being returned to Earth. There is no maybe about it." He rolled his eyes and I stopped him with a hand on his shoulder. "The Brindollan gods took Galaxy's power and gave her to the Vorna to imprison here on Earth. They gave you all the bodies needed to take more power as fast as you could, to the point that you can even somehow handle Dominions. It doesn't make sense for the gods here to take you when you meant literally nothing to any of them, but the Brindollan gods had every reason to get you the fuck away from them, since you were a threat to them."

The one who wore the cloak with the hood up, his yellow eyes glaring out from beneath it spoke with a slightly southern Hispanic lilt to his tone. "That... That fucking sucks, dude, but it does kinda check out. I mean, I'd get the only people who could get into my shit the fuck away from me if I could too. Blame anyone else, and sic them on the poor bastards that have nothing to do with this."

One of the others, shorter with flaming hair, Balmur, if I recall right, muttered, "But Radiance *chose* us, man. I was taken to the Hells for this, and you're telling me it was because they couldn't keep us in check that we ended up back here?"

The frozen, elf-looking man beside the shortest member snickered. "Don't act like you wouldn't have come back for your wife anyway."

Balmur rolled his eyes. "Well yeah, Yoh too, but still—that's kinda fucked up."

Zeke pushed my hand away gently. "Galaxy would swear to this?"

I nodded. "She would swear that it was what she believed, what all of us think, really, and that since that's the most we have to go on..." I shook my head and added, "She would swear that her children betrayed her, stole and divided her

Dominion amongst themselves, and gave her to the beings who wanted to keep her hidden away with enough of her power given to them to keep her cooped up in her prison."

Zeke's eyes widened but it was Muu who spoke in a hiss. "Her kids? Fuck, man, this is why I don't have any."

The blue one grinned. "You have to have sex with someone to make kids, man—I think you're good."

Muu gasped and crossed his arms. "Tell that to a certain green dragon there, buddy. She was all over me."

The others began to laugh and tease but Zeke was reserved and thoughtful until they quieted down. In the awkward silence that built after, he finally looked up at me and asked, "What does she want to do about it? She has just as much a reason to want to go to Brindolla as we do now, as much a right. We could make one hell of a team, Marcus."

I nodded, heart thudding against my rib cage as I bobbed my head in agreement. "We could. Stop hunting the gods here —I'm not saying don't defend yourselves by any means, but don't actively hunt them, and we can work together to try to get those of you who want to go back, back."

He raised his eyebrows and the smile returned, although a little predatory. "We're about to go meet with a bunch of gods who will likely want to kill me, and you want me to keep my hands clean?"

I snorted. "Those hands are rated E for everyone, but I definitely know you can make sure that they have to pay a fee to earn them." He chuckled at the joke and I heaved a sigh before adding, "All I'm asking is for some lenience for the innocent. If they attack you, I'll be one of the first to jump to your defense, but let's not go around picking fights. Not when I think I can get you to where you wanna go."

He stilled and turned to me, the others' laughter and bickering dying as Muu said, "What did you just say with your mouth face?"

My lips turned down at the corners at his wording, and said, "I can travel from the Null to planets and across the veils. I might be able to go to Brindolla and get you there somehow. I don't know if it's possible yet, but I'm probably the best hope we have at the moment."

There was a shifting around us, shadows lengthening and something moved from mine to Zeke's. He froze and then a raven made of pure ebon energy rose from within it, fluttering up to his shoulder with Zeke saying, "Hello. Who is this?"

I wondered too, and then I recalled what the Spirit of the Null had done. "Hey! I know who you are."

The bird leaned forward and began to crow into the fur-covered warrior's ear. He frowned, and then smiled, his teeth shining in the light. "Good. Good." He sighed and leaned his neck back, letting his head come to an upright resting position. "This is wonderful news."

Yohsuke crossed his arms and motioned to the raven on his friend's shoulder. "Dude, none of us speaks bird, or bitch, what did it say?"

"My kids have been proving they're badasses, my wife prepares to go to war with the Seelie if they keep fucking around." He pointed to me with his chin. "You've got a big supporter in the Null who's ready to ally with you, and Muu?"

Muu's ridged, scaly eyebrows raised in surprise. "What about me?"

Zeke grinned wildly. "Ampharia has something to give you when you come back."

The shock on Muu's face was evident, but the rest of the party went berserk, almost riotous as they cheered and roared at the news their friend had received. Muu just looked shocked and numbly muttered, "See? I told you she was all over me!"

CHAPTER THIRTY

With the shock quieting him, the others surged forward to make sure their friend was okay as Zeke turned to me. "When you have the time, the Void would have you pay them a visit to get a little bump in power, but for now we need to get moving."

Zeke turned to his friend, wading through the crowd the others formed around him to smack him on his shoulder and rest his hand there. "I know how daunting it can be to have someone holding something over your head like this, bud, or thinking about you like that. You need time to collect yourself and feel what you're feeling, anxiety and all that. I would rather have you nowhere but my side, but if you need to collect your wits, I'd have you step back and deal with it all how you can for a time."

Muu didn't get much chance to speak before Zeke clenched his hand, hard enough that I could hear the knuckles popping on the other man's muscle, but Muu only looked like he was coming up out of the fog before Zeke spoke again, "You're not alone. And if anything happens, you'll have us with you, and I know you can be called on if shit goes sideways. Do you want one of the others to hang with you?"

Why all this if she just has something for him? Galaxy muttered through my mind. *Why do I feel like I'm missing something here? She's just a dragon, did he love her or something?*

I just shrugged, easily as confused as she was at all the attention the green airhead was getting.

James raised his hand and stepped forward. "I got him, man, we'll talk it out." He grinned as he patted the other man's back. "Or we can just beat it out of each other."

Muu came back to himself and rolled his eyes. "Phrasing!"

The others chuckled, Balmur shaking his head as he snickered. "There he is."

Zeke nodded and waved his hand, a tear in reality forming behind the two other men. "Get your mind on it and then feel what you'll feel, brother."

There was a tenseness to it all as he spoke, but when the two walked through, he spoke to the others. "That leaves one of us with the power of a god." He stopped as he glanced my way, then grinned. "Two, sorry. And unless attacked, we won't be able to add to that. Sorry, boys."

Balmur shrugged. "No worries. I can still stab people who piss me off and who have earned it, right?" He glanced at me for that last one and I nodded. "Good, then I'm cool. Name's Balmur, by the way, didn't get to really chat when last we met."

I nodded at him. "Marcus. Nice to make your acquaintance." I looked at the others. "I remember Yoh? And Muu and James just left, so that leaves…"

The blue one laughed and said, "Bokaj, but you can just call me ready to kick some ass."

That made me chuckle and Zeke shook his head. "I love you guys so much. Let's get going."

He raised his hand as Merlin joined us and didn't offer much else as a means to stop him as we all walked through. As I stepped forward, I allowed the Mantle of the Huntsman to pull from the shadows and cover my body, hiding my humanity and identity within its protective form.

"Damn!" I turned to see Balmur and Bokaj staring at me as

I strode forward. Balmur swore softly and said, "I want something like that. Shit."

I laughed and continued my stride through the portal before us.

The building we entered reminded me almost of the Senate house. Gods, monsters—walking myths and legends untold and previously thought figments of fiction and human imagination —filled the seats, their assistants and friends behind them as they prepared to plead their cases, whatever they may be.

There were some hissed words back and forth as our group appeared and joined them, more than a few glares sent our way. I was happy to see some of our patrons at the High Table amongst them, a few friendly faces in a sea of scorn.

One such face bore a massive grin and winked at me as the owner stood and made his way to us. "Hello, Luci."

The devil grinned, a simple suit belying what he was normally willing to wear. He gave me a hug and smiled at the others. "Boys."

Zeke grinned. "Devil. What're you wearing, man? It looks damn good."

Lucifer looked confused for a second and then his eyes widened. "Oh! You know me, the devil wears Prada, I thought that was common knowledge."

Bokaj grunted. "Never saw that movie."

Lucifer and I both gasped, the other man speaking faster. "Meryl Streep *and* Anne Hathaway? What are you, man, a savage?"

Zeke nodded. "He is. Emily Blunt and Stanley Tucci were pretty damn good in it too."

Lucifer put a hand on Zeke's shoulder. "Whatever comes, you have my vote for that alone."

That made all of us laugh, but Zeke feigned pouting. "And here I thought it would be because we were friends!"

Luci pinched the other man's furred cheek and said, "That's what we get for thinking, isn't it, darling?"

"Fuck, who's the savage now?" Lucifer smirked at me as he

walked back to his place, then someone else I knew caught my attention. "Council member Amelia."

The dhampyr council member of the High Table's governing council grinned at me, her fangs out for once. "Huntsman." She allowed herself to look at the others. "I take it that your arrival here with these people means that you will support them?"

"It means I will support those who defended themselves, but recent events mean that their sights are no longer set here, and the Table can believe me when I say they're no longer the threat they were believed to be." I lowered my voice and spoke so that she could hear me, grateful my helm kept my face and lips hidden. "There is someone running about who is able to take the power of gods and use it for themselves without being a god themselves."

She looked pointedly at Zeke and I shook my head. "Someone worse, I think. They're experimenting on creatures like dragons and drakes. Sea monsters, even Atlanteans and gods. We have a common enemy, and these guys just want to be left alone to try to go home."

"Would you swear to that?"

I considered her for a moment, then simply said, "You can taste whether I'm lying or not. It's one of your many powers, no? Can you taste a lie in my words?"

She shook her head, then spoke. "But the delusional think their words true as well. And that muddles the waters—are you delusional, Huntsman? Have you been taken in with the promise of power outside your station?"

"Nope." I grinned at her beneath my helm of shadows and said, "I have power of my own now far beyond that of the gods and the Huntsman. I'm more than I've ever been and even still, I worry about this monster wielding magic that he doesn't understand against the innocent."

She dipped her chin. "I see." She turned and spoke as she walked away. "You have given me much to consider, friend of the Table. Thank you."

I frowned at that but Galaxy whispered to me inside my mind, *She was smiling when she said that. I think it was her way of saying she knows you're being honest and that she may support us.*

I feel the same. My response made me smile and I turned to find that Zeke was moving toward the bottom rows of the seats closest to where the genuine humans were. The speaker was set up pointing out, and they watched us with fear in their gaze. More than a few people watched me nervously and an officer who spoke with one of the folks down there turned and came over to me with his hand at the ready to grab his sidearm and draw as he came to me.

Rather than waiting for him to speak, I simply took the seat Merlin motioned me into and said, "Hello, officer, how might I be of assistance to you?"

He blinked and a tense smile that didn't quite reach his eyes spread on his face as he spoke. "Some of the speakers and representatives of the government have made their discomfort at your appearance clear to me, and I came to ask you if you could maybe shift into something a bit more... friendly looking?"

My eyebrows raised slightly, I looked around and realized that sure enough while some of them might be dressed oddly, none of the gods or monsters appeared overtly monstrous, unlike me.

"Forgive me, officer, I only wear the Mantle of my station. Let me try for you?" I took a deep breath and willed the armor to shift until it looked more like a suit made of shadows, tailored betwixt the stars themselves and with a little more will, I was able to partition my helm from my shoulders and make it more of a mask rather than a helm, though the horns remained. "Is this better?"

He blinked, sweat beading onto his brow as he nodded and cleared his throat. "Uh, yes, yeah, thank you."

I tilted my head forward and, with genuine genial kindness in my voice, said, "How ever I can be of assistance."

He nodded and backed away, hand still hovering near his

weapon until he turned around. Merlin cleared his throat and I watched him from over my shoulder. It looked like he was trying to keep from laughing. "I thought he was going to pee."

I shook my head at his finding that funny and began to cast my senses around the room. Dominions crowded us, cloying and inviting, almost enough to make my stomach growl. Maybe I would go hunting for a time once all this was over, go to other planets and take some of the gods there and leave mine alone.

Listen to you, sounding like a predator. Galaxy's teasing held a note of true concern under all that bravado and attempted humor. I could feel her still and she sighed. *Sorry. I know what you are now, and while I know that, it's still a little frightening.*

I would never devour you like that, my love. My own pause held a little mirth and then I added, *We will need all the power we can scrounge if we're going to go introducing me to your kids. Kinda put the cart before the horse getting married before meeting the family, no?*

That made her laugh, a belly one with all the stress she felt forgotten before she wordlessly shook her head then huffed a sigh. *I'm sorry I drew you into my ages-old family drama.*

I smirked and said out loud, "Better than changing the whole world as you know it just by being who you are and acci-dentally awakening a pissed-off-druid-god killer."

"I heard that," Zeke muttered from where he joined me to my left, taking a seat. He offered me an easy grin as he leaned back. "I like it."

He leaned back and glanced at Merlin. "Mage-to-the-Boy-who-would-be king, nice staff. Where'd you get it?"

Merlin snickered and answered, "Atlantis." He held the weapon a little tighter and lifted it to his chest. "Kinda called to me when I found it. Feels strong."

Zeke grunted. "Yeah, weapons calling to you is weird but not unheard of. Had one once, it was useful, but goddamn was it creepy sometimes." He snickered. "Needy too. But it was *really* useful."

The doors at the far end of the room opened and Marines filed in, steps in line so much that it made me brim with pride, rifles held in right shoulder arms. Then the Wardens flooded the room from that entrance and the entrances around the room as well. They sported staves and wands as well as swords and other varying weapons.

Then the president walked into the room with Warden Jetlo and another Warden I didn't recognize. He had his weapon out on his shoulder, his hateful glare searing the room as he scanned it and then stopped on me and Merlin.

"Mistress Indeth," Merlin pointed out as I focused on the woman carrying a gaudy-looking staff that radiated power close to that of a god's Dominion. "She has the Staff of Office? How?"

She smiled openly at Merlin and gave him a little wave before speaking to the president.

"Where's the representative from the Heart?" one of the gods to my right called as he stood. "Why are the Wardens armed when we all came to this place with peace in mind—at the very least until we decide on killing the murderer!"

The president raised his hands. "Friends, gods, and compatriots, we are here in peace, and while I respect and understand many of you here come with no ill intent, there are others among you capable of destruction unlike anything we've seen before and we needed to take precautions." He cleared his throat and spoke again, firmly and friendly. "This meeting is to clear the air and bring a modicum of civility between several parties: the gods, monsters, and supernatural beings who feel slighted by those they trusted for millennia, such as the High Table whose neutrality is now in question, the gods who feel their safety has been thrown to the wind, and Mr. Erebos and his friends, who believe that they were unjustly kidnapped from their place of preference elsewhere."

He chuckled to himself and then admitted, "I'll say, when I ran for office, I never saw myself speaking to all of this. Really puts you into the perspective that life is always much bigger than you, does it not?"

Several around us, likely mortals or the shorter-lived like the

Wardens, nodded in agreement, while more than a few sets of eyes flickered toward Zeke and his friends arrayed behind him. He took it in stride and leaned forward, poking his microphone to hear it respond before he asked, "May I address the assembly, Mr. President?"

The human motioned for him to speak as he said, "Brevity is king, Mr. Erebos. We have much to work on today."

Zeke nodded and stood, lifting his mic with him so that he could speak. "I know that there's a lot of hate being pointed at me and my brothers; I won't deny that I've likely earned it, despite having previously been content to remain in anonymity before being attacked by a god on my own front lawn. In my own self-defense, I killed him and his power was mine as a default. I didn't *choose* to take it." He paused there as voices raised, but the president raised his hand and while the gods looked supremely sour about it, they hushed and let him continue. "Since then, my friends and I have only killed one other god who was already dying and was a threat to our acquaintances. We've been attacked at every other opportunity by many here, to include angels and even archangels. We've only struck when we thought people were in danger or in defense of ourselves and others."

He raised a hand and smiled. "That last bit was… wrong—I took back what was mine by right, and the Seelie had no right to be there once I ascended the throne of the Unseelie. Court business aside, I really haven't gone god hunting." He took a deep breath and let it go before saying, "And here and now, I swear as king of the Unseelie that I will slay no more gods of Earth so long as they are not a threat to me and mine by way of active attack or provable machination that has resulted in them getting hurt."

There was an odd thrust of power that radiated around him after he finished speaking that then pushed outward to the rest of the world as they no doubt watched with bated breath. All of us felt the oath lock into place, and there was a visible relaxation in the gods as they realized the severity of what he had just said.

Once the murmur of it died down, Zeke continued, "I apologize for the fear and strife my actions have caused the world and the communities affected by it. Please, bear in mind my words when the time comes to cast judgment, for those actions were the only courses laid before me in hopes of survival."

"I had friends among the Seelie!" someone behind us bellowed. I turned to see a massive man standing with a cane in his hand leveled at Zeke. "You mean to tell me you had any more right to the rule of their lands than they did?"

Yohsuke craned his head over his shoulder in his cowl and called, "They're all fuckin' dead, aren't they? The law of the Fae supports the strong, and the non-combatants were given the option to surrender themselves and become Unseelie." He crossed his arms and let himself look forward. "Mercy comes to those who accepted it, and who ask. Don't put your bullshit on us."

"Mr. Erebos, I would advise you to control your subordinates," the president called over the rising din of noise, conversations breaking out all over the room.

Zeke smirked over his shoulder and Yoh did the same in return, falling silent. There was no subordinate there. Just a friend.

A gavel banged on the desk drew our attention away from the rising voice above us and the president pointed to the man. "I understand that you're upset, sir, and the time to air your grievance will come, I promise you, but for now we need to proceed with the agenda of the meeting, okay?" He shuffled some papers and then lifted his arm, then said, "We would like to invite speaker Amelia to the floor, the representative from the High Table whose neutrality has been called into question."

Amelia glided down the stairs closer to the floor and then approached the stand where the president backed away graciously, offering her the mic. She smiled and thanked him quietly and then turned to address the gathered beings. "Millennia before man discovered fire again, or wrote a single word after the darkness fell and wiped out all recollection of the before, we were. The Table, or at least those who sought to bring the ideas of it to the fore of our kind, gathered and offered refuge to the fledgling forces of those who walked the shadowed lands and forged fear into the hearts of mortals. When the darkness came and the era of peace we knew came to an end, we yet still remained and took of the tree that marked our beginning and set out into the lands where our patrons would be and we set up shop."

Muttering began along the walls, and I had to admit, I was worried too; nothing she said made any sense. *Galaxy, does Merlin know what she's talking about?*

She shook her head within me, and then smiled, *Not a clue, but the eldest gods know what she's talking about, and there are quite a few here today. Just listen.*

"From the depths of that darkness, our laws came into being, and the High Table was formed. Some of you may recall that we once did not remain neutral. We were a bastion against the ignorance of humans who knew we existed and hunted us, slaughtered us, due to fear and hate." More murmuring all around us erupted and she hushed everyone with a raised hand. "When the darkness came again and the beginning was once more, we took the stance of neutrality and instead offered ourselves as a place of respite in hopes of quelling the rage that those who remained had against their once pursuers and hunters. We opened our doors in hopes that mankind—Normies—would someday learn of us, our existence, and accept us. That this cycle of hate and distrust could finally end and we could become a haven for all and a place of peace."

"So you harbor a known god killer?" a voice called from the back row. No one stood when I turned to look, so if Amelia knew who said it, she didn't address them with even so much as a glance. Different from how they'd treated us so far, but could this be something that was planned, or just played to her game?

"We offered refuge to one who was attacked, and even then, at first, we did not know for certain who or what he was." The skillful deflection was tenuous to me at best. One would assume that you would backpedal or call light to it in a way you wanted, but instead she admitted they hadn't known. "We do not toss out those who hunt humans for coming too close to their nests. We do not ban those who sell drugs to their fellow monsters, even if they make them hollow. We do not have a say over what takes place outside of our areas of influence. Do you expect a bartender or a bouncer at every supermarket? While someone is *mowing their grass?*"

The crowd was silent as she let her eyes wander the crowd before her. "No. No, you do not, and never before did you expect it. When a god moves in on another god's territory, where do you come for impartial mediums and mediators, hmm? To the Table. Where can deities and werewolves bump shoulders and feel like longtime friends in the comfort of a safe environment?"

Someone in the crowd called, "The Table."

Amelia smiled as if looking at a child to be rewarded. "Exactly. When thousands of mortals die at the hands of a wrathful god, we stand aside and watch helplessly, as there is nothing in our laws that protects them other than our presence, but the one who commits such an atrocity is... What? Not unwelcome, are they? No! Of course they're welcomed with open arms, because it did not happen at our establishments!" She pointed to Zeke. "So he killed a god who attacked him, in self-defense. Do you know how many mortals he protected from the rifts when Janus died?"

"Who cares?" someone directly behind me and Merlin snarled. "He killed a god—someone who mattered."

Amelia shook her head sadly. "I dare say that the mortals matter now that the metaphorical cat is out of the bag, my friend." She slammed her fist on the wooden stand before her and the meaty *thunk* made some in the crowd jump. "We were not ready for our truth to be shared with the Normies. Years and years of propagandized media have filtered into their news media to persuade them to like us all, wasted for us to be outed and caught with our pants down, but here we are! And we will have to make the best of it, or another age of darkness may yet see us all to ruin."

She took a breath to compose herself. "The Normies, humans, un-magic—whatever you choose to call them—know! They know about us, and some of them are even willing to allow us to be a part of their nations! Do we truly wish to hold them accountable for something someone else did? Do we really want to forgo the benefits that we could gain from this?"

Jetlo stood from where he watched the proceedings off to the side. "What does this have to do with the Table's neutrality, dhampyr?"

"If the High Table's customers choose to remain separate, we will need to prepare for another war between humanity and the supernatural. And with the advances in technology and everything that we have seen today?" She let the thought percolate in the minds of those who listened.

And that got me thinking. If humans knew about us, that means they also knew largely how to get rid of a lot of us. With how technology was, all the answers they wanted were at the tip of a thumb, and their weapons could be modified to get rid of quite a few monsters almost immediately. I mean, I'd be fine, the faith that the gods required to feed their Dominions and replenish them wasn't something I had to care about. My allergy to silver notwithstanding, I didn't have too many things to be worried about.

An atom bomb dropped on you would be worrisome, my love. You still need food as well. If they were to level the Earth getting rid of all of you, things would become quite dull.

Grimacing, I drew myself back to what was going on. There was some pressing discussion going on as Amelia left the stand and gave the mic to the president as he stepped around to speak once more. "Do we need to reconvene or are we alright to press on for a short time?"

I raised my voice. "Press on!" The old habit never had died from my time in the Marine Corps.

Some of the Marines that stood in the back glanced at me, eyes narrowed, and I decided to give them one, "Rah!"

More than a few of them turned their heads hard enough that I could have sworn at least one of them would have dropped from the whiplash, but they were a lot harder to break than that, the different breed we were.

"The offer to allow those of the supernatural community who reside in the United States citizenship is something that we as a nation would like to offer to all of you." His words rang out through the room and those gathered just stared at him for a short time as he took a steadying breath. "War is something we don't want. Even with displays such as what happened in Columbus, with the fight involving the angels… we cannot do more than to hope for a proper peace and coexistence between all of us."

"Peace…" a wizened voice whispered against the air; it sounded like it could have been uttered from just over my shoulder as chills ran down my spine. I wanted to look over my shoulder, but I couldn't move my head. "Peace is what one gives and receives as an *equal*."

A figure *whooshed* through the doors at the far end where the president and his Marines had come through, the hood of their cloak raised. As they moved to the front of the stage, feeling in my body began to return as the strain of Dominions in my vicinity began to surge and fight back. "Thank you for bringing my body with you, Merlin, I truly appreciate that."

The figure put their hand out and something cracked me painfully in the back of the head, the figure chuckling. "Whoops, sorry about that, Huntsman. Seems I forgot my manners." The shock of the *accidental* smack was enough to fully bring me out of whatever they were doing.

"Who are you and what're you doing?"

I could see the grin in the shadows of the hood. "We're old friends." The hand not holding the staff raised and pulled back, revealing Theodorous, the former Ventricle of Columbus and the last person I expected to see alive. "Things can be faked, like deaths, no matter how magical they may appear with the power of gods at your disposal. Though I do suppose this is the first time you're meeting me and not the moniker I gave this body that I took over upon my arrival in this world."

The staff in his hand spun and as it did, the wood cracked and fell to the ground as dust, revealing a smaller weapon that was somehow familiar to me.

The library! Galaxy hissed within me, showing me the image of it sitting in the bin for staves, walking sticks and the like. The creepy thing had felt like it was watching me, *And it was, Marcus. That thing is dangerous.*

"Hubris?" Zeke muttered next to me and I blinked at the name. "Hubris, what the hell is going on? Come to me—now!"

The voice emanated from the staff and the man holding it at the same time. "No, I think I won't." The scepter swirled in his hand and then suddenly appeared as a pin on his chest, like a decoration. "You see, former master, when the gods of Brindolla sent you here, they also sent any items bound to your soul with you, like me. And with nothing to do but explore once you had forgotten me, I found others willing to assist me and a soul space adjacent to the one I could access thanks to my wretched curse from those blathering buffoons."

His laughter once more sent a chill down my spine. "Peace?" He posed once again. "What good is peace in the face of progress? The gods of the past stopped me once, when I was on the verge of a breakthrough in my research, calling my work abominations. Saying that what I tampered with was purely for the gods to deign whether it was right or not; well, who is to stop me now with all these gods at my disposal, hmm? Who will summon the guardian to stop me here, hm? No one."

"Bold statement for a stick," I growled standing to my feet. "Merlin, you ready for a fight?"

"Bit of bad news there, boss." I glanced at what he was showing me and my blood ran cold.

There was a mass of lycanthropes downtown in Columbus and all of them were led by Marik, his massive werewolf form in front of the High Table. There was a snap and a pulling shift as the whole room full of gods and monsters along with the humans meant to mingle with us was transported.

"You know Marcus, *Huntsman,* I have you to thank for a lot of this, don't I?" I blinked at him as chains rose from the ground and attached themselves to my legs and wrists. In my peripheral vision, it seemed to me like the others, gods and monsters alike, were getting that same treatment. "You ruined my plans with the Seelie whelp. You took the most promising young wizard from me before I could finish luring him to my side with his junky master's assistance. *You* were the one who kept the monsters from being outed sooner with stopping Serpath's other half from continuing her murders."

He laughed, weird from Theo's face, the level of hatred and spite that was on it as he looked back at me. "You stopped my contacts in the Night Parade, and you even managed to find my lair in Atlantis, but you know what you didn't do?"

I couldn't pass up an opportunity to throw him off his game and mess him up, so I interrupted and said, "Throw in the kitchen sink?" He paused as I grinned at him. "What, big-bad-wizard-asshole with a god complex can't handle one little Huntsman?"

The man stalked forward and as he did, he lifted his hand and Marik appeared next to him. "You couldn't take care of my pet, could you?"

I raised an eyebrow. "I could've killed him at any time."

He shook his head, a smirk growing across his face as he came closer. "No, you were too worried about the friends I'm about to sic on the city below us." His smirk became a massive grin of triumph. "Take a look around, Marcus. I thought you liked Atlantis so much, I brought it to Ohio for you. Now we have a front row seat to the fall of your city, and there's not one thing you can do. I would say that begins to make us even for how you've managed to accidentally foil my plans for a time, yes?"

Sure enough, I could see that we were on one of the larger

floating islands and floating above some of the more familiar buildings in Columbus.

I did my best to try to appear blasé but it was highly irritating to know that this asshole was taking his anger at me out on my city.

"Hubris, that means something about pride, right?" The bemused man wearing the scepter pen nodded as if at a child while I spoke. "Then how about you show some and fight me yourself, coward."

The man laughed and Zeke just sighed. "He's not gonna do that, man. We kept getting clues about him on our world, and we never connected the dots. At least, I didn't." Hubris clapped his hands politely as Zeke spoke and then scowled as Zeke spat in his direction. "He's too much of a little bitch to get his hands dirty."

"Marik." Theo-Hubris lifted his hand and motioned to Zeke. "Shut that one up, harshly, if you would. But leave him alive; he's got a Dominion I wish to play with." He turned and raised his voice. "Children of the sky beneath the deep, heed my call!"

Thousands of bird-like cries lifted to his voice and then fell eerily silent as he pointed. "This city is that of he who decimated your ranks, and the gods who love you wish for you to end them all so that we may begin this world anew."

As he grandstanded and did his best to sound doting, Marik came over to us with his claws out and a grimace on his face. As he closed in on Zeke, I asked, "So what's the wrinkled dick over there got on you that you're doing his bidding?"

Marik blinked at me, then said, "He gave me the power to be what I wanted to be. I owe him for that."

Zeke rolled his eyes. "You wanna die for it?"

Marik grimaced and shook his head. "I won't kill you, but you can't kill me either, seeing as though he has your power by the short and curlies."

I strained at my chains, trying to freeze them or cut them

with my Dominion, but nothing worked. *Must be immune to magic and Dominions.*

"Chains are meant to stop gods, man," Marik commented dryly as he looked at me. "Magic and god powers won't do shit to 'em." He turned back to Zeke and sighed. "Sorry, boss wants me to rough you up and I'm not one to displease if I can help it."

Zeke tilted his head. "What about Ki?"

Marik sneered. "It's his own personal blend of manacles bound to his power—there's no key."

That made Zeke laugh. "Oh, man, if you don't even know what I meant, then that's a *definite* no." Marik swung at him and Zeke just laughed again as he dipped his head back just out of reach. "Oh, yoohoo, *boys*."

James appeared out of a portal with a grin on his face and Muu just grabbed Marik by the scruff of the neck, the werewolf allowing a small yelp of surprise.

Muu grinned, but there was no happiness in it, only something deep and dangerous. "Daddy's baaack," he sang.

He blinked and then frowned, glancing at Zeke. "Dude back there the bad guy?" Zeke nodded as Muu motioned to Marik. "Henchman?"

I grunted. "Passably, but don't kill him, he's got my wolves under his control."

"Oh, I see." Muu shook the man in his grasp violently. "What did I tell you about pissing on the carpet, Mister Piddle Paws?"

Marik bristled, "I'll fucking gut you for that!"

James snorted. "More men than you have tried, flea bag." He bent down and used Ki to cut through my chains, the metal clanking and clattering as he worked his way through it. "We gonna go after the bad stickman?"

Zeke nodded as he pulled at his own chains so that James could get them for him. "Yeah. Marcus, can you handle the pigeons and puppies?"

I grimaced and then grinned as I saw something I hoped to

see once again as I looked at Marik. The bonds to his packs and the pack for Columbus were right there. I reached out and cycled Dominion into my fingers as my grasp closed on it successfully. The bond with the Columbus wolves crumbled before the power around the other ones ramped up and I lost the grasp, but the damage was done. Laughing, I snarled victoriously. "Never mind, kill him if you want."

Marik howled and snarled, *"Wolves! Destroy the city!"* He twisted himself and wind whipped around him as something yanked him away with magic.

"Well, that puts a damper on me kicking his ass." Muu harrumphed sadly. He cracked his neck. "Oh well. Time to go make some kindling."

With little warning, he bounded toward the distracted god tamer and bellowed, "Sticky!"

Once James finished with my chains, he stood up and shook his head then moved on to the others. Zeke grabbed my attention with a sharp whistle. "I'll make sure he doesn't use any Dominion, but I don't know what Hubris has planned other than just destroying the city and taking power for himself. You gonna be okay?"

I summoned my scythe and took a deep breath before snarling, "Commence the Hunt!"

My armor melted from my body, reforming the demonic figure I had before trying to temper my fearsome visage for the Normies, but I also embraced my Vornal form, making me grow on the spot, wings bursting from my back.

I grinned as I felt the others begin their transition into the Hunt, even the wolves who had been given back. They were mine once more.

I twisted my scythe and rammed the butt of it into the ground, casting Masquerade. Dozens of shadows flickered into existence around me and on the island, some of them close enough to Hubris and his body to touch him. So they did.

My mana had nearly bottomed out with such a massive casting, but the perks of wearing my armor and Mantle meant that it replenished quickly. I grinned as the sorcerer spun his hands out around him and pushed a dozen shadows away from him only to have them reform and attack again.

I focused on the flying enemies that surged toward the sides of my homeland to drop toward the city below. Fires began to produce smoke that filtered upward.

"Unseelie inbound. Marcus, go save the city," Zeke shouted to me from where he stood, then he turned to look at the others. "Bokaj, I need you—"

The archer raised a hand to stop him, and called out, "To provide air support, rain down hell on everyone, and provide the sickest licks this side of the veil? Got it, man. You know I got this shit."

The bow he stabbed into the ground vibrated and stayed where it was as he pulled out an electric guitar and began to play a song that made my blood boil. Launching myself forward, the shadows and I surged toward the sky as I unleashed Mako. "Clear the skies of the birds, buddy. Have a good snack!"

The drake roared excitedly and I called to the others and Galaxy, "Kill them *all*."

I saw something falling to the ground next to me and it was Merlin riding a plummeting bird person toward the ground. I grinned then pointed to him. "You and Arden need to mitigate the damage from the fires. You see Normies, save them."

He nodded and stomped on the bird's head as it tried to correct its course. "Galaxy, can you pass this on to the others?"

They know, and this time I will be joining in the fight.

I raised a brow. "You're sure?"

She laughed and pulled herself onto my shoulder. "I need to pull my weight and rent is due!"

With that she turned into a raven and screeched next to my ear as she flew toward the ground.

Something landed on my back and I turned, grasping the arm and the weapon it held only to realize that it was Balmur.

"Magic is shit up there, and I do better in crowds. Get me to the werewolves and I'll get to work."

He dug into his pocket and pulled out an earring. "Gift for you from Z, just make sure you don't yell into it, it hurts."

I pushed my armor away from my ear and he stabbed the earring into my earlobe. "Ah, god damnit."

As soon as I was about to call him a few choice names, voices filtered through my mind, first being Yoh. "Goddamn, dude, this bitch has all kinds of spells!"

Booming explosions rocked the air around us and, in the distance, massive flashes of magic spiked through the skies toward indeterminate targets.

"Just dodge them and whittle him down. The Wardens have been turned; they're working with him," James called over the airwave.

"Oh, that's going to be annoying," I muttered and Balmur cackled. "What?"

Zeke came over the earring. "We all heard that, but I get it if you have a few extra voices in your dome case like me as well." I could hear the mirth in his tone and then he snarled, "Muu! Stop beating on his shield and just go after the Wardens!"

I nodded and let myself dive, passing the word through Galaxy.

Thunder echoed below as Cassia surged from the High Table with someone running out behind her. Rogue werewolves parted like the Red Sea in front of her and the other figure and then converged.

I gripped my scythe a little tighter and roared as I swung it, ice forming along the blade and shooting forward into the crowd. I flung Balmur into the fray and then dropped in myself.

Cassia swung her massive club and clobbered a couple of the attacking monsters over the head hard enough that they fell but it wouldn't be long.

"Silver?" I called out and Cassia nodded. I grinned and

pulled it out of my Dominion, then coated her weapon with it. "Should last a bit."

A katana flashed in front of my face and I did the same for the wielder though in their armor, I couldn't quite feel who it was. Chiasa's voice rang out behind the shadows, "Coat it, Huntsman."

I grunted and did as she wished, whipping around with my scythe behind her to take care of one of the enemies that would have speared her to the ground.

Marcus! Galaxy's call pulled me away from my talking soon-to-be mother in law, glancing into the sky. *He's summoned more monsters, chimeras of some kind, and something more dangerous—people mixed with animals!*

Hubris, his hair fluttering in the wind as he grasped the veil of the world and yanked his hands down. Portals opening all over the place made the hair on my neck raise.

Fuck me... I launched myself into the air to begin looking for them and found that we were hopelessly outgunned. More and more monsters poured in and they were all armed to the teeth, and the Wardens fought us at every turn as well. This was a losing battle.

As the shadow-covered Wild Hunt raged against the people amassed against them, I took a deep breath and pushed my Dominion into my throat, amplifying my voice. "Let all who would join the Wild Hunt, those whose souls cry out for justice, judgment, and the strength to fight and defend themselves, embrace the shadows nearest them."

I cast Masquerade again and placed them all throughout the area I could see, even amongst the monsters, funneling mana into the spell as I forced it to become a channel. As soon as the shadows brushed against any of them, a change surged throughout the lines. Creatures that had been attacking my horde a mere heartbeat before began to shift away from their offensive endeavors and turned to fight their former comrades.

A vast majority of the animal-man hybrids crowded around the shadows that sprouted and clambered to touch them and our numbers swelled. And then Galaxy appeared above a crowd of them and fell on them with a raging hunger that almost scared me, and when she started swiping and painting the ground with blood, I moved on so she could focus.

An echoing bellow above us startled me and forced hundreds of beings to pause in what they were doing. Hubris and his puppet glared hatefully down at us as the tides began to turn against him and he pointed at me. "No!"

Despite the energy building in his aura, I grinned. "Oh yes, and I can feel a few people straining above you as well. Gods. Demons. Monsters who would rather give me their faith than be of use to you."

Five figures in manacles flashed into being next to him, their heads limp and hanging to the side as he pulled at a rope that was tied to each of them. "We shall see about that. I don't know what magic you used to break my barrier, but I shall see you ended now and mold this world in my own image." He sneered and pressed his hands together. "No gods to oversee us and flaunt unearned power. Only those who wish to be more than they could have ever been."

Galaxy, I might need you if he decides to do something crazy. Aloud, I spoke to Zeke and his friends. "Any chance any of you could run any kind of interference?"

There was a crackling response from one of them. "Little... bus... Fuck!"

He continued to focus on whatever he was doing and rather than staying where I was, I flew upward at him as fast as I could until a tiny dark blot against the sun began to grow. *Muu?*

The dragoon's laughter could be heard even over the wind as he plummeted toward Hubris. The sorcerer spun and his attack speared straight into the falling lance-wielder, arresting his momentum. "I think I know your tactics all too well, you bumbling puke-colored lizard."

I couldn't see him, but I could hear Muu chuckle weakly through the earring before he said, "Made ya look."

The sorcerer flinched and a hail of arrows arced at him. A

few spiked him before he was able to construct a shield and began to motion and turn them toward the fighters below. I threw everything I had into my wings and pushed myself on, my scythe slicing the air beneath me like a deadly tail and as soon as I was within attacking range, I swung with all my might.

The scythe sliced through the shield he placed in front of me without looking and bit into his leg deeply before Dominion stopped it and pushed the weapon out. He hissed, "Know your place!"

Magic gripped me once more and forced me to still in the air as if petrified by Cassia's gaze. He grinned as his right hand raised and Dominion as black as the void between the stars danced along the spell he cast, a grin spreading across his face. "Goodbye!"

A thunderous roar from my left pushed me from his attack as a meteor made of scales and hatred collided with Hubris in the form of a massive red dragon. Teeth skittered along the shield protecting the ancient sorcerer and Zeke dragged him upward into the sky, his hangers on trailing behind him as if their sleep was too unending for the fight to awaken them.

Marcus, if he continues to draw from those gods, he can really drag this fight out. Galaxy sounded as if she was trying to get me to think about it, but I knew what I was going to have to do. *I know that this will be crossing a line for you, but I don't think they would want to be seen as glorified batteries to a megalomaniac bent on remaking a world he holds no true ties to.*

As if to punctuate what she had said, a massive sword made of mana formed above the two struggling former partners and slashed at Zeke's exposed neck. There was a dull golden flash of light and a tiny black animal took his place and fell outside the strike and then the dragon was back with a roar. "You *asshole!*"

I grit my teeth and surged upward once more, using my Dominion to press me faster. Zeke and the sorcerer duked it out as titans would, James now clambering along the dragon-shaped druid's scales to get to their enemy, which gave me a bit of an idea.

"James, I need you to free the gods that he's dragging along with him if you can." The draconic-looking fighter's head turned in my direction, as if unsure what I was talking about. "Just free a couple of them and we can make sure he has less juice to work with, okay?"

He shrugged and began to walk along the scales with less resistance as the two stopped their upward climb and now plummeted toward the island below. As soon as he closed the distance enough, James leaped toward Hubris and his slumbering god batteries. His hand began glowing a strange orange color as he swiped it at the rope, but a shield barred his way, the mana thick enough to stall the scaled fighter's attack.

Until his hand started to slowly part the barrier and the aura around his hand began to sharpen and compact until it was damn near a glowing sword. Hubris shouted something I couldn't quite make out, but now I was in range as well. Using Embodiment of Lightning, I zapped my way to where he was and swung my scythe. This time the weapon was stopped by Dominion outright and that was just the distraction needed.

James's slice seared through the shattered part of the barrier and then the tethers, and I grabbed the rope attached to the gods and hauled ass away from them all. As soon as I was away from the fighting and in the air, Mako and Galaxy soared around me while I took stock. I had three of them with me, and that would be a great addition to my power as drained as I was certain they were.

We have you covered, Marcus, get to eating. I nodded and put my hand on the first's chest, just above their steadily beating heart. I took a deep breath and then shoved my hand through the slumbering god's ribs and ended them.

"Thank you for your sacrifice." My muttered prayer for their peace did little to assuage the guilt I felt, but I couldn't let it eat at me—I had a job to do. Drinking the Dominion within the god down into me, I prepared the dwelling as I had been taught and then began to settle it within me. Once it was fully contained, I moved on to the next one without really gathering what kind either of them was.

As I killed the second god, a sense of dread filled me as I felt for the energy within them. This one felt cold. Foreign. Ancient beyond measure. And as I scrounged around for the sparks of power within, something grabbed me and surged up and out of it and into me. Death. This had been a god of death. That was the only way to truly define what was trying to rampage through me right now, but as the power screeched toward my heart, my own Dominion blocked it off and shot it toward the Endless within me and I drank it down, corralling it into the cold and ice that I partitioned for it.

The energy inside the now-dead god dwindled until it was gone and then every alarm bell in my mind went screaming off as something streaked through the air at me. I used my Dominion to build a shield and parried the attack, finding Hubris and one of the other gods trying to attack me. The slumbering one with him indeed still tried to grab me as if acting like a puppet on a string.

"How dare you take from me, mortal?" The sorcerer wearing Theodorous's face looked beaten up, for all his bluster and posturing.

"I do what I want." My counter was simple and I had to ask, "So, are you Hubris wearing Theo like a meat suit? Is he in there at all?"

"We are one and the same," he clarified indignantly and I breathed a sigh of relief, but he attacked again and I had to shove him away from me. Galaxy battered the creatures she could with her wings and it wasn't going well as she fluttered around us, trying to keep them all away.

I tossed her my scythe with a shouted, "Here you go!"

She grabbed it and immediately shifted, slicing through a few of them with ease and bellowed, "I love this thing!" She was off keeping the Atlanteans busy and that left me Hubris.

As Hubris blinked at me in mute shock, I drew my pistols and unloaded, scoring a few body shots on him with my new ammo. Blood sprang from his skin and he scoffed, then the pain set in and he growled in fury.

His short window to retaliate got even shorter when a pissed off green dragon grabbed him and pulled him into a hug and folded his wings to fall toward the ground. Hubris didn't go plummeting easily, magic spells spiking into Zeke as he flew faster toward the earth. One of Hubris' spells missed the draconic druid and drifted over a flock of his own fighters, melting them like they'd been sprayed by acid.

Hurriedly, I grabbed the god that had been trying to attack me and broke her neck, pulling her Dominion inside me while holding the corpse in my arms. As I worked, I called to Galaxy mentally. *What's the situation looking like?*

A lot of the gods have been freeing themselves slowly, but the fight below us is going how it will. Reinforcements from the other branches of the High Table arrived a few minutes ago, but it's chaos. Our numbers swell, but the number of monsters coming from the portals he's made just aren't stopping!

I grimaced at that and dropped my latest meal to the ground below me, numb now to the fact that I had done what I had. I grabbed the last god and pulled them close as my fist punched through his throat, severing the spine and killing him. I gripped the muscles above the stomach and pulled the energy into me. I almost wondered where the last god had gone, but he had likely hidden them, knowing I would probably attack them to get his powerbase to the lowest I could.

I used the earrings to reach out to the others with Zeke. "The Wardens taken care of on the island?"

Bokaj answered, "Yup! Little fuckers are dead as shit, and now I'm pickin' chicken and plucking wings. What's the haps on the ground, Balmur?"

"Fucking chaos!" the shorter man responded with a snarl. "Zeke needs to stop fucking with that asshole and close these portals!"

Galaxy, can we get Merlin and Amabala on those?

There was a pause before she answered, *He's getting the fires put out with Arden, but as soon as he's free, they will begin. Amabala is still out of commission, so it will take him time to get each one closed.*

How many are there? The impression she sent back was unclear but the idea that there were many wasn't lost on me. "Okay, so then we do need Zeke to focus elsewhere. Shit."

I glanced down and realized that a vast majority of the problem still around the High Table was still the werewolves that had been ordered to destroy us, and that gave me a gruesome idea.

I lowered myself and pooled my Dominion in my hands, summoning small silver coins that I willed to be as sharp as they possibly could become. Taking a deep breath, I began to toss them into the air and ordered them to stay where they were as I kept throwing. Hundreds of coins shined in the air as I worked until I was pretty sure I had enough and then I closed my eyes and put my hands into the air and then shot them toward their desired targets.

Some hit the werewolves, others bird people who tried to use their superior mobility to their advantage, but a massive swath of our enemies fell either to injury or to their deaths. As they died left and right, the Dominion of death inside me began to grow and shift within the cage I'd built around it. The fighting excited me in a way that felt good, primal. Like I needed to be on the battlefield, and I wanted all of these beings below me to fight and die, as that was the natural progression of these things. The order of the universe.

But it wasn't the order I wanted, so I rebuked it and crushed that foreign mindset with my will. Galaxy's prideful words rumbled through me as she purred, *You learn so well, my love. Cassia and the others are working their way toward survivors who chose to hide and not answer the call, Merlin is going to work on the portals. If we can free more of the gods above us from whatever Hubris binds them with, we can turn the tide even further.*

I nodded, using the earring to speak, "Zeke, I'm going to try to free the gods up top. The portals keep feeding monsters into the area, and we're going to try to close the ones we can, but we need you to help with that one if you can."

The only answer I got in return was the enraged roar of a fighting dragon and a shouting sorcerer whose words I couldn't make out. I flew upward, using my pistols to kill any of the Atlanteans who ventured into my range. Once I ran out of ammo, I put them back into my inventory and focused on flying and trying to recover my power as I moved.

Under my own power, it was a little more difficult to focus on recuperating my Dominion, unlike when I had been hitching rides with Guide. Still, a fraction recovered during a battle like this would be better than nothing at all, and with my Mantle, I was nearing full mana now as well.

Galaxy landed on the island the same time I did and took her celestial form, her figure cloaked in a dark robe that looked more like her than almost anything I had ever seen her wear. The gods were all locked into place, though some of them appeared to only be mildly locked down, like they moved inside molasses or something equally as thick.

Glaring around the area, I couldn't figure out what kind of magic or power it was that locked them all down like this. I scoured the ground and grimaced as I still found nothing, wishing Merlin were here to assist me with this.

I closed the distance between me and the gods, looking around closely, and found that there were some monsters that were just outright chained in place and their bodies were frozen like that. One such monster was a very pissed-off-looking fallen angel.

His chain was just as immune to magic as mine had been and that gave me an idea. "Let me borrow my scythe, Galaxy." She passed it to me and I took a swing at the chain on his left arm. The chain bent and creaked under the attack, chipping a bit where the blade hit. I swung again, a third time, and finally a fourth time before I was able to sever the link.

The spell came partially undone and Lucifer's eyes widened. "That snake-fucking bastard!" He blinked and frowned down at me. "Where did he go? I'm going to enjoy feeding him to my demons."

"He's getting ganged up on by a dragon and a very pissed off dude who likes to punch things." I took a better stance to swing my scythe at the other chain holding him down when something slammed into me hard enough to make me lose my grip on my weapon.

The tackle damn near carried me to the side of the island and over the edge, but my attacker tripped and we fell, skidding to a halt on the stone ground six feet from the edge. I grunted and found Marik on top of me in a full mount, his fists rocketing into my exposed face.

The first punch irritated me. The second rattled me, because it was somehow stronger than the first. "You just had to interfere!" The werewolf alpha snarled at me, his clawed fingers coming out now.

Nails scraped across my helmet and I just laughed. "Kind of in my fucking job description, buddy."

Rather than bucking him off in a test of strength, I just grabbed his leg and launched us both over the side of the island.

He yelped and flailed as we began to fall and I just held onto him and let my wings do the work, lifting us both back up. I tossed him back onto the island and landed back on solid ground, "Get him free, Galaxy. I've got furball here."

He roared and his physical form only grew as he launched himself at me with his claws slicing. I dipped under his first strike and punched him in the solar plexus. The roar stopped with a wheeze and then I kicked him away from me.

"You murdered someone I respected, Marik." Stalking around him as he collected himself, I found that I didn't know if I necessarily wanted to kill him right now. I did know that I wanted to *hurt* him at the very least, though. "And before you spout that alpha bro bullshit, just know I don't give a shit. You took his pack under orders? Fuck you. You did it for power."

A wry grunt of a chuckle made him cough before he looked up at me and said, "So?"

I stopped pacing around him and stood very still. He wiped a bit of the blood off his lip with the back of his arm and grinned, all those sharp teeth getting a bit of sun as he pointed to me. "You did the same by becoming the Huntsman."

I grimaced. "Sure. Believe what you want." I raised my hands to my side. "I'm no one's bitch, but can you say the same? What are you, a pet? Can you really even be considered a henchman when your boss considers you less useful than a wet fart?"

He raised a brow. "Really?"

A drawn out, tired sigh escaped me as I grumbled, "Listen, I've been killing a lot of your friends and work pals, it's kinda hard to top that shit with witty banter too, okay?"

That got him and he launched himself at me, so I let him hit me and get himself covered in ice. Just a thin layer. "Enough to help you cool off, mister furry."

"For fuck's sake, just fight me, you unclever dickhead!" I rolled my eyes and walked away from him, listening to his grunting as he tried to escape, then huffed and walked back over to him, standing a foot away. He scowled at me. "What? You gonna kiss me, fucker?"

I smirked, but it was Galaxy who bellowed, "His dance card is full, bitch!"

He snarled and jutted his head forward, snapping at me, so I punched him in the throat and sent him reeling and onto the ground. That left the front of his body where it was, frozen, and the rest of what was inside him exposed and open for a killing blow.

As I was about to spear him with a massive lance of ice, a silent thanks to Muu for a trick I could use, power radiated out of him. I followed the thickening bond into the sky where Hubris floated, one arm cradled against his body, his good one pointed at Marik. The injured sorcerer spat a globule of blood onto the ground and wheezed, "Not today, you stupid mort—"

"When are you going to learn that fucking with me gets you hurt?" I threw the ice spear at him and he blocked it with a half-barrier and sneered, only for a very angry James to crash into him from his bottom right, fists glowing and already blurring into the injured old fuck. "See?"

Marik speared me, his shoulder crushing a couple of my ribs on impact, and threw me over the edge of the floating island. This time, he jumped over the side and the wind behind him churned with power and he soared straight into me with a left hook that snapped my head to the right painfully. I grimaced, rattled from strike, and reached up for his throat, only to have him claw my arm away and snarl as he punched me again.

We hit one of the smaller isles and I used the impact to throw him off me and shifted form, Vornal form taking over. "You should've stayed laying down, Marik."

He grinned his wolfish grin. "And you should've been a blowjob."

Green and blue bands of wind sliced toward me. I flicked my wrist and my Dominion solidified in front of the magical attacks in time to halt them and then the air around me began billowing and battering me from all around, buffeting my wings mercilessly.

I huffed and cast Physical Buff on myself. My body stiffened and felt much more robust than I had. My wings stilled and as soon as he was near me, I twisted and lashed out with the leathery appendage. My wing caught him in the chin and as soon as his step faltered, my clawed hands wrapped around his throat and I pushed him up in front of me with a grin. "Going up?"

He slashed me across my face, a small divot left behind in the spectral metal and a gash in my cheek and nose despite my helmet covering the majority of my head. I tensed and then launched into the stone above us. His body bucked as he hit it, then I kept pushing as I slammed my left fist into him over and over. Each consecutive blow drove him through the floating earth above us and ate away at the Dominion giving him strength until I finally got him to be still and hit him for all I was worth. We burst through the floor, tile splintering and shattering all over as we came up out of it and I tossed him down to the ground.

He hit painfully, ribs caved in a bit and his face bloodied and battered. Marik heaved in pain, writhing limply and then he stopped as his body began to heal, albeit slowly. For some reason, now that his Dominion-fed buff was gone, I wanted him to suffer more. To feel the anguish he caused my friends.

With him getting stronger, I had to wonder how powerful he was in his own right without Hubris's influence, but also how much had been given to him and what he knew.

"Alright." I took a steadying breath and decided on the path I wanted to forge ahead on. "Here's how this is going to work, okay?"

He started to try to say something, but the muscles on his jaw were a little slow on the uptake while healing so he just moved his jaw and sounds gurgled out of him.

I grunted as I shifted back into my human state so that he could see exactly what my face looked like as I spoke to him. "Gross. Shut up and listen." I leaned over him and spoke clearly. "I'm not going to kill you. I will be beating your ass— don't you ever doubt that shit because I am spiteful and vengeful and I will have my pound of flesh." He glanced over my shoulder and I followed his gaze to the meat popsicle, so I smirked and amended that. "*Pounds* of flesh. You fucked with something that shouldn't have been, but you're more useful to me alive than dead for now."

I flicked my wrist and golden Dominion flooded from my palm, and I placed it on his throat as it healed, careful not to let the energy heal him or anything weird. "This collar means you belong to me now. We're not gonna make it a kink thing, don't get excited." His glare made me want to both laugh at him and smack him, so I chose neither and carried on. "Where you go, I'll know. Who you're around, same. If you disobey me, I'll make death feel like a reprieve. But if you do what I ask and do it well, I will reward you."

I reached down and put my hand on the bare bones of his rib cage as muscle and sinew began to slowly shift over them. "There's a saying where I come from. 'The beatings will continue until morale improves.' And, Marik, I have to say, you will have the *highest* morale if you piss me off. Once all this is done, I expect you to come to me so we can have a heart to heart, am I clear? Oh, shit—ew. Just blink, you're still goddamn gross right now, man."

He blinked at me twice which I took to mean an affirmation, because really, what choice did he have? He didn't have to know which parts of that little speech I had pulled out of my ass and why. All he had to do was obey.

I reached down and smacked his cheek with mock affection as Void Frost spread down his neck to cover his body. "Good boy." I stood and frowned. "Again, not a kink thing; you should really get that under control."

I made it back to Galaxy who was slightly winded but had managed to at least chip the chains that bound Lucifer in place.

The devil stared at me in disbelief. "You're sparing him."

My eyebrows raised and I tilted my head. "That far outside the realm of what I would do, Lucifer?"

He shook his head, motioning with his one free arm. "Well, I didn't quite expect mercy from the villain of a children's horror movie about a certain mouse and his failing magic."

I groaned. "No. Not that one. Ugh." I put my hands to my eyes and grimaced. "And it's not mercy. Just think of it as deferred justice. Come on, let's get you free."

CHAPTER THIRTY-ONE

"Who has eyes on Muu?" Zeke's voice sounded tired as he spoke through the earring.

Bokaj spoke up. "I hit him with those healing arrows you made me for emergencies, then I lost sight of him in the chaos." I could see the archer in the distance, mounting a ridge on another island. "Muu?"

I spoke up. "I didn't see him after Hubris hit him with all that god power. Speaking of, where is he?"

"I snapped him in half," Zeke answered through a wheeze. There was a heavy sigh. "He made sure I paid for it, but fucker earned it. What a waste of a good goddamn tool."

"Found him." Balmur was calm as he spoke and I could see there was still a fight going on down below. My hackles raised, wondering if Hubris had come back. "This Cassia lady nabbed Muu and pulled him inside the bar. He's getting some treatment but he's pretty hurt, man. You may wanna get over here and start on the healing spells."

Zeke huffed, "Yeah, I'll be over." There was a pause and then he grunted, "Where'd they go?"

Balmur answered, "The bar, dude."

Zeke, frustrated, retorted, "No, the stick and his fucking puppet. They were *just* here."

The hair on the back of my neck raised as a stillness washed over the world around me.

"Well, Marcus, I have to give it to you and those idiots down there, you sure know how to put yourselves in the path of greatness." I turned to find the man who had formerly been Theodorous standing stark naked and looking brand new in the middle of the gods that remained. The pin of a scepter was nowhere to be seen and the man smiled villainously. "I didn't want to see if that little experiment would work, but I am *so* glad it did. How do you like my vessel now? The final god you missed, mixed with the homunculus I created to infiltrate the Wardens. What a thrill."

He lifted his hand and the Dominion around us shifted and began to pool around him. "She was an old one, and as such, her power was a little more robust than her friend's, sadly for you. She was a goddess of rebirth and creation. So what I'm going to do is destroy this planet, and just find another to restart—bad taste and memories of this one and all that."

"Ding ding," I muttered through the earring. "Company's back and he's pissed off."

Galaxy, get here. She appeared next to me and then moved next to me. *I think he's going to be trying to spike Earth with all of that.*

It makes sense, and I don't know how we're going to stop him other than maybe having you try to eat him or push the energy into something else.

Hubris grinned at me and flexed his fingers, the gods around us raising from where they were to float around him. "All this power at my disposal, and let me guess, you'll try to get to me to stop me, well guess what? I'll just come back." His grin widened, and it looked like he was the cat who ate the fattest canary. "I've figured out the secrets to Dominions and the gods' power, and I will use it to thwart you at every turn, no matter how often you might strike me down because of my new power."

I grunted, then nodded. "Yeah. Yeah, that'll probably happen."

I could feel something was off, and that was amplified when Balmur growled, "I'm comin'."

"Rebirth is crazy, right?" I paced forward slightly as ice began to build along my forearm like a shield. He hefted a hand at me and blasted me with some of the energy he gathered. I put a bit of my Dominion over the dome like a gloss and deflected it, but the hit was like taking a sledgehammer to the shoulder. My reserves were running frightfully low, but there was one Dominion that blossomed with every death around me.

"Stop moving toward me, imbecile, or I will start killing these gods here and now!" I stilled and he looked happy I listened, his control and need for it reestablished. "Better. And it's a bit odd, but nothing worse than being stuck inside a glorified cane for centuries, then having to deal with that insufferable moron for the time he used me."

He shook with rage and I could see he would have liked nothing more than to gloat, but I had other options. "Do you want a pair of pants?"

He blinked, shoulders sagging a bit. "What?"

I motioned to him. "Pants. Your junk is hanging out and I don't know if it bothers you or not, but being a stick for a few centuries kind of made you into a bit of a nudist, I guess?"

His lips pulled back as he seethed and pressed his hand forward. "How *dare* you assume that about your betters!"

Power rippled my way, distorting reality as it streaked toward me, and I pushed into it with my shield and my own Dominion. Suddenly, Galaxy was next to me and her hand was out, a shimmering ring in front of her, assisting in protecting us both. The ring I gave her augmented my power oddly and helped to mitigate the attack some, but my footing started to slip backward when a figure floated upward from beneath the man's feet.

Balmur and his weapons flashed upward and out, slashing

things I never wanted to see getting slashed. And that was the opportunity I needed.

I cast Embodiment of Lightning once more and appeared in front of the man. I took him by the throat and pressed my hand against his chest, but instead of killing him outright and chancing him being reborn, I tried to dislodge the Dominions in him. As soon as I grabbed one and tried to wrest it from him, another two would attack my will and tried to whittle me down and eject me out of him. With him regaining his wits, I was forced to react and shoved my newest and arguably most dangerous Dominion into him as my Vornal form came to the fore once again.

He stiffened and then screamed, long and piercing. "Do you think this will stop me? I will be reborn!"

I continued to push death into him, my form shifting unbidden as the power fled me, steadily letting it build and guided what I wanted to happen with my will. Below and around us, people still died and those flickering lives being snuffed out fed this power.

"I don't think you will." My Dominion began to attack and overwhelm the one in his newest body. "You've been using this one pretty regularly from all the shit you unleashed on us down there." I gripped his neck harder as Balmur continued his stabbing and slicing but sensing what I was doing, he didn't kill him. "Being born again had to take a lot out of you, and these gods' worshippers were somehow poisoned and pitted against them. Who knew that could backfire?"

Inside his body, the fight between the icy, dread-filled grip of death against the diminished and overused rebirth and creation carried on, and death and I were *winning*. "This is my home, and I have a lot of shit left to do, like buy a house, make lots of drinks, and play loads of games with the people I fucking care about. Can't have you fucking that up for me. And I can't have you screwing around and creating anything else."

His Dominion died, a dull echo of it inside him making him wail as I continued to hold him by his throat. "I've let people get away with shit in the past, but you've been far too involved in my life for a while, so this is the end of you."

Continuing to let death pervade his every molecule, I pulled him down so that I could look him in the eyes and muttered, "This is for that copper dragon you used to fulfill your fucking curiosity on."

I took the death Dominion and pushed it along my hand before sinking it into his ribs like a dagger straight into his heart. The fight, rage, and light in his eyes died slowly as I continued to dump the last dregs of the newfound power I had. I pumped every last drop of the foul-feeling energy into his body until there was none of it left in me, and then I let my fingers unclench and took his heart out with a squelching *pop*.

For good measure, Balmur stabbed him six or seven times in rapid succession before turning to me. "Why does it feel... dangerous up here?"

The energy he had been controlling still lingered and built, like someone turned on a spigot and then left their house for their whole yard to flood. I couldn't control it myself; I didn't know how or what he'd done, and if I took it into myself, I could be accused of trying to kill all of the gods and goddesses who had been his victims.

The dragon egg! Galaxy startled me and I pulled it out of my inventory. She stepped out and pointed to the ground. "We push the Dominions into the egg."

I blinked and frowned. "Will that work?"

Galaxy looked concerned for a long moment and admitted, "It could kill it? But if we don't do *something*, this much power could start to play havoc on both the planet and its population."

Without thinking too hard about that, I nodded and put the egg on the ground as close to the center of the energy as I could stand to wade into.

Zeke crested the side of the island and shifted from his massive eagle form into his normal fox-man self. "What the hell is all this?"

I glanced back at him and motioned for him to come help.

"Killed him, don't have time to explain, help us push the energy to the egg."

He huffed and joined me, but it was Galaxy who did the truly heavy lifting. Her eyes closed and the Dominion around us swirled toward herself and then she placed her hand on the egg and the god power just began to siphon toward it slowly like a growing whirlpool.

Bit by bit the egg began to drink it in.

As time went on, it got harder and harder for me to focus and my Dominion's power was flagging as I kept trying to push it before finally my vision unfocused and blurred dangerously.

And then below us, there was someone who lifted some coins and cash from the ground and threw it into the air. "Hope this helps." The coins turned to golden power as they rushed into me.

Then more began to do it, their sacrifices bolstering my strength and flooding me with renewed vigor.

Galaxy hissed, "We're going to kiss Cassia *so* hard after this!"

I laughed and with my strength back and building, I started to really push the power toward the egg. After a few more minutes, the spell freezing the gods and forcing them to sleep began to wane and the energy leaking from them all stopped. Once it stopped, we were able to completely push the freed Dominion into the egg before some of the other gods began helping us and taking some of their power back. At the end of that, I picked up the egg, warm and inviting in a way it hadn't been before, and smiled at it. "Thanks, little fella."

Once we were finished, drenched in sweat, I collapsed onto the ground, exhausted.

"First time you've had to work with that much power?" Zeke asked, his voice a bit strained.

I held up a hand with a single finger held up and Galaxy said, "Why does that sound like the beginning of a bad sex joke?"

Zeke snorted and answered, "Well, probably because we've

all been hanging out with Muu too much lately, but that's okay." He yawned and glanced around. "Think you guys got it up here; I got a friend I need to go check on."

I nodded and he stumbled toward the edge, only to pause before trying to throw himself over the edge of the island. He stiffened and lowered himself into a fighting stance as there was a rumbling noise and then a shaking of the ground we were on.

I groaned as I rolled my eyes. "Fuck's sake!"

"Got it! I got it," someone called and the shifting and movement stopped. I turned back to see a jacked muscle man holding his hands out. "Sorry, hadn't gotten to introduce myself, I'm Zeus. And yes, I'm *that* guy."

I frowned and said, "Thanks?"

He nodded and said, "Well, yeah, so we were aware the whole time you guys were fighting and I gotta say, there was a lot going on, but I appreciate what you guys all did." He motioned to Zeke. "Before, I wanted to kill you. Janus and I went way back and now, I know you weren't at fault. He was the kinda guy to really throw himself at someone whose fate and path he couldn't read and swore that meant they had to die. But, uh, seems you're doing good with his powers. So thank you. Sorry about wanting you dead."

Probably hearing it through my end, cautiously, Zeke grunted through the earring, "Yeaah, uh, sure. No worries. Definitely not the first time, and if fate has her way, won't be the last."

"Yeah, well, that's the thing, it shouldn't have happened, but I'm willing to let go and join the good ol' U S of A if that means that people here will be cool with us. I don't really want another all-out war on my hands."

There was a muttering of agreement from some of the gods and goddesses around us and I had to admit, things were looking up if they were all interested.

———

Weeks later, after cleanup was finished, and things were being rebuilt *way* faster than usual, me, Galaxy, Cassia, Arden, Merlin, and Amabala drove along the highway to get downtown for the ceremony that would be held there.

We chattered about nothing for a short time, then hit a pothole and Cassia snarled, "Fuck! All these gods fixing shit in the city and no one thinks to fix the fucking potholes?"

I laughed. "Those would never be fixed." I looked out the window and into the sky, still unable to believe that Atlantis still floated above us.

Some of the surviving Atlanteans had agreed to stay there and that the city was better here anyway. They'd been coerced and even ensorcelled into believing that Hubris had been some kind of savior for them and that had made them zealous in their following of his instructions. Their leadership, a council of surviving elders, had called to me for aid since I had eaten their gods. They'd wanted me to rule them, but I just shook my head and told them that I had my hands full with the Hunt.

They had given us a badass island, though, with one hell of a view. Turned out that having a house built there would be much easier, considering that the market was wild and we no longer had to consider ley lines or portals.

"Wild that they're all just so... carefree," Arden muttered from her place in the middle of the back seat.

I glanced back at her and she looked up from her game. "The supernaturals, that is."

I shrugged. "They don't have to hide anymore. They're citizens now, protected by an ever-growing and evolving set of laws based on what the lawmakers can do, with their freedoms and abilities taken into consideration."

Merlin snickered and said, "Never thought I'd hear that come out of anyone's mouth."

"Says the ex-Warden," Cassia shot back playfully. "You think they'll catch the Order leaders?"

"Eventually they'll slip up somewhere, and then that will be the time for us to strike." Merlin's answer seemed sure to me and I had to agree. Jetlo wasn't the type to take shit laying down and I didn't know the other one. "Besides, with their assistance given to Hubris, they've been upgraded to a magical terrorist organization, and that means all the people they used to abuse will be able to fight back with impunity now."

That last bit had been a bit more morbid than I had thought he would go for. "You okay, buddy?"

He dipped his head so he didn't have to look at anyone and answered honestly, "I will be. Just hard to recognize that they would fall so far. What had he promised them to get them to turn?"

"I don't know, but there's still a lot left to do," Arden reminded us. "We need to find my family, fix my sister, get Cassia's eyes fixed, and plan a wedding."

Cassia laughed. "I kinda like my eyes now, though it sucks not being able to really let people enjoy them up close anymore."

"And watching you sleep with a blindfold on is pretty weird," Galaxy teased her from the back.

"Does she drool on it?" Amabala piped up and the rest of us laughed as Cass groaned.

We pulled onto the street, finding that the majority of it was blocked off by cops and secret service. They verified our identification and our names on the list before searching the car and I had one hell of a time keeping the fact that I could literally pull a scythe out and kill almost anyone instantly to myself.

It was the little things that made life easier.

We pulled down the marked path to the parking lot, and then made our way to the designated area beside the entrance to the High Table. Amelia grinned at us and motioned for us to join her. "Thanks for coming to the reopening, everyone."

Cassia grinned and moved around in her lovely dress, baby bump beginning to show. "And let people miss this? Please."

Amelia laughed at that and nodded us toward the front of the doors where Kenshi, Uncle Yen, and Keith awaited us. The young werewolf cleaned up well, his new bouncer uniform and vest looking very tidy and his combed hair parted weirdly.

He growled at us, "Stop grinning like that, Marcus."

"Pass," I stated and he rolled his eyes.

Secret Service came over to us and spoke softly, "Hey everyone, thanks for letting us be here today. The president is going to be over in a minute, and we just ask that you respect his privacy and refrain from any photography or anything like that while he's over here. We have journalists in the crowd that will be happy to get you photos with him, okay?"

I nodded. "Thanks for all your hard work." He offered me a stiff smile and walked off toward the president and his other retinue. Once they were ready and the crowd was gathered, he came over to the podium and began his speech.

"My fellow Americans, in the last few weeks, our way of life itself has changed. The existence of supernatural creatures and gods was confirmed, and that world has stepped out from the shadows of our minds and through the fog of fear to stand here with us today." He nodded as the crowd burst into cheers of support and applause. He grinned and motioned to the building behind him. "For countless years, this building's exclusivity has eluded us and, for the first time, we know why—protection. Today, High Table Councilwoman Amelia who joins me and the rest of the country in hopes that from this day forward, the High Table will continue to be a place of comfort and community, and thank them for allowing humanity to step through the doors and join their super brothers and sisters for a great drink and a good time."

He stepped back and Kenshi pushed the podium out of the way so that the president and Amelia could cut the red ribbon in front of the doors. "The High Table is now open to all who abide by the rules!"

Amelia's words rang through the air and the crowd went wild.

We went inside the bar to applause and to see that some of the key players in the attack were waiting for us. Uncle Yen fixed his bow tie and called over to the president, "Sir, first round's on me, how about that?"

The president grinned and nodded. "I think I'll take you up on that, Yenasi."

I grinned and marveled at the fact that he would share a drink with us, and made my way over to the table that our new allies crowded around. When I came to it, Zeke lifted his glass. "Marcus."

I nodded at him and said his name as he smiled. Bokaj and Balmur reached beneath the table and pulled out two objects I hadn't expected to see. Zeke motioned to them and said, "Arden told Muu about them and he weaseled the list of locations out of Galaxy. We'd like you to consider these an offer of goodwill and a thanks for dealing with my constant murderous tendencies."

Arden gasped from behind me, the glasses in her hands falling toward the ground but the shorter man rushed forward and caught them with a teasing, "Almost a party foul, man."

Arden just nodded dumbly and collected the two lamps that held her family members and said nothing. "We couldn't find one of them," Muu grumbled from the other side of the woman. "Someone had raided it before we got there and the list won't update for me. I'm sorry."

She nodded and kissed him on the cheek, tears streaming down her face. "Thank you. Thank you so much."

Zeke smiled. "I take care of my people. And that's you lot now too." He tapped his table and said softly, "Once we start to move toward getting back, I'll make sure you guys are kitted out, talking the best shit money can buy and I can enchant, feel me?"

I nodded. "Thanks, man. Sorry for being a thorn in your side sometimes."

He waved that away and we drank in silence for a brief time before the president came over to us. "Gentlemen, ladies, thank you for your service. I'd like to present you all with medals if you'll have them, maybe in a few months' time."

I grinned. "Be honored, Mr. President."

He shook my hand and pointed to the ladies. "Ms. Galaxy, Ms. Cassia, you two take care. I've got a gift coming for the baby from the missus and me at the White House. We hope you'll be able to use it. Saved our necks with our youngest, I'll tell ya."

Cassia smiled. "Of course we'll take all the help we can get, Mr. President. Thank you."

He nodded happily and raised his beer to all of us. "To freedom and those who defend it."

We raised our various drinks and cheered with him, "To freedom!"

He grinned almost boyishly and went back to the people who minded him and they took him out the back to the VIP rooms to schmooze with the various gods and monsters who wanted to meet him.

Once he was gone and out of earshot, Zeke leaned forward and asked, "So, what's the plan to get us home?"

I grinned and responded, "Well. It'll involve the Null and the Void. But I think I have an idea about it." I pulled Cassia and Galaxy toward me, hugging them. "We'll need time to prepare everything, you'll be needed too, but we should be able to make it there if what I want to do is possible. It'll just take some ingenuity."

Muu laughed and startled us before saying, "Oh, we got that shit in spades, man. We're *so* going to kick some godly ass." His eyebrows shot up and then he said, "Shit, Galaxy, those are your kids I'm talking about. That was super out of touch for me. I'm not talking about abusing them or anything."

Galaxy took a drink of what she had in her hand, swallowing it with a massive gulp before she sighed happily and said, "I am. It seems Mommy needs to get home and dole out a little motherly love."

ABOUT CHRISTOPHER JOHNS

Christopher Johns is a former photojournalist for the United States Marine Corps with published works telling hundreds of other peoples' stories through word, photo, and even video. But throughout that time, his editors and superiors had always said that his love of reading fantasy and about worlds of fantastic beauty and horrible power bled into his work. That meant he should write a book.

Well, ta-da!

Chris has been an avid devourer of fantasy and science fiction for more than twenty years and looks forward to sharing that love with his son, his loving fiancée and almost anyone he could ever hope to meet.

Connect with Chris:
Facebook.com/AxeDruidAuthor
Twitter.com/JonsyJohns

ABOUT MOUNTAINDALE PRESS

Dakota and Danielle Krout, a husband and wife team, strive to create as well as publish excellent fantasy and science fiction novels. Self-publishing *The Divine Dungeon: Dungeon Born* in 2016 transformed their careers from Dakota's military and programming background and Danielle's Ph.D. in pharmacology to President and CEO, respectively, of a small press. Their goal is to share their success with other authors and provide captivating fiction to readers with the purpose of solidifying Mountaindale Press as the place 'Where Fantasy Transforms Reality.'

Connect with Mountaindale Press:
MountaindalePress.com
Facebook.com/MountaindalePress
Twitter.com/_Mountaindale
Instagram.com/MountaindalePress

MOUNTAINDALE PRESS TITLES

GameLit and LitRPG

The Completionist Chronicles,
Cooking with Disaster,
The Divine Dungeon,
Full Murderhobo, and
Year of the Sword by Dakota Krout

A Touch of Power by Jay Boyce

Red Mage and
Farming Livia by Xander Boyce

Ether Collapse and
Ether Flows by Ryan DeBruyn

Unbound by Nicoli Gonnella

Threads of Fate by Michael Head

Lion's Lineage by Rohan Hublikar and Dakota Krout

Wolfman Warlock by James Hunter and Dakota Krout

Axe Druid,
Mephisto's Magic Online, and
High Table Hijinks by Christopher Johns

Dragon Core Chronicles by Lars Machmüller

Pixel Dust and
Necrotic Apocalypse by David Petrie

Viceroy's Pride and
Tower of Somnus by Cale Plamann

Henchman by Carl Stubblefield

Artorian's Archives by Dennis Vanderkerken and Dakota Krout

www.ingramcontent.com/pod-product-compliance
Lightning Source LLC
Chambersburg PA
CBHW021436240626
47153CB00001B/176